The Truth about Adira

Anna Paulsen

The Truth About Adira

Cover design by Marianne Nowicki

ISBN- 978-1-7329049-0-3 (E-book)

ISBN-978-1-7329049-1-0 (Print)

This book is lovingly dedicated to my Mom.
She is the inspiration behind every strong woman I pen
and is my rock, always.
I am beyond lucky to have her in my life.

I love you Mom.

One leaf falling from a tree.

A moment of beauty as it cascades,
journeying toward the ground.

Soon after, another follows.

Landing on top of the other leaf.

Covering it.

Shielding it.

Engulfing it.

No longer two leaves, but one whole.

CONTENTS

Prologue

Dear Kaitlyn,

You have just entered the world, and already your future is being pondered over. As a result of my unwavering, dictated orders, you are labeled an unwanted soul, treated slightly better than a leper. They most definitely think me cruel, but no one challenges me. No one dares to disobey my commands. They will never know or even suspect that my cold, cruel heart does indeed ache for you. To me, you are a precious girl. A mere innocent that has been relinquished unto the arms of solitude and abandonment. I am well aware that I am hurting you most. I am cruel, and nothing can change that. Instead of keeping you warm, I am robbing you of endless love and returning you as one does an item that no longer works or fits to a store. You fit, baby girl, you fit, but looking at you would bring up bad memories. Every glance at your beautiful face would rub salt into my festering wounds. I know what I am doing is selfish. You will never get to experience the warmth of your mother's kiss. Your father . . . well, that is a story worth not mentioning. He left after that atrocious attack and has stayed away so you will never see him again. That is a good thing. And I, why am I writing this letter instead of holding you and kissing you? Well I, I am a mere coward. I am scared of looking you in the eyes. I do not have enough strength to tell you why just yet, but I will.

I lack spirit and charisma. I think I always did. Your mom had it all. She was perfect, but I never saw it. I am old now and sickly, and I carry such a hefty secret inside my heart. One that would make you hate me.

I ask one thing of you. Please remember that I love you and that I always will.

—A.

Dear Kaitlyn,

It is your first birthday, and I am trying to picture what you look like. When I close my eyes, I can envision a beautiful baby with golden hair and chubby cheeks. I can imagine your sweet, powdery scent and your beautiful, baby-soft skin. How I long to hold you, touch you, feel you near me. It is impossible, I know. I have made it impossible for myself with the promise I have made after your mother passed away. It is my fault, and I will die an old woman, alone and miserable with a terrible stain on my conscience. I just ask for forgiveness now, but not from you; that is too much to ask for. I ask it from myself. You would think that would be the easiest forgiveness to receive, right? No. Trust me when I tell you it's really difficult. I don't think I'll ever be able to forgive myself.

I saw a child in the park last week. It was a girl with her mother. I stared at them both until I could not bear it anymore. I went up to them and started talking to the mother. I found out that the baby was fourteen months old. Just two months older than you. Her name was Angelina. I asked if I could hold her, and her mother agreed. I will never forget how it felt to hold her in my arms. I pretended that I was holding you and I started to cry. The young mother asked me if I was okay. I did not reply. I could not because I did not want to lie to her. The queen of lies could not tell one more lie, how crazy is that? My heart felt like it was breaking in two. Right after I left the park and walked away from the baby that could have been you, from the memories that are reality, I had a massive heart attack. My heart, old and broken, could not take that much emotion in one day.

I am doing better now, until I think about you and what I have done. Then I feel my heart seizing and the tremors going up the side of my body. The pain always settles in the middle of my chest. I imagine the pain to weigh about twenty-one pounds.

I want you to know that I see you in every baby I encounter in my everyday life.

A big hug from me to you.

Love,
Grandma

Dear Kaitlyn,

I have been sick and unable to write my letters. After my heart attack, I had a stroke. Being alone and sick, I feel like that is the price I have to pay for giving you away. It is just me and my guilty conscious, my constant companion, on this slow road to recovery.

It took me quite some time to regain my speech as well as my ability to write. The stroke took a big piece of my life from me. You are three years old now. I always wonder what you look like. There are so many things I want to tell you. Yet words on this piece of paper can never do my thoughts justice.

I love you.

Grandma

Dear Kaitlyn,

Happy birthday, my child. You are four years old now, and on your special day, I make one wish. It is a purely selfish wish, one that hurts me, but one I need to make. I hope and wish and pray that I don't ever run into you. I would not be able to survive. I cannot live with what I have done . . . and with what he has done to all of us. But then again, I cannot blame him entirely. If fault lies with anyone, it is with me. I only wanted the best for your mother. I wanted her to have a life that she deserved, full of money and a husband that was worthy of her. We knew his family for years, a very wealthy and distinguished family. He was raised by the best nannies and taught by the best tutors and schooled at the best boarding school in the nation. Yet that did not make him a gentleman. He was far from gentle and far from an honorable man.

As a result of what I did, of how I pushed him and her together, it caused her to leave this world prematurely. She resented me until the very end of her life. I am sure you would hate me if you saw me as well. I am the reason for so much unhappiness in your life. It is too late for me to try to justify my actions. I need to save my breath because nothing I say could justify what I have done. It is too late. Your mother is gone. You are alone. And I am dying. My pain is deserved. Yours isn't.

I love you, my angel.

Then there was the letter that she wrote a few days after the birthday letter. She had never written them so close to one another. Five days, to be exact, separated them.

Dearest Kaitlyn,

I was on Willow Road today and I saw the most beautiful child. She was sitting alone on a swing, holding a ragged doll, tightly hugging it to her chest. I came up to the fence to get a closer look at this angel, and she stared into my eyes. It was as if she saw right through me, into my soul, and recognized me. My heart hurt after I saw the sadness that hosted itself inside her eyes. Her eyes were exactly like the eyes of the girl I knew so well, of the one I loved so deeply, the one I carried in my body for nine months, the one I loved and had to bury. I cried, and you looked at me with a look that I could not describe. Then you walked up to me and presented me with a leaf off of the ground. Your fingers touched my palm, and that gentle touch shook me to the core. I felt my blood rush hysterically throughout my body. I felt electrical currents seep into my hand. I knew that I would feel some reaction to you, but I was not expecting this kind of reaction. That is why I got scared and I ran away. When I got home, I still felt your touch, and I felt it even after I scrubbed my hands with soap for hours. It still burned me. Haunted me. As I stood over my bathroom sink, looking at the bleach I was about to soak my hand in, I realized I never should have gone there. A guilty conscience does this to a person. It plays with one's head and one does not know if it is reality or a dream. That is why I am scared to fall asleep, because in my dreams, I see a little girl crying, a young woman crying, and an old, broken woman crying. Three generations crying salty tears. Crying for the evil in the world. Hoping and secretly praying for an ounce of compassion. A grain of understanding. A drop of happiness. All this dawned on me, and I put the bleach away.

You were my granddaughter. My child's child. Though I am ashamed of my actions, I do not regret seeing you. I just regret breaking down and running away. But then again, I did what I felt, and I felt sad and at fault. That same night, I walked back there and picked up that leaf, the only present you could have given me, and held on to it. How did I know that it was your leaf? You may laugh and say I was a fool for thinking I found your leaf, but I did. There may be many leaves on the ground, but only one that you held. And that one meant more to me than anything in this world.

I knew that the leaf must have meant something to you if you decided to leave your swing of dreams and walk toward me, toward the real world. I knew that one day you would step past the gates and enter the outside world and be prepared. I could tell that you were a tough girl. A girl not afraid to dream, but one who did not base her life on dreams, but on truths.

I was your ticket to the outside world. A rusted metal gate the only thing that separated grandchild and grandmother. And that leaf was the middle ground that was able to break through the gates. I remember how your eyes lit up when the leaf left your hand and landed in mine. On the other side. I think you realized then that not everything was hopeless. That you too could permeate outside one day.

The next day I went outside to my garden and sat there for hours watching the leaves being caressed by the gentle breeze. And then one leaf dangled and slowly made its journey downward and fell near the other leaves on the ground. In that moment, I realized why you gave me that leaf. The leaf hangs on to the branch until the change of seasons causes it to fall freely to the ground. Just like life. There is a time for everything. At the right moment in time, you would also be set free. In your case, the years would set you free. You just have to be strong and wait for your time to come.

And I had to stay away. I could not offer you false hope. I could not come and visit you, so that your heart would not break when I did not take you home with me. So that my heart did not succumb to telling you I was your grandmother and why I couldn't be.

—A.

Granddaughter,

Last night I had a dream about him. The man who your mother loved and wanted to spend her life with. He loved your mother. I think I knew that then, but I tried to pretend that I didn't. I remember how easy it was for me to mock him and to say that he was poor and therefore insignificant. I shudder when I think about how badly I treated him, but I wanted him to leave your mother alone. She was born to be grand and not a poor man's wife. Her beauty alone was unrivaled, and she could have had her pick of boys and well-off men. Why she had to fall in love with him I will never know, but she did. Madly and deeply. He even had the gall to come to me looking for you after I sent you away. I could not let him have you. I did not want him to raise you. He was the reason that you did not have a mother. If he did not enter your mother's life, she would have followed in my footsteps and married into money. I may sound cruel, but I think you are better off in that foster home I placed you in after your mom died. The husband and wife, though money hungry, are pliable and do exactly as I demand of them. They gave you their last name and they promised to never hit or abuse you. I paid heftily for that service. They assured me that they would stay away from people and never let anyone inside their home. With their reassurance and their vow of secrecy, I knew that he, your mother's love, would never find you there. I knew you were safe behind those walls.

My heart was buried alongside my daughter, so you cannot blame me for doing this. This is the last letter, but I want you to know something. I made mistakes when it came to my daughter. I didn't want to repeat those with my granddaughter. If that meant giving you up, then so be it.

Yes, the foster home was the best plan for you indeed.

—A.

Chapter One

Kaitlyn Stone

I had no past. Growing up, I was a child that no one wanted. I was that girl that no one even seemed to empathize.

I was once told that I would go nowhere by people who should have nurtured me and protected me. They told me that the only reason they took me in was for the money. I would sit in a corner and stare at a dark wall until even the darkness of night concealed that wall from me, yearning for a parent's touch, hug, kiss, but that was not possible. I daydreamed about my perfect home with my perfect family, and when it was time to return from my daydreams, I was filled with simultaneous anger and despair. I pleaded silently many times, in my prayers, for someone to show interest in me and to throw me a lifeline. I was sinking in sadness, but help never came. After a while I felt that God himself had forgotten about me, so I stopped praying by the time I was six.

A couple of times I had fantasies about beating up the children I was growing up alongside, just so I could feel someone's skin as my fist collided with it, but they were in the same boat as I was, so that thought dissipated quickly every time it even crossed my mind. When my mind returned from these short but twisted day-dreams, I would retreat back to my sad, quiet existence and just live. Not caring about what day it was, what time it was, where I was, who I was, who I would be. I just accepted the fact that I would always be alone because someone gave me up. At least I knew that for sure. My foster family *always* reminded me of that.

The Stone residence was a glacial, gloomy place. Even years later, I shudder thinking about it. It was the type of place that gave you chills just by looking at it from the outside, past the met-al-spiked gates. The inside was even eerier and devoid of joy, and the energy was heavy like lead. I spent the first eighteen years of my life there, and I knew I would have to spend the rest of my life living with the memories as well as the nightmares. Both equally wretched to me.

The Stones were a perfect reflection of their home. They were cold as stone and just as emotionless. They kept away from the children and acted as if we all had incurable diseases. Sometimes while they homeschooled us, I tried to provoke them and act up. As strange as that sounds, I wanted them to hit me or push me aside. I desperately needed to feel that I was alive. Instead I got a blank stare in return, and I was quickly cast off and dismissed. The blank stare was their signature response. Their home was a place that never unveiled love. Any possibility of love, whether giving or receiving, was erased the moment one stepped through the heavy black wrought-iron doors. Once they slammed shut, you were left with an erratic heartbeat and a feeling of desolation that seeped into your bones.

I shared a room with a boy named Jackson Stone and a girl named Jessica Stone. I remember when Jessica arrived at the residence. She did not speak, but held out five fingers when I softly asked her how old she was. Five years old, just like me, yet she was so small and fragile and shy that I kept away from her. She looked at Jackson and me and would cry, and I didn't know how to stop her tears. I would look to Jax for advice, but he would just shrug, so I left her alone.

Jax and I grew up together. He was four years older than me and barely spoke, yet he always looked out for me like I imagined a big brother would. There were times that he would slip me his food when I didn't get any or give me his blanket when I was cold and mine wasn't enough. He did not do well with thank-yous or hugs, so I took from him and thanked him silently with my grateful yet always guarded eyes.

He once told me he had plans to run away before his eighteenth birthday and that he planned the escape in his head daily. That three-minute conversation was our longest ever. I remember the day clearly. I was sitting by the window, wrapped in his blanket, watching the snow fall. It was beautiful, and I longed to play in it. I told Jax that and he told me that he longed to run away. It was December 25, Christmas Day, and neither he nor I received a gift. I will never forget the determined look on his fifteen-year-old face as he crossed the room to me and knelt in front of the window, beholding the freedom before his eyes, separated by a thick piece of glass. I knew it was only a matter of time before he left. I could see it and felt his determination strongly emanate from him, and I felt so proud of him. I knew Jess watched the scene at the window too because when I turned around to look at her lying in bed, huddled beneath a thin blanket, she closed her eyes, closing herself off to me. She wasn't ready to talk, but selfishly I hoped and wished she would be ready soon. Knowing that Jax would be leaving meant that I needed her alongside me more than ever.

That wish came true not long after I made it. I was having a nightmare and crying hysterically. Jess crawled into my bed and held me closely, her arms becoming my security blanket. She told me a story about a knight, and her words calmed me. From that moment our friendship and sisterhood grew, with our roots entwining elaborately and intricately. We became soul sisters and the best of friends. She and I would huddle together, sharing stories and foggy, condensate breaths every night. Some days Jackson watched us, and I swear that one day I saw him smile when I was telling Jess about my future. It was a genuine, loving smile, and it warmed my heart. It made me believe that I could attain my story and make it real too. I felt a strong bond to him in that moment, unlike any that I felt before. That was the day that I gave Jax his nickname. When I called him Jetliner Jax through a mouthful of giggles, he looked at me silently for a long moment before grinning at me.

That was the second time I saw him smile.

That nickname fit him. He always wanted to take off like a jetliner.

And he did.

I remember watching him get smaller and smaller from my window before he stopped to look back at the house. I watched his shoulders droop. Though only seventeen, he had aged drastically before my eyes and I felt his pain and heavy sadness through the glass. He must have sensed me looking at him because he straightened up and waved goodbye. That wave stuck with me, implanted itself in my heart, more than any words from him ever could.

Jax carried a lifetime of hurt in his eyes, but he never spoke about his past or how old he was when he came to the Stones, so I didn't even know if his past silenced him or if he silenced himself. I was certain about one thing though: Jax cared for Jess and me, and we cared for him. Deeply.

Things weren't the same after he left. I missed him every single day. I can't say the same about the Stones. They didn't even notify the police about his absence.

When the time came and Jess and I left the foster home, we promised to never return to this town that left a bad taste in our mouths. We had some money stashed away that Jackson gave us before he took off. We didn't know where he got the money, and he wouldn't tell us, so we didn't press him. We just took it and hid it. Two twenties rolled tightly, resembling a cigarette, allowed us to buy two one-way bus tickets. We didn't take anything with us the day we left, just our souls, and we made sure to dispose of our dreams before boarding. We had no room for that type of baggage. We needed to survive, and surviving meant living, especially living in reality. Our journey took us across state lines, and we never looked back. Until now.

***

I was a child all over again, asking questions. Why did I get the box with letters? Why was I even considering going back to the town that had detained me for eighteen years? The same town that I had vowed to forget forever. Why was the past catching up to me at a time when I had been trying to write a future for myself? I could never move forward if my past kept pulling me back.

Sadness's offspring, I learned years ago, was loneliness. The same loneliness that had been my friend for thirty-one years. The loneliness that had pushed aside everyone that even came remotely close to me. I had no boyfriend, very few friends, no family besides Jess because I could not trust anyone with my love. I was used to living like that, and I had accepted that as my destiny.

Jess understood me because she had come from the same place I had. A place littered with questions and no answers. A place of darkness and numerous nights that involved crying oneself to sleep.

I stared at these letters and the one note from an attorney, my grandmother's attorney, that had altered the life I presently knew. The person who had nothing substantial up to this point suddenly had a home from a stranger who called herself my grandmother. *My grandmother.* How unusual that word sounded to me. Even more unusual was that I was facing the past that I so desperately wanted to find when I was a child and now wanted to bury as an adult. The one tie to my past, the one person that could answer some of my questions, was gone.

My *grandmother* was gone; she had passed away weeks ago. My past and its secrets went to the cold, dark, suffocating ground with her. Except for the letters she had written me over the years.

Letters that felt like they had arrived too late although I couldn't explain what they were too late for.

It was terrifying, I admit, to learn that a few papers could be a big link to my past.

That's why I was initially torn and undecided about going back to the place that I swore never to return to. The place where I had buried my tears and my heart and walked out holding my head high although my soul was battered and broken.

I was the mediator of the debate in my head. Me against myself. A big part of me said that I was not going to go back. I was living in the present, and I was writing for the future. Why go back to a time and a place that only left me with bitter memories? My main focus should've been my writing.

I initially got my big break by submitting an article to a local newspaper. Money was desperately needed once Jess and I left the foster home, and I was working at a local diner, and one day, someone left a newspaper open on the counter and the ad caught my eye: "$1,000 first prize for the best short story."

I had nothing to lose, and the entry was free, so I went ahead and submitted my story. I handwrote it, as I didn't have access to a computer, making sure that everything was printed in big letters and neatly. Writing had always come naturally to me. No one besides Jess really spoke to me at the Stone household, so writing had been my escape. Jess and I spent many nights sharing our stories. Jess was the romantic. She always wrote about her knight in shining armor. I used to tease her about that, but deep down a part of me wanted that knight to have a brother and rescue me as well.

Two weeks after my submission, I got a call at the diner that I was the grand winner. The editor of the newspaper offered me a temporary position at the paper. That put me in the midst of a network of writers, publicists, editors, publishers, you name it. I was apparently good because after only a month of temping, I was offered a full-time position covering the news. On top of that I also got offered an advance to write a book from a big publishing house. I was ecstatic.

My first novel had been a major success. It was a story about a girl who grew up alone on the streets of a big city. Every day was a lesson in survival for her. She eventually turned to drugs and got involved with the wrong crowd. The reckless high she lived on became her downfall, and she died overdosing on heroin. It was a dark novel that allowed me to expel all of my anger and disappointments. It had been cathartic and my therapy. It still was on days when I got overwhelmed with emotions and when anxiety and panic knocked on my door. I reached for it and let the cure of my typed words wash over me.

After the first novel, there was so much excitement and buzz around me. I was interviewed and catapulted into the limelight, and I drank all that exhilaration in. I was being called "an author to keep an eye on."

Then the night of July 15 occurred and changed everything. It was a warm evening with a slight breeze. It would have been the perfect summer night except for what transpired. That night, a big part of me died. I closed myself off completely and denied the one thing that always offered me solace. My writing was laid to rest as the passion in me, the light, died suddenly. Fear, sadness, uncertainty, and loss of hope took its place instead and branded itself in my mind.

A part of me wanted to see my grandma's house, to experience walking across the same floors she had and run my hands across her belongings. There were so many things I would have liked to know, and perhaps staying in her home would give me some clarity. There were days that I would look in the mirror and see a puzzling expression on my face as I examined my features. Who gave me my green eyes? Whose hair did I have? Why did I love to question everything in my life? Who did I thank for being a pillar of strength on most days and a soft easily breakable woman on other days? Days like today. July 15.

***

I promised myself years ago that I would not cry on this day, yet I felt wetness paving a path down my cheeks. One drop fell on my hand followed by another. I stared at the tears until I no longer saw them. The light from above me blinded me momentarily and I felt numb and so cold. I was shaking uncontrollably and my teeth were clattering. Suddenly there was no light and I was encompassed in total darkness. I knew what was happening, and I wouldn't allow that monster to win. I breathed deeply and repeated, "You are okay," over and over again until I heard a knock on the door, but I didn't move. I was too weak to get up. The door creaked open, and I was instantly wrapped in the comfort of sweet vanilla. The darkness faded away and my breathing slowed.

"I got you, baby girl. No one is ever going to hurt you ever again. I am here." She rubbed my shoulders and hugged me tightly. I cried into her shoulder, and after what seemed like an hour, I felt myself being helped up. I hadn't realized I was on the floor, in my hallway, so close to the door. So close to an escape. My body ached from being on the cold floor, and I tried to rub the feeling back into my legs. As I straightened my back, Jess headed toward my kitchen. She returned with a bottle of water, and compassion and understanding in her eyes.

"Here you go," she said softly, twisting the cap off the bottle before handing it to me.

I took the water from her quickly and guzzled it down in an instant. Jess headed back to the kitchen and came out carrying a dishtowel. She wiped my forehead with the warm, wet towel, and I tried to smile at her. I wasn't sure if it worked.

"Thank you for coming," I managed to say, my body still shaking uncontrollably and my voice breaking.

"You know I would never miss being with you tonight." I felt her hand rubbing my back, and it did not seem to help. I was unable to stop the shaking. "Do you want to lie down, under the blankets, and read a story, like we did back when we were young?" she asked in a soft voice.

I looked up at her and saw deep concern in her eyes. I nodded my head and took a few deep breaths.

"As long as there are no stories about knights in shining armor, I say yes." I attempted to smile once more, yet instead it came out looking like a grimace.

"Of course, there is a knight. He is damn fine too. And he's all yours today." She grinned and tilted her head, examining me closely. Suddenly, I felt as if I was on display, and I looked away. She touched my shoulder, checking to see if I was okay, and I closed my eyes, buying myself some time.

I knew there was no need to feel embarrassed with her or uncomfortable, but for a moment there, I did. Though she was trying to be playful and do her best to take my mind off of the traumatic night, thoughts of a knight made me feel sad. He didn't exist in my life, and I thought it was safe to say that he never would.

Sorrow overcame me, and I tried to pacify it by focusing on something else. I looked around the room, trying to gauge the time by the windows.

"What time is it?" I asked groggily.

"It's 10:00 p.m. We still have time before 11:00" She pushed my wet, sweaty strands off of my face and behind my ear. "I rushed to get here as quickly as I possibly could. I worked until five today and then covered your shift at the diner."

I looked up quickly, panic crossing my face. Jess shook her head. "Don't worry, Lisa and Jerry understand why you couldn't come in." She grabbed my hand and softly said, "They remember, so they sent me home a little earlier with a pumpkin pie for you."

I wiped the tears that fell from my eyes. Lisa and Jerry were the two sweetest souls I had met. They had been married for fifty-five years and were still very much in love with one another. They argued about everything, from the price of the specials to the napkins, but they always kissed and made up quickly. They were the best. They also never questioned me about why I stopped writing or about that night.

"Mmm, pumpkin pie. My favorite." I cocked my eyebrow. "Lisa must have made this just for me, as the only pies she has now are apple and blueberry and peach." A genuine smile hosted itself on my face now thinking about Lisa's generous, loving heart. "Aww, very sweet of her." I placed my hand to my heart, feeling very honored to have such a loving circle of support.

"Do you think you can share a slice with your best friend?" Jess tried to reach for the pie, and I sidestepped her and ran toward the kitchen. I heard my best friend laughing, and I couldn't help but feel a little lighter as well.

"Of course, but only a slice," I yelled out from the safety of the kitchen, away from Jess's fingers. I laughed under my breath as I rummaged through my drawers until I found a knife to cut the juicy pie into luscious slices. When the pie was cut, I placed a big piece on my plate and another on Jess's plate. I grabbed two forks, and with two plates in my hands, I walked back toward my friend and handed her a plate along with a fork. She groaned in pleasure as the first bite hit her tongue. I would have laughed, but I did the same. It was that good. I looked at Jess, and she instantly sensed my gaze on her. I motioned toward my bedroom and started walking. Jess followed. We sat on the bed and devoured the pie. I could hear the clock outside on the church chiming. I knew it was chiming eleven times. I didn't have to count. It never affected me, only on this day. Jess placed her plate on the nightstand and reached for mine, depositing it right next to hers. She gathered me in her arms and started telling me the story of my knight. Moments before, thoughts of my knight made me sad; however, now it made me hopeful because he was someone I would have loved to meet. Tall, dark, and muscular. Jess couldn't decide on what he did for a living, but she said whatever it was, he was darn good at it. Her story brought me peace and most importantly, strength. Strength to take the next step.

I took a deep breath in and let it out. "Jess, when I was a small girl, another small girl once told me that she would protect me from monsters and that I should never be scared. I am counting on her now to help me fight the unknown demons in my past and to help me solve a puzzle that is my life. Do you think she is up for it?"

"Sure am. I was tough then and even tougher now, so those monsters better stay away," she said emphatically. She grabbed my hand and held it, just like she used to do when we were younger. "So you really want to do it?"

I nodded. "I feel like I have to. My life is incomplete because a chunk of it is speculation. There are days when I try to forget the past, but I can't really escape it. I need to go back there even if it is just to reminisce about how I lived and how I could have lived." I stopped talking as I realized something. "Wait—you won't have any problems with taking time off from your job?"

"What job?"

I gasped, and Jess laughed, undisturbed by the fact that she was jobless.

"You didn't?" I said, disbelieving. Jess shrugged her shoulder as if quitting a job was no big deal for her. "That job was getting me nowhere. You know that the only reason I took that assistant job for the lawyer was because I thought he was hot. I just grew tired of it, you know."

"Of Jake, you mean?" I asked quizzically.

"Okay, okay. You got me. Who knew he would end up being so uptight and so boring?" She sat up and faced me.

"Why do I get the feeling there is more to this story? Did you let him down easy?" I inquired.

"Of course. I don't think he took it too hard though. Get this." She hit my shoulder gently. Jess and I were both touchy people. We always talked with our hands and touched people's hands or shoulders. We tried to stop, but it was a lost cause. "I saw him the very next day when I went to grab a cup of coffee with a tall and leggy redhead. I wanted to make him sweat a bit, so I walked over and said hi. Guess what I learned next?" she asked, her face animated, retelling the story.

I could feel my eyes widen in surprise. "What?"

"Apparently this beautiful woman was his fiancée of fourteen months and they are getting married this August. In less than a month!" she said, raising her voice. She was getting red, and I could see that this run-in affected her. Jess pretended like she didn't care, but she had really liked Jake. She had fallen for him pretty quickly.

That lying cad.

I shook my head and finally spoke, "I know I am repeating myself, but WHAT!" My mouth was wide open. I was really surprised. I met Jake the first day Jess started working at the firm. I came to pick her up after work and we all ended up going for drinks. He and Jess hit it off right away. I remember asking him if he was seeing anyone that night and he said he was single and could not stop flirting with Jess all night. He kept telling her she was a girl that could make him want a relationship. To make matters worse, I liked him. He passed my test, which shows you how bad I was at spotting the not-so-good guys.

"What happened next?" I cringed inwardly. I always had a hard time understanding people who lied. Why not come out and say he was engaged? That two-faced snake.

"I wished them a fabulous day. Oh, and I reminded Jake to send my very generous severance pay along with a glowing recommendation to me in the mail, and I walked away with a smile and my head held high."

I smiled and reached out to hug her. "That's my girl!"

I knew Jess was pretending not to be hurt by acting indifferent. It was her defense mechanism. Had been since she was little.

I knew she was disappointed. She had told me all about the promises Jake made to her and the words of love he showered on her. We now knew that they were all empty and untrue.

Jess hugged me back tightly. "There has to be something better out there for me, you know? My calling is still out there. I always wanted to teach. Perhaps I could look into programs and follow that path?" She looked at me. "That is why I need a break. In order to sort out one's life, I think you have to return to the place it started, to your roots."

I rolled my eyes at her. "Ughh, this trip is a step back into our past. A past that we wanted to outgrow, not to mention outrun so quickly." I sighed and my best friend, my only family, reached for my hand and held it tightly. She gave it a good squeeze and I felt better. She always had that calming effect on me.

"You are getting a chance to find out something more about your past. I think you would regret it down the line if you didn't go back." Sadness crossed her face. "I wish I knew about my past. About my birth parents. About how I ended up at the Stones. I would follow every lead until it gave me some insight."

Jess was so passionate about this. I had never seen her quite so fired up about our past. I was about to tease her about it, but she jumped off the bed and crossed to the bedroom window. I could tell that something was on her mind.

"We are different now. We are stronger. It'll be okay," Jess said unwaveringly, and I believed her.

"It'll be okay," I whispered, tilting my head to the side, watching my best friend intensely, remembering moments when those words were lies to both of us. Lies we told to survive.

I know she remembered. I could see it in the stiffness of her back and shoulders.

"It'll be okay," I said once more, robotically.

I hoped this time those three words were the truth.

His fingers traced the outline of the key, the key that he made many, many years ago. Its presence in his hand brought him comfort as he walked toward the windowsill, the resting place of the candle that he burned for her every night.

He reached for the box leaning against the candle and took out a match, striking it on the side of the box that contained the strip that would bring him illumination. He lit the candle and watched as the flame danced. Instantly he was reminded of a time when he danced. With her.

Many moons ago.

He closed his eyes and transported himself to a happier time, a time when he could touch her, a time when he placed an exact copy of this key around her neck, caressing her arms, her neck, kissing her.

He forgot about the lit match in his hand, and it scalded him. It didn't hurt though. Nothing could ever compare to the hurt of losing her.

He closed his eyes once more, conjuring up the happier times, and that was when he felt her presence. The scent of magnolias encased him, and his nostrils flared slightly, inhaling their scent.

Magnolias.

Her favorite flowers.

He opened his eyes and let the tears fall freely.

He blew out the candle, darkness enveloping him. He walked toward his bedroom, the scent of magnolias keeping him company.

Chapter Two

Landing Falls

Kendrew Batten

"Mr. Morris, a new box of books just arrived. Do you want me to start working on them, or should I wait for you?"

"You can go ahead and start. I'll be there in a minute," I could hear him yelling from the back of the shop. He was sixty-two years young, a war veteran who had seen it all, and nothing stopped him. I'd been helping at the shop for a few years now, as I loved antiques and considered Mr. Morris to be like family. He was the only interaction I had besides the guys at the firehouse.

I had wanted to be a firefighter since I was thirteen years old. I made a promise to myself then that I would save lives. I would without a moment's hesitation run into an inferno knowing that I might not make it out. Maybe that way I would be able to atone for my sins.

There was a reason I felt that way, and it was the same reason why I was a loner. I lived alone in a house that could easily be divided with two more roommates, but I chose not to. I reveled in the solitary life. The simple life. I didn't even date anymore, not because I couldn't get a date (I had been told I was handsome on multiple occasions), but because I didn't like the emotions involved. I liked relationships with no strings, without emotions, an even exchange where I pleased you and you pleased me and afterward we each went our own separate way. It was always the same terms with me. No strings was my thing.

I don't want to brag, but I rarely went out of my way to get a woman. I got hit on at the grocery store, fighting fires, sitting on my steps, you name it. I guess it didn't help that I was Mr. February in a firefighter's calendar. February. The month of love . . . or lust. You pick. In the picture, my six-foot-three frame, broad shoulders, and shirtless body were on display, smeared with soot all over my six-pack. I had done it for charity; all the guys in my ladder company took part in it, but after that calendar came out, the single women and some not-so-single women had been flirting with me. I didn't like to date anyone in my town though. It would complicate things. Not that I would call what I did dating. I occasionally went out to bars with the guys and almost always left with a woman. I never called her back or met her again. I never led anyone on though. I always told them that one time was all this would be. One time was all it could be. Sometimes I met the occasional woman who thought that she could "heal me." It was never going to happen. She would end up with a broken heart even after I warned her.

I loved single life, and there was no room in my quiet, solitary life for a plant let alone a woman. It was just me and my books and my thoughts.

I liked it that way.

I was used to it that way.

I didn't deserve anything else.

My last serious relationship was four years ago, and it lasted for a couple of months. She was a stewardess that was in town for a bachelorette party, and I met her at Harry's, which was a local bar here in town. It was an instant attraction, full of intense lust, and it surprised me. I liked her and she was a good girlfriend. She was away a lot, and that meant I didn't see her often, which I think was a big reason why it lasted close to four months. I tried my best to be monogamous with her because I wanted to see if maybe I could turn into a relationship guy. With my schedule and hers, we would see one another every two weeks or so for a day or two.

In the end, it just didn't work out.

It always came down to the same reason. I just couldn't give her what she needed. I couldn't truly and fully be hers. Resentment, shame, and guilt took up a big chunk of my heart space, leaving very little room for romance.

Hayley, that was her name, had left me when I wouldn't open up and commit. However, we still texted each other occasionally, and just this Valentine's she surprised me by showing up at my door with nothing on under her coat. My body ignited, but my heart stayed as frozen as ever.

Letting someone in would mean letting them see me for who I really was. That terrified me, and I refused to let that happen. There was a reason I woke up screaming and drenched in sweat every time I fell asleep.

There was a reason I didn't allow myself to love.

Everyone I love, died.

Just like he had.

I loved him and yet I had killed him.

A hand on my shoulder startled me and rescued me from my gloomy, heartbreaking memories.

"Any good finds in there?"

I looked at the hand on my shoulder and felt its strength. I borrowed from it. "A lot." I looked at the leather-bound books with dark green, maroon, and black covers and forced a smile. "This is a really great find." I showed him the book that caught my eye. He took it from me and scanned a few pages.

Jim and I especially loved going through the books. We were both avid readers and loved classics. I was stuck on Hemingway currently, but before that it was Shakespeare and Milton. After Hemingway, who knew which author would grab my attention? Perhaps one in this new box full of books?

I watched as Jim placed the book I gave him down on the table and reached for another book, running his hand across the cover.

"Wow. This will be fun." He looked my way. "You can run off if you want. I will close up."

"No, it's okay. I'll stay."

"No date tonight?" He looked at me sheepishly. "I don't believe it."

"Not tonight." I paused for a moment and grinned. "Tomorrow."

"Someone from town, if you don't mind me asking?"

I shook my head. I didn't date anyone from town. Never had and never would.

"I know someday you will meet someone who will make you want to change that." He stopped for a moment as if he was reminiscing about someone special, and smiled. "I know I did."

"I don't know, Jim," I said. "I don't want to get involved with someone when I know I can't offer them my best self."

"Perhaps the right person for you will be in the same boat as you?"

I raised an eyebrow, not quite getting what he was saying.

"Perhaps she will also think she's not relationship ready, but all she will need is your puzzle piece to match hers," Jim said.

I laughed. "My puzzle pieces are jagged." I shook my head. "Plus, where would I meet someone like that?" I said somberly. I looked outside the windows at the passersby on the street.

"Perhaps she will come find you," he said softly.

I pondered his words. A tiny part of me would have loved to meet someone special to go through life with, but I knew that was impossible. I stayed away from relationships and people I could eventually care about for a reason.

It was not for my protection, but for theirs.

The direction my thoughts were taking me only made me feel dejected, so it was time to change the subject.

I looked back at the books. "I'm grateful these beauties arrived. I think they will sell very fast." I avoided looking at Jim because I knew he would see the struggle inside of me, the internal battle between loving and closing myself off. He would see the wishes that I burned inside of myself, burying the remnants deep into the ground of my heart. Wishes that occasionally tried to rise from the ashes like a phoenix.

No, I didn't want her to arrive anytime soon, or ever, for that matter.

My life was content just as it was now.

He lit the candle and waited for the fragrance of magnolias to scent the room. He closed his eyes and waited. He finally got a subtle whiff of it and smiled. He looked at her picture hanging on his wall, and talked to it. He did so daily. He told her about his day, about the shop, about the people he encountered, and most importantly, he talked to her about the love he felt for her. After their talk, he strolled outside, leaving the living room door ajar, allowing the scent to trail after him on the porch. He sat in his rocking chair and faced the tree, their magnolia tree. In that moment, the scent of magnolias got stronger and he turned to the vacant chair next to him and held out his hand, as if he was holding hers. He felt a breeze against his palm and he closed his hand, holding onto her tightly, wishing that memories and subtle scents of magnolia weren't the only things left of her.

"I love you," he whispered. "I always will." He turned slightly so that he was facing the chair alongside his, and smiled.

Perhaps it was the wind, but the chair started slowly rocking in tandem with his rocking chair. He exhaled the breath he didn't realize he had been holding and watched the tree surrounded by fields of grass and starry skies. He watched the changing leaves fall and remembered how much they both loved to play in the leaves.

Memories, the scent of magnolia, the creaky rocking chairs and crickets lulled him to sleep, a smile on his face because he knew she was with him, and everything was okay when she was there. The pain momentarily dissuaded. Magnolias and her love had that power.

Chapter Three

Landing Falls

Kaitlyn

"Why did I listen to you?" I said while frantically pacing back and forth. "Sometimes the past is better left in the past. Why did you agree to come with me? Why didn't you talk me out of this crazy plan? Why—?"

"And why did you have to pack so much?" Jess cut me off and gave me her goofy grin that was frustrating me right now, so I glared at her. "I mean if there was no point in coming here, why pack as if we were staying here for years to come?" She winked at me, and my glare turned into narrowed eyes at her.

"Can you please be serious for at least a moment? This is serious business here." I continued pacing, wringing my fingers, reminding myself to breathe deeply.

"Which is why we had to come. Serious business means serious business." Jess found this situation amusing. "Also, you had practically two and a half months to change your mind and you didn't, so don't you dare blame me, missy." Jess was laughing, but she had her index finger in my face. I knew she was serious when she did that. That broke the tension and made me laugh. I couldn't be mad at her. She had always had my back.

She was also right. I had put off the trip a couple of times until I realized that running wouldn't solve a darn thing and set a date and kept it.

I looked around and realized we were lost, standing in the middle of a street with our luggage, a map in Jess's hands and clueless expressions on our faces.

"Now where exactly is this home? According to your directions, we should be standing in front of it, but we are in front of a cemetery, and I have goose bumps. You know I hate cemeteries." A crow landed on a nearby tree startling me, and I leaned in closer to Jess. "Also, I am freezing. So do you know where we go, Miss I Know My Way in Life?"

"Well I never did say I was an expert in deciphering directions." She rolled her eyes. "Don't worry, I think I know where we have to go now."

"Well lead the way, madam."

After circling the town for one hour and finally succumbing to asking a passerby for directions, we found ourselves in front of a beautiful white colonial home with hunter-green shutters. This house had once belonged to my grandmother, and now it was mine. I still could not believe it.

The front porch looked inviting and I could imagine my grandmother making use of it. Perhaps she even wrote some of the letters from it?

I took in the home, and even from a few feet away, I could tell the paint was chipping everywhere and the home definitely needed a facelift. It was a grand home, yet standing in front of it, it did not feel overwhelming. I felt warmth seep out from the front door and make its way to me on this brisk, early October day.

This home was just like the home I had dreamed about when I was with the Stones. In my dreams, I would run through the door up the flight of stairs to my own room that had three beautiful windows overlooking a small hill. Every morning the sun would wake me up with its warm hug, and every night I imagined myself falling asleep with the dark skies and moonlight bathing my skin. I daydreamed about sitting by the window right next to a big dollhouse. After school, I would rush home to see my momma smile at me as she was preparing to take cookies out of the stove. They were chocolate chip. Always chocolate chip.

Jess walked up the four steps leading up to the porch, and I watched her as she started to peek into windows. I could not resist shaking my head at her and laughing, because this was Jess. Always the explorer and always up for an adventure while I just stood in the driveway and took in my surroundings. Situations like this usually left me out of my comfort zone, overwhelmed and anxiety ridden, but I was surprised that I felt at peace here.

No cold sweats or shaking or trouble breathing.

My eyes settled on the white wooden distressed rocking chairs that looked very inviting on the porch. I could imagine watching sunrises and sunsets from there. I left Jess to peek into more windows, and I took a walk on the pathway that led me to the back of the house. I passed beautiful mums planted along the house in shades of yellow and burnt orange leading up to crimson red.

Ombre shades of fall.

The garden was larger than I had imagined, and it even housed a small pond. Though overgrown with weeds and tall grass, it was like stepping into a secret paradise, a garden lover's delight. There was a beautiful, large magnolia tree in the middle, sitting on top of the hill, right near the pond. As the sun set, it looked like it was on fire and glowing, calling to me. I wondered if I could talk Jess into climbing it with me tomorrow. I chuckled because that discussion would be pretty comical. Jess did not like heights at all. Just thinking about climbing a tree would break her out in hives.

I turned back around and started walking back to the front of the home. Jess was now sitting in one of the rocking chairs and was watching me. I glanced at the stairs, took a deep breath, and made my way to her on the porch. My eyes were drawn to the door with two lovely urn planters flanking it. They were filled with yellow mums, and two large pumpkins had been placed in front of them. Beside the door, above the doorbell, was a small sign with an inscription. I reached out and touched the bronze plate. I traced the words and whispered them, a smile coming to my face. It said, Welcome Home.

I knew this home would require some work before I could sell it, but it definitely had charm and potential and I would enjoy my stay there while renovating it. First things first, I needed to weed the overgrown sprawling yard in front and mow the grass. I would put a bench in the garden and a swing under the magnolia tree. Mostly for charm and curb appeal for potential buyers, but also for my enjoyment. Nothing wrong with delighting in it a bit before I sold it.

In my head, I was already creating lists and tackling DIY projects. I needed to paint the porch, the doors, replace some shutters. That was just the outside work. In just a moment, I would know how the inside looks.

I jinxed myself by saying I was not overwhelmed. I now started to feel the panic creeping in. The peace I felt moments ago was quickly replaced by the unknown, and it terrified me. I was so nervous and my hands were shaking. I dropped the keys and picked them up, mumbling under my breath.

It was silly to be so nervous about a home's interior, wasn't it? I took a deep breath and put the key in the lock.

The one tie to my past had lived here and walked these grounds that I was currently on. I wiped the sweat from my forehead and turned to Jess, who was rocking away, yet watching me closely from the chair.

"Hey, Jess, how about we leave this luggage right behind this closed door and go find some pumpkin pie and a pumpkin latte first?" I knew I was deflecting and postponing the inevitable, but I just needed some time to prepare myself.

And to kick this anxiety in the butt.

"Yes, please. We definitely earned it after all that walking earlier," she said enthusiastically.

I nodded in agreement, and we fist-bumped each other, laughing.

***

After pumpkin lattes, Jess went to the library to look something up in the archives. She didn't elaborate, and I didn't press her. I knew that if she wanted to share it with me, she would, so I walked around the town, taking in the sights and smells. Pumpkins and cinnamon wafted through the air, and I found myself soaking in the homey feel of this town. Passersby would say hello as they walked by, and everyone was so helpful and friendly.

I walked until I found myself in front of a large brick building. A building that fiercely grabbed my attention.

"Wow," I exclaimed under my breath. The structure before me was beautiful, and I was instantly drawn to it. It was a brick building, four stories high, with big windowpane windows. The bricks were distressed and beautifully weathered. I walked around the building, running my hand over it, feeling the cold, rough bricks against my fingertips.

Memories of a beard scraping my breasts assaulted me, transporting me to the time that my back was against the cold pavement, bricks of the building adjacent to me my only vantage point as I looked away from his menacing eyes.

Eyes that had pinned me down just like his body had.

I had refused to look at him. I refused to show him the fear in my eyes.

I felt the fear spread throughout my body and I fought the onslaught of nausea. I leaned against the brick and put my head between my legs for a while and fought the memories of this all-too-real moment in my life just mere months ago.

A little over fourteen months ago.

Breathe.

I am okay.

Breathe.

I will be okay.

Breathe.

I counted to a hundred slowly and felt the tremors inside of me subside.

I hoped one day these nightmares would no longer be triggered.

I had survived and would survive.

The last few months had been a testament to my survival skills, though some days were rockier than others. I was an expert at burying sadness and hurt deep within me and not allowing fear or anger to rule me.

I was stronger than that. I was a fighter.

The breeze off of the water caressed my clammy skin, and I inhaled every gulp of air that blew my way. I felt like a fish dangling on a line gasping for breath.

After about five minutes or so of this breathing ritual, I was finally feeling better. I rose slowly and walked toward the back of the building.

I focused on the allure of the building. The back of the brick fixture was even more exquisite than the front. I cautiously ran my hand over the large wood doors and traced the bronze plaque on the left side of the doors:

Historical Society Site
The MILL
c. 1816

I knew there was a reason I was drawn to this mill. I loved old antique items, but especially old buildings. I went up the three steps and looked at the view, imagining what people working inside the mill saw two hundred years ago. I lost myself and took my senses on a journey to the past, and I could almost see a child poking his head out and waving at me from one of the windows above and a woman ushering him to get back to work before peering out the window herself to see what her child was looking at. I could imagine men and women working hard alongside their young children, trying to make a living, trying to survive. All working long hours, alongside the water that never gave up, that never stopped moving.

I had always loved the water. It seemed to have a calming effect on me and my free-spirit nature. Jess always teased me that I was a mermaid who somehow got her feet, but that my soul remained half aquatic. She once joked and said that I gave up the water for my knight in shining armor.

Jess and her fairy tales.

I shook my head, but couldn't stop the smile from forming on my lips.

The sun felt so reviving on my skin and so warm, just like a loving hug. I tilted my head up and basked in its golden glory before watching the sun dance with the water, creating a beautiful display of glittering lights. I especially loved the twinkle of the sun's rays as they gleamed off of the water, the sun and water working to create glitters of colorful light. I also loved the smell of the sea, the salty feel of it on my lips, and the sound that the water made as it crashed against the coast and the rocks. Some days it was gentle, while other days rough, but it was always powerful and always in control.

I wanted to be like the water, fluid and sure of my path through the uncertain terrains in my life.

I looked up at the building once more and waved to those imaginary souls in the windows and to all the souls trapped in the past, still living in this building. Jess also loved to tease me about that because ever since I could speak, I had always believed in ghosts and spirits. Some might say I'd had imaginary friends at the home growing up since I didn't talk to anyone but Jess and Jax, but I always knew it went beyond that. I believed in ghosts, even if others thought I was nuts. It made me feel less alone, knowing that souls somehow managed to live on.

I could feel life in old abandoned buildings and in antique collectibles. It was as if I could feel the people who lived before me and their residual energy.

I shook my head at the direction my thoughts had taken me in. Always a daydreamer and always a writer, penning stories in my head.

I snuck one quick look back at the building and at the water. I started walking, wanting to explore more places in this town. I noticed a cobblestone street that was pedestrian only, and I hopped off of the sidewalk and rejoiced in walking on the cobblestone street. I felt it had an exquisite and old story to tell. I imagined all the horse-drawn carriages that pounded against it, leaving their energy behind.

I got so lost in my daydreams of cobblestones and the incredible feeling of having them under my feet that I didn't spot the stunning shop in front of me until I was practically at its doorstep. I gasped in excitement.

It was an antique shop.

I stopped myself from barging through the door, but I couldn't stop the eagerness spreading through me, anticipating what I would find, bracing myself for the treasures that I was sure abounded past the lovely, heavy, wooden double doors.

Like a giddy child about to enter a candy store, I reached for the doorknob and pushed the door open. The door creaked and the sound settled in my heart.

I imagined all the people before me who used the same door and all the history that it held.

I was transported to a safe place, and I loved it.

My eyes scanned the store and dilated in excitement, taking in the beautiful and one-of-a-kind inventory. This place was like a museum, and the energy was so astounding. The smell of old books drifted toward me, drawing me to them, and my feet moved toward the pile of books and toward the gentleman working at the counter, rearranging those books.

He looked to be in his sixties, about six feet tall with a lean physique. He was dressed in a light blue button-down shirt that was tucked into a pair of dark blue jeans. He was holding a book, immersed in its yellowed pages. Looking at him, I could deduce that he was a catch when he was younger because even now in his later years he was quite handsome. My eyes fell to the book he was holding, a book of Pablo Neruda poems.

"Good afternoon," I said softy, and watched as his eyes darted up and spotted me. Surprise filled his eyes.

"Good afternoon. I didn't hear anyone come in. I'm sorry," he said apologetically.

"No, I'm sorry for intruding." I pointed to his book, and he didn't say anything. He was just staring at me as if he hadn't heard a word I just said.

"I didn't mean to interrupt," I said, trying to break the silence. He still did not answer. He continued to look at me with a puzzled look on his face. His brows were drawn together. I watched as his gaze changed from surprise to shock. As if he had seen a ghost. I noticed his eyes fall to my neck.

Do I have some dirt there?

I instinctively touched the side of my neck, and his eyes flickered back to my face. He knew that I noticed him looking there.

I should have felt uncomfortable in a new place with a man I did not know staring at me as if he knew me. Yet I did not, and I could not explain why that was.

Deep down, I just knew that nothing bad could happen to me, that he would not allow any harm to come my way. I felt exceedingly tranquil and I intensely felt like I belonged in this shop. I gazed into his calm eyes and saw love, comfort, and compassion swimming in his beautiful, blue as the Caribbean Sea eyes. I found that I could not speak, nor could I move, so I just stood there and so did the gentleman. What should have felt uncomfortable just felt exceptionally natural to me.

Almost as if I had stepped home when I stepped through those doors.

"Mr. Morris, where did you want this box again?" A man that looked to be in his early thirties emerged from the back room with a big box in his hands. He broke the spell between me and the gentleman. I turned toward him and smiled. He was very handsome, about six foot plus a few more inches. He had dark-colored hair and was very well built with broad shoulders. He was dressed in a light blue sweater with the sleeves pushed up his forearms and out of the way. His jeans were distressed and emphasized his great body.

That man never skips leg day at the gym.

He was carrying a heavy box overflowing with old books. The kind with the leather covers and beautiful embroidered words, some gold plated and others weathered, but nonetheless priceless.

Since July 15 occurred, I had stayed away from men, but this handsome guy captured my attention. I felt my heart beating rapidly inside my chest. I looked at him trying to see if he could hear.

I was met with his beautiful, hazel-colored eyes. They were mesmerizing and intriguing, and I found myself unable to look away.

Unfortunately, the attraction was one-sided. Here I was eating him up like a double chocolate cake, and he was looking at me with an annoyed look on his face.

Was I drooling?

He probably got attention and disliked it. Probably had a wife or serious girlfriend.

I turned off my attraction to him and instead tried to be friendly.

I could do that.

Friends. Friends. Friends.

What do I do now?

Say hi.

Yes. I will say hi. Good idea.

"Hi," I managed to croak out.

My brain could not come up with any other words. Conversation totally escaped me. I was nervous, overcome with sudden shyness, and I felt my face and neck burning up. I am sure I looked like a freaking tomato.

He mumbled, "Hi," back. At least I thought that was what he said before abruptly turning away with the box of books. I watched as he quickened his pace and entered a room to the side of the cash register.

He was beautiful from the back as well.

Totally rude, but hot as hell.

I looked back to the gentleman that rude guy called Mr. Morris, and he was smiling. He looked in the direction the man walked away to and then looked back at me, a sparkle in his eyes.

He no longer looked like he had seen a ghost, but a comedy show. I could tell he was holding back laughter, and I felt myself blushing again.

What just happened? I wondered.

"So are you new in town?" Mr. Morris broke the silence. He was looking at me with interest.

I didn't know what to say. The last time I was here I was young. So much had changed. The people, the neighborhood. Yet there were many similarities as well.

Do I say no? Yes? Do you admit to being from the place that you swore never to remember? How do you answer a simple yet deep question like that?

I answered quickly before the turmoil of my thoughts showed on my face.

He seemed to be looking at me very closely. Almost as if he was waiting for my answer. He couldn't know me, right? Or recognize me?

No, it had been too long and I was so different.

"Yes, you could say that."

"Welcome," he finally said. "My name is Jim. Some—" he paused and pointed to the room to the side of him where rude jerk had sauntered off to "—call me Mr. Morris. Please call me Jim though." He reached out his hand, and I took one big step forward and shook it. His hand felt warm against my cold one.

Figured, all my blood had rushed to my face and neck.

"Kaitlyn Stone. Nice to meet you as well."

He was looking at me with questions in his eyes. I wondered if I favored my grandmother or if I reminded him of someone?

"I think you'll like your stay here. Will you be here long?"

"Not sure yet. Probably a month. No more than two. But then again, who knows?" I shrugged my shoulders. "Destiny kind of writes its own story. Mine brought me here. It just didn't specify the details. I take them as they come."

"That's the way to look at it. You are a very wise young lady. I apologize, but I should have asked earlier, were you looking for something in particular?"

"Actually, is that book for sale?" I pointed to the book on the counter that he was holding earlier.

"No, it's not."

"Oh. Too bad. I love Neruda." I couldn't help the pout that formed on my face, and I quickly wiped it off, hoping that Mr. Morris didn't see it.

"Then it's yours." He picked up the book and offered it to me.

"I thought it wasn't for sale?" I asked, taking the book from him diffidently.

"It's not. I could never put a price on Neruda's poetry. It's priceless."

"That's why it should have a price. Especially an edition like this." My finger pointed to the book. "A hefty price."

"Consider it a welcome gift. Enjoy it and feel free to come in here as often as you like," he said, looking delighted.

"Thank you so much." I hugged the book tightly to my chest, tears of gratitude filling my eyes. "I will definitely be back. This is my kind of store." I looked around, a smile forming on my lips that quickly spread to my eyes, replacing the tears.

I motioned toward the door and the foot traffic outside. "Well, I have to run. I have a dinner date with my friend that I came here with. See you soon." I walked toward the door, and as I was about to reach for the doorknob, I stopped and looked down at the book in my hand one more time and traced the embossed lettering. I looked back at Jim and saw him watching me, with what looked to be a proud look on his face.

"I will treasure this always," I told him, before turning the knob and rushing out of the store in search of Jess.

As the door closed behind me, Jim whispered, "I had a feeling you would."

Dearest Mary,

We just finished "work" today. I am cold and tired. It has rained all day today, but it still has not washed away the stench of blood and death.

What I really wanted to do was go to sleep and forget what I saw today, what I saw yesterday, and what I will see tomorrow. I am scared that tomorrow may be even worse than today was.

The only thoughts that keep me from losing my mind or going depressed are thoughts of you. In my mind I see you smiling at me, running your hand across my face feeling the contours and shadows, and most of all I see you like I saw you when I first fell in love with you. Whoever said that time spent apart made the time spent together precious deserves an award.

I wonder how you will look when I come back home. I also wonder if you miss me as much as I miss you. I really, really do.

My love, please try not to worry about me. I am safe and vow to watch over myself extremely well so that nothing happens to me. I really have to go now. It is getting very dark, and the rain is starting to seep inside our sleeping quarters. I can't wait to get a letter from you and hold the same paper that you held.

Always yours,

Jim

Chapter Four

Kendrew

I heard the door close. I could finally let out the breath that I was holding. Something had happened out there when I saw her and when I looked into her eyes.

Something that had never happened to me before.

Something that I could not explain.

Something that scared the shit out of me.

I didn't like it.

Not one damn bit.

She had caught me by surprise. I was carrying a box filled with new books that arrived for Jim's perusal. We loved going through those treasures together. I was deep in thought and so excited about the books, and I was definitely not expecting to see that beauty in the store. My eyes took all of her in automatically. She was about five foot six with a gorgeous body. Even with her jacket on, I could tell she had beautiful curves. Her ass looked amazing in those skinny jeans. Man, was she freaking hot. She had dark blonde hair and green eyes. I could tell she did not wear much makeup. She was a natural beauty. And when she smiled at me, I felt my heart speed up. She seemed affected by me as well. She started to blush, her shyness catching me even more off guard, and I saw her stuff her hands into her pockets. I remember watching her lips, wanting to taste them. I believe she mouthed, "Hi," to me.

I responded with a look of boredom and disinterest.

Classy, I know.

I had come off as a jerk. I knew it, but I had to.

I had promised myself that I would never feel emotions for another person, yet one visit to a store from a complete stranger and I was weak in the knees.

I knew Jim saw what happened back there; he knew that I was affected by her, but I would just ignore talking about it. In fact, I would ignore thinking about it. It was better that she thought I was a dick than a good guy.

Better for both of us.

After that, I hurried to my hiding spot with the books and let out a long sigh of relief. That sigh did not relieve the tension.

I closed my eyes and counted to ten, and when that didn't help, I realized that I probably needed five more minutes and a shot at Harry's and then I would be okay.

I would forget her and her voice as she laughed and talked with Jim.

I *would* forget her.

Of course, I would forget her.

I just needed five minutes and that damn shot.

***

Two hours, a beer, and six shots later, I still hadn't forgotten her.

To make matters worse, she had just walked into Harry's with a woman. Beautiful as well, but my eyes automatically went toward her. My natural beauty.

Fuck, man. *My* natural beauty! Since when was she mine? She never could be nor did I want her to be *mine*.

I argued with myself under my breath. I shook my head thinking I could shake thoughts of her out of it. No luck.

I needed alcohol. More alcohol. "Elle, hit me with another shot."

"Are you sure? Everything okay, Drew?" Elle asked warily.

"Dandy. Just dandy." I glanced behind me and saw "Hi Girl" and her friend seated by the window.

She was facing me. She was looking directly at me.

Damn.

I shot her another one of my famous looks and she quickly looked away.

I looked back at my drink and cursed. I threw back the shot and waited for the burning to start. It didn't happen. I didn't know why I even waited for it. I was numb as fuck. I didn't feel a damn thing. Even Elle's laughter in the background sounded muted, thanks to my rapidly beating heart. I closed my eyes and rubbed them with my fingers.

I looked at a grinning Elle and focused on her moving lips. "Did she turn you down, Drew boy? If so, I can imagine why you're pissed. I don't think you've ever been turned down before."

I glared at Elle and moved my shot glass toward her. She chuckled and refilled my glass and walked away shaking her head and laughing.

I felt *her* eyes boring into my back. I had to leave. I got up and sat back down quickly. I hadn't had a drink in years, and one chick had me feeling like the bar had shifted a few degrees to the left. What the hell! She was turning my world upside down because I was letting her. I had to stay strong and not let any emotion seep through my cold exterior.

Act cold.

Make an exit.

Don't fall flat on your face.

I paid Elle and got up to leave once again. I stumbled on my own feet and fell back onto the stool.

At least I didn't fall on the floor.

I leaned my head on the bar. I began my ritual of counting to ten. When I felt like I had regained my equilibrium, I attempted to get up from my seat once more. This time I rose without a problem. Well, except for another growing problem. I felt her gaze on me, and it caused something else to rise with me.

Miss Hi had me hot, and I hated it.

I couldn't wait until she took her touristy ass and left this town. Hopefully it would be tomorrow, and tomorrow couldn't come soon enough.

I walked toward the door slowly and opened it. My feet felt wonky, but I managed to step outside. The cool air hit me and it felt so good. I felt much better. Like I could finally breathe.

I started walking.

I had practically forgotten her already.

I made it as far as the parking lot and heard someone rushing after me, shouting.

"Hey, where the heck do you think you are going drunk as a skunk?" It was a woman's voice. I didn't even want to see who it was. I just hoped it was not her. I continued walking and ignored the person, hoping they'd take the hint and back off. I was not in the mood for a sermon. Or a chit-chat on the side of the road.

I was trying to ignore her and must have done a great job because I didn't even hear her approach me until I felt a yank on my shoulder.

"Excuse me," she said, her voice raised.

I shook off her touch and turned on her like a feral animal. I was about to unleash a few curse words, when my eyes collided with the same green eyes that had haunted me for the past couple of hours. Only this time they were filled with anger. There was fire in them. My dick rose yet again. Perfect timing.

Shit.

I groaned out loud.

It is *her.*

Kaitlyn.

Her name has been on replay in my mind since I first heard her introduce herself to Jim.

Fuck.

I turned my back on her, took a few deep breaths to calm myself, and turned back around to face her.

She must have thought I felt sick or something because she touched my shoulder yet again, this time gently. "Are you okay?" she asked, worry replacing the previous anger.

I pushed her hand away and glared at her. "I was okay until someone interrupted my peaceful walk home."

"Walk?" she whispered. "Wait. You're walking?" She looked around the parking lot and back at me, confusion in her eyes. "You don't have a car here?" I watched a blush color her cheeks.

She was so beautiful, but I could not let my thoughts go there. I wouldn't.

"What are you, the damn police?" I growled. I couldn't allow myself to be weak with her. Only one way to do that. Stop memorizing her face and start walking. I turned away from her and started walking slowly. I heard her call out after me.

"No, I just thought you were being stupid, getting behind the wheel and driving intoxicated. I felt like someone should stop you from hurting yourself or another person."

Her words stopped me dead in my tracks. I felt the darkness and sadness coming at me full force. I turned around and looked into her compassion-filled eyes.

The next words were out of my mouth before I could stop them. "It's too late for that."

She took a step toward me, and I saw her hand reaching out. I turned away quickly, congratulating myself on not stumbling, and started walking. This time I was not stopping until I was in front of my house.

I didn't know why I said what I just said.

Why I shared that information with her eluded me.

I just knew that I couldn't have her pity, or worse, her compassion-filled touch, on me. I would unravel.

Damn.

"Are you sure you will be okay? Perhaps I can get you an Uber?" she called out softly.

I ignored her. I didn't think I would ever be okay again. She didn't have to know that. She didn't have to know anything. I was fine and would be fine. Everything would go back to normal real soon.

I told myself that.

I also told the heat burning in my shoulder to turn to ice.

The same shoulder she had touched.

Twice.

Shit.

He lit a candle and took it to the recliner in his living room. From that vantage point, he had a view of her beautiful face. Her smile was captured in a 4X6 photograph and encased in a frame on his fireplace mantle. She was beautiful, and even in a small picture, her smile sparkled and she warmed up not only the room but also his old, tired heart. He placed the candle on the side table and watched as the flame created shadows that danced off of her face.

He closed his eyes, resting his head against the chair, and he remembered the way the snow had fallen on them as they made snow angels on the ground. He remembered the beautiful snowflakes that had stuck to her eyelashes, one of a kind attracting one of a kind. He remembered kissing her lips and warming them with his, and most importantly, he remembered what they had done in the snow: they whispered, "I love you," to each other for the first time.

He leaned down and blew out the candle. He rested his head against the recliner. He no longer saw her picture, darkness had enveloped the room, but in his mind, he saw her clearly.

The scent of magnolias encircled him as he fell asleep.

Chapter Five

Kaitlyn

He was walking home, not driving. Geez, I felt like such an idiot. I had made such an ass out of myself. I watched him until he became a blur. I really didn't know why I ran after him or why I even cared if he was going to be safe. He had been rude and inconsiderate and a total douchebag from the very first moment I met him. And that look he had given me in the bar only confirmed that. I shouldn't have cared, but a part of me did, and I followed him, keeping a considerable distance, until I was sure he made it back home safely. Only then did I turn back around and go back to Jesse.

That was my good deed of the day. Perhaps that deed would count for more than a day, perhaps a year, considering how rude the subject had been.

I didn't even know his name, but I did know I didn't want to see him hurt. For a moment back there, I recognized raw pain in his eyes. I felt his sadness. I saw it permeate his entire body. He was hurting and hiding behind the pain.

I knew there were more layers to him. Layers of mistrust, scars, and sadness. I had enough of my own layers to deal with and did not need his, but I also felt bad for him. I knew so well what it felt like to be sad and lonely and immersed in concentrated pain. I wondered what happened to him that made him such a moody recluse.

I knew I shouldn't think about him so much. It was not like he gave a damn about me or how I felt or even wondered what my life was like, so I told myself to forget him and what I felt around him. I would stop asking so many questions when it came to him.

They would get me nowhere.

He wanted to be left alone, and I would respect that. I told myself that was what I would do, but I couldn't forget his haunted eyes and the expression of pain on his face. I knew that wouldn't be something I could easily forget, because for a second, his eyes reflected the same pain I felt.

It was like looking into a mirror.

***

Jess took off early in the morning on what she called her "secret mission," and it left me tackling the house on my own. By midafternoon, I needed a break and walked into town. I stopped in for a latte and headed toward the antique shop, hoping I didn't run into a certain someone while there.

I momentarily marveled at the beautiful wood door and grabbed the doorknob, twisting it to enter. Just like the very first time, the place welcomed me home. I breathed in the scents of antiques and wood and found myself feeling overwhelmingly content within the store's structure.

"Well hello there." I turned around, and Jim was poking his head out of the side room, behind the counter. The same exact spot that the rude guy went into the last time I was there.

I mentally chastised myself for thinking about him yet again and instead focused on Jim.

"I couldn't stay away." I smiled.

"I'm glad," he responded. "Feel free to look around and stay as long as you want."

"Thank you. I might take you up on that." I walked toward him. "Just please let me know if I overstay my welcome."

"That'll never happen," he said. His eyes were so kind and also so familiar. I couldn't put my finger on it.

My eyes traveled across the counter, and right next to the cash register was a copy of *Romeo and Juliet*. I gasped and grabbed the book, running my fingers through the maroon, scratched-up leather cover. I ran my fingernail over the slightly frayed corner, loving its perfect imperfections.

"I love this play." I sighed.

"I do too," Jim said, "a tale of love and tragedy."

I watched as his eyes became sad. It was as if he was remembering something.

"I don't know many love stories like theirs."

"I do," he responded wistfully. He looked at me, and I watched as he bit his lower lip. "Reminds me of my love," he said on a whisper.

I could tell that he was reminiscing about someone, and that had my curiosity piqued. "How long have you been together?" I asked.

"Since our eyes met." I watched as tears pooled in his eyes. "I loved her the very first time I met her, and love her more every single day."

"That's beautiful. Does she help you run the place?" I asked, looking around the store. I hadn't seen anyone except for Rude Guy helping out. Perhaps she was there and I missed her?

"No," he said regretfully. I watched as a tear rolled down his face and fell on the counter. He ran his hands across his eyes and cheeks, wiping away the remnants of tears. "Not in physical form at least." He looked me straight in the eyes, and I felt a shiver run through me. "I promised to love her forever, and I never break a promise. She made the same promise to me." His gaze held mine, and I found myself unable to look away. In his eyes, I saw undying love as well as unwavering sadness.

"That is beyond beautiful," I whispered. "I haven't met anyone lucky enough to love and be loved so profoundly."

"You've never been in love?" he asked.

I shook my head. I looked to the side, making sure that the room was empty before I spoke. I wouldn't want Rude Guy to hear me admit to that. Why I cared, I didn't know, but I did.

"No. I don't have much time to date." I looked at the wall behind him, avoiding eye contact. I felt my cheeks burning up.

I watched as his hand reached for mine and gently patted it. It was a brief moment of contact before he pulled away, yet I looked up at him wondering why that touch, along with those gentle eyes, felt so familiar to me.

"It's nothing to be ashamed of. Fate works in mysterious ways to bring two people together who are meant to be into one another's lives." He paused for a moment before continuing. "You cannot run away from the intense feelings when you meet the one. They spark something in you, this awareness and this fire, and one is never the same after that. That's a beautiful thing to watch when that happens."

I watched as his eyes glanced to the side, to the room Rude Guy went into the other day.

I flinched, and he noticed. He assured me quickly, "Kendrew isn't here. Just me today."

Kendrew. That was his name.

Why did my heart just skip a beat?

I was relieved to know that rude guy wasn't there, yet also embarrassed that Jim knew how he affected me.

I looked back at the book, and out of the corner of my eye saw the room in my periphery. There was no way Rude Guy and I had that type of connection.

I looked back at the book in front of me and pointed to it. I refused to think about him any longer, so a change of topic was not only greatly needed, but also appreciated.

"Is this for sale?"

"It's yours." He smiled and pushed the book across the counter toward me.

"Are you sure?" I looked at him dubiously.

"Positive." He shook his head, his smile growing even bigger.

"Thank you so much." I beamed at him and nestled the book against my chest. "I'm building quite the book collection thanks to you."

"Enjoy, my dear girl," he whispered under his breath. "Enjoy."

My Jim,

How I wish I could send you a book. I know it would be silly and impossible to do so, but I know how much you must miss reading.

I wish you were safe and here, among your books and with me, and not so far away.

I know our circumstances cannot be changed now, so instead I find myself doing things that you love to do just to be closer to you.

Which is where the book comes in. Imagine this! I went into an antique store today and was browsing the book section, and I picked up the second edition of Jane Eyre! I know you would grin from ear to ear in excitement if you were in the store with me and saw that book.

I got the book and felt your excitement course through me. I am reading it now and love it. The pages are yellowed, and I love imagining who held the book before me. Is that why you love antiques so much? The story every piece seems to tell?

I think your love of books has definitely rubbed off on me. I can't wait to gift it to you when you come back home to me.

Please stay safe, my love, and know that I love you so much.

Love always,

Mary

Chapter Six

Kendrew

I stared into my coffee. It was as dark and bitter as my mood. I tried to eat, but the thought of food made me sick. Hopefully, I could grab some dinner later tonight. For now, I was filling up on coffee and trying to not think about last night. Thinking made the pounding in my head intensify. But I couldn't seem to turn it off.

I had been so rude to her yet again. She was only trying to help, and I almost chewed her head off. I definitely deserved this hangover for being such a massive dick.

I knew what she did for me last night. Not only did she seem to read my pain, which was fucking scary, but she also made sure I got home safely. I didn't let her know I saw her, but I did. I was aware of her. I only had seen her twice, but both times, I had felt an indescribable sensation when she was around. That sensation followed me all the way home. I owed her an apology, but I would not give her one. It was better for her to hate me. It was better for both of us.

***

An hour later, when I still couldn't stop my thoughts of running toward her, I decided to make myself useful and went to Shelby's house to chop some wood for her. The sound of the ax splitting the piece of wood did wonders for my mood. It's something that I did for her every Thursday, until she left me a note on her door saying she no longer needed it. Usually that note showed up around mid to late June, when the warm weather hit these parts.

That was our system of communication. All this time that I had been leaving her groceries or chopped wood, I had never spoken to her. I saw her in her rocking chair staring out into the space in front of her many times though. She always had this blank expression on her face. From what I knew of her and personally observed, she never invited anyone in, at least not that I knew of. She was a kind yet solitary lady, and I respected that.

I would never force her to talk if she didn't want to.

I once asked myself why the interest in her? It was simple. Miss Shelby reminded me of myself. She was a loner and seemed to like it. Like surrounds itself by like apparently.

I asked Jim about her once and he got a peculiar look on his face. He got very quiet, and his body froze, causing me to shift gears and change the subject hastily. That wasn't my story to uncover. As far as I was concerned, everyone had skeletons in their closet and had the right to air them out or not.

I looked at the wood I had chopped and smiled. I put the ax down and rolled my head and then my shoulders. I wiped the sweat off of my forehead. Who would have thought that chopping wood would help my hangover? But it did, and once again I felt useful and invigorated.

I carried the chopped wood toward Shelby's house and left it on her doorstep, up against the door. I then set off home to shower. I made it to the sidewalk before movement across the street caught my eye and caused me to stop. My shoulder started to tingle. The same one she recently had touched. Apparently, cold nor hot showers could not erase her touch. Trust me, I had tried it all.

Looking beautiful in a pair of light jeans and a sweater, with the sunlight gleaming off of her hair, she ran up the stairs to her house, coffee cup in hand. I watched as she opened her door and crossed the threshold, closing the door quickly behind her.

Even after the door closed, I stood on the sidewalk, glued to the spot, and watched.

I took in the appearance of her house. It was in slight deterioration, but nothing that some elbow grease and TLC couldn't help.

I wondered if she would be fixing the place herself? Or perhaps she had someone she was living in it with? That thought never had crossed my mind until now. What if she did have a significant other?

I didn't know why, but thinking about that made me feel like someone had punched me in the gut. I didn't like that feeling one bit. I had to stop looking at her and for her. I had to leave. Yet why I stood watching her, paralyzed in one spot, I did not know.

I just couldn't move.

I hated feeling like a prisoner of my own emotions, my own demons, but that was exactly how a life with me would look.

A life with baggage and sadness and nightmares.

I wiped the sweat that broke out on my forehead and felt a pair of eyes on me. I scanned her house and realized that it was not her. I felt the sensation from behind me, someone's eyes boring into me from behind.

I turned around quickly, my eyes colliding with Miss Shelby. She was rocking away on her rocking chair, the curtain pulled back to one side, watching me with a blank expression on her face. I shot her a smile, the one that usually made ladies swoon, which she completely ignored. She just kept staring at me, and every once in a while, she glanced across the street, at *her* house. Feeling uncomfortable at being watched so closely, I glanced away from Shelby and could not stop my gaze from doing what Shelby did. I looked across the street once more, but she was nowhere to be seen. The tingling in my shoulder dissipated and I wished that I could have it back. The house was quiet, the street was quiet, and I could feel my thoughts working overtime, wondering what Kaitlyn was doing, what Shelby was thinking.

I felt anxiety start to seep in, and to diffuse it, I started walking fast. I didn't know when my pace changed, but it did. I was running. Sweat was pouring down my face and back, and my breathing was labored. I was probably beating my own personal best running time. You would think my workout was a good one, but you would be wrong.

It wasn't. I could not outrun thoughts of *her*.

My darling Jim,

First of all, I have to tell you that I am a little upset with you. In your letter, you did not mention where you are. That would at least make me feel a little better knowing where I can find you if need be. I feel so lost without you. Sometimes I wake up at night from a nightmare, one that comes very often. It takes you from my side, and I wake up screaming, only to know that it's the realest truth. You have been taken from me.

I try to be strong, but some days those dreams terrify me. What if they take you away from me for good?

I would not be able to survive without you. Your happiness and well-being are the reason I breathe.

Every time I get a letter from you, you alone seem to have the power to scare the demons away. The ones that threaten to haunt my dreams at night. You and your love guard me, and I sleep like a baby now, uninterrupted. In my dreams, you are by my side. I feel you reaching toward me. I feel you kissing the tip of my nose and my temple. I feel your cold hands (yes even in my dreams your hands are cold) cradling my face and looking deep into my eyes.

I love being with you in my dreams, and I cannot wait to see you in person. I was wondering if there is anything you would like me to send you? I would gladly transport myself to you, but I doubt they would take such a large package.

Darling, I must go. Mother is calling, and you know that mother does not like to wait. Soon, my precious darling, soon, we will be together. Remember that I love you and am keeping you to the promise you made me. You better watch over yourself so that you do not get hurt. I love you . . .

Only yours forever,
Mary

Chapter Seven

Kaitlyn

"I am so hungry. I really think I could eat everything on the menu, including the menu," Jess teased.

She and I both had been cleaning the house today and going through some old papers, and we skipped lunch. It was now 6:00 p.m., and our stomachs hadn't stopped growling for the last hour.

"Everything looks so good, but I think I will just have the salad," I said, putting the menu down on the table.

"You are going to whittle away before my eyes if you keep eating like that," Jess scolded.

"I am not that hungry. I think it might have to do with being here." I motioned with my hand. "You know, nerves."

"Are you sure that's it?" Jess asked, raising her eyebrows. "Maybe this loss of appetite has something to do with a certain hot guy?"

I scoffed. "He *would* cause someone to lose their appetite. He is a jerk, Jess. A real low-down jerk."

Jess looked at my red face and started to laugh. "I see he really got under your skin. I don't think I've seen you this worked up in a while."

"I hope you don't see me like this again," I said, looking at her pointedly.

The waitress came over and took our order.

Thoughts of the jerk really got me worked up. I took a sip of my water and tried to focus on something else. He was not worth it.

Jess had stopped watching me with a smirk on her face and was looking down at her phone. I looked around the room and took in my surroundings. It felt so cozy in this restaurant, in this town. And quiet.

Why wasn't Jess saying anything? Since when did she stop teasing me so quickly?

I looked back at Jess and she looked worried.

"Everything okay?" I asked.

She shook her head. "I just got a text from Jake," she said, tears pooling in her eyes. "He says he misses me."

"Oh no. Sweetie. Don't fall for it. He is not worth it." I reached out to grab her hand and give it a squeeze. "He lied to you," I reminded her gently.

I didn't want my best friend, my sister, to get hurt again.

"I know. I would never take him back, but it still hurts that he has this power over me. I mean, look at me, I am crying, and I almost never cry."

"It's okay to feel, sweetie. It's okay to let it out too," I told her.

Jess was looking at the phone. I didn't think she heard anything I just said. She must have really liked that jerk because when she got silent, that's when I knew she was hurting.

When she withdrew into her shell like that, the only thing that could convince her to come out was fun and laughter. Hopefully I could make her laugh.

"I have an idea," I said, reaching for her hand that was holding the phone and touching it. Jess looked up at me. "After we eat, let's go back to Harry's and throw some darts. You can imagine you are throwing them at Jake, and I can throw some at Jerk." I grinned and watched as a smile formed on Jess's face.

"That sounds like a plan," she said, placing her phone in her bag.

Our food arrived, and I seemed to have gotten my appetite again, but it was short-lived. I felt my skin tingling. I looked around for the reason, and I found it. The reason was looking my way, oblivious to the waitress holding out two bags of food for him to take from her.

I watched as she waved the bags in front of his face, disrupting his view of me. She finally got his attention, and he took the bags from her. He reached inside his wallet for money and paid. He then said something to her, and she nodded her head, smiling at him. He reached inside his wallet for some more bills and handed them over to her. His eyes collided with mine once more, and I couldn't take it anymore.

"Can you swap places with me?" I asked frantically.

Jess was devouring her chicken scaloppini and didn't hear me. Instead of waiting for her to move, I joined her at her side.

"What's the matter?" She looked at me quizzically.

"Jerk is here. Jerk was looking at me, and I don't want to look at Jerk," I whispered, my words coming out very fast.

Jess turned around, with a mouthful food, and gasped. "Holy cannoli, he is gorgeous."

"Shhhhhhhh," I hissed at her and hit her shoulder gently. I felt my face burning. Even though she had a mouthful of food, what she said came out pretty loud. I put my hands on my face and wished I could just become invisible for a moment. "Is he still there?" I whispered, my voice muffled between my palms, the same palms that were still covering my eyes.

"Nah, he left," Jess said straightforwardly. I lowered my hands and looked at her, seeing the smirk on her face.

She finds this amusing. Welllll good for her.

I rolled my eyes at her and returned to my side of the booth.

"Good." I breathed a sigh of relief and picked at my salad.

"You and he seem to show up at the same places," Jess said. I looked at her and was about to refute her statement vehemently, but she spoke again. "Maybe . . . It's . . . Fate?" I watched her emphasize every single word, all while moving her eyebrows suggestively.

I snorted. "More like bad luck," I mumbled under my breath, and Jess laughed.

I could see understanding in her eyes. She knew I didn't believe that for a moment. It was more complicated than that. He was the first man who could raise my blood pressure without much provocation. He was also the first man I was insanely attracted to.

Though he disliked me and acted like a jerk around me, I found myself feeling safe around him. I knew that sounded strange, but I almost felt like he knew sadness and pain and that we had bonded over that. I had seen his eyes many times when I looked in the mirror at myself.

Haunted, pained, saddened, and lonely.

I doubt Mr. Hotness is lonely.

He probably has girls at his beck and call.

We changed the subject and were talking about the asshat, Jake, when the waitress arrived to refill our water glasses. "How was the food?" she asked, a genuine smile on her face.

"Delicious," Jess answered, rubbing her belly.

"It was great. Thank you," I said.

"Can I get you anything else?" she said sweetly.

I shook my head. "Not today. Can we please just have the check?"

"Oh, no need for that. It's all been taken care of already, ladies."

"Who—?"

There was a loud crash from the kitchen. It sounded like glass breaking. We watched her take a deep breath and make the sign of the cross. "Oh no, not the plates again." She looked at us frantically. "Excuse me."

We nodded our heads, and she took off in the direction of the kitchen.

Jess looked at me with a knowing look on her face. "Jerk isn't such a jerk after all."

I was speechless. For once, I didn't know what to say or what to think. Why would he do that?

He lit the candle and took it outside. He watched the wick dance with the breeze. He spotted movement across the field, in her house. He got up and watched as a woman leaned on the ledge of the window, looking up at the sky, watching the moon. It looked so much like her that he couldn't believe his eyes. The magnolia scent he couldn't explain, nor could he explain feeling her around him, but this girl looked too real to be her.

Who is that? He blew out the candle and watched as darkness concealed him from her view. She, however, was illuminated by the harvest moon. She looked so much like his love, but that couldn't be possible. He watched her close the window and draw the curtains together.

Why was she in that house?

The owner of the home died a few months ago, but from what he knew, she had no surviving relatives, except for her.

Could it be her?

His precious daughter? The one he looked for and never found?

The one who had a special place in his heart just like her mama did?

His two girls. One gone and one out there somewhere.

His loves.

His reasons for living.

Chapter Eight

Kendrew

Blood. So much blood. It was everywhere. I held Whiskers in my hands. We were both shaking. He was crying, and so was I. I was immobilized. I tried to scream, but I couldn't.

I was looking at him. The person I was just playing ball with the other day. The one who always had my back. The one who never yelled at me. His entire face was covered in blood. He had a big gash on his forehead. He wasn't moving.

I was frozen watching the car catch on fire.

I was frozen watching my dad die.

It was all my fault.

I tried to scream, but I couldn't.

I woke up screaming. It was only a dream, but unfortunately the dream was based on reality for me. Though I woke up, I never quite woke up from the reality that I had caused someone's death.

My heart was racing, and I was completely drenched in sweat. I jumped out of bed and tried to open the window. My hands were sweaty and shaking so badly that it took a few tries. The anxiety started to kick in, and I felt like a fish out of its water bowl.

I counted to three and tried to push the window up some more, needing more air. I exhaled, inhaled, exhaled, and inhaled. I closed my eyes, and I fed off of the cool breeze, remembering to take short breaths. To breathe out before I could breathe in.

After a while my breathing steadied and I closed the window. I stood in the middle of my bedroom, naked and drenched in sweat, waiting for the next phase to kick in. I remembered my nightmare, or reality as I called it, and the shaking started. My teeth were clattering uncontrollably, and my hands clenched into tight fists. I felt every muscle in my body quiver and spasm.

It would pass soon. This was usually the last step before the attack passed.

I always shook uncontrollably . . . just like I did that dreadful day.

The day I wished I had died instead.

I deserved to be in the cold, dark ground, not him.

"I'm okay. I'm okay," I repeated over and over again, like a litany.

I didn't believe it.

I felt like I would never be okay. That I would never forgive myself for what happened in the past.

And I shouldn't have. No one should've forgiven me. Not my sister nor my mom. Especially not myself. I had ruined our family. I was the reason my dad was dead. That was why I would not allow myself to be happy. He deserved to live. He had love in his life, a family, a job he loved. I had no one, and it was just how it should be and would be.

I told you all I was fucked up. Believe me, I didn't lie.

***

After my nightmare, I decided to go for a run. That always made me feel better. At least it stopped the shivering. I pushed myself to the max today and ran thirteen miles. I ran past Ms. Shelby's home and saw her by the window. I waved, but she didn't see me. She never did. All these years that I had "known" her, I'd come to the realization that she did not live in the present. Jim wouldn't say much about her, but he did tell me once that she had lost the love of her life and since then had not left her house. She had pushed the pause button on the screen of her life because another person wasn't in the screenshot anymore. The moment my dad died, I pressed pause as well. I didn't let another person near me either since then.

I was glad I decided to take this path running home. It had nothing to do with running past that sexy girl's house. She did not seem like a one-night stand type of girl. As far as I was concerned, I had paid off my debt to her the other day at the diner. The way I looked at it, we were even.

No more reason for our paths to cross. She had tried to help me. In turn, I had paid for her and her friend's lunch. We were good.

That was how I saw it.

That was how it would be.

That was how it needed to be.

I promised myself I wouldn't look her way, but curiosity got the better of me. I allowed my gaze to quickly roam over her home, my mind wondering what she was doing today. I saw some paint cans on her porch and a rake leaning against the porch swing. No sign of her though.

A squirrel ran past me and up a tree on the sidewalk, and I jerked backward. My mind was elsewhere, and I didn't even see a squirrel.

Nice job, man. You got caught off guard by a squirrel. A freakin' squirrel. I shook my head, trying to shake her out of my thoughts.

Why did I care to know things about her? I had dated women in the past and never wanted to know deeper things about them, yet three interactions—short, fully clothed interactions—and I was turning into a newspaper reporter, asking the who, what, when, where, and whys about her.

I was definitely done thinking and was more interested in a little fun today. It was my day off, and I needed a diversion. One that did not involve Hi Girl.

I needed to have sex tonight. Yes, that would make everything better. It's been a while. Some action would take my mind off of thinking, and I would concentrate on pleasure. On slipping myself inside a beautiful woman. A woman who would look nothing like Hi Girl. A woman who would stop my brain from thinking.

A woman whose eyes would be dilated in pleasure and not filled with pain and sadness. A woman who was willing and understood that I was a single man and intended to stay that way. A woman who liked no strings. A woman who did not get under my skin.

Yeah, I needed an antidote for Hi Girl, and I would find it tonight.

First things first though.

Shower.

Dress.

Grocery shop.

Beer.

Sex.

And some more sex.

I smiled the entire way home, thinking about my plans tonight. Boy, did I like those kinds of plans!

My lovely M.,

Your last letter made me so happy. That book sounds like an incredible find.

What I wouldn't give to have a book here, but it would not be feasible. I am not complaining though. Your letters are the best, and no book compares, not even Shakespeare. And you know how much I love Shakespeare.

I was thinking about you last night, and you transitioned from my thoughts into my dreams. I only slept for an hour, but an hour with you was a luxury.

I can't wait to see you, my love. When I come back home, I am running straight to our magnolia tree. Meet me there with your love and you will make me the happiest man on the face of the earth. And the luckiest.

I hope you visit my dreams again tonight and tomorrow night and the night after.

I love you, doll face.

J.

Chapter Nine

Kaitlyn

What a beautiful fall morning. The air was crisp and so fresh. I breathed in as much of it as I possibly could. Deep into my lungs. Exhaled. And repeated. With every breath released, I imagined my worries disappearing. Lately I'd been thinking a lot. Not only about my feelings, but also about my grandmother. Additionally, Jess had not been herself. I watched her writing things down, and she seemed distant. I didn't know if coming back to this town was affecting her or if it was something else, like Jake, perhaps, but whenever I tried to talk to her, she avoided me. She left the house through the back door and didn't return until it was dark. I worried, but I also knew that I could not push her or force her to talk. She would do so when she was ready.

I wrapped myself in my navy poncho and remembered the sales lady who said that I made ponchos look sexy. I knew she was only saying that to make a sale, but I still smiled thinking about it. It had made me feel good to have someone see me and acknowledge me, even if it was only to make a sale of it. I had to admit, I was glad that I bought it. It was keeping me nice and comfy on a day like today. Almost as if it was giving me a hug. I closed my eyes and imagined how it would feel to have someone hugging me now. His strong arms wrapped around me. My body nestled against his body. Him kissing my neck. Before I knew it, "he" had a familiar face in my daydream . . .

How in the world did my thoughts go to Jerk?

Yes, I was attracted to him, but his personality soured any sweetness I had for him. I hated that he occupied my thoughts. I disliked him after our run-in at the bar's parking lot, but after the incident the other day, I almost started to like him again.

Enough of him. I did not want a man in my life. Especially not someone as moody as him. Even if he was as sexy as sin.

Back to my surroundings and a safer topic, I really did like it here. I could imagine coming home from work to the house I was currently staying in. There would be a cat or two at the window watching me make my way to the door. My husband would be playing with the kids in the living room, their toys splayed all across the wooden floors and rug. He would look up, and his eyes would sparkle with love for me. I would go to him and give him a kiss . . . wait . . . husband? Kids? Where did that come from?

I really had not been myself today. First, I thought about Jerk. Then I dreamed about family. No matter how much I would love a family, I didn't think it was possible. Dreams of a loving family did not come to people like me. They never had, and I was foolish to daydream that they would. I shook my head at my recent thoughts and was about to descend the steps of my porch to go for a quick walk around the neighborhood, when I saw movement from the corner of my eye. It was someone across the street, on the steps of the old home. It was a man. He was wearing a black-and-gray flannel shirt with a black puffer vest over it. He had on a dark blue pair of jeans that were lovingly worn, from the looks of it. He was crouching on the steps, pushing two bags of groceries closer to the door. It was as if he didn't want to be seen. Why was he hiding? What was he doing?

I looked back across the street. The house looked abandoned. I hadn't seen anyone leave or enter it in the time I had been here. So why was this man leaving groceries on the doorstep? He looked familiar. I realized I was being super nosy and was about to turn away and go inside. That's when it hit me.

It was Kendrew.

Oh my goodness, what was he, of all people, doing there?

I felt my body instantly react to seeing him. My heart, upon realizing his identity, beat faster and harder in my chest. I really didn't know why I was so fascinated and enthralled by this man. I couldn't seem to move or look away when he was near. I promised myself to avoid him at all costs from now on, but having him across the street from me had me glued to the spot.

I realized that I could look at and admire his body from afar without him even realizing it. Perhaps this might "cure" me of my crush on him. I was surprised his cold attitude hadn't cured me yet, but I guessed I liked men who could be assholes. Who knew? I shook my head at that thought and laughed under my breath.

He knocked over one bag, and bread, apples, and oranges rolled out. He rushed to pick them up and put them into the bag again, all while staying low. He looked around, almost as if he sensed he was being watched, so I moved quickly and quietly before he could see me. I didn't want to look like a total stalker, so while crouching behind my wooden porch railing, I continued to peek through the slats.

It's not stalking if he doesn't know, right?

I rolled my eyes at my own reasoning sometimes. I would admit, I had some strong yet strange attraction to him. I chastised myself for having it.

Who lives in that house? Why is he staying low like that?

My mind was racing, and different scenarios played in my mind. I was so deep in thought that a loud noise startled me, and I went into panic mode and pulled the poncho over my head and held my breath. I stayed that way for a good ten Mississippis, and when I didn't hear any noise in my vicinity, I slowly pulled the poncho down a bit and with only my eyes peeking through the porch slats, I looked once again.

I saw him knock on the door, and I almost laughed out loud. That was the loud noise I heard mere moments ago. I watched him knock loudly two more times before rushing away.

I continued to watch him as he walked away, his pace quickening, his hands in his front pockets and his head hung low.

Why doesn't he want to be seen? What is going on? And why do I care?

I would be leaving soon. Stalker mode off.

I got into the house and prepared lunch for myself. I looked out the window moments later and noticed that the bags of groceries were gone. I watched as the door across the street closed. I was a few seconds too late. Had I stayed at the window, I would have seen who the person was that lived there.

Who the heck lives there?

***

I checked my watch yet again. It was 11:30 a.m. and still no sign of him. I had been sitting at my window for the past two hours.

I swore I was not a stalker. Just curious. I mean, I lived across the street. If I happened to see something, that did not mean I was nosy. It just meant that I was in the perfect vicinity to witness it. At least that is what I kept telling myself.

Truth be told, ever since I was a little girl, I had loved to watch people from the window of the foster home. We didn't have many books or toys, and the world past the window's barrier always fascinated me. It still did, till this very day, especially when it rained. I loved rain. There was something freeing and beautiful about it. I loved the way the ground looked after it poured. So revitalized and renewed. Every single rainy day, you could find me in front of a window on the inside, watching the world outside.

I looked at the paint cans I bought at the hardware store, and I sighed. I really should have been painting, but for some reason I couldn't. Instead, I sat behind the curtain, watching for any movement, watching for a sexy man with groceries, who leaves them by the door, knocks, and runs off.

I reached for a peanut butter and jelly sandwich and started to nibble on it. I also had some cashews with me and some hot coffee. I was prepared in case the hunger pangs struck early or boredom from sitting in one place for a while kicked in. Either way, I was prepared.

Truth be told, I wouldn't have minded seeing him. Watching him from behind my curtain would give me the perfect opportunity to watch him without him knowing I was interested in him.

No, not stalkerish at all.

I chuckled to myself. I grabbed some cashews and waited.

One hour and a cramped back later and there was no sign of him.

I walked away disappointed.

I knew one thing for sure. I had not missed my calling. Waiting patiently for something or someone that may or may not come was tedious. And I would've probably ended up gaining weight, considering all the snacks I ate, with limited activity. There was only one way I could get answers. I was going to be neighborly and bring a pie.

I needed to find a recipe online.

I was only being neighborly.

Definitely not stalkerish.

Just neighborly.

And maybe a dash of nosy.

My dearest and truest love,

My treasure, words cannot express how thrilled I was to get your letter. However, I cannot stand one thing. You mustn't be upset with me. If I could I would tell you what region I am in, but it is confidential. Our letters are being screened and I really cannot. Please, darling, understand that I have no secrets from you. You know me better than I know myself.

I miss your laugh, especially your giggling when I tickle you. I miss the little things. Like seeing you run up the hill to our tree. Or watching the sunset with you. It really made me realize that life is all about the little moments because they turn out to be the grandest when one looks back.

Today was another difficult day for me, but I will not go into too much detail. I don't want you to worry about me. I hope that this mission ends soon and that I make it back to you so that we can have a lifetime of sunrises and sunsets together.

I promise you, I will do everything in my power and stay strong and alert so that I come back to you whole and as soon as possible. That is my promise to you. Did I ever break a promise to you?

I don't intend to now or ever. I love you, my precious fiery angel.

I am kissing this letter and mailing it to you with all my love.

Yours forever,

Jim

Chapter Ten

Kendrew

"Bro, that brunette has been eyeing you for the past hour." I followed Jason's gaze, and sure enough, the girl smiled at me and leaned forward to sip her drink while looking at me. My eyes fell on her breasts, and they were beautiful. Big and round. The type I could nibble and feast on. I loved breasts, especially big ones. I wanted to put my head between them right here and now. Well, not only my head, if I am being honest. My eyes moved up to her face. She was pretty and different from someone that had recently made a home in my head. Unlike the natural dark blonde of the one I did not want to think about, this one was a bleach blonde. She was tanned and toned and incredibly sexy. She knew it too.

I noticed her run her tongue across her lips slowly as her eyes watched me watching her.

I moved in the seat. I wanted to feel that tongue on me. She seemed to know as well because she winked. I watched her finger tap the straw in her pink cocktail, and I felt my anatomy at half-mast and rising. Her tongue was now licking that same straw slowly. My cock liked that and wanted a piece of that action. He was more than ready for some fun and release. I smiled at her, and she waved for me to come over. I left Trent, Mike, and Jason at the bar to watch the football game as I went over to say hi.

"Hi there, beautiful. Can I buy you another drink?" I smiled at her, and from this angle I could tell I had a good eye from across the bar. Her girls were beautiful. They were big and round and were spilling from her low-cut top. The view was incredible from where I was standing. It would be even better in a hotel room or back at her place, with her naked and against me.

"How about you sit down for a minute instead, stranger?" she said, her voice raspy and sexy. She patted the spot next to her and winked. She then licked her lips and watched me watch her doing it.

I looked at her friends. "I'm not interrupting?"

They giggled, and one of her friends said, "No, Bridge wasn't with us. She was too busy eating you up from afar." They giggled some more, and I laughed.

I looked at Bridge, and she did not look embarrassed or flustered.

I sat down next to her and leaned into her, whispering into her ear, "That true?"

She turned to look at me, and our mouths were mere millimeters apart. I felt her hot breath on my lips. She nodded.

"And how did I taste?"

She looked at my lips, and I could tell she wanted to kiss me. I moved my face closer to hers, and she surprised me. I was expecting a kiss, but instead, she traced my lips with her tongue.

She knew how to make a man hot for her. I let her continue her exploration, wondering what would come next. I felt her hand on my crotch, and I moaned. I could feel her smile against my lips. She nipped my lower lip and then soothed it by licking it. I couldn't stand it anymore. My lips pressed against her lips pretty hard, and I opened her mouth. My tongue invaded and started dueling with her tongue. Her hand moved in my lap, and I felt myself getting harder and harder. My tongue continued to play with her mouth, exploring it. It definitely needed some more action, especially with a lot less clothes on.

"So good. I want more and more," I told her. I put an arm around her back and pulled her in closer, so her breasts were pressed against my chest. I kissed her again, my tongue circling her tongue as I rubbed my chest against hers.

I didn't know anything about her, but I did know this: the girl was a skilled kisser.

I heard more giggles coming from around us. Her friends were eyeing us, and they pretended to look away when I noticed it. I felt uncomfortable being watched, so I pulled away a bit and I looked back at her. She was pouting. She took her hand from my lap and I almost protested.

"I'm Kendrew Batten, by the way."

"Bridget Martin, a.k.a. Bridge." I reached out my hand to shake hers. It felt weird after what we had just done, but she held onto my hand and rubbed circles against it with her thumb.

"Well, Bridge. Nice to meet you. Do you live here, or are you visiting?"

"Visiting. I needed a getaway. Some shopping and some fun are always good, right?" she responded. She pressed her breasts against me, and my blood rushed to my crotch.

I was pretty sure I no longer had any blood in my head. Everything seemed to have pooled in my boxers.

Her hand fell to my lap again. "Are you from here?"

"Yes. I live real close," I whispered to her.

"Do you live alone, or is there a Mrs. Kendrew?" she asked, and looked at me, awaiting my response.

I laughed out loud and shook my head so hard that I was surprised it didn't come off my neck. "No misses."

"That's good. I wouldn't want to hit on a taken man."

Somehow, I doubted that would matter to her, but today that meant nothing to me. She was beautiful, she was willing and ready, and I would be stupid to question her morals. She was nothing like Hi Girl, but that was the entire reason for coming here today. To forget her. To find someone so different from her.

Bridge's hand moved lower, and I felt her rubbing circles on my knee. I looked at her top and could see that she was as affected as me. Her nipples were hard and showing through her tight top.

I needed to take her someplace quiet, but first I needed to lay the ground rules. I did not need any drama.

"Hit all you want. I am single and don't plan on changing that ever. I am not looking for a serious girlfriend either," I told her. I looked at her, watching her face closely to see if she understood what I was saying. When she nodded, I continued, "My line of work isn't easy. I am a firefighter, so I believe in just living in the moment and having a whole lot of fun." I looked at her breasts and licked my lips, imaging how her nipples would feel against my tongue.

"Ohhh, a firefighter. Can you put out my fire, Ken?" She grabbed my hand and put it on the inside of her thigh.

"That depends. How long are you here for?" My eyes darkened in lust for her.

"We leave tomorrow." She pouted, and I rolled my eyes internally.

That was perfect. She wouldn't be able to get attached to me.

"Where are you staying?" I questioned.

"At the Tree Line Hotel."

"I can't let a fire consume you, pretty lady. That would be me not doing my job." I winked at her and offered her my hand. "Let's go."

"Wait, let me tell my friends I am leaving with you, so they know not to come looking for me anytime soon. I intend to stoke and put out some fires tonight and expect the same in return," she whispered in my ear, licking the tip before turning to her friends.

I heard her tell them she was going to the hotel with me, and I heard a few "lucky yous," "he's hot," "I'd hit that too," "go get him," and I couldn't help but grin. I was so looking forward to what was going to happen in mere minutes that I must've looked like Garfield with a lasagna.

Garfield.

That used to be my dad's favorite comic strip.

Every Sunday, we would read the strip together.

Damn. Just what I didn't need. Memories from the past to come at me when all I wanted to do was forget everything right now. I was definitely not going down memory lane today. I was going down on a beautiful blonde instead.

Focus, man. Focus.

Bridge grabbed me by the hand and walked toward the exit with me.

"See you at the firehouse tomorrow, guys," I said as I passed my buddies on the way out.

"See ya, man." Trent winked at me; Jason gave me a thumbs-up.

We got outside and the air hit my lungs. I was so hot and turned on that I pulled Bridge to me and kissed her wildly. I picked her up, and she instinctively wrapped her legs around my waist. This here was turning out to be my lucky day. I walked us to the side of the bar, without breaking contact with her sexy mouth, to a little alleyway between the bar and another building next door. I felt her sucking and nibbling on my neck. I leaned against the brick wall and grabbed her nice, round ass and pulled her against my erection. She let out a moan.

I felt like a king.

I felt unstoppable.

I felt tingles.

I felt eyes on me.

I looked past Bridget and saw a woman looking my way. Her right hand was touching the left side of her neck. Our eyes locked and I heard her gasp. Her face looked flushed, and she seemed flustered that had I caught her looking. She dropped her hand from her neck quickly, and I closed my eyes to gather my thoughts. I heard shuffling and her heels clicking on the sidewalk. And then it stopped. A door opened with a creak and closed. I should have been focusing on the hot woman licking her way across my throat, her hands running against my back, touching me all over. Yet I didn't. I thought about wide green eyes and her shocked expression. Her flushed face. Her hand caressing her neck.

I replayed her gasp over and over again in my mind.

Only in my thoughts, I imagined her gasping when I entered her. Her green eyes dilated and full of passion, looking deep into my eyes as I filled her completely. I groaned loudly as thoughts of Hi Girl naked in my arms, assaulted me.

"Fuck," I said harshly and a little breathlessly.

"Yes, baby. You are so turned on for me."

I was transported back to the present, to Bridget. I opened my eyes. Bridge was rubbing herself against my arousal. Her big breasts pressed against mine. She thought my erection was for her. It no longer was. I looked around for the source of my arousal and came to the realization that I no longer felt like a king.

I no longer felt unstoppable.

I felt absolutely nothing for this woman kissing me. My boner was no longer up for Bridge. All because of Hi Girl with her beautiful blushes.

Why did she have to complicate my life?

I was fine with boners and hooking up with random girls. Why did one girl have to get me so worked up with just her eyes on me? Why did I care about how she saw me or what she thought of me?

Yet I did.

Fuck.

Damn my plan.

Beer and sex no longer were on my menu. I wanted something more delicate yet exotic at the same time. Something down to earth yet passionate.

I wanted her and could not figure out why.

How did one girl show up and change my life around so completely without even trying to?

What was wrong with me? What made Kaitlyn my kryptonite?

***

I had another nightmare again. I was up all night, thinking about Kaitlyn and what to do with my unexplained attraction to her. For a brief moment, I thought about going to her home, ringing her bell, and telling her what she did to me.

To explain that nothing happened with Bridget. That what she saw was me trying to forget her. That she was the one I wanted to kiss.

I knew I couldn't tell her, it was crazy, especially considering who I was. I didn't deserve someone like her. She definitely deserved a nice guy, one not prone to nightmares and moods, and especially not one who was the cause of a death.

I was so stupid, even for a moment, to think about going to her. To think that I could be worthy of someone in my life. I was a loner for a reason. I worked hard, played hard, and lived in reality.

I was a fucked-up man who had never even fallen asleep with a woman because the nightmares always came. With them came questions and answers I was not ready to give. So instead of seeing her and telling her everything I was feeling, I buried that idea along with the feelings and watched a movie, made some dinner, and went to bed.

Burying away thoughts of her did not work. I lay awake for hours, looking at my ceiling, so aware of the sheets on my naked body, and thought about her. I thought about how it would feel to have her here tonight, naked in the moonlight, with her hair falling on my pillow, on her breasts, all over me. I grunted and tried to think about Bridget, and that didn't work. Instead I remembered Kaitlyn's eyes as she watched me dry hump Bridget. In the freaking alleyway of all places, and in broad daylight.

It surprised me that I cared so much about what she saw. The Kendrew I knew myself to be wouldn't care if another girl saw me thrusting into Bridge in the alleyway. My reasoning would always be that I was single and not looking for anything serious, just some fun. Yet here I was feeling bad that Kaitlyn had seen what went on with me and Bridge. For some reason, I didn't want her to think that I was that kind of guy. That realization scared the shit out of me. I was so used to moving from one woman to the next. Honestly, there were some girls I slept with without even asking their names. It was all about release and me giving them pleasure and receiving pleasure in return.

I liked sex and beautiful women. And the women liked me and my body and what I did to them. I looked at it as an even exchange. That's why I never believed in leading anyone on.

I didn't want to lead Kaitlyn on either, but I definitely wanted to kiss her. Maybe she would be up for a one-night stand too?

I shook my head. As quickly as that thought entered my mind, it left just as quickly.

I knew she wouldn't.

Truth be told, if I had her in my arms, I didn't think I would be able to let her go. She did something to me without even trying.

I had gone to the bar and wanted to leave with Bridge for the sole purpose of forgetting Kaitlyn. Yet the moment I had seen her I knew I couldn't stop thinking about her. Her beautiful face. Her wide eyes. Her hand caressing her neck.

I had told Bridge I didn't feel well and that I would call her later. I knew I wouldn't. I didn't even get her number. I felt like a complete loser and so ashamed that Kaitlyn had witnessed my behavior.

A part of me wanted to get to know Kaitlyn. To find out what put a smile on her face and the twinkle in her eyes. I wanted to know why she had come to town, what other books she loved, how it felt to kiss her, and most importantly, I wanted to show her who I really was. However, the part of me that lost everything I ever cared about knew that would be a very costly mistake. For both of us. That was a risk I wasn't sure I was willing to take. Would I be able to move on after being around her, near her, with her?

That was the million-dollar question, and it was the last thought I remember before dozing off.

***

Even Kaitlyn could not keep the demons away. I woke up shaking, sweaty, and struggling to catch my breath. Some people dreamt and woke up reenergized. Meanwhile, I slept with nightmares and woke up every night with the realization that I was a horrible man. That I was the reason another person could not breathe. There were times that I welcomed the nightmares and panic attacks and the struggles to breathe because they reminded me of who I was, especially when I came close to believing I was worthy of happiness. These nightmares were my reality, and they reminded me that I was exactly that guy that I didn't want Kaitlyn to see. Who was I kidding? I was the dick in the alleyway kissing a girl that I had just met. I was a guy who didn't let anyone close.

Once my shaking subsided, my vision was clear. I was glad she had seen me with Bridget yesterday. It was better she saw me for what I was.

There was no happiness on the horizon for me. I didn't deserve it.

I would do everything in my power to stay away from her. If I thought I acted like an asshole before, I would make sure I was an even bigger asshole now.

Next time my penis took over and did all the thinking, I would let it, not caring who saw. I was a one-night stand pro, and I liked it. No one got to see under my skin, and I didn't delve deep under my hookup's skin either. It was pleasure for pleasure, and I intended to keep it that way.

I headed to take a cold shower yet again. Déjà freakin vu.

My dearest and loveliest Mary,

Receiving a letter from you turns my days filled with rain and mud into a sunny field with a gentle breeze blowing. You transport me to our favorite spot on the hill under the magnolia tree. I can't wait to tell our children one day what that tree means to us. It is, after all, where I first laid eyes on you and fell in love. You mentioned in your letter that you are strong. I know that. You give me too much credit for my strength. I think I learned being strong from you, my dear. Don't act so surprised! Right this moment, you are probably laughing and thinking that I am trying to flatter you by saying such things. (Now you're surprised that I guessed right! I know you so well.) I carry the letters you write to me in my jacket right next to my heart. I wrapped them in a little piece of plastic bag so that they don't get wet since it rains every day here. You, my dear, are the reason my hearts beat.

Speaking of my heart, it just skipped a beat when you told me that you wait for me in your dreams. My beautiful and precious girl, you were just in my dreams early this morning. It was around three o'clock, and we got the call to get some rest for fifteen minutes. Next thing I knew I was reaching for you and opened my eyes to see myself leaning against the rice paddy dikes. That was the best fifteen minutes of sleep I ever had. You felt so real. Amidst all the shouting and the heaviness of my rain-soaked flak jacket, I didn't know that it was possible to dream of someone so quickly and to wake up so calm and relaxed. Perhaps I didn't dream of you, but maybe I did visit you in your dreams somehow?

One thing I will never forget is the way you looked. You are a real beauty, and I can't wait to see you in person and hold you. I must warn you, however, I may not be able to pull away from you ever again. I am glad and relieved to hear that you are doing great. Everything I do here and every decision I make is meant to bring me home in one piece. I have never prayed as much as I have prayed since I came here, but I don't only pray for myself, I pray for you and for coming home in one piece. I love you, angel!

Yours forever,
Jim

P.S. My friend (who is very nosy, I might add) just chuckled as he read my closing. I don't care. If he only knew how lucky I am he would not chuckle but glare at me with envy (he is laughing), but then again, let him learn about love on his own. Then he will understand what all the poets of the past and present write about and portray in their pieces. But even the best poet cannot explain what you and I have. No one can. Only you and I know the intensity. I can't wait to . . . (I will fill this in when I see you in person, my love). For now I really must go . . . I love you.

Chapter Eleven

Kaitlyn

Why the hell did I look at him kissing and groping that woman?

He was a jerk. Rude. Inconsiderate. I was definitely not interested, so why had I gawked?

Apparently, he wasn't a jerk to everyone, just me. That woman he was kissing the other day and whose neck he was sucking on was beautiful. The type I imagined he would go for. No wonder he disliked me. He could have a pageant queen, why even look twice at an annoying plain Jane?

Images of them together flooded my mind. I needed some heavy-duty Wite-Out for my brain.

She was thin yet curvaceous with legs that went on for miles. Legs that wrapped around him. She had been wearing ridiculously high heels and was dressed in a very sexy outfit. No wonder he had gone for that. He had seemed to be enjoying her nibbling his neck as much as she was enjoying him.

I thought I had looked at my peanut butter cup ice cream that way three days ago. Pathetic, right?

Wite-Out. Wite-Out.

She was a blonde and had long wavy hair. Hair that he had wrapped his hand around. Hair that I had seen him gently pull back as he passionately attacked her mouth. I could hear her whimper and see her rub herself frantically against the fly of his jeans. I heard him moan and grab her ass with both hands, pressing her against his crotch. And that's when I wished I was in her shoes. I felt my breasts get hard and wetness gathering between my legs. I felt my hand going to my neck, wishing it was his lips.

And then his eyes were on me. It was as if he could see into me, into my deepest thoughts.

I knew he couldn't really because if he did, he would pity me. A woman scared of intimacy, terrified of giving another person part of herself.

I won't lie, for one moment, when I approached the bar and saw him passionately kissing her, I wanted to be her.

I wanted to be held by him that way. Kissed by him. Touched by him.

After seeing that scene, I could not stop squirming in the barstool. I needed air, but I couldn't go back out there, so I went for the next best thing. Alcohol. I had hoped that a drink would replace one heat with another.

I would change my pattern of thinking. I would think about my home, the lady across the street, the lady he brought groceries to . . .

Stop, Kait . . . stop.

I needed to forget everything I had seen back there.

I needed my heart to beat normally again.

I needed this tingling between my legs to stop.

I needed my breathing to return to normal.

I needed to stop imagining that I was that girl, in his arms.

I wanted him. I think that was why I hadn't been able look away. I had been pretending to be in her shoes, knowing I never could be.

***

For the first time in a few years, my hand traveled across my body. I touched my lips and neck and then circled one nipple and then the other. My journey continued past my belly button and rested on my mound. My breathing quickened. My nipples tightened, and I was so aroused that I could feel the wetness between my legs. My hips started moving and my body yearned for touch down there. I finally dipped one finger inside and moaned. It felt so good. I circled my nub, and electricity went through my body. I imagined Kendrew touching me. My breathing got harsher and my movements quickened. My body coiled and exploded. My toes curled, and for the first time in a long time, I felt like I was going to be okay. All because of Kendrew. He had done this without being here.

I wished he was here.

***

I needed to clear my mind of what I had seen yesterday, and I knew it was a risky idea, considering I might run into him, but I still decided on paying Jim's shop a visit. I had my fingers crossed all the way there, hoping that I would only encounter Jim there and no one else.

Especially not a handsome hunk who was making out in front of my very eyes just yesterday. He was probably still with her, considering it was 10:00 a.m. Perhaps they were still in bed, holding one another, touching, kissing, tasting . . .

I needed to stop this. Shopping usually made me feel better and took my mind off of things. I was hoping it would do the same today. Especially since I really wanted to purchase a few items for my home.

My home, I didn't think I would ever get used to saying that.

I also figured that if Kendrew was in the store, he would realize that I was not affected by him yesterday at all. I would pull off an Oscar-winning performance, especially considering what had happened last night with my hand exploring my body. I knew he affected me deeply. And I was upset for letting myself feel that way.

I approached the store and pulled the handle, opening the door. I stepped inside and automatically I smiled, realizing how much I liked coming here. It was only my third time, but it brought a smile to my face and an indescribable peace to my soul, that not only settled in me but also around me.

I looked around and did not see Jim anywhere. I decided to walk around and see if there were any items that caught my eye. I knew I would find something special in a place like this. An item pre-used, pre-loved, and pre-cherished. My very own treasure.

"Good morning. Let me know if you need some help." A man's voice permeated my thoughts, and I smiled.

I turned around and now found Jim at the table behind the counter, with a box cutter in his hands, leaning over a large parcel, his eyes not looking up from it.

"I will. Thank you, Jim. Do you need any help with that?" I asked.

I watched his head come up quickly, and his smiling eyes looked straight into mine.

"Kaitlyn. So good to see you again. How are you?" Jim placed the box cutter on the counter and walked over to me and gave me a big hug.

"I am great. I am renovating my grandmother's house and will stay in town for a bit longer before I sell it."

"I am glad you are staying, even if for a short while," he said. "Perhaps you might change your mind and come to like this town?"

I shook my head. "I like this town already. Everyone is so sweet," I hurriedly assured him, not quite sure why I felt the need to do so. Perhaps it was the truth. I truly did like this town and all the people I had met so far, minus one obnoxious man who was as rude as he was sexy.

And sexy he was.

Why do I always go back to thinking about him?

I looked back to Jim and explained my reason for this visit. "Since I am staying for a little bit, I was thinking that perhaps I should get a desk for myself." I stopped and looked around the store. "Something with character and unique. I was actually thinking of getting an antique writer's desk, if you have one, perhaps?" My voice was filled with excitement and anticipation. I hoped Jim had a desk for me, just like the one I had in my mind. It would be old and have a writer's energy to it. Perhaps that type of desk would inspire me to pick up my pen and write again.

Jim's voice permeated my thoughts. "I do, right in the back." He pointed to the right side of the store. "Actually, I have about four there. Hopefully one will be the one you are looking for." He was looking at me closely. I could tell he wanted to ask me something.

"I hope so too." I smiled and headed in the direction he pointed to just mere seconds ago.

"Would you like me to call Kendrew to help you?" He looked back behind the counter, to the adjacent storage room. The exact spot where I first saw Kendrew step out of that first time I was in the store.

It seemed like that was so long ago and yet it was just three weeks ago.

"No!" I thought that came out louder than I anticipated, so I followed up softly, "No. No. No need." I felt myself stammering. "I, um, like exploring on my own. It's much more fun that way." I forced a smile to my face and hoped Jim bought it.

Good save, Kaitlyn, good save. I gave myself a mental pat on the back.

He looked at me with a surprised and amused look on his face, not quite buying my explanation.

I tried to change the subject. "Special delivery there?" I pointed toward his box.

He hurried behind the counter, toward the parcel, and reached inside. His eyes were filled with joy, and his smile was so contagious that I couldn't help but smile with him.

"Oh yes, books, books, and more books." He smiled and lifted up one book, handing it to me. I gasped. It was one of my favorite books by Virginia Woolf.

"I love this book." I looked inside, and it was one of the first editions. I held it to my chest. "This book, as well as Shakespeare's plays, were my escapes when I was younger."

I was so lost in talking about the book that I didn't realize it was no longer Jim and me in the store. *He* was here as well. The energy in the room significantly shifted, becoming heavy and electrified. He was now standing right next to Jim, looking at the book pressed against my chest before his eyes traveled over me, from my boots all the way to my face. My eyes took him in as well, and it frustrated me that they liked what they saw. He looked very handsome in a navy crewneck sweater with his sleeves pushed up, revealing muscular, strong forearms, with dark blue jeans, and a baseball cap on his head. He looked very relaxed and startled to see me in the store. I guessed sex did that to him, mellowed him out a bit and made him less of a jerk.

I thought back to the first time I had come into the store and the attitude and mean looks he gave me and compared that to today. Sure, he hadn't said a word, but he also hadn't stormed off.

It was like night and day.

He should have sex all the time.

He probably does, Kait. He probably does.

The room suddenly felt twenty degrees warmer. I unzipped my coat, exposing my neck, hoping that would help combat the sudden heat. I felt his eyes on me, on my neck, and it took so much restraint not to look at him looking at me. I didn't want his eyes to read me like an open book, knowing that I was so affected by him. Yet my own eyes betrayed me and answered his call. His gaze was focused on me, and he was looking straight into my eyes, telling me words I could not decipher, with his eyes. I was confused, and I looked away. No longer looking into his eyes, my body started to return back to earth. I reminded myself to breathe. If he could make me feel this way with just his gaze, I couldn't help but imagine how it would feel if he was communicating with me via his fingers, his tongue, his body against mine. I felt myself flushing, and I wished I could take off the coat entirely.

Why the hell are you thinking about him and sex with him?

I couldn't stop the thoughts and images that flooded my mind, even though I tried to temper them to no avail. Images of his beautiful naked body flooded my mind. I knew he would be beautiful without a stitch of clothing on because even fully clothed, he was very muscular, tall, and so devilishly handsome.

He was solid. Yes, solid was the perfect word for his build.

I could tell that his arms were used to lifting heavy firefighting equipment without too much exertion. Not only firefighting equipment though. Women, too.

Blonde, beautiful bombshells in alleyways and who knows where else . . .

I felt myself blushing, and I mentally chastised myself for thinking such thoughts. I looked away from him quickly and back to Jim, who was looking from Kendrew to me with a knowing grin on his face.

I gave the book back to Jim and pointed toward the back of the store, toward the desks. "I will . . . uhh . . . take a look at those desks . . . um. Excuse me." I turned slightly, away from two sets of eyes that were staring at me quite intently. I scanned the store and took a step toward the back, toward the desks, and I congratulated myself on getting away so smoothly.

I knew I would regret it, but in my feverish state, I couldn't help or stop myself. I turned around slightly to steal one more glance at Kendrew, hoping that he didn't notice my glance back. Instead, my eyes collided with his. The impact of his eyes and mine was staggeringly fiery. I felt my breath hitch, and I was startled to feel a shiver run through my body. I felt butterflies multiplying in my stomach, and I felt my body's reaction to him intensify, especially between my legs. His gaze was on mine, and it did not waver. I watched him bite his lower lip, his face looking confused as if not knowing what to do. I, however, knew what I wanted to do. I wanted to lick that spot he had just bitten, and I found myself licking my lips in response to my thoughts. My eyes went back to his, and he was looking at me as if he wanted to kiss me. His lips parted, and I saw him take a shallow breath. His eyes were so beautiful, and I found myself exploring their depths.

He took a step forward, toward me, and I took a step as well. I watched as his eyes roamed over my face, as if trying to memorize it, before settling on my eyes, yet again. How strange that I always hated eye contact, especially with a stranger, yet with him, I was so comfortable and dare I say, at home, gazing into his eyes. I watched in my peripheral vision as his hand reached out slightly, toward me. Fear took over my senses and I turned away from him abruptly, surprised that I didn't trip and fall on my feet, and walked away, in search of a desk, with a curse on my lips.

Damn the man for having a superpower over me.

I headed to the back of the store quickly and sat in a chair, surrounded by a dresser, two desks, and a few large floor lamps. I focused on my breathing and getting it back to normal. My thoughts went back to what had happened when my eyes locked with his. It was almost as if time stood still. As if we were communicating without any words, with our own language that no one else seemed to comprehend but us. It was intense and surprised me. I had given up men for a reason, and for a moment back there, with him reaching for me, I had almost forgotten that reason.

Damn him for making me feel such intense things while he had a girlfriend.

This couldn't go further. It couldn't. I wouldn't let it. If not for my self-preservation, for his girlfriend's sake.

Why is this one able to penetrate my walls?

My very high walls.

Jess had once asked me why I didn't try to date after what happened. I told her that my walls were not only tall, but they were also surrounded by barbed wire on top. I joked that my heart was behind that wall, and it was embedded in ice.

Yes, I have a wall up, I thought, *and for good reason.* Just thinking about the reason made me shiver fiercely.

I put my arms around myself and rubbed a sense of security into them. What normally worked, did not, at this moment. So instead, I let my thoughts travel to him. Automatically shivers were replaced with a scorching heat inside my body. A flame for him. A man I barely knew, yet felt so strongly for. A man that made me wish I was whole and in possession of a heart that wasn't caged with an abundance of insecurities, scars, helplessness, sorrow, anguish, loneliness, and pain.

Yet, with all those doubts, and that caged heart, he seemed to know how to melt the ice temporarily and climb the walls. With him in my thoughts, I could almost see over all the walls and obstacles. He made me want to see past the pain and uncertainty to the field of dreams and hopes. He made me want to go on a date with him and kiss him and fall asleep with his breath on my neck, holding me and fighting alongside me once the nightmare came. He made me want to believe in a fairy tale. Him. One man that I had spoken to twice.

I seriously was losing it. I had never thought of anyone in that kind of light, fluffy, and embellished daydream, yet a big part of me wanted a man like him to notice me. To look at me and pick me instead of a woman like the one he was with in the alleyway. *Was she his girlfriend? Or just one of his women? Did a man like Kendrew do commitment?*

When I first met him, I thought I saw pain in his eyes. The second time at the bar, the pain was accompanied by hurt and a deep-rooted sadness. He seemed a bit of a recluse. Or perhaps that's how he was with me? Maybe he just didn't like me.

I always had been a woman who relied on facts. There were two facts. The first being that he hated my guts, and the evidence was the first day in the store and the day in the bar.

Yet why did he buy the lunches for Jess and myself?

The second was that he ignored me today. Didn't even say hi. He wanted me to leave him alone.

Yet why did he look at me like he did just a few moments ago? As if he was awestruck and dare I say it, as if he liked what he saw?

I had one more fact. He probably thought I was a stalker, especially after yesterday.

Gosh, that was so embarrassing. I was willing my mind to forget what I saw, but I knew my body would not let me forget.

I was crushing on him. Very hard.

Thankfully he didn't know that I watched him deliver the groceries to my neighbor across the street or that I watched him through the windows like a person that watches television, snacks included.

I moaned and leaned into my hands. I would find a writing desk and leave as fast as I could.

***

I looked at the two desks in front of me, and although they were lovely, they weren't exactly what I imagined writing on. I went in search of a few more. Along the way, I stopped to admire countless books, lamps, plates, an old Singer sewing machine, paintings, a dining room table, a few embroidered tapestries, a Turkish rug, and a Victorian chair.

As I was about to give up on finding my writing desk, the one I pictured in my mind's eye, I saw it. It was absolutely gorgeous. It was the only one that truly stood out, with its dark cherry finish and one drawer with a beautiful pewter handle. It also featured quatrefoils, fleurs-de-lis, and spiral carvings on the legs. I ran my hand over it and felt the hand-carved details. There was also a straight-fluted column on each end connected with a banner-and-finial trestle and a plank top. I grabbed a nearby chair and sat down in front of the desk and felt the energy of it. I traced every scratch and ran my hands over every indentation and gently touched the peeling lacquer. Some might have called this desk distressed, but I called it full of history. My mind was racing with questions. Who was the previous owner of the desk and what made him or her sell it? Was it in their way? Were they in dire need of money? Was the desk so scratched because of the large amount of work done on it?

I touched the antique pewter handle and pulled it gently, to open the drawer. I was surprised to see that it was not empty. There was a book lying in the corner. I picked it up and blew away the dust. It was a book of poetry. I traced the burgundy cloth cover and ran my fingers across the embossed wording. I could tell just by looking at the book and feeling it, that it was pretty old. I opened the book and read the exquisite cursive handwritten inscription. I felt my eyes welling up at the beautiful wording. Every sentence was filled with even more love and heart.

My dearest,

Remember that whenever I am away fighting the war that I am always with you. Distance will separate us, but our love will never die. I promise that I will love you until I no longer can, and that will never happen, so I promise to love you forever. I anxiously await the day that you become my wife. I don't know how I will last without you all those months, but I will have your picture and wedding band in the coat pocket right next to my heart. Love you, my dearest Shelby.

—Matthew Manning

I readied myself with armor and headed to the front of the store. Kendrew was no longer there; it was only Jim. I told my body that it was not disappointment that I felt, but a strong sense of relief.

"Boy, did I find a beautiful desk. I would love to purchase the dark cherry one and this book. My goodness, Jim, what a beautiful inscription." I opened the cover and showed him the handwritten dedication. He reached for the book, to get a closer look at it, and I handed it over to him. I watched as a sad smile broke out on his face.

"Theirs was a beautiful love story," he said softly.

"You know them?" I asked, surprised.

"Yes, Matthew and I served together. His Shelby lives in this town." He paused for a moment. "Matthew was an amazing friend to me." He looked back at the book. "Where was this book?" he asked.

"It was in the drawer of my desk." I smiled and corrected myself. "Well, it was in the desk I would like to buy."

Jim handed the book back to me and looked toward the back of the store. "I don't know how it got there." He shook his head slowly, a sad expression coming over his face. "I would never sell this book. He died in a battle and was found with her picture in his pocket and an engagement ring. She never married and lives alone," he said sadly, shaking his head as if that would help erase the sad thoughts.

He looked at me, a smile replacing his sadness, though I could tell it didn't reach his eyes. "So which desk caught your eye again?"

"The dark cherry one," I replied enthusiastically.

"The one with all the scratches?" His voice sounded surprised.

"I look at it as lovingly used." I laughed, and Jim joined in. I then remembered the other day and someone else being lovingly used and I held back a groan.

"I love that. And for the record, I love that desk too." He smiled, before continuing, "It's my favorite. Something about all the signs of wear and tear that makes me wonder who used it, you know?"

"Yes!" I exclaimed. "That is exactly how I feel about it."

I handed Jim my credit card, and he asked me when I would like it delivered.

"Kendrew and I can drop it off at your home and set it up inside. Just let me know when you will be home and we will come on by."

He rang me up and handed me my credit card back.

"I'm running around a lot these days. I really don't know when I will be home or not. Difficult to say." I felt horrible for lying to Jim and averted my eyes for a moment, pretending to be looking in my purse for the wallet to put the credit card back in.

"Perhaps you can just drop it off and leave it on my porch. That definitely works."

"Are you sure?" Jim looked at me curiously.

"Positive." I stopped and thought for a moment, a thought coming to my mind. "Better yet, how about we hold off on the delivery for a week or so? That will give me enough time to sand and paint and clean up before moving the desk in." I looked at Jim. "I don't want to get the desk dirty. It's so gorgeous." I smiled. "Is that okay with you?"

He nodded his head, a grin spreading across his face. "Yes, of course." I watched him jot down, "Delayed delivery 1–2 weeks," on his copy of the sales receipt.

He looked up at me. "We will be in touch in one to two weeks' time, then."

I gave Jim a thumbs-up, and he chuckled.

"Thank you, Jim," I said a little too cheerfully. I was pretending not to be affected, but I was. All by someone that I had seen for a mere minute today.

I was in trouble and had to stay away from Kendrew.

He had someone and loved having her from the looks of things.

I had to stay away. That meant no more stalking, errr, watching, from the window.

And definitely no letting him inside my house.

I managed to get myself an extra one or two weeks to get over him.

And I would.

Somehow.

Then in two weeks, when the desk was delivered, it would be left on the porch. I would manage with that somehow as well. If I didn't, then perhaps a writing desk on a porch would work? Daily inspiration. Fresh air. People-watching.

No, it wouldn't work, as I would watch for the one person I had just sworn to not watch for. I felt so stupid. This guy didn't even say hi to me, and here I was worrying about how to avoid him. I'm pretty sure he had done that already.

That Oscar performance was still mine to play, and I would. Starting now.

Actress Kaitlyn.

Enter stage.

Jim was asking me a question and looking at me as if I had two heads.

"I'm sorry, I got lost in thought a bit," I said sheepishly.

If only he knew what my thoughts were about.

He smiled. "I was just asking your address so that I could write it on this receipt for delivery."

"It's 48 Mulberry Lane."

He jotted the address down quickly. "Small world." He smiled. "The lady that book belongs to lives right across from you, in the old Queen Anne-style home, dark blue with white shutters. Bad shape." He shook his head. "She won't let anyone inside to help her. It's almost as if she died the day Matthew did, and she doesn't change anything. No one has ever seen her outside either." He bent and picked up another taped box and reached for his box cutter.

I felt my jaw dropping. "I was wondering who lived there." I thought back to the book. "Do you think I could have that book? I have been planning on visiting her. This way, I can give it to her."

"I don't think she will let you in, but you can try," he said. He paused and opened his mouth to talk before closing it. He looked at me and bit his lips. "Your grandmother died recently?" he said in a way that made it half question, half fact. He was looking at the box cutter in his hand, his head down, but I could tell he was awaiting my response. As if he was bracing himself for what I would tell him next.

"Yes, I never got a chance to know her," I responded sadly.

"May I ask her name?" he asked, slicing open one side of the box.

"Amelia."

The box cutter nicked his skin, drawing blood. "Amelia," he whispered, disbelieving his own hearing.

I ran behind the counter to help him. "Do you have a first aid kit?" I placed the inscribed book on the counter.

He pointed to the desk behind him, and I hurried to get it. I cleaned off his hand with peroxide and slathered some ointment on it before wrapping his hand in a gauze bandage. His hand was shaking.

"I knew you looked familiar," he whispered and looked deep into my eyes. "Did you change your name to Kaitlyn?"

"No. That's the name I was called since I was a little girl," I said, thinking back to the first time I heard myself referred to as Kaitlyn.

"Did you know her? My grandmother?" I asked.

"I'm sorry, Kaitlyn, maybe we can talk some other time? I am not feeling that well," he said, sounding very muddled.

"I understand. Get some rest. I could stay here while you go home and rest. Or I could call Kendrew? You look very pale. Or I can walk you home, make sure you get home safe—"

"No," he cut me off. "I will be okay. It's just a little cut." He waved his hand as if it didn't bother him at all. "Kendrew left for the day, he had to be at the firehouse." He looked at me. "No need to stay. I am fine." He waved his cut hand. "This is nothing compared to some of the injuries I received during the war." He sounded sad and reflective.

"I'm sorry," I said.

"I'm not. I made it back." He pointed to the book I placed on the counter. "He didn't."

He turned his back and walked toward the window, and I took that moment to return the first aid kit to its rightful place behind the counter. I put the kit away and noticed something I hadn't spotted before, since I was in such a hurry. The gleam caught my eye, and I reached for the item. It was an antique heart-shaped key. I ran my finger over the metal and smiled. It was so beautiful. I found myself looking at it and holding it for far too long. I realized I was snooping, so I put the key back down into its place and looked across the room to see if Jim had seen me touching it. Thankfully, he hadn't, so I closed the drawer quickly.

I cleared my throat, trying to get Jim's attention. That didn't work. He was standing with his back turned to me, staring out the window, oblivious to all that was going on around him. I looked out and saw a man walking by, waving to him, yet Jim didn't wave back or acknowledge him in any way. In fact, it was almost as if he hadn't seen him. I didn't want to disturb him while he was deep in thought and wishing to be alone, so I decided to walk out quietly. I grabbed the book from the counter and pressed it against my chest. I passed him, and he still didn't look my way, so I let myself out.

Once I was outside, I glanced back at the store. I scratched my head, wondering if I should go back and check on him just in case. It was then that I noticed the still-moving sign that said, "Sorry, we are closed," and no Mr. Morris anywhere in sight.

Chapter Twelve

Kaitlyn

Jess left the other day. She said that she had to check on something and that she would be back in a week or two. I could tell that she had been preoccupied since we arrived here. She had been spending a lot of time at the library researching something and seemed like she was on a mission to uncover some secrets. She wouldn't tell me what she was researching; she just asked that I trust her, and I did.

I missed my friend immensely and had been trying to keep busy. I had cleaned the entire house twice, gone through my grandma's drawers, and gathered three big black garbage bags full of clothes that I donated. I raked and picked up all the leaves in the yard, and at present, I found myself with nothing to do. I was getting bored and did not feel up for painting the interior of the house or the exterior today. Thankfully tomorrow I would start a part-time job at the florist and hoped that would keep me busy until she returned.

On my morning run to the coffee shop, I had found out that a lovely florist in town named Irma was looking for someone to cover for her three days a week. Her husband was battling cancer, and she accompanied him on his chemo and radiation visits to the hospital. Instead of shutting the place down, I was going to help out and run it.

I loved flowers. It seemed like the perfect fit.

I had also picked up baking. I looked down at my masterpiece.

Pumpkin pie. I had made pumpkin pie. Who would have thought? Me, a pie maker! I looked down at it with glee and felt my teeth gently sinking into my lip. I did that when I was unsure of something. In this case, as happy as I was that I baked a pie and did not burn the house down, taking my neighbors' homes with it in the process, it was not quite what I expected it to look like. It especially did not look like the photos on the website that I got the recipe from. Theirs did not have a sunken-in middle and a slightly burned outer rim.

Proud of myself, I took a picture of it and texted it over to Jess. She did not respond. Maybe later.

My pie, though not the best in the looks department, smelled absolutely divine. I would definitely call this a valiant effort. A head-held-high moment.

I stopped staring and smiling at the pie and hoped my neighbor would like it, or at least appreciate the effort.

Introducing myself to my neighbor across the street was long overdue.

***

I rang the bell and waited, but no one came to the door to let me in. I was about to leave the pie and walk away, but I felt eyes on me. I took the initiative and extended my hand toward the doorknob. I touched it, and before I lost my nerve, I turned it and walked into the dark, chilly home.

"I knew you would come," she said in a sure voice.

"How?" The only word that managed to come out of my mouth sounded so puny now. I could have asked another question or said something entirely different, yet the only word that came to my mind was that one small but powerful word. However, it loses all of its power the moment someone ignores it and does not answer. The old lady looked at me with a determined look on her face that made me regret coming inside. After looking me up and down, she finally spoke.

"You are just like her. She would not give up either. You look like her so much, but most importantly, you have her spirit. She was the only one I allowed to enter my home, and now you."

"Thank you so much. I was worried that I might be intruding—"

"No, you weren't worried about intruding." She cut me off and a smile formed on her face. "Courtesy just makes you say that."

My jaw dropped. That was exactly what I was thinking. "You are good, but that is scary that you know that. You just met me."

"But I knew your mother. We were best friends, and we never grew apart." She said that as if it was supposed to be enough. "Girl, remember that we don't need to bother with any of that courtesy business here. You speak only what you feel in this house, even if it hurts or is just plain unconventional. And remember you are welcome here any time. You can never intrude."

"Thank you very much." I smiled. "So you knew my mother well?"

"I did. I still do," she said cryptically.

"But how? My mother passed away right after I was born." I looked at her, needing her to tell me more about my mom.

She looked away. "Death never takes anyone from you. My Matthew is the only reason I am still alive. My heart lives for the both of us. Our love is kept alive that way." She turned to look at me. "Your mother never left you. She is always near you because she lives in your heart. Believe that, and you will witness the never-ending miracle of love." She must have realized that she had ventured off the topic of my mom, and she steered the conversation back to her.

"She was like my sister. She was younger than me, but she acted like the older one; she was so overprotective of me when I was at my weakest. I could never be as strong as she was." Her eyes flew to my hands. "What do you have there?"

I was so intrigued and entranced by this lovely lady that I had completely forgotten what I had come to her with. The sunken pie.

"I brought some pumpkin pie. I'm not sure if you will like it." I fidgeted and looked down at the pie in my hands. "It's my first time making a pie." I looked at Shelby and smiled. "Honestly, my first time baking anything, for that matter." The lady looked at the pie and back at me, and I could tell she was holding back laughter.

"It's okay. You can laugh," I told her, giggling. Shelby joined in until tears trickled down her face. I watched her wipe them and look at me with a serious expression once again.

"Sit down, girl, and let me take a look at you."

I felt her gaze sweep over my entire body. I did not know where to look while she examined me, so I looked at the older lady and took in her appearance as well. Her face, I could tell, was once a beautiful one. Although now time added wrinkles to it and a certain sadness seeped into her features, she was still very pretty. She wore a plain black dress that looked to be old-fashioned. It made her pale skin look even paler. Her hair was salt and pepper and was swept up in a tight bun on top of her head, making her thin face appear even thinner. Her eyes were a washed-out blue as if years of crying had wiped away the vibrancy they once possessed. Her hands were gently folded in her lap, and I noticed that she wore a thin gold wedding band on her left ring finger. She finally sat back and smiled showing off beautiful, straight teeth. For that one moment, sadness seemed to escape her body, temporarily creeping into a tiny hiding space, ready and waiting for the moment when it could return to its rightful home once again. "You are beautiful. I always knew you would return here. I was so upset with your grandmother for not bringing you here sooner."

"My grandmother passed away. I never got a chance to meet her. If it weren't for the letters she wrote me, I would never have found out about this place—"

"She was always scared to look you in the eye," Shelby said, shaking her head. "She had her reasons," she whispered, her voice sounding like it was miles away. She was looking past me, at the house across the street. My grandmother's house.

My house now.

Shelby looked back at me. I tried to break the silence and come up with a topic I would love to hear more about. My mom.

"I would give everything I own"—I point to the house across the street—"just to have my mom and grandma here now." I looked at Shelby, whose eyes filled with tears. She smiled and placed a hand on her heart.

"Yes, you are like her." A tear trailed down her cheek and she let it, her gaze unwavering. "She never cared for money. The most important things in her life were things that could not be purchased: a laughing fit with me in school, the way her heart beat when she was in love, the butterflies in her stomach whenever he kissed her—" she stopped to take a deep breath, and continued "—and the smile you gave her when she would lay you to sleep." I watched the tears continue to make their way down Shelby's face. I went over to her, leaned down, and wiped Shelby's tears with my fingertips. I then planted a kiss on her weathered cheek. I inhaled her lovely floral scent.

Gardenia.

One of my favorites along with camellias, irises, and peonies. Tears clouded my vision, but I fought to keep them under control.

I inhaled a deep breath. "Thank you so much. It's these little words, these recollections . . . they mean the world to me. You are my gateway to her."

Shelby smiled and looked over at the pie. "All this crying has got me hungry. How about we test your baking skills?"

"Oh boy." I put the pie down on the side table and asked about a knife. Shelby pointed me to the kitchen, and I returned with a knife and two plates. "Would you like me to make some tea for you?" I inquired.

"I don't own a tea kettle. Or tea, for that matter," Shelby said.

"Well we'll just have to change that, now, won't we?" I smiled and was shocked to see that Shelby smiled back at me, with genuine affection in her eyes. With a faraway look on her face, she whispered something under her breath, but I heard it and suppressed the tears that threatened to pool in my eyes yet again.

The statement followed me home.

"It's as if Mary was here," replayed in my thoughts over and over again, long after I left Shelby's home.

***

I stood at the door, trying to work up the courage to knock. The dark wood was beautiful, the grain was unique, and the handwork on it was exquisite. I took a deep breath, picked up the oiled bronze circular doorknocker, and announced myself.

I waited a few moments, and when no one appeared at the door, I knocked louder. Finally, I heard movement and the door opened. I watched Jim jump back slightly. I thought I was the last person he expected to see, but I wanted to check in on him and see how his hand was.

"It's me," I exclaimed. "I hope I'm not intruding. I just wanted to make sure all was okay with your hand." I looked at his hand and saw a bandage wrapped around it. He looked down at his hand too and then back at me, a smile forming on his face.

"This is nothing. Clumsiness in my old age." He shrugged.

"Are you sure you don't need to get it checked out?"

"No, it'll be okay," he said.

I stood in his doorway, looking at him, not knowing what to do. I should've left, as he didn't invite me in, but I found my shoes glued to his porch.

"This door is beautiful," I told him, trying to break that silence. I ran my hands across it.

"I made it," he said. I could tell he was proud of that fact.

"You did?" I said in awe.

He nodded his head. "I always liked to work with my hands. Wood and metals are my favorite mediums."

"It's breathtaking," I exclaimed.

Silence once again.

"Would you like to come inside for a cup of coffee or tea? I was just sitting in my living room, going through some of my books that I was thinking of bringing to the store." He looked behind him, inside his home. "I'm running out of room here." He smiled.

"I would love to come inside and perhaps help you go through them."

He stepped to the side, and I entered the room. I saw numerous books spilled across his living room. Some were on the floor, some were scattered across his rug, and then there were some on chairs and tables.

"Wow, you weren't exaggerating when you said that you had a lot of books." I marveled at the different book covers, sizes, colors. He could've opened a library with his collection of books.

"Please help yourself to anything you would like." He looked at the books and at me. "I will be right back with something special that I saved just for you." He took a step back and crossed to his foyer before making his way up the wooden staircase.

My gaze took in his living room space. It felt homey and lived in. The floors were a dark mahogany wood, with a wool rug in varying shades of jewel-tone colors, in the middle. There was a coffee table on top of it and two recliner chairs flanking it. The chairs were facing a stone fireplace. A beautiful wood mantle, with hand carvings, hung above it. Light filtered through the bare windows and formed little rainbows across the floor. I moved my hand and marveled at the rainbow of colors on my hand. I walked to the mantle and looked at the candle, but something else captured my attention.

Though the picture was black and white, I could tell that the woman in the picture was a colorful personality. She was beautiful, and her eyes were radiating love and amusement. She was staring back at the camera with such a rawness that permeated through the paper, through time, until it reached me. I reached out and touched the picture and felt electricity course from it into my body.

It was probably the rug and then me touching the frame that caused the jolt.

I felt like I knew her, like I had seen her eyes somewhere. I picked up the portrait and turned it around. The frame was coming undone, and I lifted the corner, spotting some writing. I was being nosy and I knew that I shouldn't read it, but I went ahead and did so.

My true love, the only man I can ever and will always love. Thank you for your friendship, and for your love. Though we may be young we know what we feel. They know too or else they would not work so hard at keeping us from each other. Sometimes words cannot express my emotions. They just can't do them justice. They are but mere words while what I feel for you is so strong and special, I know that we will always be together. My love, cherish this picture and look at it when I am not near, although that is hard to imagine since I am always with you, in your heart.

I love you. A simple statement. Three words yet the meaning is so deep.

I do. Two words. The meaning even deeper . . .

Your girl,

M.

I wanted to love someone so much that the person was always living in me, in my thoughts and in my heart. This girl loved Jim so much. No wonder he could not forget her or move on and marry another woman. He was faithful to his one true love whose name was a mystery.

The initial M., who can it be?

I stared at it, losing myself in her gaze. Her eyes were so familiar.

I can't place my finger on where I have seen them before.

I continued looking at her until a door closing upstairs snapped me out of my trance. I heard footsteps coming down the stairs. I readjusted the picture, making sure it was positioned exactly the same way that I found it. I walked away from her, toward the chair. I moved the books from the chair to the floor, and I sat on it. Jim's footsteps were getting louder. I looked up at the picture once more, and from where I was sitting, I noticed that the chair had been adjusted so that when Jim sat by the fireplace, he could enjoy it with his beloved girl M.

The floor creaked, and I turned toward the noise.

"Here is a book I have been meaning to give you. It's a book that I got as a gift from an old friend, and I would like to give it to my new friend." He extended the book to me, and I took it instantly.

It was Ernest Hemingway's *To Have and Have Not*. I touched the book and opened it, running my fingers across the slightly yellowed pages. The scent of aged paper filled the air around me. I loved the smell of older books, and I breathed it in. "This is beyond incredible. Thank you so much, Jim."

I rose from the chair, and with the book in my right hand, I wrapped my arms around him, hugging him. I felt him hug me back, and it felt so good. I looked back at the portrait, and it was almost as if the figure was real, watching us, approving of our friendship.

A floral scent encompassed us, replacing the scent of books. It was subtle yet noticeable. I pulled away from Jim slowly and looked around the room, looking for a magnolia bouquet, but saw nothing.

The scent seemed to leave, and I looked at Jim and saw that his eyes were welling up. He was looking at the picture on the wall and smiling through the tears.

"Thank you, Jim. You are spoiling me with these amazing literary treasures." I was so grateful for the beautiful gifts he had bestowed on me, along with his easygoing nature and friendship. "Should we get started with the books?" My gaze swept across the room.

He shook his head. "How about a rain check on that? I feel like I need a nap. Age, you know?" He chuckled, and I joined in. Jim was very fit, and from what I had seen, always on the move, keeping busy, so I didn't think he would nap. I thought his wanting to be alone had something to do with the portrait, with the way he stared at it with overwhelming emotion just moments ago.

It was as if he needed a moment to be alone with her.

"Rain check sounds good." I smiled. I hugged the book to my chest and watched as his gaze traveled to me and then back at the lady in the picture. I took the cue and walked toward the door, and Jim followed.

"Thank you for this amazing book once again," I said. The magnolia scent seemed to follow me, softly hugging me with its warm and soft scent. "I'm glad your hand is okay." I opened the door and looked back at Jim.

He smiled. "You're welcome. Feel free to visit anytime."

"I will." I clutched the book to my chest and stepped outside.

I closed the door behind me and scanned the area for magnolia trees growing nearby, but I knew it was not possible for blooms this late in the year. The only magnolia tree was the one on my property.

I scratched my head as realization dawned on me. That was my magnolia tree! All this time Jim had been my neighbor and I hadn't known.

That magnolia on my property that I loved so much was the midway point between our houses.

I made my way toward the lovely tree and ran my hands across the thick bark. I walked around it in a circle, feeling so comfortable and so at peace under its massive branches. I smelled the sweet floral scent once more and closed my eyes, inhaling the scent and pulling it deep inside of me, into my soul.

I opened my eyes and started the very short walk home. I got my foot tangled in something, and I fell to the ground, landing on my hands and knees, the book knocked out of my hands. I reached for it, dusting it off on my shirt. I placed the book under my arm, safely cocooning it while I dusted off my hands and rose to my feet. I looked for the culprit of my fall and saw a small hole in the ground, probably caused by a gopher or a squirrel hiding its food.

My eyes then focused on something peeking from under the dried leaves. It was so impossible, yet I touched it and felt its softness. I inhaled its scent and felt tears enter my eyes without knowing why I was getting so emotional. I looked around to see if I could spot others, but there were none.

I walked home, a book in one hand and a single perfect magnolia bloom in the other.

There was a path. It was muddy and very difficult to cross with all the gear we carried. It wasn't like any other path that I had encountered or crossed before. It scared me. The rain made it slippery and we could not stop. We pushed on harder and faster. In order to survive, we needed to. As I looked at the path with heavy eyes, it looked so long. We walked for hours, and it only seemed to get longer. I tried focusing on my friends in front of me. I adjusted the rhythm of their shoes against the muddy land to mine. I was cold, and my teeth clattered uncontrollably. My uniform was soaking wet, and I struggled staying upright as my backpack was pushing me toward the ground. I didn't think I could make it. I was the last one in my group. I knew that I had to find the strength and walk faster, but instead I dropped to the ground. The mud seemed to cool my already cold body, and I knew that this was it.

I once heard a man talking about his darkest hour and how he thought he was going to die. He said that he felt death in every bone of his being and that only then did he start to pray. He didn't how the words of the Lord's Prayer left his lips, as he hadn't uttered the prayer in over twenty years. When he was telling his friends in the bar that story, they laughed at him and his sudden return to God. He did not care. He told them he got a second chance and he promised to drink less. They mocked him, and I listened to him. Now, as I lay on the ground, without the strength to move, I could almost hear him whispering in my ear, "Our Father." So I started praying for the strength to go forward, for the strength to get back to you in one piece, and for the soul of the man in the bar. I felt drops of water make a trail down my face, and I licked my lips and tasted their saltiness. The water continued to fall on my hands that were covered in the wet earth, and I realized I was hysterically crying. The sound of the rain muted my anguished prayer, and I was scared that he did not hear me, so I prayed louder, until the words meant something to me. What started out as a mechanical "Our Father" turned into a plea to a higher power to spare my life and to bring me home safely to a woman whose heart I held.

I begged for him to become my rock, to make me strong. To help me carry the load to safety. I prayed until I could no longer, and then I stopped and let the rain cleanse me as holy water does a sinner. The rain no longer chilled my bones, but seemed to warm them. I then realized that the sun had come up from behind the clouds and lit up the path that I was supposed to take. It warmed my achy bones, and I got up and started walking. My friend Matt turned around and waited for me. I looked at his face, anxious to see his reaction. I wanted to know if he had seen what had happened back there. Or if he had heard. Somehow, I couldn't ask or didn't want to ask. I acted as if nothing unusual had happened. As if my darkest hour had never occurred. We started walking together, in silence. I was grateful for his presence. I looked up at the sky and felt comforted.

That day two miracles happened. I found my strength, and I realized God was listening to me.

When our end location was nearing, I thought I saw my beautiful girl standing in the middle of the path with arms outstretched waiting for me. I ran the remaining mile and collapsed.

What seemed like moments later, Matt took my backpack off and helped me up. We dropped our belongings in an old shack. This would be our hideout for a couple of hours. A lot of the guys fell asleep, grateful for the reprieve, even if for a short time. Some even slept with their gear on. Some slept leaning against the wall. Some just stared ahead. Matt looked at me and smiled. He jokingly punched my arm. "Let's find some water and wash ourselves up a little."

I looked at him puzzled. I didn't know why he worried so much about being clean, but I followed him. As I passed a cracked window, I got a glimpse of the person staring back at me. It was the reflection of a man whose face was caked with dry mud with a trail where my tears had run. At that point, I knew Matt had seen and heard what had happened. In his own way, he was telling me he would never tell anyone. My secret was safe with him.

I had respected him before, but after this, I hero-worshiped him. I still do.

He never made it home. He took a bullet for me.

***

He lit a candle and sat in front of her picture.

"I had my nightmare again, Mary." He took a deep breath. "He should have lived. He should have come home to Shelby." His voice broke, and tears fell on his hand.

This nightmare came and went, but the guilt always remained. It was why he kept away from Shelby. He couldn't face her knowing that she lost her love because of Him. He shouldn't have made that decision to take the bullet. It shouldn't have been his choice to make.

"I call it a nightmare, but it's real." He stopped for a moment. "Everything in that nightmare happened."

He closed his eyes and was transported back to 105-degree weather and a very damp climate. He could smell death mixed with fear and blood.

Soon, the scent of war disappeared, replaced by magnolias.

He opened his eyes, looked at her, and silently thanked her.

Chapter Thirteen

Kaitlyn

My visits with Shelby continued.

I loved listening to her stories. They filled me with happiness and joy. She was a special link, a rare bridge, to my long-gone mom, and I loved walking on that path of memories alongside her. I was learning about my mom through Shelby's words, through her laughter and her tears, and through her beautiful recollections.

I loved Shelby, and her life story fascinated me, but the link to my mom made it that much more special. It warmed my heart hearing her say that I had my mother's twinkling eyes, or mischievous smile when I was planning something. It really made me beam to know that my mom loved to run in the rain and climb trees.

I was my mother's daughter, and I loved it.

Shelby loved talking about my mom and never held back, but whenever I tried to ask about my dad, her eyes got dark and she stopped talking. She shut down completely, and I did not know what to make of her reaction. Being a curious creature as I was, I tried to weave him into our conversations, and it never ended well.

Like today.

I just asked what his eye color was and how he was as a person, and she looked away from me, pulling up a visible wall around herself.

We sat in silence. I could hear the clock ticking away, almost getting louder by the minute.

Tick-tock. Tick-tock. Tick-tock.

I realized I was holding my breath while listening to the sound of the clock. I released it and rose from the couch, walking toward the round table, where the plate with the shortbread was as well as the English afternoon tea in its beautiful, hand-painted blue-and-white teapot that I had gifted Shelby.

I heard Shelby whisper something. A name. I turned around, and her eyes were clouded over, her forehead wrinkled, deep in thought. I recognized that look.

She was miles away.

I grabbed a shortbread cookie, placed it on a plate, and awaited Shelby's return from the past. She would come back when she was ready.

I figured that I might as well have some tea while I waited for her return, so I poured myself a cup and sipped it while walking toward the couch slowly. I sat down and took in my surroundings. The walls that were once chalk white, were now time kissed and aged a warm shade of creamy beige. In the middle of the room there was a beautiful brick fireplace with crackling firewood that was keeping us comfortably warm. My eyes settled on the two beautiful rocking chairs that sat in front of the window. They were identical, yet one was visibly used and the other covered in dust. My gaze lingered on the rocking chair, and after a while, I broke contact with it. I glanced at Shelby, and she was focused on me. Her gaze was no longer clouded.

She was back from her visit.

I put my plate and tea on the coffee table in front of me and got up to get some shortbread and tea for Shelby. Once filled, I placed the plate on her lap, and she reached for the dainty teacup, taking it from my hands. She took a sip and I waited, knowing that she would hand it over to me to put on the coffee table. She always did that, and today was no different. Our fingers touched, and she patted me on the hand, gently, with a smile on her face. Yes, she was back.

I sat back down and watched her. Her eyes were glued on the rocking chairs.

"I always believed that I would rock my baby in that chair." She lifted her right hand and pointed in the direction of the chair, her fingers gently curling into a fist. I heard her take a ragged breath before she continued speaking. "I would hold it in my arms until it fell asleep, all of its worries rocked away by its mama." She looked at the chair lovingly. "The other chair would be filled by my husband, who would watch me nurse our child, with love and devotion in his eyes." She looked down at her lap and touched her ring-clad finger, circling the slim band with her fingers.

Her wedding band. A symbol of an unending love. A love that was not buried with a body, yet lived on in memories and in the soul and heart of Shelby. Her wedding band, though put on her finger long ago, was placed by her one and true love and never taken off. It symbolized their connection beautifully.

A circle had no end. Just like her love for her husband.

I looked at my purse, and I made the decision. It would be difficult, but it was something I had to do. I reached inside my purse and touched the hard cover, tracing the lettering. I took two consecutive deep breaths.

How do I give her his book without upsetting her? How can I make this easier for her?

I debated back and forth in my mind on how to give her the book. I didn't want to upset her or overwhelm her.

"What's wrong with you today?" she remarked. The words startled me, causing my head to shoot up. I was thinking so hard about how to give her the book, that I didn't realize Shelby noticed my unease. "Nerves don't look good on you," she teased.

I swallowed nervously. "Shelby, I have something for you. I . . . ummm . . . found this in Jim's antique store. He was not quite sure how it ended up with him, but it belongs to you . . . with you."

I reached into my purse, taking out the book slowly. Shelby watched me in silence. Every movement of my hand was met by her unwavering gaze. She finally saw the book, and her eyes brightened. I got up, and with the book gently cradled in the palm of my hand, I brought it over to her. I offered the book to her, and she reached for it with excitement. I watched as she held the book in the palm of her left hand and traced the leather-bound cover with her other hand. She followed the ridges of the worn cover with her fingertips before opening the book to the first page. She traced the handwriting she had memorized ages ago.

Though she was smiling, tears fell on the page, one after the other, and blended with the paper. She wiped her eyes quickly, terrified of blurring the words on the paper. I watched and felt my heart expanding, filling with love for her and Matthew.

I decided to leave her alone, with him and his words, and I slowly backed out, leaving her to revel in her newfound treasure.

Closing the door quietly behind me, I caught a glimpse of a beautiful moment that I knew I would remember forever. Shelby kissed the book and brought it down to her body to the area where her chest was beating and held onto it tightly. It was as if her own heartbeat gave the book life and Matthew's words poured right out.

I sat on the stoop unable to walk, unable to forget the scene I had just seen. By the time I was ready, dark night accompanied me across the street a changed woman. A woman wanting to take a chance on love, a woman determined not to let fear stop her. A woman who yearned for the type of love that Shelby and Jim experienced daily, even after a loved one's passing.

A woman who wanted to feel like a woman.

Chapter Fourteen

Kaitlyn

It was a very quiet day, the rain probably the culprit, keeping those that did not have to be outside their homes, nestled indoors. I was covering for Irma as she went with Harold for his chemotherapy treatment. I was rearranging some greeting cards that were in the front of the shop by the cash register, when I heard the bell ding and the sound of rain filling the space before the door shut out its rhythm and beat. The smell of rain mixed with an earthy, woodsy scent made its way to me, and I inhaled it. I had a customer, and judging by the scent, a male.

I put the cards that were still in my hands, down on the counter. I would tackle those later. I turned around and faced my customer. "Welcome. How can I help y—"

The words lodged in my throat. Only one person had been capable of doing that to me so far and he was standing right in front of me. He was rain-soaked, dripping on the shop's floor, filling the space with his masculinity. All of a sudden, the shop felt so small and I felt on top of him. A hand reach away from touching him.

I gazed at him and saw the droplets running in rivulets from his hair to his face, and he tried to wipe them off. I watched as the droplets hung on to his eyelashes, not wanting to leave him.

Just like the blonde in the alleyway.

He was looking at me, and for a moment, it was just us and the scents surrounding us. His unique scent mixed with the lingering aroma of Stargazer lilies that had been delivered earlier today and the rain. If I could bottle this scent up I would, and I would spray it on my pillows every night before bed.

I shook my head to clear out the fog in it, and I smiled at him.

"How can I help you today?"

He blinked back, as if surprised that I was so cordial.

It was my job to be professional and to put my customers and this store first, and so I did.

"Hi," he said and looked around the room. "I, uh—would like a bouquet of flowers."

He ran his hand through his hair. I could tell he was uncomfortable. He looked around, and I watched as his shoulders shrugged involuntarily. I had a feeling he did not know what flowers to get or even what the names of the flowers were.

"Do you know what flowers you would like, or what colors?"

He looked at me as if I was speaking another language. He ran his hand through his hair once more, and I found myself wanting to do the same to him.

Focus. Kaitlyn. Focus.

"Perhaps you can tell me what occasion and I can offer some suggestions," I politely inquired.

I patted my back for being the ever-consummate professional.

"Not really any occasion . . . just giving someone flowers," he whispered.

Ohhhhhhh. Blonde bombshell. He is probably getting her flowers.

I didn't know why, but sadness and disappointment coursed through me and I felt myself shudder involuntarily. My eyes met his, and I watched his gaze fall to my lips. I took a big step back.

He has a girlfriend. Or at least a girl he is interested in.

He is buying her flowers.

Cool it.

"Any idea what she likes?"

He shook his head and took a step toward me, negating the space I just put between us a few moments ago.

"What do you like?" he asked softly.

That question was so loaded, and I think he knew it the moment the words were out.

What do I *like?*

I like you.

I like the way you smell.

I like the way you feel in close proximity to me.

I like the way I feel alive when you are near.

I like the way your eyes look at me, as if they are undressing me.

I like your lips, and most of all, I like the way you look this very moment, soaked from the rain.

I like you, Kendrew, and I can't.

"Sunflowers," I croaked out. My throat felt dry, as if I had been wandering the Sahara for days, so I walked toward the floral coolers, stopping for a moment to get a sip of coffee from my coffee mug that I had placed by the cash register. I continued toward the coolers where the flowers were stored and opened up the glass doors. I felt him right behind me. The cold air from the fridge hit me, yet I still felt on fire. My throat felt parched yet again, yearning for his wet lips to hydrate me. I shook that image from my mind and turned sideways to face him, holding the door awkwardly with my knee. He walked up to the coolers and held the door for me while I grabbed the flowers.

"Thank you," I whispered. He didn't say anything, and I glanced at him from the corner of my eye. His face was unreadable.

Blank.

I felt dumb for being so affected by him when he could care less. He was here buying flowers for his woman friend, girlfriend, hookup, whatever you wanted to call her.

"These have always been my favorite." I pulled out five sunflower stems and brought the flowers to my nose, and I giggled. I didn't want him to think I was completely off my rocker, so I explained the giggle. "I always find myself drawn to smelling every flower, even those that have no fragrances, like these beauties." I looked at him and smiled. I watched him look from me to the sunflowers.

Okay. Too late. By the look on his face, he probably already thinks I am cuckoo.

He didn't say anything, so I looked around the store, trying to give him other floral suggestions. Perhaps he didn't like the look of the sunflower bouquet I was presenting him. I pointed out roses to him as well as delphinium and lilies as wonderful substitutes.

"No, I'll take those." He pointed to the sunflowers in my hand.

He was all business, while I was all fool.

I was so embarrassed that I just wanted to go outside in this downpour, pretend I was sugar, and melt.

"Good choice." I smiled once again. Only this time, I didn't wait for his smile. I knew it was not coming, so I turned away from him quickly and walked toward the table right next to the cash register. I congratulated myself on that task. I wrapped the flowers in a clear plastic wrapping paper, grabbed a blank note card and a plant-food packet, and taped it to the clear wrapping.

"Would you like a bow?" I asked, looking at the different colors of string lining the wall.

"A what?" he said abruptly.

"A bow." I finally looked up at him, and his eyebrows were drawn together.

He was looking at me with uncertainty, and I pointed to a bouquet that I made before he came in. It was an online order that was awaiting pickup. A dozen red roses and a big satin string wrapped around the stems, finished off with a big bow.

He shook his head vehemently, almost as if he wouldn't be caught dead with a bow, and I couldn't help but grin. I grabbed a piece of burlap and wrapped it around the stems. I tied the burlap with a piece of beige string. This made it more rustic yet romantic at the same time.

I admired the way it turned out. Sunflowers and burlap were two of my favorite things. Very rustic chic.

She, whoever she was, would love it. I twirled the flowers around once, making sure the bouquet looked beautiful from every angle, and it did.

This bouquet made me smile and think happy thoughts, imagining how I would feel getting such flowers from such a handsome man as Kendrew.

I exhaled the idea and put the flowers on the counter swiftly, as if they were burning a hole in my hand. I looked up at him, and he was looking at me and then at the flowers and then back at me again.

I was behaving like such an idiot. He was looking at me as if I had two heads.

I ignored the confused look on his face and told him the price.

I glanced at the cards I was arranging before he walked in and turned my insides into jelly, but out of the corner of my eye, I saw him reaching into his pockets and taking out his wallet. He took out his credit card and handed it to me. My fingers touched his momentarily, and a spark shot up my arm. He pulled his hand away, as if burned, and I dropped the credit card.

"Oops, sorry," I mumbled.

I rang him up and returned the credit card to him, sliding it toward him so that we did not accidentally touch again.

"Thanks," he said. I watched him take the credit card and shove it in his wallet. He grabbed the flowers and looked at me, as if he wanted to say something, but was holding back.

"You're welcome." I smiled. "I hope she likes the flowers."

He looked so beautiful standing in the shop, with his wet clothes clinging to his body and the sunflowers in his hand. Truth be told, if he showed up at my doorstep looking like he did right now, as much as I loved sunflowers, I would be elated to just have him as my present.

He nodded and opened his mouth, as if to say something. I held my breath, willing him to speak. He didn't. Instead, he gazed at me briefly with what appeared to be a pained expression and turned and walked away. The door opened, and I welcomed the sound of rain. It calmed me at least momentarily before the door closed behind him and it became muted once again. My heart was beating erratically, and I closed my eyes, hoping to calm it. I breathed in his lingering scent and found myself walking toward the glass window to watch his retreating form.

I still must have been breathing heavily because I looked at the glass and it was foggy, obstructing my view of him. I wiped at it quickly and gasped in surprise. There he was standing in the rain, the yellow flowers standing out against the gray backdrop, breathing in the sunflowers.

Just like I did.

My heart skipped a beat. I watched as my hand involuntarily rose and reached for the window, reaching for him. A force pulling me toward him. Wanting him yet knowing that I could not. Needing to feel him, but instead feeling cold, foggy glass.

Sobering, I remembered who he had gotten the flowers for, and my head dropped. I walked away from the window of dashed dreams toward the greeting cards I was reorganizing earlier.

I would rearrange the sympathy cards, as I was in no mood for congratulations or wedding cards. My mood turned as dark as the sky outside, and I felt moisture, so similar to the rain, only this moisture pooled in my eyes and trailed down my cheek and clenched my heart and twisted it.

I looked down at the card in my hand, the writing resonating powerfully.

So sorry for your loss.

Chapter Fifteen

Kendrew

When I walked into the store, I had already braced myself. I knew she worked there. It was a small town and word traveled. I had gone in there thinking I could turn over a new leaf with her, but fear won out in the end. I was breathless and couldn't speak. It felt like someone punched me in the chest when she turned around and her gaze met mine. I found it difficult to breathe, I could barely speak, my heart was beating so loudly, and I felt frozen to the spot.

Before coming in, I practiced what I was going to say. I practiced how I would walk in and act unaffected. I would be friendly and normal, yet the moment I walked through the door, leaving the safety of the outdoors, and found myself in front of her, surrounded by her beauty and charm, by her energy and grace, I was speechless.

My brain was muddled.

My Kendrew GPS was off.

It did not stop me from moving toward her though. It was like my body had a magnet and reacted to her magnet. I could not explain it, but I knew I would never forget it. I also knew I would never feel it for anyone else again. How I knew this I couldn't say, but I just did.

The rain now beat against my face, but instead of rushing home, I stopped in the middle of the sidewalk, devoid of passersby, and looked down at the bouquet of sunlight in my hands wishing that I was holding her and running my fingers through her golden hair instead. I touched the petals gently and they were soft, just like her fingertips when we accidentally touched. I could still feel the electricity shooting up my arms from the unintentional meeting of our fingers. That jolt not only electrified my hand, but it also electrified my heart. She didn't know, but I wanted to take those fingers and kiss each one. I had done everything in my power to remain a rock, and I think I succeeded.

In my mind, I thought about the accident and I felt ominous. Thinking back, I probably came across rude once again, but it was for her own good. She did not need to know that I had come in wanting to turn over a new leaf with her. That I wanted to tell her the truth about Bridget, about my feelings for her, about the past.

That was what terrified me. I wanted to tell her everything, even the parts of me I kept buried deep, especially the parts I had hidden away for years. It was a struggle, but in the end, instead of kissing her, I embraced the part of me that was bereft of any and all emotion.

I knew the exact moment when she realized the flowers were for a woman, and though they were, they were not quite for the woman she thought. I saw her initial surprise, and then I saw a bit of sadness cross her face before she pulled herself together and acted like she did not care.

I knew she cared because I felt the same.

She and I, as strange as our connection seemed to be to outsiders, understood one another. It was like we communicated with glances and unspoken words, with sighs, and all while wearing masks.

Not many could tell which mask we had put on, but we could.

We fooled no one.

Though that strong, unexplained connection was the basis of my fears, it was also the anchor that kept me calm.

A woman like Kaitlyn could have me thinking about happily ever afters in a heartbeat, and that wasn't me. It wasn't me *anymore*. I didn't deserve it. I couldn't be that man even if I wanted to. So instead, I let her think they were for the blonde in the alleyway, or some other female, for that matter. She probably thought there were a bunch of them, and although she wouldn't be wrong, none of them ever meant anything to me. None of them made me feel things on a deeper, soul level like she did.

Ever since I met her, I felt charged. It wasn't only physical with her, although I did find her drop-dead beautiful; it went much deeper. I wanted to protect her, and I knew that I couldn't. It was for those reasons that it was better that she thought I was a player.

It was better for her heart.

It was better for her life.

I wouldn't risk injuring or hurting her.

The raindrops landed on the sunflowers and shifted my attention from her, but not for long because the droplets in the center of the flower reminded me of her. So fragile and so pure, clinging to the flower, trusting it to protect her. I watched as another droplet fell on to one of those droplets and splattered it, wiping it away. Just like that, in the blink of an eye, the beautiful bubble was gone. The flower petals, though they cradled it, could not keep it safe and whole in its cocoon.

I would burst her bubble too.

I knew it and I cared enough not to go there, not to hurt her, even for an ounce of happiness beside her.

I would not be the reason that her light diminished.

I couldn't.

So instead, I would give her the space to grow and face the sun. To stand proud like a sunflower. I looked down at the flowers and smiled. They smelled just like her, fresh and sunny. Though often overlooked for roses, the sunflowers, in my opinion, were even more beautiful. They didn't need a fragrance to charm you; they did it just by being bright and sunny and unique.

I had to stay away from her and I would. In the meantime, I embraced the rain falling on me and surprised myself, when instead of walking, I bent down to smell the sunflowers.

Just as she had.

And I smiled.

Just as she had.

The flowers had captured her scent subtly and held it inside the petals. I inhaled deeply, closing my eyes, relying only on my sense of smell and touch. I was enveloped in her bouquet of lightness, beauty, and freshness. I touched the petals gently and imagined myself running my fingers across her body, tracing her cheek, her lips.

I forced myself to open my eyes because the path of my thoughts was not safe. I focused on being glued to this spot, plastered to the heavy rain falling on me, on the sunflowers and on the sidewalk so that I did not return to the store and kiss her and feel her body against mine, warming me.

Against my better judgment, I glanced back at the store, hoping to see her watching me, hoping to see something in her eyes that would give me permission to take her in my arms. Instead, my eyes, though still hazy from my daydream, saw all too clearly. They found a fogged-up window and her figure retreating from me.

Walking away from me.

You see, if I was the sun, she would turn toward me, just like the sunflowers she loved so much did.

However, I wasn't the sun. I was everything dark and I sucked any and all light into my darkness, enveloping it in dark clouds.

I put my head down and started walking quickly. I told myself that putting my head down was to protect my face from the rain. That it had nothing to do with this sadness that had overcome me, that it had nothing to do with the fact that she could not be mine.

That was a lie.

I blamed the rain on the wetness traveling down my cheek.

That was an even bigger lie.

Leaves the color of gold and copper were dropping at our feet. Laughter was permeating the brisk air. He would rake the leaves into a big pile with his hands, and she would watch him. Her eyes would widen with anticipation. He stepped aside, and she ran and jumped into the pile, giggling uncontrollably.

"I am glad one of us is having fun," he grumbled jokingly.

She laughed and took a few leaves and threw them into the air. They cascaded and made their way back to her. One big red leaf landed in the middle of her hair. It was a vivid contrast to her light brown hair kissed with the sun's highlights.

"You are having fun too, admit it. I mean, you get to watch me."

"Mighty sure of yourself, are you?" He tried to be serious, but a grin spread across his face.

"Mmmhhhhmmmm." She smiled and watched as he approached her and knelt on the ground, inches from her face.

It was moments like these that he loved, moments like these that he cherished. Lying on a heap of leaves, being herself, she was the most beautiful person on the planet.

"You are right. I love watching you. You know that, don't you?" His hand reached out and touched her skin. She looked deep into his eyes, losing all ability to speak. She just nodded her head.

"You are a beauty. Just like this leaf." He took the fiery red leaf off of her head, and taking her hand, they traced the outline of the leaf.

"I know I blush a lot when I am embarrassed, but do I get that red?" She started to laugh, but noticed that he was deep in thought. She knew him so well to know that he was not done saying what he needed to say. She had seen that distant look before. She looked down at the leaf that he was still tracing.

"The color is beautiful just like your lips after I've kissed them well." His hand now traced her lips. He leaned in closer; he could feel her breath on his face. He was about to kiss her, and she pulled on his jacket, and he fell on top of her. This time he joined in her laughter.

"I could get used to this," he said, grinning.

"I thought you said you weren't having fun?"

"I am now." He kissed her and rolled her on top of him. A gentle wind passed and more leaves fell on top of them.

"Me too."

"But I was having fun before too," he said.

"I know," she responded.

"You know me so well."

"I know," she said.

He laughed and she snuggled closer to him. "What's so funny?"

"I just love the way you say, 'I know,' with such confidence," he told her.

"I know," she repeated, and he laughed. "I am a confident gal."

"I know," he replied, and both of them laughed this time.

"I could fall asleep like this with you in my arms. I never knew that leaves could be so much fun."

"They are when you have great company. And I am amazing company," he said in a teasing tone.

"That you are," she agreed.

"I know."

"Now who overuses that word?" she teased.

"I love you," he said.

"Now that you can say as much as possible," she said with a sigh.

"I do, my fiery gal."

"Oh no, speaking of fiery. Where's the leaf? Oh no, I must have dropped it." She looked around frantically and tried to locate it. There were too many leaves, different shapes and colors. She picked up another red one. "You're the expert, is this the one?"

He shook his head. "It must have fallen when you rolled me over."

"Or when you fell on top of me," she said, pouting.

"Do you know that there are no two leaves alike?"

Her eyes widened. "Really?"

"We just have our memories."

"That's nice, but I want to save that leaf and retrace it with you someday down the line, when we are old and gray." She looked around the fallen leaves again. "Is this the one, maybe?" She held a red maple leaf with a small tear in the corner. Her eyes told him that she knew it was not it, but she still held out hope for finding their leaf, their memory captured and embalmed in it.

"Nope. But you are the one. My one and only."

They kissed, more leaves falling on their bodies.

Chapter Sixteen

Kaitlyn

I balanced the cookies in my hand as I reached for the doorknob with the other. The cool air hit me and I shivered. Perfect coffee or tea day along with some peppermint cookies I had baked. I hadn't burned them, which was a success for me. I carefully stepped over the threshold and closed the door behind me. These cookies were losing their heat quickly, so I walked down my steps and across the street to Shelby's as fast as I could without tripping or dropping the platter of just-baked peppermint goodness.

"Good morning, Shelby," I opened the door and called out from the doorway. "Can I come in?" I cheerfully asked. It'd been a week since the interaction with Kendrew at the flower shop. It had taken me an entire week to put how I was feeling behind me.

He bought flowers for another woman.

Oh my gosh. I was such an idiot to have such strong emotions toward a man that bought flowers for another woman.

He was never interested in me.

Telling myself that I wasn't desired by Kendrew hurt, but it was necessary.

I did not believe in fairy tales or knights in shining armor anymore, so I knew I would be okay.

It would take some time because my body seemed to change whenever he was around. I became aware of every part of my body, and my breathing changed, as did the beating of my heart.

I had never felt that way, and I thought that was why it confused me.

However, this past week, I had focused on working around the house as well as at the flower shop. It was a difficult feat to enter the shop and to wipe away his presence long after he left, but I think I finally managed on day five. On day six, I could look at sunflowers without feeling jealous and sad simultaneously. On day seven, I found my mojo again and started baking.

"Come on in, dear," I heard Shelby respond from the living room. "Come quickly. Whatever you brought smells divine."

I chuckled because Shelby and I shared the same sweet tooth.

"Peppermint cookies," I proudly said as I entered the living room. Shelby was sitting on the couch, her back to the door. I showed her the cookies before depositing them on the coffee table. I walked back to Shelby and pressed my lips to her cheek. I felt bad for not coming to see her for an entire week.

That kiss was my apology, as were the cookies.

I felt her arm pat my back gently, and as I pulled away to sit down next to her, I found her watching me. I jumped up and grabbed two plates from the kitchen as well as a knife and utensils.

"Busy week?" Shelby asked.

I nodded. "Very." I looked at the rug so Shelby could not read my eyes and know I was not telling her the entire truth.

"Hmmm."

I waited for Shelby to say more, but she didn't.

I knew I couldn't avoid eye contact with her much longer. I looked up and saw knowing in her eyes.

I didn't need to explain. She knew I would tell her when and if I was ready.

I grabbed three cookies, placed them on a small plate, and handed it to Shelby. I did the same for myself and sat down. "Oh, I completely forgot. Would you like some tea or coffee to go with this?"

"Yes, I just made some Earl Grey tea moments ago. Would you mind getting it for me? It's in the kitchen."

"Of course not. Earl Grey tea sounds amazing." I rose from the couch, smiling at her.

I brought out the teapot and poured us both a cup. I grabbed another cookie before sitting down. I felt Shelby's gaze on me, watching me intently.

I nodded toward the cookie in my hand. "I know I shouldn't be such a glutton, but I think these came out better than the pies." I took another bite out of the cookie, a gratified smile plastering my face. "Mmm, delicious," I said. I looked at Shelby and she still was watching me. "Would you like to try one?" I gestured toward the mound of cookies on the plate.

"Are you seeing someone now?" Her question caught me off guard and I stuffed the rest of the cookie in my mouth, to keep from answering her right away. I was not sure how to respond. Did I tell her the truth or did I lie and say I had someone back in the other town where I lived before coming here?

I chewed slowly and decided to tell her the truth. Partially. I mean there was no need for me to tell her about the reason I had given up on men.

"No, no boyfriend for me," I said, pushing my chair back from the table a bit, away from the cookies and their deliciousness.

"Why is that?" She looked at me fixedly. "You are a beautiful woman. I am sure someone catches your eye from time to time?"

"No, not really," I said, my voice feeling tight all of a sudden. I took a sip of tea, trying to clear my throat, and I ran my hand across the doily on the table, tracing the crochet pattern. Anything to not look at Shelby's inquisitive gaze.

"Hmm, I could swear that was you," she said and watched as my head shot up before continuing. A small smile formed on her lips as she regarded me for another second before she continued. "You know, that day, behind your porch railing, watching a certain handsome man who also happens to leave me groceries?" She took a sip of her tea and looked me straight in the eye from behind the cup.

My eyes widened, and I took a sip of tea, trying to buy myself some time to respond. I ran through many responses, and only one would work.

The truth.

I placed the cup on the table and looked at Shelby, ready to admit that the person she saw was, in fact, me.

"Oh no, you saw that?" I groaned inwardly. I put my hands up to my face and covered my eyes.

"Yes," she chuckled. "That was quite a performance." She looked at me with amusement. "Who needs television when I have that?" She pointed toward my home.

I felt the laughter building inside me, and when I heard her laughter, I couldn't help but join in. Tears ran down my face and I wiped them. I needed that laugh.

"How long have you known that he was bringing you groceries?" I asked her softly. I watched Shelby smile slowly and look straight at me. She looked so much younger and so at peace while she smiled.

I mentally gave Kendrew props for making Shelby feel so special.

"Since the first day." She laughed, her eyes wrinkling in the corners. "He also chops my wood." She stopped to ponder something, her face tilted upward to the ceiling in thought, before turning to me. "I guess I like him," she said with surety and sincerity.

"That's really nice of him to do that for you." I took another cookie and bit into it, savoring it, all while thinking about the man who helped little old ladies out.

I knew about the groceries, but the chopped wood was new to my ears. He was so difficult to understand. I didn't know where to begin with him or if I should even bother understanding him.

"I have always been able to read people," Shelby continued. "And he is a good person." She leaned in and said gently, "He is very hurt and has a protective wall around himself, but for the right person" —she pointed to me—"I feel he would break down that wall and bare his heart." She looked at me affectionately.

I shook my head. "No, not me. He has a woman." I pointed to my breasts and put my hands way out in front of my chest, emphasizing that she had big breasts. "I accidentally saw them kissing in front of the bar, and he also brought her flowers last week."

Shelby waved her hand dismissively. "Whoever she was, she wasn't the right one for him." She pinned me with her gaze.

"How do you know she wasn't right for him?" I asked her breathlessly. For some reason, I found myself holding my breath, hoping that Shelby was right.

"She wasn't you, was she?" she said pointedly, her lips pursing. "You don't think I see him run by your house every morning and look for you." She smiled, and her voice softened. "Or the way he looks at you when he thinks no one is looking at him." She tilted her head to the left and looked at me, a sweet smile on her face.

"He doesn't see me—" I croaked out, shaking my head. I chewed on my lip and thought back to all the times he had ignored me or acted rude to me.

Her eyes widened. "Are you sure?" she asked, looking thoughtful. She did not wait for my response. She gestured toward the window. "You were entering your home one day, and he froze in his tracks and watched you, mesmerized. He felt me looking and tried to play it off, but I saw his face." Shelby tilted her head, a gentle grin forming as she recollected what had happened. "He tried to cover a deep yearning, and when he realized it, he tried to walk away, but did so reluctantly. I saw hunger in his eyes, and that was him seeing you for a few seconds." She was about to say something else, but stopped.

She shook her head. "No, let me tell you this as well. He runs by your house and looks at it every time. Sometimes I catch him stopping and looking for you. You both are drawn to one another yet are fighting it."

Kaitlyn tried to speak and Shelby stopped her. "He is fighting his feelings for you just like you are fighting your feelings for him." She clenched her jaw. "Life is too short for that game." She leaned forward and her hand touched my cheek. "Kiss him. What's the worst that could happen?"

I chewed the inside of my cheek, thinking about what she had said. I was so confused. Why was Kendrew acting one way with me and another when I didn't see him?

She swallowed visibly.

"He already thinks I am nuts. Why give him a reason to prove that he was right by kissing him?" I asked. I studied Shelby, my expression calm yet my feelings confused.

"People in town think I am nuts for not going outside after Matthew died, but he comes by and helps. So maybe he likes nuts?" Shelby said with a twinkle in her eyes. I giggled.

"Put up some mistletoe by your door. You never know." She winked.

"How about we change the subject?" I asked with a grin on my face. "What pie should I try next week?"

"Kaitlyn, I will gain weight with all your baking." She rubbed her mid-section.

"You look fabulous."

"I've been meaning to ask you something, Kaitlyn." She paused and looked at me.

"Sure," I said.

"Your name, Kaitlyn, is a beautiful name, but—" she stopped and looked at me, a question in her voice "—it's just not something she would have named you. I don't know, it just doesn't seem like her . . . not to mention you."

"Sometimes I feel like that's not me. Do you think it's possible that it isn't my name?"

"I think it is very possible. Your mother mentioned a different name for you before you were born. She said she would name you something that meant the world to her. She would name you so that she could live on in you after she passed on."

"Deep down, I think that I have a different name." I looked at Shelby, who was listening to me intently. "I mean, one day I was walking down the street and my friend called out, 'Kaitlyn,' and I kept walking. It didn't seem to register. Until my friend caught up with me and chastised me for pretending not to see her." I sighed. "Some days I don't recognize it myself." I looked back at the older lady for guidance.

"I never want you to question who you are. Yes, the past is important, but it is not the indicator of who you are. You paved your own way. You are a smart, beautiful, young woman who just wants to find out where she comes from. There is nothing wrong with that, but just never question the present and who you are now."

"With all due respect, I think it's easier for you to say that because you were never in my shoes."

"What do you think is worse? Trying to find a past while living in the present or living in the past and being lost in the present? That is me. Ever since Matthew died, I seemed to die. It was a slow disintegrating death, but a death nonetheless. I live in the past, with my memories and a love that was so strong and comforting to me. Sometimes I feel like I should let him go and have him wait for me on the other side."

"I am sorry. You are right."

"You are a great girl. Remember that she is proud of you and the person you are now."

"Thank you." I crossed to Shelby's side and hugged her. "Now what do I do about the name thing?"

They looked at each other, bound in silence, deep in thought, the question thick in the air.

I just remembered something that Jim mentioned the first day in the store.

"I think Jim knows something," I said.

"He does," Shelby whispered.

"Why didn't you tell me?"

"It's not my story to tell." She looked me in the eyes. "He will tell you when he is ready, not a moment sooner."

"What—?"

Shelby cut me off. "I can't. Trust me on this one. The time isn't right yet. In the meantime, get to know Jim. He is a great person and I think the more time you spend together, the more ready he will be to trust his instincts and will fill in the missing pieces."

I wanted to press her to tell me, but I knew it was hopeless. She wouldn't. For some reason she wanted me to talk to Jim. I liked him a lot, so that wasn't a problem, but I just wished everyone would stop keeping secrets from me.

A moment of silence ensued as Shelby finally took a bite of her cookie and groaned. She looked at me. "This is so good."

I smiled at her, still deep in thought about my name and the mystery of Jim.

"Don't forget the Kendrew thing," Shelby said, breaking the silence.

"I should get going." I was not in the mood to talk about him anymore.

"Before you go, can you please grab my book for me?" she said. "It's on the nightstand in my bedroom."

I saw a twinkle in Shelby's eyes and didn't know what to make of it, so I just put it aside temporarily and did as she asked.

"Of course." I walked toward her bedroom. I knew this place by heart now. Sometimes while Shelby read or napped, I cleaned the place up for her a bit. It was the least I could do for her, my mom's dearest friend. Plus, the dusting helped keep my mind off of other things and off of certain people, and it calmed me. I was truly at peace when I was tackling a cleaning project. The harder I worked and the more exercise my muscles got, the better I seemed to sleep at night.

I walked into her room, and my eyes automatically looked for the picture of her and her love. The happiness that came off of that picture of them together was mystically magical. It was something I would have wished for one day, many years ago.

Definitely not now. Not anymore. Not after what happened to me that dreadful day.

That day I realized that wishes were not automatically granted, that stop did not always mean stop, that help shrieked into the night did not guarantee that help would indeed come.

No, my wishes had died with a part of me that day.

That didn't mean that I didn't wish for other people to be happy or rejoice in their happiness at a point in their lives.

My eyes traveled across Shelby's room and the two frames, yet this time, there was something new that caught my eyes. My gaze was seized not by the nonexistent book on the nightstand, but by the flowers in the vase.

Sunflowers that looked about a week old, wrapped in burlap. Some petals had dropped, but their beauty still remained.

Beautiful, cheery, happy sunflowers.

I found myself walking toward them, and my hand reached out to touch them. The petals, though slightly aged and dried up at the tips, were still full of light and life. Involuntarily, I leaned into the petals and closed my eyes as I inhaled deeply.

Instead of sun, I smelled the rain.

And Kendrew.

"I don't see the book in your bedroom," I called out to Shelby.

I would pretend not to have noticed the flowers.

I would put on a mask and hope I pulled it off.

I knew Shelby had good intentions and wanted me to give whatever these feelings were with Kendrew a chance. However, she didn't see how he acted with me and around me. He was not interested in someone like me. He had made it clear quite a few times already.

I didn't want someone to feel forced to like me, or feel forced to talk to me. I wanted . . .

What I wanted did not matter because he did not want the same.

I squared my shoulders and walked away from the framed couple so in love, captured in time, frozen smiles and enveloped in love, staring at my retreating back.

I felt my heart, like the sunflower petals, break apart piece by piece, with every step I took away from the room, away from his lingering scent on the flowers, away from all thoughts of him.

By the time I walked from the bedroom to Shelby's living room, I was ready for the performance of my life. I entered the stage, also known as Shelby's living room, plastered a smile on my face, and faced her.

"Perhaps you left it in another room," I said. I looked at Shelby and saw her watching me intently, her right hand rubbing her left shoulder. Over and over again.

I held her gaze and she looked away, toward the chairs facing the window and my house.

"Perhaps," Shelby finally whispered. "Perhaps."

He lit the candle and brought it to his bedroom. He sat on his bed and reached to the nightstand on the side and pulled open the drawer of treasured possessions. He saw it looking up at him and gently took it out, cradling it in his hand, touching it, reliving the moment.

Seven parts, the veins still visible. The color still fiery. The memory even more vivid.

Jim sat in front of the fireplace and remembered that day. He felt so guilty for taking the leaf, but he was so transfixed with it that he could not give it up. It was as if he knew deep down that one day that would be one more thing to remind him of her.

His chest felt the same pain it had felt for a number of years now. He had lost track of how long it had been, but the pain seemed to be deeper and seemed to last longer.

He lay down and fell asleep cradling the leaf in his hands, reliving that beautiful day when he came to possess this leaf.

Chapter Seventeen

Kendrew

The next three weeks flew by. December was in the air, and although the weather was warmer than it had been last month and the clouds clear, I found myself restless.

I was working overtime and covering for an injured firefighter, and I could not help out at Jim's. I would come home beat and sometimes so exhausted that I fell asleep on the couch. The best thing about working these longer hours wasn't the pay, but the fact that I didn't get my nightmare every night. I think I was so tired, physically and mentally, that my mind just shut down and I finally got uninterrupted sleep, except for that one night where my dream seemed to be on replay and played over and over again in my mind.

The part that I hadn't liked so much about working the extra hours was that I hadn't seen Kaitlyn since that day in the flower shop. I hadn't been able to help Jim at the store or Shelby with the groceries, but I did leave a list at the grocers and money with one of the teenage kids, as well as a delivery schedule so that Shelby could still receive her items uninterrupted. I left her a note explaining I would be back to doing it myself soon.

Here I was, three weeks later, walking toward Shelby's with three bags of groceries, and my gaze wandered to Kaitlyn's home, following the path of my thoughts. My attraction and connection to Kaitlyn hadn't dissolved at all. I figured not seeing her for almost a month would cure me of her, but instead it intensified my need to see her, talk to her, and touch her.

My thoughts were interrupted by laughter. I turned my head and followed the sound. It was coming from Kaitlyn's house. She was in the yard, to the right side of the house, alternating between raking leaves and throwing them in the air, and watching them cascade around her.

Damn, she was beautiful. Her cheeks were rosy from the crisp air. Her eyes were shining, and she looked so at peace in her surroundings. I found myself stopping to take a mental picture of her. I would catalog it and save it to memory to look at over and over again. Perhaps that picture of her would replace my nightmares?

She truly was an exquisite work of art. She had the type of face I could look at for hours and not tire of. Her green eyes seemed to draw me in, welcome me, flaws and all. Her lips were rosy and full, and I could imagine them fitting perfectly against mine. Yes, she was a beautiful woman, but her beauty was more than skin deep. Her beauty was her laughter, her loving heart, her ability to see the brightness on a gray day. She looked so content and happy playing in the leaves. She tossed them in the air and giggled as they fell down her entire body. I watched as she lifted her arms up, revealing her trim stomach and her belly button, and I instantly found myself wanting to kiss and nuzzle it.

Three weeks away and I missed her like crazy. Three weeks and I wanted to kiss her and shelter her in my arms and keep her safe always.

Three weeks had done that, and I hadn't even touched her or kissed her or truly spoken to her, for that matter.

I debated between going over and kissing her and leaving without a backward glance. A big part of my heart awoke when it saw her. It was stirring and the ice around it was melting. She set me on fire every time I saw her. She made me want to try to let someone in again.

After so many years of being alone, that thought scared me a lot. Letting someone in meant letting someone see you for how you were, the lightness of your soul along with the darkness. Would I allow myself to tell her about my past?

The other part of me, my brain, reminded me what loving someone did to the person I loved. It destroyed them. It hurt them, and in one case, killed them.

I was falling for this girl from a distance.

This was heartbreaking.

I was under some kind of spell and could not do anything about it.

Well, there was one thing I could do.

I would keep my distance. I felt my hand tightening into a fist. I would stay away until I was sure that I could tell her about my past. Until I was sure that I could let her in completely. Until I was sure that my actions and the darkness inside me wouldn't overpower her light.

I wouldn't break her heart.

I'd rather break mine.

My love,

Mother took my last letter from you and ripped it, so moving forward, please send your letters to Shelby and she will give them to me. When my mother ripped your letter, she seemed different. A little too calm. Afterward, she apologized and claimed that she longs for friendship between us. I would no sooner trust her than I would a wolf. No, actually, I would trust a wolf more. Something is up, Jim, but I don't want you to worry. I had to tell you so that you sent the letters to Shelby.

I won't let my guard down and I won't let her trick me. How sad is it that I can't even trust my own mother? I sense she wants something from me, but I just don't know what it could be.

Dear, enough talk about her. Soon enough I will meet you at the train station. I bought myself a new dress and can't wait for you to see me. I think I look a little more grown up. I can't wait to see how you look now. I know you will look even more handsome than ever. Oh, how I wish you were on your way back now. It is late and I must go to bed now. But I am kissing this letter and hoping that you imagine how that feels when you open it and hold the envelope where my lips pressed against it. I hope you visit me in my dreams again this night.

Love you always and truly,

M.

P.S. I am sending you a picture of me so that you do not forget what I look like. I wouldn't want you getting close to a nurse just because you forgot about me. This way you can always remember me.

Chapter Eighteen

Kaitlyn

"I can't believe it is mid-December already," I said to Irma. Harold was resting at home today, and Irma was at the store. She told me to take the day off, but I wanted to help. A big order of merchandise was delivered today, all Christmas flowers and plants, and we had to unload and price them and prepare them for sale.

"I know. Look at all the poinsettias, Christmas cactuses, amaryllis, and little tabletop Christmas trees. It looks like Christmas overload in here." She laughed. "Very beautiful though."

"There is no such thing like too much Christmas," I said, smiling. I felt like a kid surrounded by all this holiday spirit and joy. I walked over and touched one of the Christmas trees. "I love the smell of Christmas trees, especially spruce and fir."

The doorbell jingled and both Irma and I looked up. It was one of the town's firefighters, named Ben.

"Hi, ladies." He smiled.

"Hi, Ben, how can I help you?" Irma asked, smiling up at him. "A bouquet for your wife, perhaps?"

Ben laughed. "Not this time, Irma. I'm here on official business." His eyes twinkled as he pulled out raffle tickets and a list with handwritten names.

"I have been designated the official raffle ticket seller." He looked at both of us with excitement, his pearly whites on full display. He was a charmer and he knew it. "The money will go toward new equipment for the firefighters and a new roof for the firehouse." He shook his head slowly, sadness incoming on his face. "That last storm did a real number on the firehouse."

He looked down at the paper in his hand. "Can we count on you ladies buying a ticket or two? We would be really grateful." He winked at both of us, turning on his charm. I watched him reach for his pen, hopeful.

Irma looked at Kaitlyn and grinned. "I'm not surprised they chose you. Who can say no to you and your dimples?"

Ben laughed heartily, the just-mentioned dimples on full display. "Many women did before my wife took pity on me and married me."

Irma and I joined in on the laughter. After the laughter died down, Irma turned to me. "I can't say no to this handsome man. Can you?"

"Oh, no," I replied. "He had me at, 'Hi, ladies.'" I looked at him with a twinkle in my eye as I pretended to fan myself dramatically. "Count me in for twenty tickets," I said.

Ben whistled. "I really am good." His smile spread to his eyes.

I looked at him closely and compared him to Kendrew. Both were handsome and tall, with broad shoulders. The only difference was hair. Ben had reddish hair and blue eyes, while Kendrew was dark haired and had hazel-colored eyes.

"I'll take twenty as well, Ben," Irma said. "What is the grand prize this year?"

"Well, that's a good one." He handed us the raffle tickets, and we gave him the money. "We all sat down to think about the prizes, and we all voted that we wanted something different this year. You know, not the regular television or iPhone prize." He looked very excited. "There are three grand prizes. A $500 gift certificate that you can spend on whatever you want, wherever you want."

He looked at Irma and me and leaned in closely to whisper, "Are you ready for the second prize?"

Irma and I nodded and Ben grinned.

"The second and third grand prizes are dates with the single firefighters at the firehouse."

Irma whistled and Ben laughed, and before we know it, we were all laughing and chatting about the candidates for the dates.

"Single firefighters? Hmmm." Irma tapped a finger on her lips, deep in thought. Her mouth opened in surprise and her eyes lit up as she came to a conclusion. "That leaves us with Kendrew and Trent."

She nudged my shoulder. "Oh wow. Those are great prizes indeed. Those two are handsome as sin, and I know many women in this town and the next town over will want to be the lucky ladies going on those dates."

Hearing Kendrew's name made my heart speed up. I just had been thinking about him, comparing him to Ben. I remembered what I saw in the parking lot, and all of a sudden, I felt very warm. I felt myself blushing.

Wait, Kendrew is single after all?

Ben and Irma were watching me. I realized they were waiting for me to say something. I needed to come up with something quick.

"It's for a great cause. I'm sure that whoever wins the prize will be happy that they did their part to help the community and the firehouse."

"Indeed. Thank you for your support, ladies." Ben wrote down our names and the number of tickets we bought on the piece of paper and turned to leave. He stopped suddenly at the door. "I almost forgot. The raffle is being held before the Christmas tree lighting in the town square this Sunday. See you there."

***

I walked home from work thinking about Kendrew going on a date. Deep in thought, I passed my home and had to walk back an entire block. I finally reached my porch and grabbed my mail. I chastised myself for not collecting my mail for a few days now. It was a big mailbox, but it was still overflowing. I took out my letters and cards, along with a small box.

Who knew I was so popular?

The cards were Christmas cards from Jim, the town's optometrist, and from St. Lucy's Church in Hope Falls.

I sat down on the chair and opened up the envelope from St. Lucy's first. The cover of the card was a beautiful red cardinal sitting on a snow-covered evergreen tree. I read the contents of the card.

Wishing you a Merry Christmas filled with love, illumination, and happiness. May the cardinal bird always show you the way.

When you are ready, please come see me in Hope Falls. This is a town two hours north from Landing Falls. I have something for you that your grandmother left behind.

Keeping you in my thoughts and prayers.

Sincerely,
Father John McMara

I would visit him in the New Year. Hopefully with Jess. She should be back home with me for the holidays.

I reached for the box next. There was no return address on it. I wondered if the box was addressed to me or if it was delivered by accident. Maybe it belonged to a neighbor?

I turned it over and saw my name written on it. It was for me after all. What could it be? I didn't recognize the writing. It was handwritten, all in caps. Very neat writing.

I shook it and laughed out loud. I just needed to cross my porch, open my door, go to the kitchen, get a knife, and open the box and see.

Instead, I shook it once more and laughed. For someone very curious, I was surprised that I was prolonging the suspense. I finally walked inside and grabbed a knife and tore open the package.

I was caught off guard at what was staring up at me: *To the Lighthouse* by Virginia Woolf.

Mr. Jim. What a sweetheart.

I opened the cover and an inscription caught my eye and took my breath away. I read it once and reread it again and again until it sunk in.

Kaitlyn, I heard you talking about this book the other day with Jim and saw how much it meant to you. I, too, love this book, and it's been my escape a few times in the past as well.

Hope you enjoy it and perhaps are able to reread it under a tree, or better yet, surrounded by falling leaves.

Merry Christmas.

Kendrew

Kendrew! The gift was from Kendrew! Oh my word!

I was overcome with emotions reading his note. I was grinning like a big fool, from ear to ear. Then I was crying because this book, which might not be much to someone else, meant the world to me. Him being the one who gave it to me meant even more, especially since I had these unexplained feelings for him. I reread his words until I had them memorized, and even then, I kept looking at his handwriting. I could not stop touching his neat cursive writing and feeling the same yellowed pages he had touched. My fingers traveled to his name and traced it, his name on my lips as I voiced it aloud. I automatically felt warmth seep into my heart. I felt it stirring and waking up from a long hibernation.

Besides the books from Jim, this was the first time a man had given me a gift.

It touched a chord deep inside of me. I was so impressed that he had done this and that he alluded to Virginia Woolf's quote about trees and changing leaves.

I wanted to shout for joy at the top of my lungs, but another part of me wanted to keep this gift to myself. Stow it away in my heart and access it on days when I felt alone.

I walked up to my bedroom, clutching it to my chest, hugging it almost as if I was hugging him. Tears blurred my vision and I closed my eyes, thinking about him. I knew I would never forget what he did, that I would never forget this gift, and most importantly, I would never forget him.

I woke up the next day, with the book on the pillow next to me, wishing it was his beautiful face looking at me.

However, in the light of day, I saw things a little differently, a shade brighter and clearer. I was in trouble of falling for him and I had to stop. I had practically fallen in love with him last night over a book. Imagine what would happen if he kissed me, or held my hand. I knew that I had to stop reading into the gift so much.

This was probably his way of saying that we were good. That we were both adults and could face each other in this small town. In fact, we could even say hi in passing or chat about the weather if we ran into one another at the grocery store or at a restaurant.

I loved the gift and would cherish it always, but I would not read into it so much or make up these fluffy stories about how he was professing his love for me with a book left in my mailbox.

Someone once told me that I had a knack for writing a story that wasn't there.

I believed them now because last night, in my mind, I imagined Kendrew caring for me when in reality he was only being neighborly.

I had to remember that and focus on facts and not sensationalized fairy tales and wishes that didn't come true.

***

The tree was twenty feet tall, and when the town's mayor hit the switch and the tree lit up, the gasps of delight could be heard all around me. The lights twinkled before my eyes and reminded me of what I never had at the foster home. I looked around and saw the joy reflected in the children's eyes, and I felt happy watching them.

The tree was stunning, and I found myself lost in its beauty. I closed my eyes and listened to the sounds of laughter, caroling, and joy surrounding me, and I did what I hadn't done in a long time.

I made a wish.

And what I wished for surprised even me.

I wished for love. True, without limitations, love.

When I opened my eyes, I felt goose bumps appear on my arms and I tried to rub them away, thinking it was the cold weather. They didn't go away; in fact they intensified. I felt the feeling of being watched and I looked around, and that is when I spotted him.

He was standing to the side of the tree and he was looking in my direction. He was wearing his firefighting gear. His black turnout coat was open, and I could see the light blue shirt underneath. My gaze wandered to the belt at his waist, to his bunker pants, all the way down to his boots. He was so handsome, and suddenly I felt scorching hot.

I felt my mouth going dry.

I focused on not falling in these heels.

I couldn't believe I was so nervous seeing him all of a sudden. Then, I heard singing.

"Silent Night" permeated the air and seemed fitting. It was silent. I no longer heard anyone around us. It was just me and him, and he was looking at me so absorbedly.

In my mind, I practiced what I wanted to say. I wanted to say hi and thank him for the beautiful gift. I wanted to tell him I would cherish the book forever.

I smiled and waved to him. I started walking toward him, practicing in my head the friendly words I wanted to say, but instead I watched his head jerk in surprise at my movement toward him. He turned away hastily, without a wave back or a smile or even a glance back at me. I watched in disbelief as he walked, no, raced, toward the town hall.

What just happened? Why is he being so hot and cold?

As handsome as he was, he was also as infuriating.

The nerve of him.

There went my "him being neighborly" theory.

I watched people starting to stream into the town hall right across the street, but I couldn't go inside just yet. I felt humiliated and not in a place to come face-to-face with him. Actress Kaitlyn needed a moment to come out. I looked around and spotted a bench a few steps away from me, and I sat down, ignoring how cold the bench was. My dress and wool winter jacket was no match for it. I felt the cold seep into my bones, and I welcomed it. Perhaps if I went numb, I wouldn't feel the sadness I felt now after he had spited me.

I only need a moment, one minute. Tops.

I replayed what happened a few times before standing up and following the stream of people filing into the town hall, readying myself in case I saw him.

The grand prize.

I rolled my eyes and ran up the stairs, heels, tight dress, and all.

Actress Kaitlyn was entering the stage.

The sound of Christmas carols being sung outside accompanied me to the town hall, which was beautifully decorated. It was like a scene out of a Christmas movie with all the fake snow and trees, lights, and baked goodies. Irma and I were in charge of creating the floral arrangements, but everyone in the community came together to string the lights and bake some delicious treats, and the eggnog flowed freely. Wherever I turned, I heard laughter and joy. Everyone was having such a wonderful time.

I looked around the room and saw so many loving neighbors and a tight-knit community, all looking out for each other. Everyone was dressed festively, in Christmas colors—shades of greens and reds—and I even spotted a few "ugly" Christmas sweaters, which were so amusing and silly that they made me laugh.

I felt a little out of place in my little black dress and red four-inch heels, but it was the only pretty dress I had brought with me. After tackling some DIY home projects, I had run out of time to go shopping for a more festive, colorful dress. The shoes would have to be festive enough.

The home had been on my mind a lot recently. I wanted to get everything patched up and looking beautiful so that I could sell it and move on. Everyone had been so kind and sweet in Landing Falls, but when you grew up like I did, it wasn't always easy to feel part of a community, especially when the majority of your life had been spent living on the outskirts of a community. As a child, I was always watching the world from my window. As an adult, not much had changed. In fact, there were days when I felt I was on the outside looking in. Take for instance, today: everyone was laughing and telling stories and exchanging pleasantries, and I was walking around, in circles, listening and smiling, yet not feeling like I completely belonged.

I scanned the room, nervously pulling at a curl, trying to see if he was there. I mentally scolded myself and released the hold on my hair. I had spent close to an hour curling these medium-length locks and did not want to ruin them.

It did feel good to dress up though. I hadn't done that in a while. The dress, those heels and the makeup and hair had nothing to do with a tall sexy firefighter who had left me a gift. Really.

I didn't even believe myself. The truth was, I wanted to impress him tonight. I knew I would see him, since he was the prize at the raffle, and I wanted him to see me in a different light. I knew he wouldn't act on it, but I wanted a guy like him to notice me with admiration in his eyes.

Darling Jim,

I miss you so much. So very, very much. I should have started this letter asking you about how you were doing, but I could not help myself. Without you by my side, I feel an emptiness that nothing and no one will ever be able to fill. It scares me when I think about where you are and how unsafe you are every day. I count the days until I see you again and hug you and never let you out of my sight. Everything is okay with me, so don't even bother worrying about me.

I picture our reunion every single day. I know it will be even better in real life than in my daydreams because I will get to touch you and kiss you and feel you.

Know this, my love, when you come back, I am never ever letting you go. I hope you are okay with a lifetime of me attached to your hip. I'll make it fun, I promise.

It is late night already and I must go to sleep. I hope you visit my dreams again. Kisses.

Love always,

Mary

Chapter Nineteen

Kendrew

"What the hell happened back there?" I asked the reflection in the bathroom mirror.

I replayed the scene in my mind, reliving every single moment since I saw her outside, by the tree.

I remembered seeing her and seeing nothing else around me but her.

I recalled her starting to walk toward me and then me running for the town hall and the safety of the bathroom, where I locked myself into the one-person stall.

I was still locked in the stall now.

Thankfully there were other bathrooms with more stalls in the building, so I didn't feel that bad about taking this bathroom hostage, but I needed some space. Some time to myself. Away from the chief and the other guys. Away from Miss Matheson trying to pinch my butt, or anyone else, for that matter.

And especially away from *her*.

Most definitely *her*.

Truth be told, I didn't know why I ran when she started walking my way. Something about her smile and the way she looked tonight made me terrified. I wasn't terrified of her, but of what she and I could become. Of what she could make me be just by being in my world.

I had put on this show for so long. I was a bachelor leading a fun lifestyle, doing what I loved every single day at the firehouse, picking up beautiful women and sharing good times with them. Yet in the blink of an eye, that Kendrew wanted to retire the moment she was near, and today, I wanted nothing more than to meet her halfway and kiss her and hold her hand.

Hold her hand?

Since when did I hold hands?

I shook my head vehemently, hoping to shake the idea right out of it.

I didn't recognize who I was becoming. For so long I had told myself I didn't deserve commitment and a happily ever after because I had taken that from someone who really deserved it. I promised myself as a young teenage kid that I would never let myself be happy or fall in love ever.

Those promises went out the window whenever I saw her. My body reacted to her, and it angered me, and in turn I acted like a real loser and took it out on her. I cringed remembering the look on her face going from happiness to confusion to sadness before my very eyes in response to my actions.

I had thought watching her from afar was innocent enough. I never thought that she would find me looking at her. There was something ethereal about her tonight, standing in the middle of the town square, looking at the large tree, with something that looked like hope shining in her eyes. It was beautiful. Then I watched her close her eyes, and I wanted to be beside her, kissing her eyes, kissing her lips. Kissing her neck.

Instead, I had just watched from afar with naked hunger displayed on my face, my thoughts and actions not working symbiotically. When she looked in my direction, the heat just spread throughout my entire body. I saw her checking me out, and I saw something different in her face tonight. It looked a lot like want and need, and dare I say it, longing.

My instinct to run had kicked in and I knew I had left her confused.

When I left the book in her mailbox, I didn't think twice about what it could mean. I wanted her to know I saw her, that I noticed her, that I cared, yet I couldn't bring myself to say any of those things.

So instead I had left the book I knew she wanted in her mailbox with a quote that hinted about leaves. It was my cowardly way of telling her she looked beautiful wearing leaves and that she should do it more often.

I wanted her to somehow read between the lines and know that I saw her playing in the leaves that day. Even if I stayed back in the shadows, I wanted her to know that I saw her clearly and vividly.

I knew I was giving her mixed signals. Hell, I was giving myself mixed signals, but when it came to her, I truly could not help it. She made me want to reach out and touch her, even though I knew there were a hundred reasons why I should not.

One of those reasons was that I was a killer and she did not deserve someone so fucked up in her life. It really came down to that. My body wanted her, but my mind knew to hold back.

The face looking back at me was that of a liar. I didn't want her body alone. I wanted all of her, every part of her, even the parts she'd kept hidden. I wanted to explore those most of all.

If I was a different man, a man deserving of her, I would be courting her every single day and showing her how beautiful and priceless she was. I wasn't, so exploration of her mind, body, soul, and heart were off the table.

It had to be.

And that was no easy feat.

It was for that reason that I was hiding in a bathroom, scared to face her. Scared to look at her beautiful body in the sexy dress she was wearing today.

If I was a different man, I would tell her about Bridget and how she ruined other women for me with just a glance at me. I would tell her that she was constantly on my mind, that she made me want to be the best Kendrew I could ever be, that she was amazing, smart, and drop-dead gorgeous. I would take her home with me and hold her in my arms until morning.

I'd done the part about taking a woman home.

The part new to me would be holding her in my arms until day broke.

That's what I wanted to do with her.

And not just once.

Now you know why I ran?

I never hid the fact that I was fucked up and complicated. I was. I was so much more too though.

The battle inside me raged on and I truly didn't know who would win.

Can light ever truly win? Can a chance at love be in reach for me?

Or had I just cemented the road leading to her with lies, hurt, and past fears?

I ran a hand through my hair roughly. I was so confused and didn't know what to do after I left this bathroom.

She must've thought I was a jerk. First, I acted rude to her, then I bought her and her friend lunch. Then I practically ignored her, yet sent her a book for Christmas with a handwritten note only to run away from her.

I felt like such an idiot.

I looked at the man in the mirror and shook my head. He was fucking spineless. Sure, he rushed into burning buildings, but he was scared to ask this one girl out.

I turned on the cold water and splashed my face.

I needed to leave this safe space and go out and face everyone, especially her.

I wouldn't blame her if she hated my guts. I hated myself now too.

My Mary,

A lifetime joined to you at the hip sounds like a dream come true. I never want to let you out of my sight or arms ever again either.

I am young, but I have seen death. I have seen lovers pulled apart forever, and I will make sure I come back to you, with a heart beating. I would never want you to go through life without me.

You and I were made for each other. I think we were put on this earth to love one another.

I don't want to make this letter serious, so I will tell you something that hopefully makes you smile. Matt and I were arguing the other day about who loved his lady more. I said I did, and of course he said he did. We decided to throw rocks to see whose landed farther. Guess what happened, baby doll?

He threw his rock pretty far. It was my turn, and I did my absolute best. I gave it my all. When he and I went to inspect who won, my rock was on top of his. We had a good laugh. Apparently, Matt and I are both madly in love with two amazing gals.

I love you always and forever,
J.

CHAPTER TWENTY

Kaitlyn

"Ladies and gentlemen, can I please have your attention?"

A loud booming voice shook her from her stream of thinking and got her attention. It was the chief. Everyone gathered closer to the stage, and the room quieted down.

"Thank you all for coming here tonight to support the firefighter fund." The chief looked around the room and smiled. "We are so grateful for this community's support. With your generous help, this fundraiser was a huge success. We raised $10,280, and with an extremely generous and anonymous donation of $5,000, we raised in total $15,280."

The chief clapped and the room joined in. A few people whistled, and the joy in the room was contagious. I, too, joined in the cheer and clapped joyfully, happy for the town.

The chief continued, "How about we start this raffle now?"

The room erupted in a few more cheers. I grinned and looked down at the raffle tickets in my hand, numbers 01271 through 01291.

"I invite to this stage Jonah Walsh. He won the spelling bee in his second-grade class just a few days ago. Jonah will be the one reaching inside and pulling the winning tickets." Jonah approached the stage to a round of applause. He was dressed in a suit, and his hair was combed back. He acted very serious, and you could tell that he was definitely proud of his role in the raffle. The chief offered his hand, and Jonah shook it.

"The first prize is a $500 gift certificate that can be used anywhere and everywhere that credit cards are accepted. The lucky winner of this ticket is—" The chief knelt down and Jonah reached inside the box and pulled out a ticket.

"01352."

I looked down. It was not my number. I heard someone shout from the back of the room, "It's me!" A woman around my age, who I had not seen around town or run into yet, hurried onto the stage and claimed her prize. After having her picture taken with the chief and Jonah by the local newspaper, she headed off stage to her circle of friends, happy for her win.

Aside from Jess, I had never had a circle of support like that lady. Sadness settled over me at the emptiness in my life, devoid of friendships and support networks.

"Onto the next prize," the voice on the stage boomed. I looked back to the stage and tucked away the onslaught of seriousness that entered my mind just moments before. The chief was grinning and could hardly contain his joy.

"This prize is for a date with Trent Hanson. One of our town's finest and bravest. He is six-foot-tall and loves riding his motorcycle, and, ladies, he is single and ready to go on a date."

Trent came onstage without a shirt, in his firefighter uniform.

"Number 01129."

I heard a shriek to my left. It was a beautiful redhead in a killer green dress. She was beautiful, and Trent definitely looked like a happy camper. She ran onstage, they took a picture, and she and Trent left the stage, chatting away.

Looked like those two would enjoy their date.

There was movement on the stage and my breath hitched. *He* had come onto the stage and looked like he would rather be anywhere but there. His eyes scanned the crowd, and they focused on me.

I quickly looked away and walked toward the table with the drinks, hoping that the eggnog wasn't only eggnog, but that it was infused with something stronger. I held onto the tickets in my left hand and grabbed the drink with the right. I felt my cheeks getting hot. They were on fire from embarrassment.

I tasted the eggnog, and to my disappointment, it wasn't infused with alcohol.

Gosh, it got terribly hot all of a sudden, with all those people surrounding me.

I told myself that the heat had nothing to do with the muscular, tall man onstage with his smooth chest.

I licked my lips and watched him. He seemed to be doing the same to me.

I heard the chief in the background; his voice sounded miles away. "Kendrew Batten is up next. He is six foot three inches."

I was imagining my hands on that chest.

"Loves Classic Literature."

And then tracing it with my tongue

"Likes to hike."

Tasting his skin.

"He is looking forward to this date."

Feeling his skin against my skin.

"And the lucky winner is 01271."

Feeling his hardness against my body. Feeling him on me, against me, in me.

Shit. 01271.

Shit. It can't be.

I almost spilled the drink I was holding.

I went into panic mode and told myself to breathe.

I put the cup of eggnog on the table momentarily to look at the number on my very first raffle ticket, to make sure I didn't make a mistake.

Number 01271 was staring back at me.

The universe is playing a cruel joke on me!

I win a date with a guy who does not even wave back to me, a guy who turned his back on me.

Oh, hell no!

I heard the rustling as people went through their tickets, looking for the number. I heard a few of the ladies' disappointed sighs. The chief repeated the number again, and I looked at the ticket in my hand and at Kendrew.

He was looking at me with a gleam in his eyes. Challenging me to step forward. Daring me.

He *knew* I had the ticket.

I had to think quickly. I scanned the crowd around me and spotted just the right person. I moved to her side quickly, mentally congratulating myself on not tripping in those heels, and placed the winning ticket in her hand.

"Consider this my Christmas gift to you," I said. She looked at me with excitement and questions in her eyes. I smiled at her, patting her hand, encouraging her to step on the stage and claim her date. I didn't look at him, but I knew he was boring his eyes into me. I *felt* it.

The truth was, I wanted to look at him, but I couldn't. I couldn't let him see how much I wanted to go out with him. I couldn't let him see how sad I was not to go out with him. I couldn't read into the gift he had given me. I had to look at facts.

"Are you sure, dear?" Miss Matheson asked me, her head nodding toward the stage and the man on it. "I am positive *he* would love to be on a date with you instead of a vintage lady like myself."

I nodded my head vehemently and reached down to kiss her cheek. "Merry Christmas," I whispered. I turned away, unable to take being in this room any longer. I looked around and spotted my escape route. The red exit light was my salvation in this overly hot room. I hurried toward it before I changed my mind.

I wanted that date so badly. He was intriguing and sexy, but a big part of me knew why I had to distance myself from him, quickly. He hated my guts.

I had honestly thought the book was an olive branch between us, but I was wrong. His reaction moments before proved it. I was not even sure he was the giver of the book anymore. I wouldn't have put it past Shelby to play matchmaker like that.

It just didn't make sense that a man would send me a gift and then treat me as a perfect stranger. Worse, he treated me like a contagious disease one runs from straight to their doctor, or better yet, the CDC, for a preventative vaccine.

I heard the chief's voice announce with laughter Miss Matheson as the winner as I stepped into the cool December air. I looked at the tree where I had just made my wish a mere hour ago, and it blurred before my eyes.

Funny how my wishes never came true for me in a way I wanted them to.

I wished for the love of a man. True, limitless, passionate, and pure love.

And I got him. Someone I felt so connected to, but who could never be mine.

I felt the wetness on my cheeks, and I looked back at the twinkling tree once more; only this time I did not make a wish.

No point in doing that. Wishes did not come true.

At least not for me.

Chapter Twenty-One

Kendrew

I knew she had the winning ticket. I could tell by her face when she kept looking at the ticket, then at me, and then back to the ticket with a frozen, slightly panicked look on her face.

I had been against this raffle until I realized she had won the date. I wanted that date with her badly. It was my way of going out with her without having to make a fool of myself by asking her out. Plus, this way, I figured she wouldn't be able to say no.

When she won, I felt excitement course through my body. I felt like the universe was giving me a second chance, or third or fourth chance, to make things right with her. She looked stunning tonight. That dress hugged her in all the right places, in places that I longed to hug. The dress showed off a little bit of her cleavage and hugged her backside lovingly. And those shoes. Wow. She was sizzling tonight.

But just as quickly as she had frozen, she recovered and gave the ticket to Ms. Matheson. An eighty-year-young cougar who loved touching men's muscles.

I was in for an interesting night.

I would laugh at my predicament if I wasn't so affected by her tonight. Why did thinking about her cause my heart to race so quickly? And most importantly, how did I stop that from happening again?

Perhaps what she had done was right. A date would have complicated things. I almost had complicated things with the book I left her. I just saw how much she loved it and felt compelled to give it to her. I was a jerk to her the first time I met her and just wanted to apologize, and that book was my vehicle for the apology.

Liar.

Truth was, I had wanted to put a smile on her face. I wasn't good with words when it came to her, so I figured the handwritten note would show her I cared about her as a person. That she mattered to me even if I didn't say it to her.

My thoughts went to the book. Perhaps she was upset that I gave her the book? I mean, I had no right giving her presents. As much as I was in my head and debating the subject, I knew I had done the right thing. I would do it the same way again. That book was meant to be hers. I wanted to say sorry and that's the way I chose. If she didn't like it, well, that was her problem.

I felt a pinch on my left buttock and I snapped back from the visit inside my head. Ah, Miss Matheson never disappointed. She was always the same. A cougar to the max degree.

I looked at all the smiling and happy faces in front of me. None happier than Miss Matheson though. I put my arm around her and gave her a sideways hug.

You know, now that I thought about it, I was glad that Kaitlyn didn't claim her date with me. She and I would never work. I loved being single, and one-night stands worked for me. Being single had its perks, and I loved that lifestyle.

It was safer that way.

My heart was protected that way.

Why change what worked and risk getting hurt?

Most importantly, why risk hurting her?

No, I was grateful that her sexy butt had walked out without claiming the date with me.

This way, we both won. She wouldn't get hurt and neither would I. Well, except for a few bruises on my buttocks from Ms. Matheson's pinches. Yes, her walking away was a win for me too.

Yet why did this "winning" feel so shitty?

***

"The desk," Jim said. "I forgot all about Kaitlyn's desk." Jim had a worried look on his face. He looked at me, and I could tell he felt really bad about forgetting. So much had gone on in the store since I was away, working extra-long hours and extra days. I felt bad for not being there for Jim, but those extra hours really took a toll on my body. I would come home and crash. One day, I didn't even make it to the bedroom and fell asleep, with my clothes on, on the living room couch.

It was my first day back and we were trying to catch up on all the orders. We were unloading a crate that had come in two weeks ago.

"I'm sure she understands. We will get it to her as soon as possible." I reached over and patted his shoulder. "Don't worry so much. We got this."

Jim nodded, yet I could tell he was still worried. He believed in going above and beyond for his customers. A late delivery to him was beyond reprehensible. "Do you think you could drop it off today?"

"Yeah, I can do that." I took out what looked to be a painting from the large crate. It was a painting of a man and woman, dancing in the rain, oblivious to the wet clothes plastered to their bodies. The background was somber, dark, and cloudy, and they were both wearing white clothing. The man was in white pants and an open white shirt, while the woman was wearing a white sundress, and a white panama hat lay on the ground nearby. It must have fallen from one of their heads while they were dancing. Or perhaps the owner of the hat wanted to feel the rain on his or her body and did not want anything in the way of that experience? What really captured my attention about the painting was that it was black and white, except for the little rays of yellow surrounding the couple. It was as if in the midst of rain and dark, heavy clouds, they were creating their own ray of sunshine. For all the darkness, the painting seemed very light and full of harmony. Their feet were bare and the smiles on their faces were so carefree. One glance at them and you could tell how much they loved one another. Their bodies were captured in a pose on canvas, yet every stroke of the paintbrush seemed to create movement. The artist did an incredible job, and I knew I wanted to buy this painting. I needed this painting, and that seemed to catch me off guard. All these years of helping Jim at the store and I never felt compelled to purchase any artwork. In fact, my walls at home were bare. Yet when it came to this painting, I knew that I had to have it. It reminded me of something and I couldn't place my finger on what that was. This scene settled inside me though and I tucked away that feeling, to explore it another day. We were too busy here today for me to reminisce and get philosophical.

"Do you want to take the car?" Jim's voice permeated my thoughts. I placed the painting on the ground, leaning it against a nightstand. I felt the trembling inside of me, and I congratulated myself on successfully placing the painting when I did. If I still had been holding it, it would have probably fallen out of my quivering hands to the ground.

The car.

Driving.

A car.

I went into panic mode.

Not many people knew that I didn't drive. In fact, no one knew, not even Jim.

I felt myself breaking out in a sweat, and I wiped my forehead. I could feel the sweat trickling down my back. I looked at Jim and he was watching me, worry etched into his face.

"I, ummm," I stammered, wiping my forehead with the back of my hand, yet again. I felt the panic rising inside of me. I was taking mouthfuls of air and still gasping. I turned away from Jim and leaned down, my head in between my knees, trying to get my breathing under control, all the while thinking of how to get myself out of this situation.

The thought of how I would get the writing desk to her never had crossed my mind. All of our customers had cars, and I would load their items into their cars for them.

I was watching the ground, thinking of a plan, of a way out of this mess, when Jim put a hand on my shoulder and started speaking in his calming voice.

"I can go get my pickup truck and bring it around in about an hour or so if that's okay with you," he said gently. "We can load the desk and I will drive us to Kaitlyn's."

I looked up, relief filling every pore in my body, and saw deep concern in Jim's eyes. Not only concern, but also understanding. He suspected something, he knew something, yet he wasn't pushing me to talk about it.

Words could not begin to describe the respect I felt for Jim and the gift he had just offered me. The gift of not needing to explain my reaction or reason to him, the gift of understanding me without words, so instead I just nodded my clammy head, my heart filled with gratitude.

***

You could set a clock by Jim. An hour later, with the desk loaded in the truck, we were off to Kaitlyn's home to drop off the desk. The desk was heavy and I worried about leaving it on the porch for her to deal with it, but that's what she wanted. I bit my fingernail, worrying how she would manage to move it.

What if it rains?

I had promised to stay away from her, for her good. The last thing I ever wanted to do was hurt her, and I would. If she found out about my past, she would hate me. She would judge me, and I didn't think I could stand her eyes looking at me with pity or shame.

So instead I remembered her words that day in the store and replayed them until we were outside her home. I would be doing what she had asked.

After the day I saw her raking the leaves, I promised myself I would stay away. Yet here I was, with her desk, on her porch, staring at her door. Jim dropped me off and claimed he had to be somewhere just now, and he grinned and waved before driving away. It took me a good moment to recover and realize what he had just done.

The last thing I needed was for him to play matchmaker now.

I stood in front of her house not wanting to go in. I considered leaving the desk and running off, like I did with Shelby's groceries, but I found myself not being able to do that.

Perhaps a part of me wanted to see her. To be a friendly neighbor, at the very least.

I knew I wouldn't allow myself to hurt her, but I could be friendly.

I talked myself into ringing the doorbell, and I heard her shouting, "Come in."

I grabbed the doorknob and twisted it. I was about to announce myself, but my breath was knocked from my body.

She was standing on a chair, barefoot, on her tiptoes, in the tightest pair of jeans I had ever seen. She was focused on the wall in front of her, a roller brush in one hand and the other hand busy moving the hair from her face. Her ponytail must have come undone as she was leaning down to wet her roller with paint. Her left cheek was splattered in paint.

"Just one moment," she said without looking at me. Her focus was on the wall in front of her. She moved the roller a couple of times before placing it in the tray. She looked at the wall once more, with a triumphant look on her face, before finally turning to me.

She let out a gasp, and I realized I was the last person she had expected in her house.

My J.,

I just received your letter today. I have to admit it, I am the most blessed person who ever lived. You make me want to do better, be better. You make me want to dance in the rain, giggle in church, lie in the grass with the dew drying itself on my clothing and infusing my hair with the fresh scent of raindrops and grass, walk barefoot through the mud, feeling its coolness between my toes, and screaming from the top of my lungs from the top of a hill for no reason other than the simple fact of doing it. I miss doing all of these things with you. I will never forget the first time you asked me to meet you on our hill when it was raining. The look on my mother's face was priceless when I came home looking less than perfect. I could not contain my laughter, and I didn't really want to, in all honesty, when she demanded I tell her where I had been and what I had been doing. I told her the stains on my dress were only mud and grass and would wash out. She looked positively livid. Oh, what great memories. And they only get better!

I can't wait to do some more outrageous things, and you are the perfect person to start such mischief with. The way your eyes sparkle when we do these things warms my heart and infuses me with extreme happiness. I know that with you by my side our world will be vibrant. On top of that, you are so handsome. I never told you before, but you took my breath away that day when you stood before me with a smile on your face, your hair wet and clothes plastered to your skin. I won't say that I fell in love with you then because that would be a lie. I loved you a while ago already, but that day you captured a piece of my soul. A piece of me. No matter what happens, you will always be one with me because the soul lives on. I know you felt the change. You looked at me and read it in my eyes . . . I know you did. That was spectacular.

I bet you are wondering why I mention this now? Yes, you are! (I know you so well!) Well, it's raining here and the letter I received from you was splattered with rain as well (I could read everything, no worries) so it is also raining where you are. Miles and miles away. Do you think it's the same rain? I just opened my window and held out my left hand. It felt cold against my palm. I'm going to tell you what I did next, but you have to promise not to laugh. I looked at my hand and kissed it thinking of you.

It seems like the rain is our connection. Every time it rains, I remember how my soul fused with you that day. So, darling, whenever it rains, please think of me. I am every drop that falls from the sky needing to feel you close . . . I love you.

—M.

Chapter Twenty-Two

Kaitlyn

I was about to jump off the chair, when I suddenly saw him rush forward, toward me. His hands were around me and I felt my heart jump. Just a gentle brushing of his hands on mine and my breath felt labored. My eyes dilated and I looked at his lips instinctively.

He pulled away so quickly.

"I thought you were about to fall," he said, looking at the chair I was standing on.

He seemed to be avoiding eye contact with me.

The air was filled with intense energy, the type of energy between a man and woman who have intense chemistry but have not acted on it. Instead, it builds up and builds up, until it is so intense and strong.

"I'm so sorry for keeping you waiting," I managed to speak first. I pointed to the wall. "This wall has been giving me a hard time all afternoon, and I can't tell you how happy I am to be done."

I smiled, and his gaze dropped to my lips. I took a step back away from him, away from the heat. Away from temptation and ultimate rejection. Though our bodies might have recognized each other in a strange way, his hesitancy to be friendly with me was warning enough to respect him and to stay away.

"Where is your ladder?" he asked. His tone was serious as he scanned the room looking for it. His gaze was fixed on mine, and I felt myself blushing.

"I, um," I stammered and looked behind me, to the chair I was just painting on a few moments ago. My teeth were biting into my lip as I admitted the truth. "Umm, that's my ladder." I pointed to the chair and looked at him. Laughter. I felt my lips shaking, and

I was holding back laughter. How silly all this must've looked to serious, stern Kendrew.

I looked at him and watched as his eyes tore away from mine and he spotted the chair. I watched him shake his head and cover his mouth with his hand, but not fast enough to hide the smile forming on his lips.

"That's not safe," he mumbled.

"I'm glad you didn't see me earlier then." I giggled.

I watched as he bit his lower lip. I could tell I had his curiosity piqued, so I was not surprised when he wanted to know more.

"What happened earlier?" he asked warily.

I pointed to a box. "See that box." He nodded his head and I continued my story. "Well, envision me standing, just like I did moments ago, on the chair; only this time imagine that box under my feet on the chair."

What he did next astonished me and warmed my heart.

CHAPTER TWENTY-THREE

Kendrew

I felt the laughter build inside me. I tried to hold it in, but I couldn't. I pictured how she looked, barefoot and standing on a box that was on a chair, painting.

The lighthearted laughter astonished me. It had been so long since I had allowed myself to truly laugh. I mean, I joked around with the guys from time to time, or smiled at something Jim said, but I hadn't laughed like this since I was a kid, playing games with my family. She joined in laughing, and before we knew it, we were both laughing so hard that my sides hurt.

Game night had been big at our home. My mom would make popcorn and my sister and I took turns picking the game we would play every Saturday. My favorite was always Monopoly. My sister loved Twister, and my parents both loved Battleship and Jenga.

We used to have so much fun, and sometimes we laughed so hard that tears trickled down our faces and our stomachs hurt from laughter. Exactly like it was now.

Kaitlyn transported me back to a good memory, and I was grateful to her for that.

Surprisingly, thinking about my family and reminding myself of that memory didn't hurt as much as I expected it would. In fact, it made me happy to remember it.

I finally caught my breath and wiped the tears from my eyes and looked at her. She was doing the same. In the process of wiping her eyes, she smudged some paint and reapplied it to places on her face, where it wasn't before.

I took a look at her once more and laughed. She looked at me questioningly, and I pointed to my face and then at hers.

I watched her go to the mirror and gasp. I heard her laughing. "Oh my gosh, why didn't you tell me earlier?" she said. I watched her head into a room off the side of the hallway. I assumed it was the kitchen because I saw a wet paper towel in her hands and she was trying to wipe away the paint.

"It wasn't like that before," I answered. "You just smudged it now."

She was standing right in front of me, smiling, and I could still see some paint on her nose. I reached over and wiped it. She watched my hand reach for her and tilted her head up a little more, giving me clearer access to her face.

She chuckled. "Am I paint-free now?"

"I think you are far from being paint-free," I said, teasing her. My eyes roamed across her body and settled on her chest. She was in a heather-gray V-neck T-shirt, and I could see the valley between her breasts was splattered in paint. I dared not touch that, so I changed the subject.

I stepped away and pointed to the porch. "I have your desk here."

She let out an excited shriek and ran to see it.

I watched her do a silly happy dance in the door before she stepped out on the porch. I watched her run her hand across the desk, a big smile appearing on her beautiful face. The sun's rays bounced off of her beautiful golden hair, and she looked as if she was shining. She was so exquisite. A goddess. She was unlike anyone I knew. She was so bubbly and kind and genuine.

Even after I acted like a jerk, she had always been kind to me.

I took a few steps and stood right beside her. "Where do you want the desk?"

"Can you just leave it there, in the hallway?" she asked, pointing to the little foyer area.

I looked at her with questions in my eyes. "Here?"

"Yes." She nodded her head. "I am a little behind my painting schedule and I am painting the room where this desk will be tomorrow, so I will move it there after it is painted."

"It'll be heavy," I exclaimed. "Are you sure you don't want me to move it there and cover it so it doesn't get splattered in paint?"

"I'm positive," she said. "I will move it once I am done in there."

"Okay," I responded. "If that's what you want, but at least please let me drop off a ladder for you for tomorrow."

"I don't want to inconvenience you," she said hesitantly.

"It's not a big deal." I shrugged.

"Well, I appreciate it so much. Thank you." She extended her hand and I looked down at it, not sure what to do next. I swallowed the big lump stuck in my throat and slowly reached out to shake the hand she had extended toward me. I gripped it tightly, feeling its warmth and its strength. Most importantly, feeling the tingles and electricity that ignited when our hands met. I heard her gasp and looked at her. She was watching our entwined hands.

I felt my body tighten and respond to her touch and her gasp. I pulled away from her at lightning speed.

"No biggie," I croaked out before turning away, rapidly walking toward the door like my feet were walking on hot coals.

I hurried outside and closed the door behind me. I was standing on the porch, looking back at the door separating us. I wanted to go back inside and kiss her, but all the reasons why I shouldn't assaulted my thoughts, and I shook my head, clarity returning. I walked down the steps and focused on getting home.

Against my better judgment, I looked back at her house once more. I looked down at the hand that just held hers and I felt myself smiling. My hand felt different after touching her. I yearned to do more of that. I looked at her home with unsuppressed yearning evident on my face. Little did I know that she was watching me with the same hunger on her face, with the same tingling in her hand spreading across her body.

Chapter Twenty-Four

Kaitlyn

Ding-dong.

"Who could that be?" I wondered, looking across the hallway at the door. I could see someone's frame through the crackled glass door, but could not make out who it was.

I had spent all morning stripping paint from the door frames and doors leading to the living room and lost track of time. The doors were a special project that I wanted to tackle. They were antique and French inspired with such exquisite woodwork carvings. Someone had decided to paint them a hunter-green color, and my mission was to restore them to their natural wooden splendor. Perhaps I would then apply a little stain to make them dark cherry before finishing them off with lacquer to seal them. I wasn't sure about that yet, but I definitely did not want any paint on them.

The walk to the door, short as it was, felt like a workout. My thigh muscles were sore from me crouching on my legs for so long. I dusted off some dry paint and looked at the grandfather clock in the corner and saw that it was 11:00 a.m. I had been at that project for the past two and a half hours. No wonder my muscles were so tight and sore.

I slowly reached the door and pulled it open and could not stop the smile from forming on my lips. It was Kendrew, with a ladder, paintbrushes, two rollers, wide grin, cute ass, and all.

I was in trouble.

I took a good look at him. He was wearing jeans that fit him beautifully. They had a small rip on one knee. He had on a white T-shirt. On any other man the look would be super casual and relaxed. On him it was something different. It was sexy with a dash of rugged and masculine, and I was really losing it over this guy. I looked up at his face and watched him looking at me just as closely. I smiled and opened the door wider, stepping aside to let him enter.

I grabbed the paintbrushes and rollers from him and our fingers accidentally touched. I felt the electricity shoot up my arm, and I looked at him.

He didn't seem to notice.

He took a few steps before placing the ladder down and setting it up.

I walked the two feet over to him and left the paintbrushes and rollers on the steps, spreading them out. I was not sure where he wanted them, and I seemed to be tongue-tied at the moment.

He was looking at the French doors I had been working on. "Busy morning, huh?" He nodded his head toward the doors.

I followed the direction of his gaze and then looked back at him before a satisfied grin spread across my face.

"Yeah, I couldn't sleep that well, so I went for a run and then decided to tackle those doors."

He smiled. "They look beautiful."

Just like you, I wanted to say. Instead, I felt myself blushing at his compliment and my drifting thoughts. "Thank you," I whispered.

"Shall we get started?" he asked.

I felt my eyebrows drawing together, my forehead lifting in confusion. "We?" I asked. "You're not working today?"

He looked at me. "I am—" he looked around the hallway and pointed to the walls "—here."

"Here?" I whispered.

"Yeah, it's my day off. Why not make myself somewhat useful?" He shrugged his shoulders, and I watched him. I couldn't seem to talk to him like a normal person without being overly aware of every tiny movement his body made. I looked up at him and saw him watching me, a slightly confused look on his face. I realized he was waiting for a response from me.

I shook my head, pretending like I knew what I was doing. Anything to be away from his body. "That's okay. I can do it, and I can just return the ladder and brushes when I am done." I was talking quickly. That always happened when I was nervous. "I don't want to inconvenience you."

He took a few steps toward me and was so close that I could smell his clean scent. It smelled like rain in a meadow. He had probably just gotten out of a shower before coming over here. My innocent thoughts of him showering were replaced with a vividly erotic picture of him in the shower, and I felt my blush intensify. I looked down at my feet and thought about his scent.

Yes, that is safer.

It was clean. Fresh. Manly. With a hint of oak and some spice. I couldn't put my finger on the kind.

This wasn't working.

I couldn't seem to think with him being so close, so I succumbed and allowed myself to feel, to soak in this moment, and what I felt was electrifying and terrifying at the same exact time. It caused a fire to spread through my body, and I felt it pool in the area between my legs. I was squirming now and hoped he didn't realize why.

This was so embarrassing. My body did not have a filter when it came to him. It just seemed to have a switch that was always turned to "on."

I must've looked like a tomato right now. My face was on fire.

I was still looking at my feet and felt his hand lift my face up gently to look at him.

"I would like to help," he said gently. "Truly." His eyes were looking into mine, and I found myself mesmerized. No longer embarrassed, but strangely comforted and accepted and so in tune with his gaze. I never wanted this moment to stop, but I knew it would, so I knew I would accept his help.

Anything to have him alongside me for a little bit longer. I would hold onto this memory for the lonely nights ahead of me.

I looked at him and nodded my head in agreement, and he smiled at me. The smile seemed to spread across his face and reached his eyes, making them shine. He looked so different right now.

So at ease.

It was almost as if he had let down his guard with me.

If he could do it, I could as well.

"I really appreciate it," I responded and took a step back, needing some air. I pointed to my French doors. "I'll, umm, finish stripping those doors." I took a few more steps backward, unable to tear my gaze from him just yet.

He looked at me, his eyes running from my face all the way to my feet before asking, "And where do you want me to paint?"

I looked around and saw that my paint job yesterday wasn't that great. In the morning light, I could see the streaks and uneven paint distribution. I laughed, and his gaze followed mine.

I pointed to the wall, laughing. "Right about there looks good?"

He looked at the wall I painted yesterday, his eyes going wide before he looked back at me and chuckled. "Yeah, I think that's a good place to start." He laughed.

He pointed to the paint can sitting on the floor in the hallway, by the little corner table, housing the faux magenta orchid in a white vase. A large painting of a grassy field with a magnolia tree hung above the table. It was so exquisite and always grabbed my attention. I found myself looking at it every time I entered and left the house. It deserved something nicer next to it than a faux orchid.

I made a mental note to replace that with real flowers soon. I never liked artificial flowers. There was something about genuine flowers that made me feel good. Perhaps it was the fragrance, or the fact that I loved to watch blossoms bloom. I even liked to see them wilt before my eyes. I know that sounds weird, but I liked the way they changed. I guess you could say I appreciated their life cycle. Artificial flowers always remained "perfect," never as unique or original as a live flower. They never browned, artificial buds never opened, and they just always remained the same.

Yes, I needed a live flower or plant to put there. Perhaps violets or a Christmas cactus? Or maybe a fern would look great there?

Or a fig tree.

Yes, a fig tree would look great.

His voice interrupted my thoughts. "Is this the paint for this hallway?" He pointed to the paint can on the floor.

"Yes." I watched him lift the paint can, his muscles flexing and his shirt stretching with his movements.

I was doing everything in my power not to drool.

I was so mesmerized by him. By the way he looked, by the way he was acting. He probably got that attention from women all the time.

I couldn't help but wonder why he was helping me today. Did he feel something too, or was this his way of making up for the rocky start he and I had had?

The book definitely had made up for our rocky start. This, him being here today, was something far greater to me, and I really appreciated it. My thoughts went back to the book and the note he had written me.

He was still holding the can of paint, watching me, and I realized that I was blocking his path. Instead of moving aside and letting him pass, I cleared my throat and used this time to say a long-overdue thank-you.

"I, um, never got a chance to say thank you for the book." His face turned toward me, his gaze colliding with mine, making it difficult to focus. I averted my gaze and instead looked at the artificial flowers. "I loved it. I—thank you so much." I walked over and gave him a hug before I lost my nerve and chickened out. My arms embraced his waist and I found that I didn't want to let go. It felt so right, yet I did let go because I felt him freeze up and stand frozen, with his arms to his side. I pulled away quickly and walked to the opposite side of the room, needing space to process his reaction.

Why did I hug him?

He definitely did not enjoy it. His body was as cold as a polar ice cap.

"You're very welcome," he whispered so quietly that I barely could make out the words. I went back to my hunter-green doors and crouched down to work on them some more. I stole a glance at him and was surprised to see him painting.

What did you expect, that he would be standing looking at you and smiling?

Get it through your thick skull, he does not like you like that.

I picked up my paintbrush and tried to focus on the job. I needed to focus on revamping this place and selling it. There was no room in my life for childish dreams and wishes of romance.

All would be well if I remembered that.

I tried to focus on the job ahead of me, but I found myself not able to focus. The green doors would have to wait until tomorrow. I grabbed a roller and joined him in painting the walls. Only this time, I made sure my paint was distributed more evenly, but my mind quickly went back to him. It was like I was drawn to him and unable to focus on anything other than him. I glanced at him quickly and saw he was still very much focused on painting.

I had to admit that I liked being near him today. It felt different in this room with him in it. I knew I had to stay a safe distance from him, and I would, but I also knew that I would feel every single move he made. That's how cognizant I was of him. My body especially seemed electrified and my thoughts kept going back to how amazing his body felt when I held him.

I knew I would be in trouble watching him and his muscles, but you know what, I would enjoy the trouble.

This trouble easily put a smile on my face and just as easily, if not more, lit a fire in my furnace.

This trouble was damn fine.

Chapter Twenty-Five

Kendrew

Her legs. God, her legs were amazing. I couldn't stop staring at her. Everything about her was beautiful. Her gorgeous legs in those skinny jeans and her killer curves were making me crazy. I wanted to grab her hips and pull her to me. Grab her ass and . . . damn. She said something. She was waiting for my answer. I just smiled.

She looked at me puzzlingly for a while and tilted her head to the side, looking at me with a beautiful smile taking over her face. She crossed the distance between us, and I felt like I was drooling, watching her hips move and her legs as she came closer and closer.

"Do you think this paint will cover in one coat after all?" She looked at me.

Brain, work. Answer the beautiful lady.

"It should. It's a paint and primer in one so . . . " My voice tapered off and I looked at the wall she had tried to paint yesterday and scratched my head. "Um, yeah, we shall see."

"Hmmm." Kaitlyn tapped her jaw with her finger. "So why didn't the paint cover evenly for me?" I watched as she bit her lower lip gently, looking at the wall, then back at me, before looking at the streaky wall again. "Guess they don't make paint like they used to. Everything is about cutting corners now. Damn shame." She shook her head in disbelief.

"Perhaps it wasn't the paint's fault, but the painter's?" I watched her jaw drop in surprise. I felt so playful around her this very moment and so safe that I didn't want to hold back the big grin from my face. I just let her see it, see me, happy around her. That's how she made me feel.

"What did you say?" she finally said in between giggles. "Something about the painter's fault, huh?"

I found myself liking this banter, and I relished the feeling of my lips turning upward. I shook my head and she laughed. I joined in.

Wow, we sure turned a corner.

She took a step closer and playfully punched my arm gently. "Oh, that was pretty low," she said, chuckling.

"Hey, I say it like I see it—" I grinned and pointed to the wall "—and those are some uneven strokes."

That word, innocent on my lips, turned really dirty in my mind. I shook my head as if to shake the image I just got, out of my mind. I tried to hide my wicked, dirty thoughts and instead focus on her. I watched her put her hands on her hips, pretending to be upset with my opinion of her painting. I knew she was joking because she was working hard to suppress her laughter.

"I actually think it's fabulous," she said, lifting her nose proudly in the air, a smile spreading across her beautiful features. "Kinda boho and artsy, don't ya think?"

"Well, art is subjective so . . . " My voice trailed off, replaced with some more chuckles. Next thing I knew, she joined in with me and we were both laughing and crying at the same time. When we both finally got our composure back, I looked at the wall and smiled before looking back at her, into her eyes. I took a few steps toward her. I was now standing right in front of her, my fingers brushing against hers. I looked down at our touching hands and she did the same. My thumb gently traced her hand, rubbing circles. Feeling her hand against mine brought me to a place of serenity that I had never visited before. I felt my breathing intensify and shifted my eyes upward, toward her green orbs. She was looking at my lips with yearning and want plain as day in her eyes. I pulled away in alarm.

Too close.

Breathe.

Too damn close.

In and out.

I exhaled and scanned the room, looking for something to take my mind off of her touch and her gaze. I focused on the roll of paper towels lying in the corner on the floor. I took a few shaky steps toward the roll. My legs felt like jelly and I put all my focus into ripping a few paper towels, even though I didn't really need them now. I just needed something to do.

"It's our little secret," I said.

"Secret?" she asked inquisitively, her eyebrows drawn together.

I nodded my head and pointed toward the "artsy" wall.

"Ohhh," she said, her voice tapering off.

That's not what I meant.

I wished that I could have the courage to tell her the truth.

That I loved what we both just shared, that I loved how amazing our touching hands felt.

How I wanted to guard this and keep her and these newfound emotions that surfaced between us. And how I wanted more. And how wanting more scared me.

What should have felt innocent started to feel confusing. I wanted nothing more than to walk up to her and kiss her right now. I wanted to run my hands through her hair and feel her respond to my touch. I wanted to hold her and press her against me while I cupped her backside with my hands.

I needed a break. I needed a shower or a long walk, but some water would have to do. Cold water.

It was as if she read my mind.

"Ummmm, would you like something to drink?" she asked, and my head jerked up. I felt like a child that was caught stealing a cookie from a cookie jar right before dinner. I was trying to change my course of thinking, but she was not helping. She had her back turned toward me, her assets facing me, and I couldn't function. She looked over her shoulder, in the doorway leading to her kitchen.

She had mentioned water.

"Sure," I responded.

"Coffee or water are your very limited options."

"Water is good." My throat felt so parched, as if I had just returned from a trip across the Sahara Desert.

Water. The drink of life. Nothing like water to quench a thirst. I wondered if it would quench my thirst for her too?

"Okay. Be right back," she said perkily.

I watched her ass as she walked out of the room. God, she must have had me under some kind of spell. How long had it been since I looked at a woman with such want and desire? I can tell you it'd been a while. Yes, I'd been around. I loved the company of women, but never found myself craving one so much, so often, and for so long as I had Kaitlyn. And she caught me looking too, and I, the man who never blushed, felt myself blush like a teenager. What the fuck?

I heard her humming in the kitchen, and it was driving me insane with need. I couldn't think about anything other than her and the noises she would make as I took her in every room in this house. My mind was heading in a one-track direction and I needed to focus. I was helping her out. I would treat her as a sister, and I would believe that last lie I told myself just now. For her good and mine. I didn't do commitment or steady, long-term relationships. Plus, she was leaving town in a few weeks or months. No point in starting something that could hurt us or create a cord of longing between us. I was a player and I needed to act like him. I was not going to lie, but with her, I didn't want to be him. I wanted to be someone she was proud of, and that scared the shit out of me. I had nothing but nightmares to offer her. She deserved so much better than me. She deserved light and sunshine, and that was not me. I needed to change my thoughts and I needed to play the part of a detached, unaffected, unemotional guy. I could do this. I gave myself a pep talk and then I called out asking if she needed my help.

I waited for a response, and when one did not come, I headed toward the kitchen, toward her, ignoring the pull I felt as I drew closer to her.

My body felt her before I saw her. The room was filled with her sweet, clean scent, and I closed my eyes, memorizing it so that when she left, I could remember this moment, this feeling, this scent, her.

I leaned against the doorjamb in the kitchen and took in the splendid sight. She was bending at the waist, with her head in the fridge, reaching to the back to retrieve two water bottles. I had to hold back from rushing to her. The need to feel my body against her, my lips kissing her neck, was so strong that my body responded instantly. I felt myself harden, and I groaned involuntarily. It came out louder than I thought it would. I watched her turn around hastily. She was holding the water bottle at chest level and was gazing at me with a startled expression on her face. I wanted to turn and leave, run far away from her, yet I couldn't. I felt glued to the doorjamb, hard-on and all. So instead I stood there, as if I was made of stone, my tongue glued to the roof of my mouth, looking at her, remembering to breathe.

Thankfully I remembered to do that. Imagine me passing out and falling on my hard-on.

Ouch. We cannot break that prize piece.

I chuckled inwardly and tried to focus my attention on anything but her. It didn't work. Whatever was happening between us was too strong for me to battle.

I felt myself blushing. I almost never blushed. The heat in my cheeks was searing. I'd battled some pretty big fires and had not felt the heat like I did at this very moment. She offered me the bottle and I reached for it, hastily, like a castaway on a rescue boat. I welcomed anything cold now. A cold drink. A cold shower . . . I needed to take a sip and just walk away. Perhaps a quick walk or run around the block would do the trick. Before I could tell her I needed to get something and that I would be back in a few, I watched as she approached me. When I thought she would stop, she didn't. She kept it moving. I felt her lightly punch my shoulder as she passed by me. "Paint job, here we come."

The spark ignited yet again. It coursed through my entire body and landed in one spot. The spot. She felt it too. I watched her stop and look at me from the corner of her eye. I could swear I saw her breathing become more labored and her skin flushed. She turned around and we were face-to-face, so close thanks to the doorjamb, and I secretly congratulated myself on picking this spot. I saw desire in her eyes. She involuntarily took a step toward me before turning away abruptly. I watched her walk toward the living room, water bottle in her hand, head held high, shoulder a little bit too stiff, and I told my brain to follow her. Yet my body did not listen to my brain. Instead, it stood in the spot, envisioning another "job" and another "come." I pinched myself hard, knowing this insanity I was exhibiting had to stop.

I only knew one way to stop thinking like that. To stop feeling what I didn't deserve.

I rewound and went back to that time, to the scene embedded in my mind and heart and every cell in my body.

I remembered the snow, the blood, the fear, the smell. And his blank eyes looking up at me, devoid of life.

I was once again focused.

I was once again impenetrable.

My love,

I wish I knew when you were coming back. It would make this waiting a little more bearable. I would count down the days and have something to look forward to.

I have something to tell you. Mother did something so horrible the other night. She found your letters to me and burned them before my eyes. I don't know why she is so cruel. So heartless. So cold.

I didn't cry though. I didn't give her the satisfaction. Instead, I looked her straight in the eyes and started to recite one of the letters she burned, word for word. I saw the vein in her neck throb as I left whispering, your words on my lips a silent comfort.

I memorized every letter you wrote to me. Your words and my memories live in me and keep me alive. They are my air. My water. My food. My shelter. Everything I need to survive.

I kiss this letter and hope that you are still able to feel the kiss by the time it gets to you.

I love you forever and always,

Mary

Chapter Twenty-Six

Kaitlyn

He wanted to kiss me! Oh my gosh! I wanted it so much too. The last thing I wanted to do was pull away, but I had to. I had felt on fire since yesterday. I felt so turned on knowing that he was watching me with a hungry gaze. It felt so good to feel wanted by a great man. By someone like him. Someone who didn't trust easily. Someone so very much like me that it scared me and electrified me at the same time. I felt his body reaching for mine and I wanted it. I wanted him with an intensity. When I heard his groan in the kitchen earlier, I wanted him behind me, kissing my neck. Biting my shoulder as his body pressed into mine. I felt my body responding so quickly and so fervently that I had to shut it down. I was only here until the house sold.

One to two months tops.

I did not need this.

This could make a girl start believing in foolish, girlish dreams of love, and I didn't have a place for that. That wasn't the whole truth. Honestly, I didn't think I could handle having him and having to give him away. All the shitty things in my past hadn't broken me, but I strongly suspected that walking away from him after giving him a piece of myself that I never wanted to give to anyone, would break me into pieces.

I was already broken. I was that favorite broken plate that was salvaged and glued. It may look like one piece, unmarred, from far away. However, upon closer inspection, and a simple run of the hand across its ridges, it was obvious that the cracks and breaks were there. That it could no longer be a serviceable plate again.

***

I was admiring the wall and how great it had turned out. I had to admit, it looked much better than my sad initial attempt. Painting with him was so much fun, though the project ended way too soon. I loved the moments when he and I let go and worked as a team. Then there were moments when my body would turn on and watch him, wishing he would make a move. I caught him looking at me too, multiple times. The tension then would be so heavy, but we both tempered it and focused on painting.

I remembered how hot he looked in those ripped jeans. I closed my eyes and conjured up his image. I smiled when I thought about his magnificent profile. He should've been on display somewhere, on some dollar bills or something. Or better yet, on the cover of a steamy, raunchy romance novel. I would have bought it in a heartbeat and slept with it every night, staring at the cover and rereading the story all while wishing and imagining . . .

Priorities.

I needed to sell this place and form no attachments. I was leaving ASAP, and that plan was not changing. Not for anyone or anything.

My home was *elsewhere*.

The only problem was I didn't know where *elsewhere* was.

Ding-dong.

I rushed to the door, expecting to see him. Instead it was Jess. She was back. I screamed and jumped into her arms.

"Missed me so much, huh?" she teased, patting my back.

"So much!" I held her tight, not wanting to let go.

"Is that who you were thinking about when I opened the door a few seconds ago?" she teased me. I pulled away quickly.

"You looked like you were mid-orgasm." I felt my mouth opening, and Jess laughed loudly, clapping her hands.

"You saw that?" I said, feeling embarrassed. I put my face in my hands and groaned.

Jess nodded her head. "I mean, that's a beautiful wall you got there, but I don't know if you should be feeling that way about it." She wiggled her eyebrows.

I punched her shoulder playfully. "It's not for the wall," I muttered.

"Hmmm how about a coffee and you tell me all about what I missed?"

***

Two coffees and a leftover chocolate cake that we devoured later, Jess and I were caught up about Kendrew. We were now outside, weeding the garden, to burn off the calories. I grabbed a garbage bag to pick up the weeds, and Jess held it for me.

"I'm leaving, babe," Jess said somberly.

"Yeah, I am a bit tired too." I groaned in pain. "We did two days' worth of work in a few hours." I cringed. "Sorry for putting you to work the moment you got back."

I reached back a hand to massage my neck and the back of my shoulder. We'd been bent over and weeding and pruning for hours, without stopping for breaks. The area surrounding the pond looked magical now.

Jess shook her head. "No, I mean I'm leaving . . . here."

"Wait, what? When?" I asked, surprised by the news.

"Tomorrow," she said.

I looked at my best friend and saw a determined look on her face. A look I knew so well. She had something on her mind, and no one, not even I, could stop her from going for what it was she wanted.

"That's fast," I said somberly.

"I feel like it's time," she responded just as somberly.

Her response was a bit cryptic, but I knew not to push her. Instead I walked toward her and put my arms around her, squeezing her tightly.

"Is everything okay?" I whispered in her ear. "Are you okay?"

I felt shudders go through her body. She took a deep breath. "I will be."

"I am going to miss you so much."

"I'll miss you too, Sis," she said. She pulled away from the hug and looked me straight in the eyes. "I wanted to tell you earlier, but I wasn't able to get the words out." I watched tears fill her eyes, and I grabbed her hand, rubbing circles in it. It always calmed her when we were little.

"I will call you every day and hopefully Skype you daily too because I need to see your beautiful face every day."

"Yes to both!" I said. "Do you know where you are going?"

"I've been using the library computer and researching a bit, and I found something that might tell me where I was born. From there, I hope to find *someone* who knows *something* about me. Your grandma, the letters, have inspired me to try to dig deeper into what my life was before the Stones."

I understood the need to know about one's past, so I fully supported her. I would help her in any way that I possibly could.

"We should go out and celebrate your last night."

"Shower, dinner, and drinks. Yes to all three." Jess laughed all the way to the house. I followed her laughter, knowing I would miss it and her so much.

***

After a delicious Italian dinner, we entered the bar and scanned the room, looking for an open table. It was a full house tonight, so there was only standing room in the corner of the room, near the bar. Jess and I made our way through the crowds, accompanied by the Journey song "Don't Stop Believin'" starting.

Man, I loved that song.

There had been many times that I had made a fool of myself listening to it. Especially while driving. The looks people gave me when I sang out loud ranged from shock to laughter to some shaking their head.

One lady once yelled at me and told me that my car was no place to belt out a song. That I should do that in the privacy of my home.

I just laughed and kept singing and dancing in my seat.

That song always made me feel free. It brought out happiness and extreme playfulness in me. And I liked that feeling.

The words seemed to infiltrate my skin, and they moved through me.

I felt my hips moving and watched Jess's reaction when she realized what the song playing was. Her grin was so big, and when she met my gaze, with the gleam in her eye, did I know that it was on. It was one of her favorites too. I had a feeling we would be making ourselves seen, in this cramped corner, very soon.

Jess and I were now belting out the song. A few people next to us joined in, and before we knew it, the entire bar was singing, laughing, and dancing.

Jess and I didn't like to be the center of attention, but that song always seemed to bring out our adventurous sides. It was almost like it lit our fire.

I felt someone touch the top of my shoulder, and I turned toward the person. It was a girl in her early twenties that I had never seen before.

"This song rocks," she said, her grin wide. She was holding a beer in one hand and gyrating her hips, all while talking to me. She must've not been drunk yet. I was not really coordinated, and even without a drink, I would have spilled the beer on me, or worse, on someone else, or fallen flat on my butt.

Perhaps it was her age. I was probably ten years her senior, after all.

"I love it too!" I answered excitedly.

She raised her beer. "Want one?"

"Yes, please, but after this song. I just want to dance now."

She winked and continued to sing and dance with Jess and me.

At this point, the bar had turned into a dance club. I must have gotten carried away and lost in the moment, as I looked around and I was no longer near Jess or our new friend, whose name we forgot to ask. I was in the middle of the bar, right next to a large table with five wooden chairs, all of which were empty. Everyone was standing and dancing. Everyone but one person, who was looking at me and the room with a bemused look on his face.

I felt my face start to burn.

I was blushing.

"You sure know how to liven up a place." He grinned.

"That song holds all the power, trust me." I laughed. I looked at him and saw that he was smiling. My eyes felt pulled to his eyes, and what I saw there sent shivers down my spine.

Passion.

Happiness.

Joy.

Raw hunger.

Most importantly, no walls.

The music trickled off, signaling the end of the song, and the room quieted down a bit. My heart was beating wildly, and I worried that everyone in the room could hear it. That the man standing in front of me could hear it and could decipher it.

Can he tell that it beats so strongly for him?

Seconds felt like hours before another song began. From the sound of it, it was a country tune.

"Would you like a drink?" Kendrew asked, his voice permeating my thoughts.

"Yes, please. What are you havin?" I pointed to the many drinks on the table.

"Guinness." He lifted a glass and chugged what was left of it.

It wasn't much, just a little bit wetting the bottom of the glass, but I watched in awe as his Adam's apple bobbled up and down.

I want to kiss that spot and hear him say my name while I do it.

He was so sexy and made everything around him look sexy by association. I laughed inwardly at my thoughts, yet I was still very much riveted by the man in front of me. I noticed every single breath he took, every single movement he made, and I memorized it. I stored it for the future days, when I could pull them from memory and relive the moments over and over again.

I realized I sounded crazy and that I was acting so out of character, but I couldn't help how he made me feel. A way unlike I'd ever felt before.

I watched as he licked his lips, and I did the same. I realized he was waiting for me to speak, to tell him what I would like to drink. I composed myself and focused on beer and not him, at least for a moment.

"I'll have the same," I whispered, my voice suddenly feeling like sandpaper.

Can you throw in that lick of the lips too, Kendrew?

Oh my gosh, what is happening to me?

My thoughts were dangerous with him. Thankfully he didn't know what was going through my mind.

He looked at me with a question in his eyes, and I just answered him with a smile. I couldn't tell him what I was really wanting or thinking.

"Want anything else?"

You.

Your body.

Your lips.

Your body pressed against mine.

Your kisses.

Your touch against my skin.

You.

I want you.

"No, just the Guinness." I managed a smile though I suddenly felt a bit sad. I wanted more, and I didn't think I could have it.

"I'll be right back with your drink." He flashed me a big smile, and I needed to sit down for a moment. My knees felt weak and wobbly and I couldn't even blame it on the alcohol.

From my seat, I watched him walk toward the bar. Instantly, the bartender sauntered in his direction, ignoring the other patrons that were there before him. I watched her say something to him. His laughter carried all the way to me, enveloping me so that I felt less lonely. I watched as the bartender looked at me briefly before turning back to him. She leaned in and whispered something into his ear, and he shook his head vehemently and pointed at me. Her gaze followed his and I could swear I saw her eyes narrow at me. He winked at me before turning back to her. She handed him the drink and I watched as he paid and was turning to walk away, yet she grabbed his left hand, the one not holding a drink, and he turned back toward her. I watched as she leaned over the bar, her breasts spilling out of her tiny tank top. She said something to Kendrew and he leaned in and whispered something in her ear before walking away.

I should not have cared what he was saying, but I did. I hoped he didn't have a late-night date with her tonight. By late night, I meant a hookup.

I tried to think about something else. Where was Jess? I looked around the room and she was dancing with a very handsome man. As if sensing me looking at her, she looked my way and our gazes locked. She winked at me and I gave her two thumbs up. I could hear her laughter across the room as the handsome stranger twirled her before wrapping his arms around her.

I looked back toward the bar, and Kendrew was no longer there. The bartender was filling drink orders and Kendrew was walking my way. I bit my lip and took in the sight before my eyes. The words of the song captured my attention.

This girl can make me lose control

And I will not fight it

You see, she makes me think of kisses and lovin

Bet she doesn't know these thoughts are what I'm thinkin

Bet he doesn't know what I'm thinkin of either. I touched my cheeks and they were on fire. I needed that cold beer quickly to quench this thirst.

"A Guinness for the lovely lady." He handed me the drink and our fingers touched. I felt a spark, and the electricity coursed through my body. No one pulled away from the touch this time.

I took the beer from him, pretending none of that just happened. I took a very big sip of beer, followed by another one. Before I realized what I had done, half of my beer was gone.

I looked at him and he was watching me.

"Guess I was thirsty." I shrugged my shoulder, feeling a little self-conscious.

"I'm glad I replenished you." He winked at me.

He was flirting with me. Oh my, it felt great.

I felt myself blushing, and I looked away from him and his flirty self. I spotted Jess, and she was now in a lip-lock with the handsome stranger.

I pointed her out in the crowd. "Looks like my friend met someone."

Kendrew looked in their direction. "That's my man Trent. He is a good guy."

"The Trent from the raffle?" I asked, remembering that night. I *knew* he looked familiar.

"Same one." He chuckled. "He didn't get a cougar like I did." He laughed and I joined in.

Yes, I remembered that night very well. So much had changed since then. He and I were actually holding a conversation.

And I loved it.

The butterflies in my stomach multiplied every time he spoke or looked at me. I had been swooning internally since our conversation started.

"Did you have fun on your date?" I inquired sheepishly, looking him in the eyes.

"I would have had more fun with the original winner." He grinned and winked at me.

I looked away, feeling a blush come on, towards Jess and Trent.

"Is he dating someone?" I asked, biting my lip in worry. "Perhaps that woman from the auction?"

He shook his head. "No, but by the looks of things, probably will be real soon."

"She is leaving tomorrow," I told Kendrew and found myself shocked that I had told him about Jess's plans. We were both so guarded usually and didn't talk about plans to strangers.

Technically, Kendrew isn't a stranger . . . perhaps that's why I felt comfortable telling him?

Without knowing when or how, a wall seemed to have come down between me and him.

"Where is she going?" His brow furrowed. "Are you leaving too?" he asked quickly. He looked down at the table and traced a big scratch with his fingernail.

"I don't know. I don't think she knows yet," I responded. "As for me, I am staying here for now."

I watched as his head shot up and worry was replaced with happiness.

"You are stuck with me a bit longer." I smiled and bit my lip.

"How about a dance to celebrate?"

"Celebrate?" I asked, puzzled.

"Celebrate me being stuck with you." He grinned, and I couldn't help but laugh. He extended his hand and I placed mine in his. He rubbed his thumb against my finger and pulled me in close.

I lost all sense of time and place. All I knew was that I was with Kendrew. My heart was beating wildly with the music, and I was so at peace. I closed my eyes and breathed him in. He pulled me to his chest, and though the song was upbeat, we slow danced.

I could feel his heat melt into mine, and I surrendered to the feeling.

We swayed to the words of a man in love.

This girl, man I wanna scream out loud

She makes me hot and cold at the same time

Hot for her kisses and cold when she leaves me

Alone, for a minute

Girl, don't leave me alone no more

I want you next to me, pressed into me, holdin me tight

Lovin me

I groaned, and Kendrew must have heard because he was looking at me intently. I looked at him with eyes filled with hunger and let out a soft sigh.

He leaned down, and his lips touched mine. Our bodies moved in unison to the music while our lips took as much as they could. His tongue touched my tongue and I couldn't help but groan. I ran my hands across his back and he did the same to me. I asked him without words to take the kiss deeper and harder, and he complied.

This man, he makes me think of tomorrow

Nothing I want more than to be next to him

Kissin him and lovin him,

Losing control

This kiss was everything I needed and did not know how to ask for. It filled every crack in my heart and filled it with hope and endless possibilities.

He moved from my lips and placed a kiss on my neck. I felt him make a trail toward my ear, and he licked it before taking a bite out of it. I moaned and move against him. This time he hissed.

I could feel his arousal, and it was so hard and hot against me. I wanted to wrap my legs around his waist, but the song broke through my thoughts, bringing me back to the moment.

You make me wish on drops of rain,

On stars in the skies, on the moon in the night

Oooo you make me want to take a chance

Baby, ooooo I lose my mind when you are around,

Your body, your kisses, your touch,

Make me want to let go and trust and believe

You, make me want to take a chance on love

That's what he was making me do. He was making me go lose my mind in public, in a roomful of people. I took a step back and watched as he looked at me, trying to read what I was feeling.

"I'm sorry. I have to go find Jess." I looked at the ground. "Thank you for the beer and the dance." I walked away from him, from the heat, the comfort, the protection, on wobbly legs.

"Anytime," I heard him whisper.

***

"I don't want you to go," I whimpered. I was holding onto Jess super tightly.

"I have to do this," she said, running her hands across my back.

"What about Trent?" I murmured.

She was silent for a moment. She started to speak, but hesitated. "I . . . um—"

She stepped away from me, breaking our hug. She moved in a circle before looking at me and speaking. "I like him a lot, babe." She nailed me with her gaze. "Like a whole lot. Like forget who the hell Jake is a lot." She sighed. "Dancing with him made me dream about what could be. The girl who hadn't allowed herself to feel felt something potent, and frankly, it scared me." She looked at me, and for the briefest second, sadness planted itself in her eyes. "How can I give myself to someone and love someone when I don't even know who I am or where I come from?"

I shook my head, disagreeing with her. "I'm sure he likes you just as you are," I reassured her. "It sure looked that way from where I was sitting."

A small silence ensued. Her eyebrows knit together and she expelled a big breath. "I just need to go on this journey, this rediscovery of who I am, before I can let anyone else in." She shrugged. "If I find out something about my family, I will come back, and if he is still single, maybe he and I can try to go on a date or something," she said, looking thoughtful.

I looked at her curiously. "Jess, did you tell him you were leaving?"

She shook her head and mumbled, "Nope."

"You didn't want to?" I asked softly.

She shook her head again, emotion overwhelming her. "I couldn't." Tears slipped from her eyes. "If I did, I wouldn't be able to leave."

There was so much I wanted to say to my friend, but I didn't. Instead I just hugged her and told her a short story about a firefighting knight that waited for her return. She sniffled, but didn't let go.

I told my sister that I loved her and wished she found what she was looking for. I told her to do it quickly so that she could return to me.

She planted a kiss on my cheek, and I laughed loudly. It was wet and sloppy and it was what she always did when we were growing up. I would always wipe it away dramatically, my face laden with disgust, but today, I left it on in remembrance of what I was lucky enough to have.

I loved her and I always would. So very much. Sloppy kisses and all.

Chapter Twenty-Seven

Kendrew

I ran my hand through the fluffy yet silky fur from the top of his head to his tail, back and forth, a Zen-like calm coming over me and Whiskers. He was purring wildly, and wildly, and it calmed me even more. He turned over and was now on his back, his tummy begging for the same treatment that his back just received moments ago. I smiled, relishing in the fact that my cat loved my presence so much.

I leaned down and nuzzled his tummy, breathing in his softness. Surprisingly, for a cat that loved salmon and tuna and used the litter box, he smelled very fresh. His fur tickled my nose and I giggled. It startled him and he jumped away from me. I coaxed him back by extending my hand toward him. He looked at it momentarily, almost as if he was debating whether he should take the peace offering for scaring him while he was in a kitty coma of ecstasy.

After a few more "come here, Whiskers," he sauntered toward me and lay down right against my chest. A human cat cuddle with me being his big spoon. We fell asleep like that, and that was the best sleep I had ever had to date.

Beep. Beep. Beep.

The alarm on my phone went off. I looked down and saw that it was set for 4:27 a.m. It was my day off today, but I must have forgotten to turn it off.

I stretched my hands above my head and touched my headboard.

The wood felt cold against my fingertips and so smooth. Images flashed across my mind of her legs feeling smooth against my fingertips.

The idea to go for a run crossed my mind and I felt so energized by that idea. I should probably do some groceries too, I thought. The thought to hit the bar for some beer with the guys also crossed my mind, but just as quickly was dismissed. It should have excited me to go out among my friends; it always did in the past, especially if there was the possibility of meeting and hooking up with a woman, but it didn't. Instead, I looked at the ceiling and thought of her and of sunflowers.

I felt myself hardening against my stomach. My hand trailed down my stomach and I touched myself, imagining that she was touching me instead. I felt the precum seeping out, and I lubricated the length of my cock with it as my hand slid up and down, creating a friction and rhythm that I loved. Moments later, I cried out her name as I shot a load of cum that landed on my thigh and my stomach, and another load that ended up on my sheets.

As good as getting rid of this hard-on felt, I knew that it was nothing compared to how she would feel if she was here with me now.

Man, I need to get laid. I had to do something about how she made me feel. My worry was that she might be the only one that could help this situation. I chewed the inside of my cheeks, debating what I should do.

Since Whiskers, I had never allowed myself to feel something akin to love and protection toward another being.

I failed him, I failed my family, and I would fail her. It was who I was.

I hopped out of bed angrily, kicking at the cum-covered sheets that entwined themselves around me like vines. I kicked at them some more, and once they were lying in a defeated heap against my bedroom door, I ran a hand through my hair and tried to calm my frustrated self down. I wanted her, and beating up my sheets wouldn't change that.

I needed to go for a long run and take a hot shower. Then I would do some laundry and get breakfast going.

I dressed quickly, grabbing my sweatpants, a T-shirt, and my sneakers. My body was on autopilot. My body knew the drill, knew the path I would take. My feet hitting the pavement over and over again, my breathing labored, sweat running down my face and back were things I always looked forward to. My runs always took out the weariness from my bones. It was the only time I shut off my mind and my thoughts and just felt, well, besides sex, of course.

When I was halfway through the run and approaching her home, I realized that I had dreamt of Whiskers and I didn't scream.

It wasn't a nightmare.

It was a loving memory.

The truth hit me at the crack of dawn, and it stopped me dead in my tracks. My feet were glued to the spot, right in front of her house. I had had a codependent relationship with my nightmares since I was a kid. They owned a piece of me, lived in my heart and mind, and I had usually let them.

I glanced at her home and saw her light turn on. I was immobilized, in front of her house, looking at the light filtering through her blinds. My breath hitched when I saw her shadow moving around the room.

And I did what I hadn't done since I was a kid, cuddled with Whiskers. I just let myself be in the moment, not worrying about tomorrow or the day after. I savored this moment, acknowledging what I felt, and did not let fear infiltrate. I closed my eyes and felt at peace, just like I had waking up this morning.

Perhaps that rainstorm was cathartic? Perhaps spending time with Kaitlyn was cathartic? Perhaps she was the reason I did not wake up covered in sweat, screaming and shaking in fear this morning?

Perhaps she held the key that would set me free from this self-inflicted prison I lived in?

I opened my eyes and looked back at her window, needing to see her shadow, needing her to pull me from the darkness some more. Only this time I didn't see her shadow.

She was standing in front of her window, illuminated by the light in back of her, and highlighted by the colors of the sky that she was facing. She looked stunningly beautiful in a white tank top and was looking straight at me. The sky was a mixture of pinks and purples and oranges, and it was incredible. However, it would be incomplete without her beauty. I was lost in a moment, standing before her, with everything I was on full display, with my walls semi pulled down and a certain lightness in me.

Infused with the knowledge that I had a dream and not a nightmare about my past, I reached for an even bigger and better dream, knowing that it had the power to hurt me and to hurt another person. A person I admired so greatly, standing about twenty-five feet from me.

I reached out like I had that day with Whiskers. I raised my hand and waved. I held my breath, just like I had that day so many years ago, waiting to see if Whiskers would answer my call.

I watched in awe as she waved back at me.

My face broke out in a smile. A true, deep from within smile that traveled all the way to my toes. I felt butterflies dance in my stomach as I saw a smile appear on her face.

I waved one more time and waited with my breath held. I released it only when she waved back.

I pulled my gaze away from her window and ran toward my home with a renewed spirit and a spring in my step.

Yet home didn't feel like home anymore. I always used to hear the saying about home being where the heart is, and I never had gotten the full meaning behind it. I thought I finally understood that phrase now.

A big piece of my heart stayed with the girl in the white tank top, whose hair was sticking out in every direction, waving to me from her window with a smile plastered on her face that broke down and smashed all my fears into little pieces that could be swept up and discarded.

My beacon.

Chapter Twenty-Eight

Kaitlyn

"What if he doesn't come?" I asked myself in the mirror for the tenth time.

I glanced at the clock and saw that it was 6:18 a.m. I let out a breath that I didn't realize I was holding. I looked back at the mirror and liked what I saw. I was wearing black leggings with mesh inserts on the side of my legs. Comfy, yet cute at the same time. I paired that with my neon orange sneakers and a matching orange sports bra covered by a plain white T-shirt.

I looked back at the clock. *He should be here any minute.*

This was me taking a big risk, but I figured, why not? He surprised me by waving the other day, and I hadn't stopped thinking about it since.

I'd never seen him smile like I had that day. It made him look so boyish. In that moment I wanted to be the recipient of more smiles like that.

One more quick look at the clock and I pulled my hair into a ponytail. I walked toward the door.

It was now or never.

I pulled open the door and stepped out on my porch. I looked down the street for any sign of him, and I didn't see anything. It was eerily quiet.

I pretended to stretch, all the while looking for him.

I sat back down and started to feel defeated. Instead I watched the sky changing before my eyes.

"Mornin."

I whirled around and smiled.

He was standing in the same spot, just like two days ago when the magic had happened.

He looked so handsome. He was wearing a pair of shorts and a navy colored Navy Seals T-shirt.

I walked toward him and watched as he took steps toward me.

"Going somewhere?" He pointed to my running getup, a smile breaking out on his face.

"I was hoping to join a certain someone on a run." I bit my lip, smiling up at him. I realized I was flirting with him, and I loved it. "Know someone who might want a running buddy today?"

He scratched his head and pretended to ponder the question. "Hmm, no. Sorry, no one comes to mind." He burst out laughing.

I joined in and reached out to him to playfully hit his shoulder. "Oh, you," I said.

My fingers felt warm where they had touched his shoulder. I felt him flex his muscles, and I could not stop touching his shoulder. I looked into his eyes, and they were looking at me intently. The air seemed so thick and yet so right at the same time. I stepped toward him, and my face was mere inches away from his chest. I closed my eyes and inhaled.

I felt him leaning into me, and he pressed his lips against my forehead. His lips on my skin, his body pressed into mine felt like a homecoming.

We stood like that until a car passing by took us out of the moment. A moment that I knew I would always remember, especially when I was gray and reminiscing about my life. This special moment of timelessness and of feeling deeply without fear.

His hand reached for my face and took a strand of my hair and pushed it behind my ear. His hand moved to my neck and cradled it.

"Now that I think about it, I might know this pretty darn cool guy that runs in this area around this time, you know." The twinkle in his eye shone brightly, and I loved the teasing side of him.

"Think he can keep up with me?" I asked, amusement in my eyes. "I'm pretty good."

"Let's see." His lip quirked up in a smile. He leaned down and gave me a peck on my forehead, momentarily dismantling me. I watched as he took off, and I ran after him, unable to contain my laughter.

***

Forty-five minutes later, a lady dreaming of her lost love looked out the window, greeting the new day. Movement across the street caught her eyes. She saw Kendrew with someone on his back, carrying them piggyback and laughing and more carefree than she had ever seen him. He and the bundle on his back were heading toward Kaitlyn's porch. She squinted to see more clearly, and she smiled when she realized the bundle on his back was in fact Kaitlyn.

She wiped the tears that fell from her face and whispered to the man she talked to daily. The man no one else saw, yet she felt all the time.

"They have what we have, my love."

She knew that he agreed with her, and her heart overflowed with happiness and hope. Those two lovely souls before her eyes were on the fast route to falling in love, bringing her that much closer to going home.

***

"You're late," he said, pointing to his imaginary watch on his wrist. He was grinning, but as I came closer, his eyes darkened a bit. He was waiting for me on the sidewalk, right across from my home.

"Morning to you too," I responded playfully, skipping down the steps, looking forward to our run. Most importantly, looking forward to spending time with him.

"Morning." He smiled. The sun was rising behind him, and it was beautiful, but it couldn't compete with him.

He took a hold of my hand and pulled me toward him. My body reacted instantly to his touch. Goose bumps spread across my body and I felt myself being pliant in his arms.

He wrapped his arms around me and groaned into my neck. In response, I squeezed him tightly, needing him to stay like this for a little bit longer. It was like he knew I need this contact, and he didn't let go.

"You smell amazing," he whispered, his hot breath playing with my sensitive skin.

"Mmm, so do you." I smiled. "Straight out of a shower fresh." I inhaled deeply and closed my eyes, savoring the moment.

He pulled away and I mentally groaned. I looked up at him, and his eyes were filled with so much passion that I felt like I should pinch myself to see if I was truly awake or dreaming. He leaned down and kissed me, and I knew for a fact that I was awake because every cell in my body felt that kiss. I responded and kissed him back with everything I felt. I felt his hands settle on my lower back.

My hands traveled across his upper torso, mapping his muscles with my fingertips, wishing that his T-shirt was not in the way.

We kissed until we were both breathing heavily. We pulled away, our lips slightly open and moistened with each other's saliva. He pressed his forehead against mine and our breaths mingled, and I was transported to another place, a place where I felt safe. I didn't know how long we kissed or how long we stood, our breaths intermingling, but I finally, slowly, felt myself come back down to earth.

I reluctantly took a step back and felt wobbly on my own. He noticed and smiled.

"My kisses leave you weak in the knees, huh?"

I couldn't lie, so I just smiled at him instead.

"It's okay, I feel the same," he said. He took my hand in his and started walking.

"We aren't running?" I asked.

"What would you say to me taking you somewhere special this morning?"

"Lead the way," I answered, feeling daring and bold.

***

We strolled hand in hand down Main Street, and then past Main Street, until we were walking on the side of a quiet road. We cut through a field and then hiked a trail until we reached the top of a small mountain with a view of Landing Falls. To the right, you could see trees for miles, and to the left, a view of a stunning lake.

"This is my favorite spot," he said, looking down at the trees before glancing at me. "I come here when I need to clear my head or when I just need to be alone."

"I can see why. This place is beautiful," I said wistfully.

We sat in silence, our bottoms planted on the cool earth, our thighs touching gently, and my hand found its way to his. We sat like that watching the sky change before our eyes, watching the sun make its presence seen and felt in the sky.

"Thank you for bringing me here." I glanced at him.

"I only bring special people here," he said. He brought my hand that was encircled in his palm to his lips and placed a kiss there.

"Hmmmm," I pondered aloud. "Let me guess, I'm the ninety-ninth girl you've brought here?"

He burst out laughing.

"I knew it, I hit the nail on the head," I laughingly teased him. "What will lucky number one hundred get . . . fireworks?"

We both laughed and sat in silence some more. I watched birds flying in circles above our head, and I lost myself in the tranquil sounds around us.

Silence interwoven with birds' chirps, water rushing, and our hearts beating.

"Only you," he said on a shuddery breath, looking down at our entwined hands. I looked at him with questioning eyes. He looked at me closely but didn't say anything. I didn't rush him nor did I speak. I let him tell me what he wanted on his own terms, on his own schedule. I looked away and focused on the body of water below, but I was tuned into every single move he made. I watched from the corner of my eye as he ripped at a long stem of grass growing beside him. He threw it over the side of the overhang, and I watched as it spiraled down.

After a minute his voice filled the silence, "No one else has shared this space with me here. I think I knew deep down that I had to wait for someone special one day to show it to . . . that I had to wait for you."

I looked at him, deep into his eyes, and saw the truth reflected in them. I felt tears pooling in my eyes, threatening to fall, and I blinked them away frantically.

"I debated about coming back to this town, but I always felt a strong pull toward this place. I feel like I had to come back here, for you." My voice was cracking and I cleared my throat, trying to clear the emotions lodged in there. It was useless. The tears came.

"Don't cry," he said softly, letting go of my hand to wipe at my cheeks. "I never want you to cry for me or over me." He stopped as if he was pondering something. "It's why I tried to stay away. I tried so hard. I didn't want to hurt you or cause you any pain . . . ever."

"I'm glad you didn't stay away."

"It scares me that I couldn't stay away," he said solemnly.

"Why?"

"I hurt the people I care about." He looked back at the overhang, at the trees and the water below.

"I don't underst—?"

His voice, low but clear, interjected, stopping me midsentence. "I killed my dad." His eyes bored into mine, reading my reaction.

"I don't understand." My brow furrowed and I reached for his hand, but he pulled away.

Birds chirping excitedly cut through the quiet and the tension. I followed their path across the sky once more.

I felt his gaze on me, and I looked his way. I offered a smile, and he winced.

"You are too good," he said.

"No, I just know you." I looked at his clenched jaw and wanted nothing more than to kiss it and ease the tension in it and in him. "You run into burning buildings to save people, risking your safety and life for others. I don't believe you intentionally killed your dad." I pinned him with my gaze.

"Intentional or not, he is dead and it's my fault," he said coldly. "I should have died that day, not him."

I reached over and touched his hand, and this time he didn't pull away. I placed it into the safety of my hand, on my lap. I wanted to cocoon him in my warmth and offer a safe place for him.

"I never talk about it," he whispered, shaking his head. "No one knows."

"I am here if you ever decide that you want to talk about it."

He looked at me and smiled. It was not the smile I knew. It was a smile filled with sadness and difficult memories, and my guess, nightmares.

I thought back to that night when he was walking from the bar and I thought he was driving. That night he lifted the curtain, allowing me to momentarily see his grief. I knew then in those three seconds or so that he carried a very heavy burden, and I completely recognized it. I understood it. I, like he, was a survivor living with grief mixed in with anger, hurt, despondency, and sorrow.

Perhaps that is what made our connection so potent? Perhaps going through a traumatic event had bound us with this invisible and impenetrable thread, bringing us together to possibly heal?

Whatever the explanation for our paths crossing and our connection was, I was grateful for it and welcomed it because I welcomed him into my heart; and my heart, as a result, rejoiced in his presence.

I needed to feel more of him, to perhaps give him a piece of me so that he could possibly store it in his heart as well. I leaned my head on his shoulder and closed my eyes, offering my silent support. I felt my body syncing with his beats and breaths until we became one. In and out. Beat for beat. One.

"I was thirteen," he said, breaking the silence, "and I had a beautiful cat named Whiskers. Whiskers and I were inseparable. He showed up on our doorstep in a winter storm, half frozen, and we brought him back to life. I fed him with a dropper when he couldn't eat and held him until the frost left his tiny shivering body. After he got better, he shadowed me and I him. I loved him so much." His voice started to break and I felt his body starting to shiver. I shifted and encircled him, my arms going around his stomach. My head continued to rest on his shoulder, offering myself. My understanding. My empathy. Myself.

"A few weeks later, another snowstorm hit the area and I took Whiskers outside to play with me while I built a snowman. It was so funny watching him being back in the snow, how he pranced around in it. Surprisingly, after all he went through, he was not scared of it." I could feel his smile through his words. It made me smile as well.

"I turned my back on him for just a moment and he wandered into the street. Something must have spooked him, and he started running. I took off after him. It took me a while to catch up to him. He ran for about three blocks, and I was scared he would get lost or worse, hurt. I finally spotted him in the middle of the street, walking slowly. He was no longer running. I called his name, and he looked back at me. I waved for him to come to me, to move to the side of the road, where I was. He took a step towards me and stopped. I moved towards him and he purred. That's when I heard a car fast approaching. In one fast motion, I bent down and scooped Whiskers up and tried to make my way off the road. And the rest happened so quickly. The road was slippery and the car swerved to avoid hitting us. It hit a tree instead." His voice cracked and filled with agony. His tears fell on my arm and the side of my face. My skin drank in his sorrow, hoping to ease his pain. I unwound my hands from his waist momentarily, to rub his back, only to return my strong grip on him. I wanted him to know I was here for him and going through this alongside him.

"I recall the cloud of smoke, and a moment later, the smell of blood. When the ambulance came and opened up the passenger side door, I remember the blood trickling into the snow, staining it red. My dad didn't survive." He sobbed into my shoulder.

"It was an accident, Drew. You were only a child trying to save your pet."

"I shouldn't have left Whiskers alone. I should have held him in my arms and my dad wouldn't have died."

"I am sure your dad would have done anything, even give up his own life, to save yours." My voice broke and tears puddled in my eyes. I wanted him to believe this. I wanted him to stop blaming himself.

After what happened to me, I had blamed myself too. *What if I hadn't walked on that street, what if I had taken a different path home? What if I had screamed louder? What if I stayed at work later?*

A lot of what-ifs and no answers.

Hearing his story made me look at mine from a different angle. Yes, perhaps Drew and I had crossed paths to heal one another after all.

"That's why I became a firefighter, but not before running away from home when I was sixteen. I slept on streets and in empty warehouses. I took odd jobs, dirty jobs that many turn down. I had planned that escape since the accident."

We have another thing in common.

"Running away was difficult, but I felt like my mother secretly blamed me. She never made me feel like I was guilty of his death, but I saw the light in her go out after my dad's death. She didn't laugh much or go out. She just holed up at the house, and her movements became robotic. I don't think she knew how to deal with the grief, and she didn't talk about it with my sister or me. I had to leave. Perhaps not seeing me would give her another chance at a happier life. At least I hoped so." I felt his body shudder.

"I called her once, on my twenty-first birthday to tell her that I had become a firefighter. I wanted her to know that I risked my life for others, that I knew I didn't deserve to be here while my dad wasn't. I told her I loved her and never spoke to her again." His voice cracked.

"I'm sure she didn't blame you," I whispered softly.

"No, she told me she didn't, but I just never believed it." He pulled away from me and wiped at his eyes and nose. "I felt like I reminded her of that day, of that loss."

"Can I ask you something?" I asked gently.

He nodded.

"Is that why you don't drive a car?"

He nodded his head in agreement. I watched as he lowered his head and stared at the ground. I kissed his shoulder and pressed my cheek against the same spot I had just kissed.

"Thank you for sharing that with me. I'm always here if you ever want to talk about it . . . or anything else, for that matter."

I felt him nod his head. His palm reached over to me and caressed my cheek, and I leaned into it.

"I'm always here if you want to talk too," he said.

I felt myself freeze up. I looked into his eyes, and in that moment, I knew that he recognized my sadness and pain in the same way had I recognized his that night in the parking lot.

How would he feel after I told him my secret?

Would he offer a shoulder to lean on and an open and listening heart?

Or would he turn away from me?

I was not ready to know the answer to that question yet, so instead I placed my cheek back against his shoulder, closed my eyes, and welcomed the feeling of being at home in his arms for as long as I possibly could.

***

After our talk on the mountaintop, I felt like Drew and I went from slow to fast in a second. We spent every waking moment in each other's company. I told him about my life in foster care and about Jess and Jax. I filled him in on my grandmother's letters, and he would share memories of his family with me. I felt like I could tell him everything, yet I wasn't quite ready to tell him about July 15 just yet.

After we gave up on fighting our feelings and just lived in the present, we just fell into this routine and it felt so natural. Today we were having a picnic in my garden, right under the magnolia tree.

Kendrew spent his day off this morning mowing the lawn, and I spent my day off from the flower shop lying on the grass watching the sky and him. I especially loved watching him.

His scent combined with the freshly cut grass was one I would always hold on to. I stowed that lovely scent memory away, locking it in the chest drawer of my heart.

The one that collected all my lovely memories, pretty much all having to do with him.

I felt him lie down next to me and take my hand into his, interlacing our fingers until we were one. I moaned at how good it felt. He looked at my lips and leaned in to plant a kiss.

I broke the kiss and he grumbled.

I had something better in mind.

I rolled toward him and got on top of him, stretching out until my chest was flush up against his. My hair cascaded over his face, blanketing us from the views of passersby. I felt heat go through my body everywhere we were touching.

It burned.

I kissed him passionately, giving him all of myself. I put every feeling and emotion I had toward him into that kiss, and hearing him groaning and pressing up against me made me so happy. He grabbed a hold of my butt, and it was my turn to groan and gasp. I gyrated my hips, and he rolled over with me so that he was now on top of me.

He kissed my lips, gently nibbling on the lower lip before licking it, soothing it with his tongue.

He looked at me with intensity in his eyes. It was evident that he and I wanted to take the next step. I was surprised I wanted to after what happened, but I did.

"Date night at my place tonight?" he asked, his breathing labored.

"Mhhmm," I responded before kissing him passionately.

My love,

Words cannot begin to describe how happy your last letter made me. I am so proud of you. I could imagine how you looked reciting my letters. I am sorry that she burned them, but it doesn't change a thing. I love you and will always be there alongside you. I think she should start getting used to it. I'm not going anywhere, you know!

Speaking of letters, I am carrying your kiss in the shirt pocket, right next to my heart. I fall asleep with your letter in my hands and wake up with your kiss staring at me. I kiss the letter every morning and night, imagining I am kissing your lips. Matthew caught me the other day and laughed. He promised not to tell anyone else. He said his angel did the same for him and that he carries her letters right next to his heart as well and rereads them. We both laughed because we memorized letters from you gals by heart already, having read them so many times. But I love looking at your cursive writing and imagining you biting your lip as you write to me. (You know you do that when you are deep in thought, right?) I love it. I love everything about you.

I might not be able to write for a while. We are about to move locations and it might get a little dangerous, so my focus has to be on staying alive. Please know that I am thinking about you every single moment of the day and night. Please do not worry about me. I made a promise to be with you forever, and I intend to keep it.

Sending you all my love,

Jim

Chapter Twenty-Nine

Kendrew

I pulled out the zucchini lasagna from the oven. It smelled so good.

I made this for the guys at the firehouse sometimes, especially when we needed a respite from an overload of pasta, usually before the firefighters' calendar photo shoot. We all watched what we ate then, as we knew we would be hanging in other people's homes.

Knowing that she liked veggies, I figured this would impress her.

I *really* wanted to impress her.

The food was taken care of, and I had wine, beer, and sparkling water ready as well, as I was not sure what she preferred, so I wanted to give her some options.

Did I mention that I really wanted to impress her?

I glanced at the clock. *She should be here any moment.* I ran to my bedroom to change my shirt.

I thought she'd like me in the gray polo.

Ding-dong.

She was here. My heart just skipped a beat.

No, I thought, *the navy works best.*

On second thought, gray it is.

She'll like me in that one.

***

"I was always surrounded by music in my family. And when I was about eight, I got an acoustic guitar for my birthday. My . . ." I stopped talking. I looked down at my hands and she reached out and put her hand on top of mine and left it there. I looked at her beautiful hand, her long fingers, and the one short, bitten fingernail. I chuckled and touched it. She laughed as well and I looked into her eyes.

I found peace in the emerald pools and the strength to continue talking.

"I initially hated the guitar, but my dad finally got me to join him in playing it. He was a very big fan of acoustic guitars. There wasn't a night that he didn't play. Even if it was five minutes, he took it out and played a song." My voice shook. "I wish I hadn't been so difficult. That I did more with him when I had the time."

"All kids are like that. Don't blame yourself too much." She placed her other hand on my chest and laid her head right next to it. "You are an amazing, sweet, and considerate man, and I can bet that your dad knew that even when you were being a little headstrong."

"You inspire me, Lynnie. Like I want to be a glass-half-full kind of person like you are. You truly are amazing." I kissed her on the nose and then left feather kisses down her cheeks, across her eyes, and on her lips.

She laughed. "Wait, did you just call me Lynnie?"

I looked at her with a surprised look on my face. "I did. It just came out like that. I can stop if you don't like it." I felt my cheeks reddening.

"No, I love it. No one has ever given me a nickname before—" she smiled, and just like that the room lit up, as if we were in a field of sunflowers "—or called me a cute pet name, so I absolutely love it." She moved from my chest and I was about to protest, but then she climbed onto my lap and straddled me, and I moaned instead. She kissed me slowly. Her tongue touched mine. I tasted her and she tasted me, and we both gave and took equally. My hands moved over the small of her back and up toward her shoulders. Then they traveled back down and touched her beautiful round booty.

She moved on top of me and I groaned. I looked at her and she was flushed and her lips were red and moistened. She was biting her lip, and that twinkle in her eye was getting bigger with every movement of her hips.

"I want to, baby, but not like this. I want our first time to be special."

"This is special," she said, pointing to the couch and the room. "It's you and me. What can be more special than this, than us like this?"

"You deserve so much more, and I will give it to you." I winked at her. "But first, Lynnie darling, I have a little gift for you."

"Ohhh, a gift? You didn't have to."

"No, actually I did. It's thanks to you I picked up the guitar once more. You healed a part of me that was broken. Your wave in that window seemed to clear the muddy prints from my past that were dragging me down into deep murky waters. You, my precious sunflower, showed me what light and hope are all about." He smiled. "I wrote a song for you."

I grabbed her hand and placed a kiss on her palm. I rose from the couch and walked over to the guitar. I strummed it while walking back to her. I sat down next to her and faced her.

I looked deep into her eyes and started speaking to her through the chords.

She is everything, everything that is nice and sweet.

She brings the sun to my day, and when the skies are gray,

She shines brighter with every drop of rain.

There is no stopping her light.

It's deep in her heart.

And shines so bright.

Guiding me always

Like a lighthouse guides a ship on the stormy waters

She is the prettiest girl I've ever seen

Her beauty is deep from within

Deep inside

She is inside my heart

She holds a special place there

She makes me happy and at peace

She is everything that is good

She is everything

"Oh, that is so beautiful. No one ever has ever written a song for me before," she said, tears pooling in her eyes.

"I'm glad I could be the first." I pulled her close to me and wrapped my arms around her. She was lying against me, and I was cushioning her from the couch, just like a pillow would.

"So now you know music is one of my passions. What are yours?" I asked. I wanted to know everything about her.

"Old movies," she said automatically. "I love black-and-white movies and shows."

"Mmmm, let's plan a movie date night in to watch some. How about next Wednesday night if you're not working?"

"My place or yours?"

"Your pick," I exclaimed.

"Mine," she said enthusiastically.

"I'll bring the popcorn and treats."

"It's a deal," she said, a huge smile spreading across her face.

"It's a date."

Happiness filled my body and settled in my heart. I closed my eyes and just felt so at peace and happy and loved. I heard her heart beat against me, and it was more beautiful than any song I could ever pen. I listened to the rhythm, my heart syncing with hers. I felt my eyelids closing, and I didn't stop them. I reveled in this closeness and this immense feeling of peace that blanketed me and my heart.

Chapter Thirty

Kaitlyn

I could feel him. He was stronger than me, bigger than me, and he was hitting me. I screamed and tried to kick him. I couldn't. He was on top of me. Threatening me. He had a knife to my neck.

"Scream, bitch, and I slit your throat."

I cried internally as he entered my body. The pain made me want to scream. The shame of what was happening made me want to throw up. I felt the bile rising in my throat.

He was going to kill me.

I couldn't help it. I threw up.

"You bitch." He slapped me once, twice. He did not stop. I lost track of counting the blows.

I closed my eyes, waiting to feel the knife. Waiting to feel the blood ooze out of my body. He might as well. I felt dead already. Numb, empty. Hollow. I felt nothing.

I opened my eyes and saw that he was gone. I let out a shriek, and tears started streaming down my face, just as darkness enveloped me.

It was only a dream, I repeated over and over again.

And dreams die the moment a person wakes up.

It was a lie and I knew it, but I keep lying to myself in hopes that it would help.

My eyes focused on my surroundings and the arms around me. I was at Kendrew's place. We must have fallen asleep on his couch.

I inhaled through my nose and exhaled through my mouth. I focused on breathing and felt myself start to relax. Strong, powerful arms embraced me, only these arms didn't scare me. I heard him whispering words of comfort in my ear.

I moved my hand and held onto his forearm that was lying across my chest. I held on tight, like it was my safety raft in the middle of a rough sea, with waves crashing against me, trying to pull me under, unable to because of his vicelike grip, that kept me floating above water.

All of a sudden, I felt him let go of me, and I panicked.

"Kendrew," I whimpered, my hand frantically reaching for him.

"I'm right here, sweetheart. Just wanted to grab the blanket that fell on the ground." He showed me the blanket and wrapped it around me and then did what I needed the most: he wrapped his arms around me. I was not cold, yet I couldn't stop shivering. I could taste the fear rise up in my throat. I closed my eyes and just thought of him and his arms around me. His strong body became my armor and his arms my medicine.

What if he looked at me differently after I told him what had happened? What if he ran? What if he was disgusted by it?

My thoughts were momentarily interrupted when he turned me around so that my face was nestled against his chest. He kissed the top of my head, and in this moment, for the first time, I understood what feeling safe meant.

I watched him slowly release a breath, and I breathed it in. I was safe. He was my life raft. When my oxygen ran low, he would give me his breath.

"I got you. No one will hurt you when I am here."

His left hand wiped away my tears while his right hand continued to be nestled at my spine. It traveled up and down, my very own security blanket.

The last time I had the dream was on the anniversary when Jess found me on the floor shaking and crying.

I thought being in Kendrew's arms reminded me of *his* arms. Reminded me of being at *his* mercy.

Memories began to assault me, and I pulled away, embarrassed that Kendrew had to see me like that. He let me go, but I could feel him watching my face closely.

I looked down at my feet and was paralyzed and could not move. I felt my hair was in my eyes, yet I was frozen and could not move it away. I breathed in and out and counted to ten.

I looked up and faced him, my gaze locking with his through the strands of my hair.

I gasped at what I saw.

Blood was coming down the side of his cheek. I could see three deep scratch marks on his left cheek. I was so ashamed, and tears welled up in my eyes.

"I am so sorry." I touched my own cheek gently, imagining I was touching his, but was too scared to reach out for him.

He probably thought I was nuts. Who had nightmares like that? Who attacked an innocent person like I just had?

He looked at me with sadness and what looked to be understanding in his eyes.

I looked back down at my feet and wrapped my arms around my stomach. I walked toward the window, away from him. I was surprised my feet cooperated, but I was so grateful that they did, as I was so embarrassed. I needed to get away. I needed to leave. It was for the best.

How did I even start to apologize for hurting someone so bad?

Jesus, his scratches are deep.

I closed my eyes, trying to close out the image of him hurting because of me. Bleeding because of me, and I couldn't. Closing my eyes did not make the situation better. Closing them did not wipe it away.

I wished that memory could be erased like a raindrop from a windshield when the wipers were turned on, but it would need some freakin serious heavy-duty wipers.

I knew I had to tell him the truth. I owed him that much. And then I would walk away and stay away if that's what he wanted.

"I'm sorry," I whispered. "I'm so sorry." My voice broke and I felt tears forming in my eyes. I tried to blink them away. I was frustrated to feel my tears making paths down my cheeks. I wiped at them erratically.

"Don't apologize," he whispered. His voice hugged me everywhere I needed to be hugged. And most importantly, it seeped inside and calmed me. "I know that nightmares are really scary, but you're awake now. Nothing can harm you anymore; it would have to get past me," he said confidently. I didn't doubt for one moment that he could keep me safe. The question was, would he want to after knowing the truth?

"Your face." My voice cracked, stopping me from speaking momentarily. I looked at a bird flying across the sky, free, and I wished that I could do that right now. Just fly away and disappear.

"I didn't mean to hurt you. I thought you were *him* and I wanted *him* to stop." My voice broke. I felt his hands on mine, turning me so I could face him. I couldn't. I was looking at my feet, my cheeks red in shame. He lifted my head up gently to look at him, eyes to eyes.

"Do you want to talk about it?" His eyes were warm and filled with worry.

I was surprised that I found myself nodding my head. What did I have to lose? If he wanted to leave, better that he did it now.

He walked with me to the couch and wrapped me in a blanket. We sat in silence, and when I finally felt like I could talk, I started telling him about July 15.

"I was told that I was crying when the police found me. I was described as not being 'present.' I was mumbling and shaking and staring past everyone that had gathered at the scene. When a male police officer touched me, I tried to claw his eyes out." I stopped for a moment, transported to that moment temporarily. I drew in a shaky breath and didn't realize I was holding it until he touched my jawline gently, and I exhaled. I looked at him and saw his eyes filled with warmth, compassion, and understanding. It gave me the strength to continue. "They were pretty certain that I had been raped, without me saying a word, and they were right, so they wrapped me in a blanket, bloody thighs and snotty nose and bruised face and all."

I looked him straight in his eyes. "I blamed myself for that night, for what happened. I thought if I left earlier, I would have been safe, or if I had taken a different path, that wouldn't have happened. Or if I fought harder, yelled louder . . ." I sobbed, and he reached to embrace me. I was shaking in his arms and trembling, but his hard chest was offering me solace and a safe place. I felt his calm seep into my body, calming the trembling and shivering coursing through me.

"A beautiful and smart woman once told me on a mountaintop that what happened to my dad was an accident, that it wasn't my fault. She was right. I wish she would take her own advice. This was a horrific attack on you, but it wasn't your fault. It was the creep's." He stopped for a moment, a thought entering his mind. "Did they ever catch the guy?"

I shook my head. "No."

He cursed under his breath and pulled me in closer, holding me tighter than before.

"That scared me, knowing he was out there and could do it to me again or to someone else," she said. "The police had a theory that he was passing through and not local, but it didn't stop me from being paranoid and suspecting everyone, especially men. I vowed to never ever have a man touch me again, and I vowed never to cry again."

He pulled away from me suddenly. He was watching me closely. I took in the change in his body. His fists were clenched and I watched the tick in his jaw, wanting to kiss it away. I could tell he was mad that I had gone through that. I didn't want him to be anymore. That was the past, and he couldn't change it anymore than I could. He was right. The words I told him on the mountaintop belonged to me as well. Call it a breakthrough if you want or turning over a new page or just moving forward. It was me living in the present, acknowledging the past and what had happened, but no longer being trapped in a nightmare called my thoughts and memories, day in and day out. I couldn't promise that I wouldn't be triggered or that I wouldn't get nightmares, but I would deal with those demons, hopefully with him by my side.

I was ready for a new start. A happy start, to see where this feeling between me and him would take us. To do that, I needed to trust him and break down a few of my impassable walls, and build a pathway that he and I could walk on hand in hand.

"I broke one promise, and as for the second . . ." I looked his way, biting my lip, feeling so vulnerable and uncomfortable. I didn't know how to say it. I was embarrassed to tell him. He mistook my hesitancy for something else.

"I understand, baby. I am so sorry for what you went through. I'm sorry I made the moves on you. I never would have if I had known what you went through." He ran his hand through his hair, leaving it disheveled. I loved it. He looked so handsome just like that. So real. So almost mine. I wanted to run my fingers through it, following the path that his fingers just took.

"I won't touch you again." He jumped off of the couch. "I won't even look at you if it makes you feel better. God . . ." He took steps toward the couch, sitting on it for a few seconds before rising off of it rapidly. He started pacing, almost as if unsure of where he should stand or sit or what he should do. He stopped by the window I had been staring out of earlier. "Can you forgive me?" he whispered, his back turned to me.

I started to laugh, and he turned, his frown deepening. Confusion marred his handsome face.

"I was going to say . . . as for the second one . . . I am about to break it. I need you, Kendrew." I looked at him, putting my feelings for him on display, and I watched as he blinked a few times before starting to pace again.

"I need you so much," I said once again, with surety in my voice, and it must've cut through his confusion, as his pacing stopped. He was looking at me with hope in his eyes as well.

I reached out my hands, and without hesitation, he crossed the distance to me.

He grabbed my hands and placed kisses on them, some landing on my fingertips, some scattered on my wrist, and some making their way to the center of my palms. I loved those best. Those palm kisses shot straight to my heart. "Are you sure?" he asked.

"Positive." I kissed his hand back.

"Tell me if I go too far."

"You haven't done a thing yet." I chuckled.

"But you'll let me know if I do?"

"I doubt I'll have to."

He got up and started his pacing again. He stopped, looked back at me, walked around in a circle twice, and faced the wall. "Safe mode," he said.

"What?" I asked, thoroughly confused.

"Safe mode." He sat back down. "Please say 'safe mode' when I go too far and you want me to stop."

I burst out laughing. "Deal. I want you to go past safe mode now. I want you in the fast zone, so come on and kiss me already!"

CHAPTER THIRTY-ONE

Kendrew

My tongue danced with hers while my hands moved from her breasts to her stomach and back up again. As my hands explored her body, she did the same to me.

I felt her hands move from my back and trail lower until they were touching my buttocks. I felt a pinch on my left buttock, and I nipped her lip gently in response.

"My turn," I whispered.

I lifted Kaitlyn's hands up in the air. "Don't move," I pleaded with her.

She nodded in agreement.

"You trust me?" I asked softly, my finger grazing her cheek.

"Completely," she responded without hesitation.

I traced her lips with my tongue. Her mouth parted, inviting me in. I reluctantly pulled away, but she was wearing too many pieces of clothing. I had to change that.

I reached for her shirt and pulled it slowly over her head. My eyes went to her olive-green lace bra, and my hands reached out to cup her breasts. The bra was concealing too much from me. I wanted to know what color her nipples were. If they were hard for me. If they were ready for my tongue. While I kissed her neck, suckling on her sensitive skin, my hands reached behind her back and unclasped the hooks of the bra. I disposed of it in one quick move.

I lowered her hands and they instantly went to her breasts. I watched as she cupped them, all while looking at me. Her areolas were a lovely shade of dusty pink, and her nipples were hard and ready for my mouth.

I reached for one breast, and she leaned into my hand. I encircled the nipple and tapped it gently. I did the same to the second breast. I took both breasts into my hands and cupped them.

"You are so beautiful. So damn perfect." I kissed her breasts and alternated between licking one and then the other. When both had been lovingly suckled on and sensitized, I blew on her nipples, watching them harden even more. She was moaning and moving her body against me.

"You promised not to move," I reminded her and backed off a little bit.

She cried out and reached for me. "Don't stop."

I chuckled. "Oh, baby, this is just the beginning." I moved closer to her and gently nibbled on her neck. Our chests were touching and I felt her nipples even through my shirt and I rubbed against her. The friction from my shirt must've felt good against her naked upper torso because she moaned.

I looked at her face and she was watching me intently, her mouth slightly open, breathing harder.

"I bet you are so wet for me. Do you want me, Lynn?"

"Yes!" She bucked against me. Her hands moved across my lower back.

"Soon, baby. I can't wait to be inside of you. Feel you enclose me, take me deeply," I whispered, breathing heavily. "Make me cum."

I watched as she squeezed her legs together and moaned. I reached for the button on her jeans and slowly pulled the zipper down.

"Do you want me to touch you here?" I placed my hand into the unfastened jeans and ran my fingers over her panty-covered mound.

"Yes, all over," she panted.

"All over?" I pushed her lace panties aside and felt with my finger just how wet she was.

So wet.

For me.

"Yes" – she was gasping now – "touch me all over, kiss me all over. Please, hurry."

"Tonight we take our time, Lynn." She started to object, and I touched her clit, eliciting a moan. I watched her bite her lip. "Rest assured, not one inch of your skin will be untouched." I moved my finger inside her. I moved it slowly, in and out, exploring her heat. She was moaning and moving against me. I added another finger and she gasped. I moved slowly and felt the friction of her body against my finger.

I pulled my fingers out slowly, my thumb grazing her clitoris in the process.

"Ohhh, yes," she moaned, "that is the spot."

I wanted to explore more of that spot, but needed better access to it.

I pulled away and reached for her socks, which I took off. We had taken our shoes off earlier to cuddle on the couch, so that was one less thing to remove. Once her socks were off, I pulled her already open pants down her hips. She lifted her butt off the couch to assist me with their removal. Once her pants were off, I tossed them across the room. She was just in her lacey thong. I spread her legs and knelt in between them. I touched the inside of her legs, from her knees to her thighs. I lowered my face, pushed her panties to the side, and breathed in her scent.

"You are soaking wet."

She whimpered as my fingers found her opening once again. Her hips bucked as my finger went in and out of her. My other hand found her clit and joined in the fun. She cried out and I kissed her on the mouth slowly and passionately.

I took her thong off and she was now completely bare for me. "Perfection," I said. I knelt on the floor in front of her, between her legs, lifting her hips and placing them on my shoulders so that she was level with my mouth. I kissed her clitoris and circled it with my tongue. I suckled on it and she moved against my mouth, gasping and panting loudly. Her hips were moving in circles and I felt her wetness against my tongue. She told me she was close to coming, and I pulled away.

She watched me, her eyes hooded with passion, confused about why I stopped.

"Not yet, baby," I said. "I want to feel you cum while I am inside of you." I brought my fingers, wet with her juices, to my mouth and licked them clean. Her eyes widened, and I watched her take a breath.

I reached for my shirt and pulled it over my head quickly. I then reached for my belt, which I swiftly unbuckled. I unzipped my jeans and they fell to the floor. I was standing before her in my boxers, my manhood evidently pressing against them. I looked at her lying on the couch, watching me undress, and she was a sight to see. Her naked body was flushed and her nipples were glistening from my earlier kisses. One hand was touching her neck like it had that day in the parking lot. The other was between her legs. She watched me pull down my boxers, and I smiled when she looked and gasped.

Darling Jim,

I miss you so much. So very, very much. I should have started this letter asking you about how you were doing, but I wanted you to know how badly I miss you and how deeply I love you. I am getting frustrated being these words don't feel like enough. I want to show you how much I love you and care about you. I want to hold your hand and kiss your beautiful smiling lips. Without you by my side, I feel an emptiness that nothing and no one will ever be able to fill. It scares me when I think about where you are and how unsafe you are every day. I count the days until I see you again, not knowing when that will be, yet I still count away. When you come back, I expect to get extra time on our hill, hugging you and falling asleep in your arms.

As for me, everything is okay here. Mother is still Mother (rolling my eyes), and I am always expected to be the perfect daughter. How I hate playing a role. I am a girl that loves to run barefoot, that loves to spend time in the kitchen, helping the cook. I am a girl that loves to make my own bed, and most importantly, I am a girl that loves someone wholeheartedly who loves me as well.

I always tell myself that, especially when Mother throws these big parties at the house and invites all these obnoxious big shots and their children. I'm not one of them, but I have learned to play a role. I'm only truly myself when I am with you. It's almost as if you complete the missing pieces in me and make me whole and as if I complete the missing pieces in you and make you whole.

You showed me how strong I am, and nothing is testing this strength as much as this deployment, but I will make it. WE WILL MAKE IT. I know it. This type of love is worth the wait. And so are you. It is late night already and I must go to sleep. I hope you visit my dreams again. Kisses.

Stay safe, my love.

Love always,
Mary

CHAPTER THIRTY-TWO

Kaitlyn

He was amazing.

His body was hard as a rock.

All muscle.

Firm to my touch.

His chest was dusted with a light coating of hair. His stomach was chiseled, just like I imagined it would be. I couldn't wait to explore it further. And taste him.

His member was rigid and erect, and the tip was glistening with a bead of precum. It was ready for me, and I was wet and ready to feel him inside me. I rubbed my clit, which was so sensitive from his ministrations, and I spread my legs wide for him so that he could watch me play with myself while I watched him undress. He seemed to like the view because his breath caught and his member twitched.

He looked around the floor of the living room and found what he was looking for. He picked his jeans up and reached into a pocket, pulling out a couple of condoms.

He was prepared. He wanted this as much as I did. That thought excited me so much. He dropped his jeans back on the floor, ripped one packet apart, and was about to put on the condom, and I stopped him.

"I want to taste you first." I moved to position myself on the couch so that I was level with his cock. I reached for the condom packet, and he gave it to me without hesitation. I placed it beside my stomach, on the couch, within reach of both of us. We would need that a little later. Now, I had other plans.

I was on my knees, my booty in the air and my elbows resting on the arm of the couch. I watched his eyes roam over my buttocks and my legs. I extended my hand, gently running my fingers across his abs. He bucked forward, and his cock was inches from my mouth. I grabbed his hips and pulled him closer. He took a big step forward, and his cock was now touching my lips. I traced the head of his cock with my tongue and lapped up the glistening precum. He was breathing heavily and watching every move I made. I kept both of my hands wrapped around his hips, and I took him into my mouth. He was hot pulsing against my tongue and hard as steel. I sucked on him and took him deeper, until I felt him at the back of my throat. I gagged slightly and pulled away only to try again. I had him deep in my mouth and felt Kendrew move slightly, pushing himself into my mouth slowly. I took everything he offered. He was moving in my mouth and I was keeping up with him. My lips were wrapped around his cock, and I was breathing through my nose. My mouth had gotten used to his size, and I was able to take him deeper without gagging anymore. I heard him breathing heavily, and my eyes looked up at him. He was watching his cock slide in and out of my mouth.

"Fuck," he groaned out. I felt him pulling away, and I released him. I ran my tongue over my lips and felt his saltiness on them.

I loved the taste of him.

"Wow, you are one little hot vixen, aren't you?" He spanked me gently on my left buttock. "I was about to cum. I don't want to cum just yet. I want to be inside of you when I do."

He reached for the condom packet that had shifted with my movements and was now by my knees. He tore it open. I watched him put it on without breaking eye contact with me.

He joined me on the couch. I was still on my stomach, and he lay on top of me, his hands keeping him up from crushing me. One hand moved between my legs, checking to make sure I was still wet. He groaned in pleasure when his fingers found me so ready for him. I moved against his hand, needing to feel him there.

He raised my hips slightly and positioned himself so that I could feel his cock pulsing against me. I whimpered. I wanted to squeeze my thighs to relieve some of the pressure, but I knew it wouldn't help. I needed him.

"Please." I didn't need to say more. He knew what I needed, and he complied. He entered me slowly, and every inch forward felt like paradise. When he was fully inside me, he groaned. It felt so perfect. So right.

There was something so different about the way he felt inside of me, the way we fit one another. It felt spiritual, as crazy as that sounds. He leaned forward and kissed my shoulder, and then he gently nibbled it. I jerked against him and moaned loudly. He continued to glide in and out, and the speed increased. I matched it by pushing onto him. He had his hands on my hips, driving his cock home into me faster and faster. I felt myself slipping from the couch.

He slowed his movements, and I protested.

"Your eyes," he said, breathing heavily.

He pulled out and turned me over so that I was on my back and we were facing each other. My eyes locked with his.

"I want to see you when you cum all over me," he whispered, and my breath hitched. "I need to see you," he said softly, almost as if he was saying it to himself. He looked at me, really looked at me, and I saw how he felt about me reflected in his eyes. He entered me, and I raised my head slightly, to look at the point where we were connected.

Watching him entering me and stretching me was so sexy. I pushed onto his cock, and he responded by moving faster and thrusting deeper, meeting me thrust for thrust. I heard the sounds of our slick bodies meeting each other, and I realized I never wanted to do this with anyone else but him. We were both panting and our breaths were mingling together, becoming one. He was breathing for me and me for him.

My toes started to tingle. I was about to come. My eyes closed and my breathing increased. He reached between our sweat-slickened bodies, his fingers touching my clit. It was swollen, and when he pinched it, I cried out.

My body shaking, I called out his name. My body was clenching around him. He thrust deeply one more time, his movements jerky. He called out my name, spilling his orgasm into me on a moan of surrender.

***

"Taking pictures of sunrises," I whispered quietly. My backside was flush with his stomach. His arms were around me on the couch, spooning me and shielding my naked body from the morning sunlight filtering in through the windows. He placed a kiss on my neck, and I adjusted my body to give him more access to my skin.

"Hmmmm?" he said between kisses across my neck and back. He cupped my breast and circled my nipple, playing with it with the pad of his thumb. My nipples hardened instantly, and I arched back against him, a gasp of surprise falling from my lips when I encountered him hard and ready, nestled against my backside.

I tried to focus on the window and on the sunrise, but I was finding it very difficult to ignore my body's response to him. I tried.

"You asked me earlier about what I loved besides old movies. Well, I love this." I motioned toward the window with my head.

He pinched my nipple and started rocking his hips slowly against my back.

"I love this too." He licked my earlobe, eliciting a gasp from me. He laughed.

"Ohhhh, so do I." I pushed against him, my breathing becoming more and more labored. "I was actually talking about this killer sunrise."

"How about sunsets?" he asked between nibbles. His fingers left my nipple and traveled downward. He traced my belly button before going lower. He dipped a finger inside me and groaned. "So wet, so ready. I like that, baby." He circled my clitoris, and I wanted to scream. I groaned instead and focused on what he had asked me.

"Only sunrises," I answered breathlessly.

"Tell me why?" he asked. His breath was hot against my ear. His fingers were working magic inside of me, and I needed him so much. I pushed against him, needing to feel him inside of me.

He continued teasing me with his fingers, and I felt myself losing control. I tried to answer his question, but I couldn't think straight. All I felt was this man and what he did to me. I glanced at the sun rising outside his window, the colors magical, but I closed my eyes as my own burst of light happened inside of me. Colors danced behind my closed eyelids, and I felt myself floating before falling back to earth, slowing. I released everything I was feeling, everything he made me feel. I now got why some people said orgasms were earth-shattering. Man oh man, he took me to the sky with this one.

He kissed my shoulder. "Now that's how I like waking up."

I turned my head and kissed him. I needed more. I turned my head back to the window, back to the magical display, and nestled my backside against his hard member. I reached back and touched it, feeling the drop of precum, and I spread it over his member. He moaned, and I increased my hand's tempo. He stilled my hand, reached over for a condom packet that was now on the floor, and ripped it and put in on in record speed. He caressed my breast again while pushing himself into me.

I pushed backed, and he increased his speed. I watched the sun paint the skies in hues of pinks, purples, yellows, and oranges while the man I was falling in love with pumped into me from behind. He held onto my breast, alternating between rubbing my neck and pinching my nipple, until I screamed his name. I felt him increase his speed and groan. His head fell on my shoulder as his orgasm subsided. He didn't pull away. Instead he wrapped his arms around me and held me tighter. We watched the beautiful piece of ever-changing art before our eyes.

"I love sunrises too," he said with laughter in his voice.

I joined in with the laughter. I adjusted my body, wanting to see his face. I turned toward him and cringed as my muscles protested. Apparently, a sex-filled night on a couch required some serious stretching exercises beforehand.

I watched as he took the condom off, tied it, and threw it on the floor.

"I'll get that in a minute and throw it out. I just want to hold you a bit more." His head gestured toward the used condom.

"Why sunrises?" he asked.

"Sunsets are so overrated, ya know?" I smiled and drew a smile from him as well. I watched a small dimple make its presence known in his right cheek. I had never noticed it before. I had a feeling there were many more firsts with him. "Sunsets can be seen by many. I mean, they can be experienced even if you weren't planning on experiencing it, just by being out and about in the late afternoon or evening. However, sunrises are another story. For a sunrise you need a plan. You need to set an alarm, wake up extra early to experience it." I smiled. "Plus, it's so quiet at dawn. There is dew on the grass, the chill in the air, even in summertime. It's beautiful. It's like Mother Nature letting us in on her awakening. It may sound crazy, but I find sunrises so comforting. After a dark night, light emerges, and it does so in an array of colors. Almost like a curtain rising on the day's stage and we the actors are up for the performance." I stopped suddenly and looked into his eyes. "I'm yakking. Sorry." I kissed him gently on the lips and then on the chin. I loved kissing his jawline for some reason. Loved feeling the stubble and the strength of his jaw.

He was sexy, and every part of him was beautiful, but there was something extra special about doing that to him. He let me and didn't seem to mind, so that was a plus.

"Don't apologize. You are always free to speak your mind with me." He looked into my eyes with an intensity I had never seen before. I felt exposed and looked away, focusing on a freckle on his collarbone. Wanting to kiss it. His voice pulled me away from the wicked path my thoughts were starting to take me on.

"That was beautiful. I don't think I'll ever look at a sunrise the same again. You have a way with words." I felt his words coming before he even delivered them. I braced myself and tried my hardest to not tense up, but it didn't quite work.

Here it comes.

"Have you ever considered writing?"

And there it is.

The words fell easily from his lips, not knowing how much hurt those five words were inflicting on me, on my dreams that could no longer be. On a dream that had withered away, the decaying roots the only remains left in place.

I shut my eyes, trying to shut out the pain. I was not ready to discuss my failure as a writer, so I just said, "Yes." It was a very hushed yes wrapped in disappointment. All my dreams, all I ever wanted, all I thought I was, I had put into my writing, and that one day took it all away from me.

I felt him watching me, and I looked up at him and gazed deep into his eyes, divulging everything with that one look. A soul-to-soul conversation without words. He opened his mouth to speak and then closed it. He started to rub my back gently, and I looked back at him and smiled.

He understood me without words. He listened and heard everything I couldn't quite put into words just yet. I watched him nod once, and then he kissed my shoulder. I had never thought it would be possible, but that one kiss seemed to ease the pain of disenchantment and replaced it with understanding, hope, and dare I say it, love.

I knew in this moment that when I was able to talk about my past, as a writer and everything else, that he would listen and understand. That he would speak when words were needed and would do so without judgment.

I didn't think I could love him more, but that was a lie. Looking into his eyes, watching the sun reflected in them, his face covered in the morning's rays, I realized I had fallen even more in love with him than I ever thought possible.

I would never look at sunrises the same way again.

No, I would worship them.

Chapter Thirty-Three

Kaitlyn

It was a beautiful warm day for March, and we were painting the shutters a mid-gray color. He was on one ladder and I on the other, about seven feet apart. I looked over at him, with his ripped jeans and his flannel shirt, and I thought he was the sexiest man on the planet.

Maybe I could stay here after all.

He must have read my mind.

"So, what's the plan?" his sexy voice said.

I looked over at him and found him looking at me.

"What plan?" I asked.

His hand pointed to the house. "With this home." He looked at the house and then at me, before continuing, "Will you be staying around here, or are you still going . . . ?" his voice tapered off.

"I haven't really made up my mind yet. I mean, I have nothing to return to in my old town." I glanced at him. He stopped painting, but did not turn my way. He was just looking at the shutters in front of him, his teeth biting his lower lip.

I continued, "That apartment over there was rented, while this here is all mine." I took in the home and smiled. It was the first and only place that I could call my own.

I could feel he was looking at me, so I turned to him and saw that he had a serious expression on his face. "I sense there is a but . . ." he mumbled.

I laughed gently and nodded my head. I looked away from him, from the questions in his eyes, and dipped the paintbrush in the paint and continued to focus on evenly painting the shutters.

I did not want him to see how much I wanted to stay. That scared me. Especially after spending every day with him.

"But, I don't really feel at home here. This is beautiful, I mean its special because it was my grandmother's and she wanted me to have it, but it seems to be missing something." I turned to him to see his reaction to what I just said. He was turned slightly toward me on the ladder and was watching my face closely. I wanted to explain how I felt about this home, especially to him, as he deserved to know. "You would think that after not having a home and then finally out of the blue having one, it would be amazing. And it is, please don't think me ungrateful." I shook my head, my gaze going from the home to him and back to the home again. His face was expressionless and I didn't know what to make of it. My heart wanted to ask him if he would like me to stay. His answer would weigh heavily on my decision, but I couldn't. I was terrified of his answer. Instead, I turned back to the shutters and he did as well. After a while, I broke the silence and the sadness that seemed to have entered and said, "It's just, I don't know, I guess it's a little more complicated. I'm making a pro and con list, so we'll see . . ." My voice trailed off. I wanted him to know that I really was giving this home, and us, much thought.

I was thinking about so many things in this moment, that I didn't even realize that my paintbrush was no longer spreading any paint. I laughed under my breath and dipped the paintbrush in the can. I could feel him looking at me, but I held myself from looking his way. In the corner of my eye, I saw him dipping his paintbrush and continuing to paint the shutters on his side.

Silence, save for the birds in the trees and our movements on the ladder, was our companion. I didn't know why I felt so sad all of a sudden, but I did.

A big part of me did not want to leave Landing Falls.

A big reason for that was painting alongside me. I didn't know what to make of his silence, so I pretended it did not hurt.

A big part of me wished that he had said something, but he did not. He didn't even nod or shake his head. He just bit that sexy lip and kept on painting.

A few moments later, his voice broke the silence. "I shouldn't say anything, as this is your decision to make, but I *really* hope you stay," he said, spitting the words out quickly.

My head jerked toward him and I almost fell. I steadied myself in time, but before I knew it, he was behind me, his arms enclosing me in his strong embrace.

"Are you okay?" he whispered into the back of my hair. I could feel his breath on my neck and his hands close to my breasts, the only barrier my bra and shirt.

"Yes, but I think we need a break." My words were soft, my voice breathless.

He did that to me.

I felt him cup my breasts, causing me to moan and move against him. He kissed my neck and murmured softly, "I agree."

We barely made it through the door before my shirt was off. I undid his jeans and he quickly got rid of his shirt. We were clawing at one another. We didn't make it far.

We were on the floor and I was on my knees. He was holding on to my hips, and I felt him enter me from behind. I watched his face as he watched my ass move against him, and I couldn't help but feel sexy. I saw intense passion in his eyes, and I was so ecstatic that I could make him feel like that. That I was the reason behind the look of amazement on his face.

"Fuck yes," he said. "I can never get enough of you." He leaned down and grabbed my breast, pressing himself deeper into me. He knew I loved this position. The feeling of him behind me, entering me, while he pinched my nipples and played with my clit. Sometimes he even gave my booty a nice, gentle, yet effective swat.

"Yes, baby. You feel so good." I moaned, and he entered and withdrew. "Deeper." I turned my head to look him in the eyes, and he winked at me.

He complied and filled me completely, all while holding and massaging my breasts. I bucked against him and felt his right hand travel from my breast to my clitoris, and I moaned. I breathed deeply and pushed against him harder and harder. He applied a little pressure to my clit and I lost control. I screamed his name and my body spasmed. I floated away. I was no longer on my knees, but lying on my stomach. I felt Kendrew moving harder and faster on top of me, his hands spreading my ass. He was breathing heavily. I could sense he was coming. I wiggled my butt against him and rolled my hips. He moaned and plunged deeper. He moved in me two more times before I felt his orgasm come.

I loved listening to him cum. His breathing and his deep voice moaning, calling out my name.

He was lying on top of me. We were both sweaty and tired. I felt him turn on his back and pull me into his arms. He kissed the tip of my nose and I smiled. I put one arm around him and the other on his chest. I could feel his heart beating, and I loved falling asleep like that. With my hand on his chest and his on mine. Connected via our heartbeats.

"So, I think this—" he pointed to us both, lying naked on my floor "—should go on your pro list for staying here."

I burst out laughing.

***

After painting and jumping one another's bones, Drew and I were making dinner. Having him in my kitchen felt right.

Truth be told, having him in my life felt right.

I watched with interest as he prepared the ingredients and then as he stirred them, creating a culinary masterpiece. I watched his movements across my kitchen with googly eyes. When he turned off the stove and turned toward me, I was beyond smitten. He looked sure of himself, but not cocky. The kitchen smelled wonderful and the dish looked delicious. I was definitely impressed. My stomach was too. It grumbled loudly, and I placed my hand on my stomach and laughed.

"Someone is excited to try my eggplant cacciatore." He laughed.

"I won't lie. I am." Another round of loud rumbling came from my stomach and I giggled. "It smells so good."

"Just trying to add more things to your pro list for you to stay." He winked at me and I felt warmth spread through me.

"Cooking amazing meatless dishes for me will definitely go on the pro list for staying here." I stopped and thought about the passionate encounter in the hallway earlier. "Along with other things." Now, it was my turn to wink at him.

I knew he was thinking about earlier too. I saw it in his eyes and in the way his breathing changed.

Unless I turned away and changed the subject, he and I would not eat any food, and I was starving. I reached for the roasted vegetable quinoa side salad I had made.

"So why no meat?" he asked.

I looked up at him and shrugged my shoulders. "Well, at first, it wasn't really a choice. We just didn't have enough money at the foster home for any kind of meat, not even canned ham. We grew our own vegetables, and occasionally my foster dad brought home a squirrel or deer, but that was extremely rare, and I would never eat that."

I shuddered at the memory, my body going stiff before starting to shiver. I spoke quickly, hoping that Kendrew didn't feel the shudder and coldness that had seeped into my body. Hoping that he didn't see how the memory of the past still had a chokehold on me. I closed my eyes and felt tears behind my closed lids. And then I felt a warmth spread around my shivering body. It was Kendrew holding me tightly and pressing gentle soft kisses on my shoulder. Wrapped in his embrace, I found the strength to keep talking. With one hug he broke my iron chains tying me to the bad memories, and with one kiss warmed my shivery body. He deserved to know, he wanted to know, and I wanted to tell him. No backing out now.

Deep breath in and out.

"When I was in foster care, there was never a day that I felt wanted or loved. We never received any Christmas or birthday gifts. I never told anyone this, not even Jess, but one night, on Christmas, I lost hope and found it at the same moment." I smiled, reliving the memory. "I saw a beautiful deer with her baby. She came up to my window and I felt a tug at my heart. She looked me straight in the eyes and then turned to her baby. She licked its head and played with it in the snow. As her baby ran toward the dense trees, the mother turned around and stared at me for a moment. Her eyes seemed glossy, and I felt my eyes tear up. She looked behind herself and then back at me once again, as if contemplating coming toward me. When she made sure that her baby was safely playing in the snow, only then did she approach me. I could see her fur, almost feel its texture through the glass separating us. I reached toward her and touched the cool glass. She put her nose on the glass where my hand was, and it was at that moment that I felt loved. She showed me that I was not alone. That I was seen.

"I never told anyone this, but I always believed that the deer was my mom coming to check on me to make sure I was okay. To let me know she cared. I never shared that because it sounded crazy, but it brought me hope in a time when I felt everything around me was hopeless, including myself.

"Then she turned around and ran to her baby and disappeared behind the dense foliage. Emotions I never knew coursed through me and I cried. Even though she was a deer, I felt like she had come to comfort me and to offer me hope." I stopped and let out a breath. "After that I always felt a connection and a deep special bond with deer."

He moved my hair and kissed my neck. "That's beautiful," he whispered near my ear.

"There is more," I said hesitantly. I continued talking, knowing that if I stopped now, I would be unable to speak later on. "A month or so later, I walked into the kitchen and saw a bloody deer through the window, its eyes staring back at me, its mouth open as if its last breath was a scream of agony, and I wondered if that was the deer that visited me and brought me hope of freedom, hope of escape—" I paused briefly "—just hope . . . you know . . . that one day, I would be free too."

I started to choke up, tears pooling in my eyes. He reached for me, pulling me to his warm, hard chest, and it relaxed me instantly. I inhaled his masculine scent. Woodsy and slightly spicy and very fresh. A haunting scent that I knew I would never forget.

A scent that I knew I would fall asleep imagining. A scent that would greet me in the morning. A scent that would travel with me to the next place I moved on to. A scent that would always linger, in my memory, in my heart, embedded deep in my soul.

A scent that I would never forget, no matter the distance or circumstances between us. That, I knew.

After minutes of him holding me, offering me his warmth and protection and his comfort, I tilted my head and looked up at him, a smile spreading across my face, reaching my eyes, telling him everything I felt for him without words.

Honestly, thank you wasn't even enough. I owed him so much more. I wished that I could give him all that, but I knew that it was impossible.

I was scarred and broken. Like a mirror that had shattered into tiny flecks. Once broken, it was impossible to put back together again without the cracks being visible to the naked eye.

He deserved someone whose pieces weren't jagged and raw and capable of causing pain and drawing blood.

He deserved so much better than me.

"So, yeah, that's why I don't eat anything that bleeds." I pulled away from him, turning to the salad I was tossing moments ago and away from his intense gaze. I could not look up no matter how much I tried. I was ashamed that I was such a weird-fitting puzzle piece in his life. I wished I was smoother and less rough around the edges, but I wasn't and didn't think I would ever be.

Had I looked up though, I would have seen what I was feeling in my heart reflected back at me in his eyes. I would have seen a man, an abstract puzzle piece himself, longing for the same.

***

I woke up and saw his eyes looking at me, his body facing me. I nipped his chin and made my way to his lips.

He stretched in his king-sized bed and sighed like a satiated man after having a big plate of food.

"Good morning," he said with a grin.

"Mornin, birthday boy," I replied.

I swung a leg over his hip and he turned with me. He was now on his back and I was on top of him. I pressed my nipples against his chest and heard his groan. I felt his cock spring to life, twitching and pressing hard against my belly. He groaned, and I couldn't help but smile. I did this to him, and I knew that I wanted to do this to him every single day. It should've scared me more than it did, but somehow, with Drew by my side, I was sidestepping my fears and obstacles and roadblocks of my own making.

His hands moved from his sides and landed on my butt. He clasped both buttocks in his hands and I moved my body against him. He gently slapped one butt cheek and then the other. I put my hands on his chest and pressed off of him, raising myself so that I was straddling him. My hips were moving against his erection. It felt so good, especially when my clit came into contact with the tip of his cock and I ground against it.

I desperately needed to feel more of it.

I needed to have him inside of me.

I needed to give him all of myself today.

I raised myself slowly and swung my leg over to the right. I was on my knees to the side of him, taking him in my hand. He was pulsing in my hand, and I loved watching, knowing that I was causing that with my touch. His eyes were filled with passion, fully dilated and filled with desire and a need for me. He bucked against my hand and I smiled, knowing what he needed. I ran my tongue across my lips and watched him watch me. I moved my hand up and down his cock, spreading the moisture that had accumulated at the tip. Sweat broke out on his forehead, and his breathing was labored.

He was so beautiful. My birthday boy. Mine.

I stopped only to grab a condom from the nightstand, quickly opening it and placing it on him. I positioned myself onto his cock and slowly lowered myself onto him. I groaned when I felt him, deep and full inside of me. My clit was rubbing against the neatly groomed hair nestling his cock. This time I was the one that couldn't stop groaning and panting hard.

I moved and felt his arms on my ass again. He was kneading the muscles there and pushing me harder onto his cock. I felt his balls come in contact with me, our bodies slapping against each other, our breathing mingling. I looked at him and saw him watching me ride his cock. I moved my hand toward my clit and started rubbing, increasing the speed with which I was riding him. He slapped my butt, urging me to go faster and faster. His pelvis was rising, meeting my hips as they came down on him. We were in perfect rhythm. I continued touching my clit, watching him. He was about to cum, and that knowledge pushed me over the edge. I felt the spasms all over my body, starting in my toes and going all the way up to my head. I touched my clit one more time and came on him. My spasms must've pushed him over the edge because he called out my name and groaned loudly. I could feel him pulsing inside of me. I collapsed on his chest and felt his erratic heartbeat. He was sweaty, and I licked a bead of sweat that rolled from his neck to his chest, tasting its saltiness. He continued to whisper my name. I heard him, but at a distance because it felt like I was floating in the air, lounging on a cloud of fluff. I listened to his breathing matching my own. After a while, I heard him chuckle before speaking.

"Wow. What a way to wake up in the morning." He ran his hand from my back all the way down to my butt, before squeezing it. I giggled, feeling ticklish all of a sudden.

"You're an early riser—" I wiggled my brows at him "—so I had to get an early start on your birthday festivities." I winked at him.

I fell to the side and he moved to his side as well, so that we were both facing one another again. Just like we were before our amazing morning sex. I entwined my legs with his and embraced him. My cheeks rested against his chest. I felt his heart beat, and it hit me how much I loved him. How much I lived for him. How much he impacted my life. How much *his* heartbeat meant to *me.*

I pressed my hand against his chest, right against that beautiful, beating heart. I felt his hand enclose mine and hold me. We stayed that way for a while, soaking in this moment. Time seemed to stop for us, for this precious moment. Being this way with him felt so right. For the first time ever, I could say that I felt like I'd truly come home. This home was filled with love and acceptance and honesty and respect. It was beautiful and nourishing and soul replenishing.

I thought back to the day that Jess held me in bed, when I had my "dark nightmare" and she told me about my knight in shining armor. I guess that story wasn't a fairy tale after all. My knight was here, holding me, being my strength when I needed it and my foundation when I stood on shaky ground. And I was his. We were two pillars supporting one another, each drawing from each other's pools of strength.

My knight wasn't perfect to the average fairy-tale reader, nor did he fit the typical knight's shoes or armor. My knight had nightmares and a sad past that had left him scarred, but that was one of the reasons that made him perfect for me. I, too, had scars and a sad past. I understood him and he understood me. I thought about what Bronte once wrote, so many years ago, yet so relevant today, applying to both of us, "'He's more myself than I am. Whatever our souls are made of, his and mine are the same."

Yes, my knight and I were cut from the same cloth, and by some miracle we came together and learned to heal parts of our souls that needed it and replaced the sadness with hope and possibilities.

It couldn't be, was it?

Oh my, it was!

Was I ready to share that with him?

This realization hit me hard and strong, causing a deep throbbing in my heart, and tears filled my eyes. I had found my home, and it was in the knight's embrace. The sudden clarity should have terrified me, but it didn't because by my knight's side, I was able to conquer and slay my fears.

"I love you," I whispered so quietly that I started to wonder if he even heard it.

I had not planned on saying that, but something about his heartbeat, the way it beat against my hand, gave me the courage to say it.

It was the first time I'd ever said that to a man. The first time I'd ever said it to someone other than Jess.

I waited and didn't hear anything. He was motionless, so I stole a glance at him and saw that his eyes were closed and that he was asleep.

"I love you, my knight," I said once more, feeling more confident the second time. I kissed his lips and rolled away, heading to the shower. I was tempted to look back at him, but I didn't. I knew that I would rush back to bed and would cuddle with him when I wanted to make him some special birthday breakfast. So instead, I walked toward the bathroom with a heart filled with love, not only for myself, but for the sexy man in the bed behind me, who claimed my heart and inhabited my thoughts.

***

After the shower, I felt so good. The signs of lovemaking were washed from my body, but not my memory. I stood in his bedroom's doorway, naked and still wet from the shower, watching him sleep. Imagining how a lifetime beside him would look.

We would definitely need more furniture.

I chuckled at the directions my thoughts took me, but I couldn't say I hated that direction. In fact, I loved it and would jump at the opportunity to live with him.

Perhaps he could move into my house? It was roomier and felt lived-in. Besides his king-sized bed and the two nightstands, his room was pretty bare. There was one dresser adjacent to the bed and a small shelf on the wall, devoid of any pictures or personal objects.

We had always slept at my place or in Drew's living room, nestled on his roomy couch, but last night, he had brought me upstairs and carried me straight to his bed. I recalled how he laid me in the middle of the bed, kissing the entire length of my body, asking me to stay the night.

Last night and this morning had been amazing. When he . . .

I heard his phone ring downstairs, pulling me from my passionate thoughts, and I rushed to get it so that it did not wake him. I ran naked down the stairs and laughed at how silly I must've looked.

I grabbed the phone and answered it and heard silence on the other line.

"Hello," I said once again.

"Is this Kendrew . . . Kendrew Batten's number?" a puzzled voice asked me. It was a female voice.

"Yes, I just grabbed it for him as he is busy right now." I smiled, knowing that I had given him a pretty good workout this morning. *Focus, Kait. Focus.* "Can I give him a message?" I looked around and spotted a notepad on his kitchen table and a pencil. I grabbed both. I pulled out a chair and cringed when I sat on it with my naked body. This was so out of my comfort zone.

"Yes, can you please tell him his mother called to wish him a happy birthday."

"Of course. It's so nice to talk to you. How are you?" I asked hesitantly. I knew that Kendrew didn't talk to his mom, but maybe he would consider it again. Perhaps they could start afresh, like he and I had? Perhaps I could be the bridge that connected them once again?

"I am fine. How are you?" she asked, her voice a little surprised.

"I am great. I am about to make your son a big birthday breakfast."

"That's nice. And you are—?" her voice tapered off.

"Oh, I'm sorry. I'm Kaitlyn." I didn't know what else to say. I didn't want to say "girlfriend" without talking about that to him, so I felt like my name was sufficient enough. For now.

"Nice to meet you, Kaitlyn." Her voice sounded so sweet, though a little sad. "How is my son doing?"

"He is good, ma'am. Do you want me to go get him so you can hear from him yourself?"

"No, he wouldn't come talk to me."

"I'm sure he wo—"

"Please just tell him I said happy birthday." She paused to take a breath. I heard her voice breaking and sensed she was holding back tears. "That we all said happy birthday and that we love him."

"I will," I reassured her. "I definitely will."

"Thank you."

"I hope to meet you one day soon," I said, infusing hope into my words.

"Goodbye," was her choked response. Along with tears.

I felt tears pooling in my eyes and a feeling of being cold. I hugged myself and walked up the stairs to borrow a shirt from Drew. Mine had been ripped last night when we tried to disrobe as quickly as possible. I spotted a pant leg of my jeans peeking out from under the bed, and I pulled at it as quietly as possible. I put them on without my thong, as I didn't know where that or my bra was. Dressed only in pants, I walked over to Drew's dresser.

I felt sad after talking to Drew's mom. It was so obvious that she and Drew missed one another, but I also knew from what he had told me, that he felt guilty about the accident. I didn't know what to do for now, so I put away that phone call and focused on happier thoughts.

What would I make the man I loved for breakfast on his birthday?

I pulled open the first drawer of the dresser. It was his boxer drawer. I chuckled at the boxers with the beer bottles staring up at me.

Hadn't seen those on him yet.

I moved onto the second drawer, and that one held his socks. The third contained some T-shirts. I reached for the top one, a gray T-shirt, and felt something nestled under it. I pulled it out. It was a picture. I turned it around and found myself looking at an older man and woman with two young children in front of them. The man had his hands on the boy's shoulders, and the boy looked up at him and smiled. The woman had her hands around the little girl. It was a beautiful photo of a loving, tight-knit family. The one I had always dreamed of. I looked closer at the boy and realized it was Kendrew. If I had to guess, I would say he was about twelve or thirteen in this picture. He looked just like he did now, but only mini-sized. I smiled. He was so cute and his eyes so sparkly and loving. I would have recognized his eyes anywhere. Why didn't he have this photo hanging up? Why was it in his dresser drawer? I knew it wasn't my business, so I was about to put it away, when I noticed writing on the back. I shouldn't have looked, but a little peek wouldn't hurt, right? I mean, hopefully it would help me understand why he had hidden this picture.

> *We miss you so much. The entire family misses you, Son. Please call or visit. It would mean so much to your sister and to me. You know where to find all of us. We love you so much and always will. Please respond.*
>
> *Love,*
> *Mom*

I turned the picture over and ran my fingers over it. "Why are you holding that?" Those words delivered so coldly startled me. I dropped the picture. He was standing in front of me. I must have been so engrossed in my thoughts that I didn't hear him move from the bed. He picked up the picture, looked down at it, and then looked at me. His eyes that mere hours ago looked at me passionately were now narrowed at me and filled with deception, fury, and pain.

"I am so sorry. I was looking for a shirt. I wanted to make breakfast, and then I saw that"—I pointed to the picture—"and—"

"And you thought it was okay to look?" he interrupted me. I could tell he was upset with me.

I reached out my hand to touch his, and he pulled away from me. I flinched.

"Drew, I'm sorry. I just came across it, and being curious, I looked. I know I had no right to look at it and should have respected that you put it away for a reason. I did not go through your things intentionally. I was looking for something to wear, as my shirt is a little ripped." I smiled at him, hoping to get a smile out of him. Hoping he remembered what happened last night and into this morning. "I was borrowing a shirt and then was off to surprise you with breakfast."

"You sure surprised me." His voice was filled with venom. "There is a reason that picture is not on display . . . Why that frame on that shelf is empty." He pointed to the shelf I had looked at earlier. His hand was shaking, and I could tell he was very upset.

He did not look at me when I started to speak.

"I know I shouldn't have looked at the picture or read the back," I explained quietly, trying to get him to understand.

He gasped and turned his face toward me quickly.

"You read the back?" He glared at me, his eyes narrowing.

I could not speak. I felt like I wanted to cry, so instead I nodded my head. He cursed under his breath and walked away from me to stand at the window. I moved toward him and kissed his bare back. I felt his body tense.

"I am so sorry. I of all people know that certain things in the past are difficult to talk about, but I see your pain and I know it has to do with your family, but it can be fixed. They love you so much. Please talk to them. I want you to please try for me."

"What I want . . ." his voice was cold and taciturn ". . . is for you to leave."

"Drew . . ." I reached for him and touched his cheek.

He turned and looked me in the eyes. "Please go."

I flinched at those two words. Just last night he had whispered, "Please stay," and now he was saying, "Please go." It felt like a blow to my heart. I knew I should never have looked in his drawer. I never should have taken out anything from his drawer that wasn't a shirt, and I definitely should not have looked at the picture and read the writing on the back. I was snooping. It was a big flaw of mine, and I knew he felt betrayed, as his privacy was violated.

"I didn't go through your things intentionally. I came across it by accident. I didn't know which drawer held a shirt for me to put on, so I looked through three drawers before finding the shirt. You know I've never been in your bedroom before and didn't know where anything was," I said, trying to make him understand. "I won't do it again. I respect your privacy and trust that you will talk to me about it when you feel ready."

"This won't ever happen again. Us having sex last night was just that. Sex. A release we both needed." He gestured toward her and the rumpled bedsheets. "This does not give you a right to go through my belongings. You and I did what I've done countless times with other women. We satisfied a need, a hunger with our bodies. It was nothing else. I realize now that the only mistake I made was to bring you into my bedroom. I never did that before and I shouldn't have now," he said cruelly. My eyes filled with tears. I tried to hold them back, but what he had just said pierced my heart. It was bleeding and he didn't even care. He dismissed me, turning his back on me. He stood at the window and I could tell he did not want to see me or hear me.

I did what he had asked of me.

***

I had to leave. I was just a booty call to him. All this time I thought that what we had was different and so special, yet it wasn't. I was replaceable to him when he was one of a kind to me. I had let him inside my body after not letting anyone else since the rape. I looked at our lovemaking as healing for me, and he just saw me as a hookup. I, too, wanted to help his wounds heal, just like he did with mine. Yet he made it clear. I was another willing body . . . nothing special to him.

I was so embarrassed and on the verge of sobbing. I would not let him see that. I refused to let him see that.

Through the tears, I spotted my undies peeking out from under the pillows. I grabbed them as well as my ripped shirt. I couldn't find my shoes, but remembered leaving them in the living room, where our making out session had first started. I didn't know how I managed to see where I was going, as my eyes were filled to the brim with tears. I refused to let him see me cry. I held it together as much as I could.

I felt his eyes on me, and that hurt me more.

He was probably wondering what was taking me so long. I shuddered at how naïve I had been.

Head held high, eyes filled with tears, and heart shattered, I walked out of his bedroom and took the first steps out of his life.

I finished dressing in record speed downstairs. I grabbed my coat and stuffed my underwear in its pocket. I pulled on my shoes, and just as I was about to leave, I glanced at the phone and remembered his mom's message that I had written down. I placed the piece of paper on top of the phone so that he could easily see it. I looked past my shoulder at the living space I knew so well. My eyes roamed over the spot where I told him about my rape, the same spot where he and I first were intimate.

The memories hurt my heart and I looked away. I walked quickly toward the door, let myself out, and ran. I didn't stop running until my throat was raw and the pinch in my side was unbearable.

I held my side and felt the underwear sticking out from my coat pocket. Anger replaced the sadness and the hurt.

My M,

Laughter. What I would give to share a laugh with you, to see the sparkle in your eyes and the dimple in your cheek as you laughed. Here, laughter is scarce. War makes a person more serious, grown up. Boys become men, and their hearts forget happiness and only remember pain and sadness. Despair haunts dreams at night. You are my salvation. Every time I open your letter I feel you, I imagine your hand scraping against the paper, writing. I imagine your hand folding the paper. Your scent fills my space and brings a smile to my face. Memories take me back to a time when only love mattered. To a time where only having you in my life mattered. Now I must worry about taking care of myself and my brothers so that I can return to you. Remember, I made you a promise, and I will keep it. I will come back, and we will be together. I can't wait to see you, hold you in my arms, and kiss you. If your mother read that, she would topple over. (See, I still have the jokes in me.)

I remember the day that you so vividly painted in your last letter. I could never forget how beautiful you looked standing a few feet from me with your hair curling as rain clung to it, your eyelashes, the tip of your nose, and your lips and made its way down your body. The reason that I did not utter a single word for a good five minutes was because I was stunned by your beauty. The intensity of you. I, too, felt a piece of my soul leave me and merge with you that day. Talking was impossible at that moment, as I was having difficulty remembering to breathe.

I want to tell you something that I never told you before. Before you entered my life, my one wish was to find a girl someday who would take my breath away. Someone whose eyes I could look into and lose myself. I knew that if I ever found that girl, I would not need anything else to be happy. I would know that she was "the one." You are the one for me. My one and only. For eternity. I knew that the love we shared was special, but that day it showed me that our love was also magical. Strong enough to last through anything.

I am so glad that you love my mischievous ways. I love seeing you having fun and not being proper as your mother always demanded of you. The earth is beautiful and is meant to be experienced with all senses. I have a few new ideas and places that I want to show you when I get back. Whenever I have a free moment over here (which is scarce) and when I am unable to sleep, I sit on a little hill (yes, I have one here too; it's not as beautiful as ours, but it's still great), and I just sit on it, trying not to think. To just see and feel. Usually the rain is pouring, which actually feels good, as it is so hot here. The bad thing is that when I am soaked like that my clothing feels like a ton of bricks. It's almost impossible to stay dry here. I look at the rice dikes below and the greenery and think that this is such a beautiful country, a place that I would like to show you one day. I don't mean to sound like a pacifist, but war seems to destroy the beauty that Mother Nature took such trouble to create. I sit and follow a bird flying across the sky, unafraid of being shot, or perhaps just being very bold. I look at the rain pounding against the mud, the puddle getting deeper. The sounds of water coming in contact with rain trying to wash away the anxiety of a gunfight.

I am sorry, but I have to end this letter. We are on the move and are getting ready for combat. Remember my promise. Don't worry. Did I ever let you down yet? (I never would nor ever will!)

P.S. You are always with me. I feel your presence. It rains every day here. LOVE YOU SO MUCH.

Yours forever,
J.

Chapter Thirty-Four

Kendrew

Seeing her in pain and trying to hold back tears hurt me so much. I felt like a jerk telling her to go, but I was ashamed of what she found in that drawer. That person in that picture looking up at her was a kid filled with hope. The person standing in front of her now was hopeless. He was a man that still had nightmares of that day.

A man that hadn't seen his family since he ran from home.

A man that still harbored a broken thirteen-year-old boy inside his heart.

I knew she wasn't to blame for looking. I believed her when she said that she was looking for a shirt. I ripped her shirt last night, which made me feel even worse for overreacting, but my past always made me feel jumpy, cautious, and unsure.

I cared about Kaitlyn so much. I loved her entire body last night and into the morning hours. I cherished it and treated it like a temple. And in the blink of an eye, I turned on her, telling her I did this with women all the time.

It was true; I had only had one-night stands before her, except for Hayley, who I used to fuck every now and then, but sex with Kaitlyn went beyond sex. It was different. I bared myself to her when our bodies joined. With every kiss and touch, I told her what I couldn't with words. It was never like this for me before. When she told me she loved me, it scared the shit out of me. These feelings were brand new to me and I didn't know what to make of them.

I knew she of all people understood secrets and difficult pasts. She had never known her family and growing up in the foster home wasn't easy for her, yet she turned out to be such an incredible and strong person.

On the other hand, I had had the perfect family and managed to bring sadness and heartache to their doorstep. After I killed him, I was no longer a happy thirteen-year-old kid. I was the kid that had taken away a beloved dad and husband. My school grades suffered and I got into fights almost every day. I took my anger out on everyone and even myself on some days. I somehow made it until I turned sixteen and left home for good. That was the last time I had seen my mom and my sister.

Since running away, I had managed to keep away from people. I guarded myself as well as my heart. No one ever slept the night in my bed, and I didn't believe in cuddling or falling asleep with a woman in my arms. Most importantly, no one ever made it to my bedroom. The living room couch, the kitchen counter, the bathroom, and my car were some of the places where the magic usually happened. Never in my bedroom.

That was my space and my space alone. I did not share it with anyone.

Until Kaitlyn.

She was different. She was scarred just like me, yet she was more courageous than I ever would be. She deserved someone better. Someone who faced their past and did not run from it like I did.

That was why watching her leave my bedroom, with so much courage, broke something inside me. I wanted to be better for her. I wanted to run after her and tell her I had overexaggerated because I wasn't used to feeling or caring for another person like I did for her. I wanted to tell her that I was still a scared thirteen-year-old boy on the inside, afraid of losing someone I loved so much again.

Hearing her say those three words to me felt like heaven, but it also terrified me. She thought of me as her knight, and I wanted to be that for her, but I was scared. I never wanted to hurt her.

Am I strong enough to protect her from myself? From the fucked-up emotions coursing through me?

I wanted to go after her and tell her that although she knew about my dad's death, she didn't know that I feared love. I feared letting her down. I feared hurting her. I feared feeling.

Instead I watched her from a foggy window, running from me. It pained me knowing that I had wounded her. I stood like that for a while, watching her get smaller and smaller. When she was out of sight, I looked at the glass that was foggy from my breath. I wrote two words that I was good at uttering.

I'm sorry.

I stared at those words and angrily wiped the glass with my hand and walked away. I looked down and realized that I was still holding the picture in my left hand. I wasn't aware of that until now.

I walked to my dresser and opened the drawer. I looked down at my shirts and closed the drawer quickly. Somehow it no longer felt right for me to hide it. I walked over to my wall shelf and placed it there instead, where I could see it every day and every night.

I sat on the edge of my bed and looked at the picture of my family in its new spot. For the first time in a long time, I smiled. I knew it was her doing.

I could still smell her on my sheets.

She was everywhere.

I raced out of my room and down the stairs, where I was assaulted by even more memories of her.

I walked around and realized that her being here with me had changed this house. It made it feel like a home full of love.

She loved me.

I ran into burning buildings without fear, yet I was terrified of falling in love.

Falling in love.

I hadn't fallen in love with her, had I?

The truth was in my heart, and I heard the answer instantly.

I was *in love. I* am *in love.*

I always *would love her.*

A piece of paper by my landline phone caught my eye. I walked over to it and read it.

Your mom called when you were sleeping. I didn't want the phone to wake you, so I picked it up. She wanted to wish you a happy birthday. She also said she loved you so much.

téng **ài**

I went upstairs with the note in my hand, her beautiful cursive words looking at me, comforting me. I looked up the two words she had written on the bottom of the paper on the internet browser on my phone. The word *téng* in Chinese represented "hurt," and ài represented "love."

I felt tears fill my eyes. Kaitlyn had written two words that had such a deep meaning. It hit me straight in my heart and almost knocked me out with its force.

My mom had called, and in a brief call, Kait had seen what I had not. I was hurting my mom, who loved me and had nurtured me and always gone out of her way for me. I had stayed away and ignored her calls, tossing away her love, yet she still called and reached out to me out of love even though it must've hurt her to get no response.

My mother's love was unconditional, and it was for me, no matter how much of a jerk I was to her.

My mom was the reason I had a landline phone. When I turned twenty-one and became a firefighter, I called her from this number, knowing that she had Caller ID. All these years, she kept calling even though I never answered. I thought she hated me for what had happened, and I started to believe that story I made up, yet my mom didn't hate me. She loved me and always would. And I had hurt her in return. Just like I had Kaitlyn. It took Kaitlyn to remind me of that. I fell back on the bed, looking at my family's portrait, asking my dad in heaven for forgiveness and closure.

***

I spent the rest of my birthday in bed, overcome with emotions. I fell asleep crying, and I woke up talking to my dad before crashing yet again. The day was emotionally draining, and I welcomed my bed. No nightmares came, and I knew that she had healed me.

Her love had healed me.

I had to talk to Kait tonight and apologize for being such a jackass, but first I desperately needed a shower.

I realized I had overreacted earlier today. It was only a picture and I almost bit her head off. That same picture was proudly on display on my shelf now.

Again, thanks to Kaitlyn.

She was a special girl, and my thoughts went to her as I lathered the body wash all over my skin. I remembered her rubbing her hands all over me and tasting me with her tongue. I hardened instantly remembering her touch.

I heard the doorbell ring and cursed. I was hoping for some release in the shower.

I should've probably ignored it, but what if by some miracle it was Kaitlyn?

I shut the water off quickly and grabbed a towel, wrapping it around my waist. I looked down at the tent in the towel and hoped that it went down before I reached the door.

The bell rang again and I rushed down the stairs to open it. My mouth dropped open. I was not expecting her, of all people, to show up.

Fuck.

My precious Jim,

I don't want you to worry, but something is bothering me. I overheard my mom talking about my future, and it is so vastly different from the future I have planned in my mind. The future I want is one with you by my side, watching our children play under our tree from our front porch. My future is filled with laughter by your side and precious moments spent under a tree watching sunrises and sunsets in your loving embrace.

The future she wants for me is cold and barren. It gives me shivers. I would do everything in my power to run from her ideal life for me.

Please know that I choose you every single day. I will always choose you no matter what. You carry my heart and I yours. It beats in me. I kiss the key you made me every single morning and night. Know that my love is unending and strong like that key. Its shaped by us and no one else.

Please never doubt my love for you. I will always love you and will remind you of my love daily. No matter where I am. Know that I love you so much and that I always put you and your well-being before my own.

I love you forever and ever. I am only yours.

Mary

Chapter Thirty-Five

Kaitlyn

I was so tempted to call him all day, but I figured it would be better if we spoke face-to-face. I cared for him so much and didn't want to end our relationship like we did this morning. I knew he cared for me too; it was evident in the way he looked at me, made love to me, and shared his past with me. I remembered him taking me to his favorite mountain and how special he made me feel, even when he first tried to stay away and fight his attraction. I wasn't giving up until I had one more chance to talk to him. I felt like we both owed it to one another.

The walk toward his place took me longer than usual because I took my time and planned what I was going to say to him along the way.

As his home came into view, I stopped for a moment and closed my eyes to calm my nerves. I took a deep breath and released it. I opened my eyes and noticed a woman entering his house.

I got closer to his home and saw his blinds were open. I peeked inside, and my jaw dropped at what I saw. Kendrew was in the middle of his living room, with droplets of water cascading down his back. He had a towel wrapped around his waist. A woman stood in front of him, and before my eyes, she opened a trench coat and revealed her naked body. I saw Kendrew look down at her and quickly look away. She caressed his face and she turned his face toward her and kissed him on the mouth, rubbing her naked body all over his. His towel unraveled and fell. I felt the tears clouding my vision. I blinked them away, and even though every cell in my body was screaming for me to run, I couldn't. It was almost as if I was cemented in place. It was like déjà vu again, only this time he wasn't in the alleyway, he was in his own home. I couldn't see his face as his back was turned toward me, but I could see the passion and sultriness on the face of the woman in front of him.

I watched as Kendrew took a step back from her. I saw that his mouth was moving and she was listening to him intently. She touched his face and went to kiss him, and he turned and she caught his cheek instead. That was when I felt her eyes turn to me. She locked eyes with me for about three seconds, and then she lowered herself to her knees in front of him. I watched his head look down at her, and I turned abruptly.

I couldn't watch anymore. I had definitely seen more than enough.

I was played for a fool. I meant nothing to him.

I must have imagined him caring for me.

I was such a damn idiot.

And for the second time today, I ran as fast as my legs could carry me. Memories of the time spent with him replayed in my mind like a short film. I felt a sharp pain in my side, and this time I didn't slow down. I ran through the pain and the tears. I ran through the silly dreams and memories. I chastised myself for thinking that I could be with him. A plain girl like me with so many scars? It was a joke. He had a model with him right now. Tall, beautiful, sultry.

Everything I wasn't.

Everything I never would be.

I got to my porch and covered my face with my hands and cried, rocking myself in the chair.

I needed some time away from here, some time away from him, to forget and pretend like he and I never happened.

Should I go back to my old town?

I kept replaying him and the bombshell in his arms. It helped me pack in record speed. I didn't know where I was going or for how long, but I would figure it out tomorrow morning. I was so tired and my eyes were so puffy that I fell asleep easily, on the couch, holding my pillow to my chest, pretending it was someone else. Even after feeling so hurt and dejected, he still lived in my thoughts. And in my heart.

I woke up at 5:00 a.m. to the sound of birds, thoughts of what happened yesterday an afterthought. Thanks to those birds, I knew where I was going.

***

Anyone who saw me now could tell by the look in my eyes and the sadness in my step that I was leaving, but reluctantly. I was leaving with a heart filled to the brim with sadness and emptiness. I got on the 8:00 a.m. bus with a weekender bag slouched over my right shoulder. It was overfilled, and I leaned slightly to the side as I boarded the bus. Yet I did not buckle under. I stood proud and strong. Independent. I needed some time to be by herself. I wouldn't admit it, but I longed for the other day to be a dream. I longed for that special someone who stole my heart to run up to me and kiss me passionately. Instead, I hugged myself and reminded myself that wishes did not come true. People were never who they claimed to be, and actions and words sometimes cut deeper than the knife I once had pressed against my neck. I boarded the bus and watched as it pulled away moments later, leaving the other half of my heart in Landing Falls, with someone who didn't want it.

Problem was, I didn't know how to get it back.

He sat on his porch watching her leave. She had come by yesterday, telling him that she needed to get away for a bit. That things didn't turn out the way they should've with Drew. She said that she needed some time away from him to forget him. He listened; that was all he could do. He couldn't tell her to stay or that she would be leaving her heart behind, that running from him wouldn't work. Those two were meant for one another, but he sat silent.

Sometimes we need to go on our own journey to find out who we truly are.

He held the key in his hand before kissing it, imagining he was kissing her lips. He ran his fingers across the initials and smiled.

"She will come back, my love. I know she will," he whispered. "She just needs to go on this journey to find herself for a little bit. I don't blame her. She found out some serious information recently, and there is more that she will find out soon."

The potent scent of magnolias surrounded him.

Chapter Thirty-Six

Kaitlyn

The church was on the smaller side, a dark stone building with a round window with the mosaic of Jesus on the cross looking at me. I walked the little path and stood in front of the house attached to the church, which I guessed was the rectory. I looked around and debated whether I should ring the bell or leave. I walked away from the door and walked to the back of the church where there was a small garden. I walked across the labyrinth-like stone walkway and took in my surroundings and felt comfortable yet uneasy here.

I was so deep in my thoughts that I did not even notice the gentleman's voice ask me who I was looking for. He was about sixty years old. His hair was still a dark black with a couple of gray hairs by his temples. He was dressed in black pants and a black shirt. He was carrying a bag of potting soil in his hands. He looked at me as if trying to figure out if he knew me, and if he did, from where. He seemed like the serious type, but I had a feeling that once he smiled, his face became friendly and his demeanor welcoming. He was a handsome man as well. He stood at about six feet tall and was average shaped with broad shoulders. I figured that he must be the groundskeeper, and I smiled at him.

"I was told that I could find Father John here," I said.

"You can," he said, slowly looking at me more intently now.

"Perhaps you can show me the way to him." I was a little taken aback by his strange behavior. "I would be grateful," I said as he just kept looking at me. I looked around and watched as he shook his head gently.

"Excuse me," he said softly. "I'm so sorry for not being present there for a moment. You just seemed so familiar." He reached out his hand to shake mine. "I am Father John."

"Nice to meet you, Father. I am sorry to interrupt. I just wanted to pay you a visit in person, especially after receiving a Christmas card from you." I looked at him and watched as his eyes widened and understanding dawned on him.

He took a deep breath and faced me. "You're her granddaughter?" He meant it more as a fact than a question. In fact, he did not wait for my response. He took me by the arm and steered me toward the rectory. "Come. We will talk. How does a cup of hot tea sound to you with gingersnap cookies?"

"I would like that very much, Father. I have a few questions to ask you, and hopefully you can answer them for me. But can you please make it a cup of coffee instead?"

"Of course," he said. "You know, your grandmother preferred coffee over tea too." We walked inside and made our way to the kitchen. He started making the coffee in silence, staring blanking at the wall as if deep in thought.

"Father, I was a wicked mother. I was the problem. It was all my fault." Her words were muffled as tears and sad cries impaired her speech. I instinctively grabbed her hand, trying to comfort and calm her.

"Back then you thought you were helping her. Sometimes one crosses the line. You crossed the line far too often, I must say." I chuckled and she sent me a look through narrowed eyes and pursed lips. "Don't deny it. You know it's true. Just like you know that the past cannot be changed. You can only make sure that you do not repeat the mistakes of the past by leaving things with your granddaughter just as they are."

"If only I could . . ." her voice choked and she whispered, "I would." Her hand trembled and I rubbed it, trying to warm her hand yet knowing she did not tremble from being cold. I had to find a way to warm her heart. I once had, but not enough. If I had done my job properly Amelia would have reunited with her granddaughter years ago.

"I will tell you what I should have told you years ago. Tell her the truth. She deserves to know – " I paused momentarily before finishing my sentence with finality " – everything."

"She will hate me," she said, pain hosting itself on her face momentarily.

"At least she would know who to hate and the reason for hating you."

"I can't live knowing she despises me. My name would sound like a curse coming from her lips. She would damn me to hell."

"I think you are doing a good job of that yourself," I said honestly, and she glared at me. "Now calm down. I can find her and bring her to you. Don't get upset. I will bring you some tea to calm your nerves."

"No," she barked out.

"No?" I asked, and she shook her head. "No to what?"

"All three," she said, tears filling her eyes.

"The doctor said – "

She interrupted me. "I am dying. I have been dying for years now. The doctor saying it does not change a damn thing." Cynicism and anger replaced the sadness and tears from just moments ago. "If you want to kill me, you go right ahead and bring me a cup of tea. Otherwise, I want a strong cup of coffee. Black."

"I'm sorry. My mistake. But don't change the subject." I pointed my finger at her. "You know that you don't want to go this way. I know that you cannot rest peacefully until you have told her everything. I know all this just as I know that I am a priest." My eyes nailed her.

She nodded her head in agreement. "You do know me so well. You always did." Tears pooled in her eyes and she looked down. "Except when it comes to tea. You know I'm not a tea drinker." She wiped her cheek with her free hand and managed a smile.

"Please. Tell her." I gave her hand a slight squeeze and headed for the door.

"Can you bring me a pen and some paper with that cup of coffee?" she said in a confident voice. There was a hint of excitement in it as well.

I turned around and smiled as tears made a trail down my right cheek.

After the coffee stopped dripping, Father John seemed to return to the present. He poured the coffee into two mugs and placed several cookies on a plate on a large tray. He turned back toward me, smiling. We sat down at the kitchen table.

"Your grandmother was certain that you would come here," he said.

"How did she know?"

"I'm not quite sure. She left you something in my safekeeping. I wanted to send it to you, but she made me promise not to. She asked me to send you a Christmas card, and she was certain you would come on your own when you were ready." He looked at me. "I think it is time for me to get it."

I nodded my head in agreement and watched him walk away. I heard his footsteps going up the stairs, and moment later, I heard them coming down again.

I was anxious to see what he had for me. What my grandmother had left for me.

He was a few feet from me, and I turned around and watched him. He was carrying a small wooden box in his hands, which he placed in front of me.

I touched it and was about to open it, when I pulled my hand back. I was terrified what a little box like this might contain.

He placed his hand over mine, encouraging me to go ahead and open it. I looked at his hand and then up at him. He was comforting, and I felt his strength seep into me, making me that much stronger. He moved his hand, and I took a deep breath and opened the box.

I looked inside and found yellowed letters. Almost similar to the ones I already possessed. Only I had a feeling these letters filled in a few more gaps.

I took the first letter out and skimmed it. I saw that Father John was mentioned in the letter, so I decided to read it aloud.

Dearest Grandchild,

"The moment I understood love was the moment I cried and you wiped my tears. I fell and you picked me up. I pushed you away, yet you stayed."

My mother used to always have that special saying. It was her favorite. I was never there to wipe your tears, nor did I pick you up when you had fallen on the cold, hard ground. I was scared of being near you. I was terrified that when you found out how your mother died and why it was my fault, you would hate me with a fervor. So instead I went on with my life, pushing you to the back of my mind. There were some days that you would pop up and I would imagine what you were doing. Then there were days that I felt you crying, and a couple of times I grabbed my keys and jumped in my car, only to break down and sit in the car, immobilized. I could not move, I could not even think of the reason that I was in my car in the first place. I did not mind when I blacked out like that because at least I forgot about you in those few precious moments. You also haunted my dreams at night. It got to the point where I would not sleep at night, only during the day, and only when other people, like my housekeepers, were around.

I don't know what hurt me the most. The fact that I gave you away or the fact that my daughter killed herself because of me. I still don't know what pain is worse—losing a daughter because of my actions or losing a granddaughter because of my choices. I once tried to answer that question, and I made a list. I was upset and overcome by chronic sadness and could not believe my eyes at what I wrote. I always knew that I was stern, but I didn't realize how wicked I was until the list stared me in my eyes. The list I wrote with my own hand. The same list that was supposed to help me answer a question that nagged me. I will not tell you the outcome because you would hate me. Your mother would hate me. Who would hate me more? I think God only knows.

Funny that I mention God. I stopped believing in him ages ago. I blamed him for giving me the free will to do the stupid things in life. I blamed him for not guiding me. For not blessing me with a heart. It made me feel a little better sometimes that what I did was predestined. I even talked myself into believing that God wanted me to give you up. I held these beliefs for years until I ran into a priest who changed my life. I rejected religion yet found myself leaning on a man of God. I don't know what it was about him, but he gave me the strength to go on. He made me question all the wrongs of the past. He reconnected me with my soul and reintroduced me to the church. As I would sit in the last row in church, in the darkness, I would marvel at him saying mass, illuminated in the light. He became my salvation.

Before I met him, I was on a dark lonely road and I was lost. In my darkest moment, he reached out his hand and saved me. He paved a new road for me, one that was well lit. I remember the first steps I took on that road. My feet were shaking but he urged me forward. He said, "I am with you. I will catch you should you fall." I remember our conversations like they happened yesterday. When he was transferred to a different parish, miles and miles away from me, we would still keep in touch, but it was no longer the same.

I always wondered why he entered my life when he did. He also was the one who urged me to find you and tell you all of this. He said, "God has a plan for you and soon he will call you to him so that he can examine your life and what you did on your temporary journey on earth. Make sure you tell your granddaughter about your hardships, about the shaky ground you were stomping when you gave her up. Make her understand. Make her forgive you." I remember laughing and then regretting it. The coughing fit that followed left me breathless and weak. He passed me a glass of water and said, "She should be near you." I remember answering him, "Just like I was near her." I was full of venom again. I knew I was dying and that my secret would die with me. He looked at me and grabbed hold of my hand and said, "All those years ago, God sent me to you so that I could help you find your way. I was meant to be the shepherd that finds the lost sheep. The moment I found you and led you the green pastures and running water, I was sent on another mission. Your soul was on the way to being healed and your heart was beating once again. All these years later, I am sent to you again so that I can lead you on the right path once again. Please let her know. She deserves it."

I knew that I would listen to him. At that moment, he could have asked me for all the stars in the galaxy and I would have gathered them and laid them at his feet. I knew that what he was saying was true. I was dying, and I still had a few moments granted to me from God to right a couple of wrongs. I looked into the eyes of the one man I trusted and asked him one question: "Why?"

The why stood for so many things. Why did I attempt to live my daughter's life for her? Why did I choose who she was to love for her? Why didn't I accept him? Why did she kill herself? Why did I give you up so easily? Why did I stay away from you? Why did I lose my way? Why did I not listen to the one person who tried to save me all those years ago? Why? Why? Why?

"Sometimes we do not understand the will of God, but in the end, we know that the path he has chosen for us is the good path."

Until this day, I am not sure if I voiced the questions out loud or if he was somehow able to read my mind. I remember feeling awkward as I listened to him continue. He walked over to the fireplace in my bedroom. I stared at him and wiped tears that fell from my eyes. I never knew when I fell in love with him. I knew it was wrong, but I couldn't help my heart. He stared into the fire for the longest time, and my breathing got labored. The heat in the room started to engulf me. I felt that this was me foreseeing hell. I knew what direction I was heading after I died, and the thought made me feel bad. I was surprised to find myself wanting to right all the wrongs so that the man standing in front of me with his back turned looking into the fire could one day stand in front of my tombstone praying for me with his head and eyes raised to the skies as I look down at him and smile. He started talking again.

"Sometimes we meet certain people for a reason. I know why I was meant to meet you. All this time you thought that I helped you, but you helped me immensely. I was on the road to leaving the church when I met you. I took you as a sign that God wanted me to stay and help people."

He turned around and walked over to me. I extended my hand and he took it. For all that heat in the room, my hands were cold, and he shivered.

I looked him deep in the eyes. "Father, I would like you to listen to my confession, please. My last confession."

He sat down, anticipating my confession to be long. He sat hunched over me listening to my whispered story that I called my last confession. Then after he absolved me from my sins, I noticed tears in his eyes. He said the rest was in God's hands now. I gathered the letters that I wrote to you but never sent you. I was preparing them for your eyes. After that I wrote my will. I asked him to send you a Christmas card and to also make sure you got the house and the other letters.

As for this letter, that you are reading now, I wanted him to give it to you personally. There is one more letter underneath this one. It contains something I would like you to give back to him. It's your mother's key. There is also another letter that will answer all your questions. It's a special letter. I wouldn't give it to anyone but you.

My darling, please thank Father John for me again. Please tell him I was a better person those last months with his help. That I wrote the will and these letters only because of him. He gave my life meaning and purpose, and I owe him a great debt. He showed me what it meant to have a heart again.

I love you always,

Amelia

I looked up and through the tears in my eyes saw that Father John was wiping his eyes as well. This time I reached out and held his hand. I could feel his hand shaking and I slowly rubbed it.

"Thank you for being with her those last few weeks," I said softly.

"Given a choice, I would have done it over and over again." He looked at me, more tears falling down his cheeks. "She was a troubled woman who realized her mistakes a little too late."

I watched him take out a handkerchief and wipe his tear-stained cheeks with it before looking back at me.

I was filled with so much emotion reading my grandmother's letter. But with a better understanding of who she was, there was still so much I didn't know.

"Can you tell me more about her, about how she passed and when . . . ?" My voice trailed off. I felt tears coming into my eyes again, and I halted them.

He nodded his head before whispering.

"The day that she was dying, her housekeeper ran over to get me." He took a deep breath before continuing. "I came to her side right away. She asked me to pray for her after her death. I knew her story. I knew what she was scared of and what she lived for. I also knew her deepest and darkest secrets as her confessor." He looked at me, tears puddling in his eyes. "I also knew that she loved you with all of her heart. That she was scared that you would hate her. She was a tough woman but very fragile when it came to her daughter and granddaughter. She was raised tough and wanted to make you tough for the world."

"Thank you, Father, for telling me this. I understand her and I forgive her. I understand . . . I love her." I could barely speak. I was choking back tears and thinking about my mom and grandma and wishing they were here now.

"She was an amazing woman," Father John said, looking past me, almost as if remembering Amelia. "Misguided, but in the end, she got everything off her chest. Her words still live on in me, and her last confession was a model one. If only others faced death as prepared as she was."

"Thank you so much for saving these letters for me," I whispered. I got up and walked over to him to hug him. He hugged me, and I could feel him crying. I was on the verge of crying too, so I changed the subject. I pointed to the box. "I will cherish them."

He pulled back and looked at me. "Don't forget, there is one more letter in there. Your grandmother cherished that letter, and she wanted you to have it. She always told me that she was keeping it safe for you until you could have it."

I nodded and smiled, thanking him once again, before stepping outside, into the fresh air. I welcomed the breeze against my wet, tear-stained cheeks.

I looked back at the door and saw Father John watching me. I waved and walked away, pondering how I would find the strength to read my mom's letter. I'm not going to lie, I was scared to open it.

***

As I walked away from St. Lucy's church, I found myself struggling to breathe. Emotions were overwhelming me.

I had so many questions and nowhere to go. I walked around the town aimlessly, until I found a bench in the park to sit on. In that moment, with the sun setting, I finally found the courage to open the letter. To my surprise, it was another letter from my grandmother, and I wasn't expecting that.

Dearest Granddaughter,

This is my last letter to you. I promised myself I would write you every year on your birthday, but that did not happen. My health did not permit it. I could have asked someone to write it for me, but that would be wrong. This is my story to tell to you although the word story does not quite fit. This isn't really a story, it's your life. This letter is part two of my confession. The priest just listened to my first confession, and now it is time for me to purge my soul in this letter, for you. I find my health is leaving me rapidly and I am on the verge of death, but today I feel I was gifted my last strength to tell you everything before I die.

There was a beautiful girl who was seventeen years old. She was a true beauty, with a heart of gold. She loved everyone and all animals and she never believed badly about another person. Many men vied for her attention, but she had eyes for one boy who her mother did not approve of. The mother had her daughter attend extravagant balls and dinner parties. There was one boy that she liked for her daughter. His name was Thomas. He was the son of an affluent business owner. He was twenty-three. He loved her daughter very much and would act like her shadow. He laughed at her deep relationship with the poor boy and called her childish for standing up for him so many times.

When Thomas leaned in to kiss her one night, she pushed him away. He only laughed and said he would be patient a while longer. He lasted a mere twenty seconds before he started at it again. This time, he did not hear her frantic no. ***He kissed her, but not like a man kisses a woman he loves. There was nothing gentle or sweet about him. He crushed her with his lips and his body, and she could barely breathe. She cried and he laughed. She cried for nine months after that. Until she could not bear it any longer and she took her own life at the magnolia tree.***

That was her special place with him. The place she and the poor boy fell in love and would meet.

The day she died, I found a letter she had addressed to you, under your pillow. I have never opened it. I did not think it would be right to do so. I was the reason she took her own life. I did have moments where I wanted to destroy her letter out of fear of what my daughter, your mother, said about me. I know she must have hated me in the end. I was the reason her life turned upside down. I took her plans and her dreams from her. She never even told anyone what she named you, so I came up with Kaitlyn when I brought you over to the Stones. That letter is in my home, behind a painting. You'll find it; just look for a painting of the beautiful hills and the magnolia tree in the springtime.

You deserve to hear her voice through her words. She had such a beautiful voice . . .

Hopefully, now you understand why your mother did what she did, and why I couldn't raise you. Or see you, for that matter. I was the reason she was dead. I pushed Thomas on her and she was physically, emotionally, and spiritually scarred as a result. She blamed me through her entire pregnancy, but never with words. She spoke no word since the day she was attacked, until that last time I saw her. Even giving birth to you, she was silent. How much she must have hurt (both physically but also emotionally) to not utter a moan or cry.

Why couldn't I accept her choice? Why couldn't I accept the love of her life? He was and is an amazing person. I now know I made a huge mistake. It is too late, but I can try to fix it. They both taught me that love is not measured in dollars but by butterflies in the stomach and tingles when two lips meet.

Why did I have to force her to entertain Thomas? I can't . . . it still hurts after all these years . . . one never forgets the death of their own child . . . it shouldn't have happened that way, but it did . . . I . . . can't do this . . . I'm sorry.

The last words were very crooked and hardly legible. My grandmother's last letter written with her last ounce of strength.

As much as I wanted to rush back home and read my mom's letters, I couldn't. I wasn't ready to see Kendrew again. My heart couldn't take it. I'd lived for so many years without knowing my past. I could live a little longer without that knowledge.

I decide to stay here, in Hope Falls for a while. Until the time was right for me to return.

Tears cascaded down my face.

One leaf falls from a tree.

Soon another follows.

Landing on top of the other leaf.

Shielding it.

Fitting together perfectly.

As one.

He sat by her grave, his body shivering from the cold, but he did not feel it. It was during the cooler nights that he wished to be by her side, to comfort her, to keep her warm. He knew that he should be heading home soon, but he felt so at home next to her, his hand on the cold marble, his voice trying to soothe her with a voice so familiar to her. A voice that talked to her every day. A voice that would never let her go.

The sound of a distant dog's barking transported him back to the present. He got up and ran his hand through the engraving on the tombstone, the same way he used to brush her hair with his fingertips. He smiled, and before walking away, whispered the same words he had for years. The wind seemed to carry his melodic voice and amplify softly the lyrical whisper. The words, "I love you wholly fully and deeply, forever," accompanied him home along with the scent of magnolias. Always magnolias.

Chapter Thirty-Seven

Kendrew

"Fuck me," I grunted, rolling over in my bed. I had a massive headache.

Last night was a night I hoped to forget. I had plans to go see Kaitlyn and apologize and tell her how I felt, and I was set on doing that after my shower. In fact, when I heard the doorbell, I ran out of the shower, thinking it was her.

I hoped it was her.

I wanted it to be her.

I needed it to be her.

It wasn't. Fuck. Fuck. Fuck.

I was beyond surprised when I opened the door to find Hayley instead.

She came inside and saw me in my towel and dropped her coat before I knew what was happening.

I shouldn't have been surprised. She had always come and gone as she pleased and done this whenever she wanted some sex. I had always liked it. Except now. I wasn't the same person I was a few weeks ago.

I was falling in love, and the only person I wanted to see naked in my house was Kaitlyn.

In fact, she was the only person I ever wanted to see naked.

Surprisingly, that did not scare me. She was special and made me feel special too.

She made me feel like I could move on from my past and build a future with her. Kaitlyn, a girl with barely a past, taught me to dream of the present and to lay foundations for the future. She taught me to live in the moment. To cherish every moment and not regret anything that you couldn't change.

As Hayley showed me her naked body, I quickly glanced down and thought of Kaitlyn right away, and I knew I couldn't do this with her. My body was not reacting to her at all, and right then and there, I knew I was in love with Kaitlyn, and I fucking loved that feeling.

Just moments before I was hard in the shower, thinking about Kaitlyn, yet felt myself go limp in front of a naked, sexy woman. I was about to tell her to leave, when she put her hands on the sides of my face and kissed me.

I looked for the heat to return, and instead I felt uncomfortable and like I was cheating on Kait.

She started rubbing herself against me. Nipples to nipples and my towel came undone.

I pushed away from her and told her to stop.

She looked at me for a moment and then tried to kiss me again. I moved my face and she got my cheek. I told her I was seeing someone and that we couldn't do this.

I felt her freeze up and gasp.

She said she understood and looked in the direction of my windows, before kneeling down to get her coat and give me my towel back. I watched her as she did that. As she stood before me, wrapped in her trench again, she told me something that really struck a chord with me.

I kept replaying her words over and over again.

"She must be special for you to give up your bachelor ways."

"She is," I told her. "She is everything to me."

"Why, Kenny dear, did you fall in love with her?" she asked in a teasing tone.

I thought about Kaitlyn and smiled. "How could I not? She is everything I ever wanted and yet told myself I didn't deserve. She and I connected from day one and I fought it hard. Yet nothing has ever felt so right to me than when I am with her." I looked at Hayley, and she had tears in her eyes.

"I never thought it would happen, but it looks like it did." She touched my arm. "But if you don't work out, call me. We always had amazing sex, baby."

I would never call her. In fact, I would do everything in my power to show Kaitlyn the depth and intensity of my love for her.

I touched Hayley's arm and led her away, toward the door, and out of my life. Out of the life that I knew before Kaitlyn. A life that seemed full of numerous fun, gorgeous women and great sex, but in reality was empty. With Kaitlyn, I had fun, beauty, brains, a compassionate heart, the best sex ever, passion, and deep love. The kind that embeds itself deep in your heart and grows stronger daily.

"Take care of yourself . . ."

"You too. Remember what I said."

"Goodbye." I looked her straight in the eye. That was me telling her it was over. Telling her to no longer drop in like that. When I said goodbye, I meant it.

I closed the door and headed to the liquor cabinet. I thought about the fact that I had fallen in love with a girl so unlike anyone I had ever known. She had taken my heart, and I didn't realize it until another woman stood before me, naked, and I didn't feel anything for her.

I realized I should have gone to see Kaitlyn right after telling Hayley goodbye and talked to her, but this realization had rocked me to the core. It was scary to care for someone like I cared for her.

It took someone who I used to have casual sex with to really open my eyes about how I felt about Lynnie.

I needed a drink or two to calm the nerves before I saw Kaitlyn.

Going to see her now would be different. I would no longer be looking at her as a bachelor who likes a pretty girl, but as a man who had fallen hopelessly and deeply in love with a woman for her heart, her personality, her smile, her charm, her entire being.

I was madly in love and I couldn't even tell you when it happened or how long I had been suppressing this information. It no longer mattered. All that mattered was that I loved a woman who loved me too.

I took the bottle to my bedroom and thought about how my life had changed since I met Kaitlyn.

I would go see her tomorrow and tell her everything.

I needed tonight with my newfound feelings and this bottle of whiskey.

Fuck me, I had fallen in love and loved it!

***

Knock, knock.

No response. I put down the large parcel in my hand. It was my gift for her. I was ready to tell her I wanted a future with her, that I wanted to be with her, always. I walked down the steps and looked up at the windows, trying to spot any movement. I didn't see anything. Most importantly, I didn't see her. I walked around the house, gently knocking on the windows that I could reach on the first floor.

Nothing.

"Kaitlyn," I yelled softly, walking toward the front of the house. It was still 10:00 a.m. I didn't want to wake up any late-morning risers. I originally had had plans to come see her yesterday morning, but there was an emergency and I had to go in to work. I had finished my shift early this morning and showered and grabbed the parcel and ran to Kaitlyn's. I needed to see her, and I started to feel dread filling me. Something felt off, like I was missing something.

I ran up the stairs once more and knocked louder. Despair and anguish were filling my body. I felt unlike myself and I couldn't explain it. All I knew was that I had royally fucked up and I hoped Kaitlyn would hear me out. I knew that I had acted like a complete ass with her the other day, saying things that I truly did not mean.

What if I had lost her for good?

I could not suppress the shudders that moved across my entire body, so I knocked harder and louder until my knuckles hurt. I alternated between knocking, smacking my palm against the door, and gently kicking it with my foot.

After what felt like hours, but was probably closer to five minutes, I heard someone shout my name.

I turned toward the voice that was coming from behind me, from across the street. From Shelby.

"She's not there," Shelby shouted. She was standing in her doorway, one foot crossing the threshold of her door, the other foot safely inside her cocoon.

I darted across the street and stood on Shelby's first step. I was looking up at her, waiting for her to say something more, but she didn't. She just looked at me, and I noticed her eyes going toward the large parcel leaning against Kaitlyn's door.

"Is she working?" I stammered. My heart felt like it was beating a mile a minute.

"No," she said flatly. "Harold is done with his treatment, so Irma is back at the shop full time . . ." Her voice tapered off.

"Do you know where I could find her?" I asked, hating the desperate tone to my voice.

"I don't think she wants to be found," she said, her eyes challenging me.

"I messed up, Miss Shelby." My eyes were pleading with hers. "I need to apologize and tell her how I feel."

"A day and two hours too late," she replied cryptically.

"Where is she?" I demanded.

"Gone," she said sadly.

"Gone," I repeated.

Gone. Gone. Gone.

Oh my god. She was gone.

"Gone where?"

"Didn't say, but she looked very hurt. She took some belongings with her and boarded a bus this morning." Shelby was looking at me. I could feel her dissecting me.

"She left for good?" I asked, disbelieving. "What about her home?" He gestured toward the home.

Shelby shrugged her shoulders. I looked at her with despair on my face and I felt the burning in my eyes.

I was crying. I hadn't cried like this since my dad died.

"I love her," I whispered, my voice breaking with emotions that I was trying to hold in. I felt a sob escape and I covered it with a cough.

I looked at Shelby, and I saw a knowing look on her face. "I believe you."

"She thinks . . ." I started and couldn't finish the sentence. *She thinks I used her because I was a jerk and said cruel things out of hurt.* I couldn't say that aloud though because I was too ashamed of myself. "I will win her back. I will search every town if I have to, I will."

I felt a touch on my arm. I looked down and saw Shelby's wrinkled and pale fingers on the tanned skin of my right arm. She had crossed the distance to me without me noticing because I was so wrapped up in plans about how I would win Kait back and where I would begin my search.

This woman, who I had known for years, had never taken more than a step outside of her door, yet here she was, crossing her line of comfort and safety to reach me, knowing I needed her this very moment. I put my left arm on top of hers, thanking her in my own silent way, knowing how much stepping outside cost her.

"I will find her, Shelby. I will," I promised her, and I watched her shake her head.

"No," she said.

No?

I looked at her with sadness and anger mixing with despair, unable to speak momentarily.

"She needs to go on this journey alone." She looked at me, a serious expression on her face. "Accompany her. Talk to her every morning you wake up and every night. Talk to her soul. Speak to her and tell her everything, but leave her to find the answers she needs now."

"But I need her to know I didn't mean what I said," I pleaded with her.

"Deep down, I think she knows." She looked at me. "Anything you tell her now, she won't believe. So instead show her." She smiled. I tried to speak and she shushed me. "Be the best man you can be so that when she comes back"—she looks me straight in my eyes now—"and I know she will, she will pick you all over again."

I didn't know what to make of her advice. Did I leave her and listen to Shelby, or did I fight for her?

Shelby must've seen the struggle inside of me on display on my face. "It won't be easy, but true love never is. It's messy and complicated and has its many tests. It's how you survive those tests and tribulations that determines how true and grand the love is. For true love, even with physical distance, never withers away. It lives in you. In your heart." I watched Shelby touch her chest.

I shook my head. "I need to explain how wrong—"

"She made me promise to not tell you where she was, and I never break a promise." She looked at me, and I felt myself going pale before her eyes. I felt lightheaded. Would I ever see her again? Did she hate me so much that she would leave for good?

"She said she needed to be alone right now." She stopped and continued after a moment of silence. "She didn't think you would come looking for her, but I asked what I should say in case you did come. She said to tell you that you got your wish," she said sadly.

I felt my legs buckling under me and grabbed the porch's banister. Shelby watched me and didn't say anything.

I nodded my head, her words sinking in.

I could not speak. My tongue was lead and I felt sick to my stomach.

I glanced at her home and saw the gift I had brought for her.

Nothing mattered anymore. She was gone and it was my fuckin fault.

I had asked her to leave. I had *wished* for her to leave.

"Congratulations, Kendrew. Yeah, your wish came true," I muttered under my breath, unable to look at Shelby. I turned away from her and jogged toward the parcel. I threw it across the yard. I walked toward it and I stomped on it and broke it until all I had were little pieces of wood and irreparable canvas scattered on the ground around me. I walked away, head down and shoulders slumped, putting distance between myself and the destroyed remnants of the happy couple dancing in the rain. I felt destroyed, just like the painting, my heart ripped into pieces.

There would be no more dancing. No more happiness. Just dark, dreary days.

Without her.

My love.

***

I battled a three-alarm fire yesterday. It was the worst fire our department had ever seen. It spread quickly, and unfortunately three lives were lost. Two children, ages two and five, and their grandfather lost their lives. It broke my heart. Why did innocent people die when scum like me got to live? I almost didn't make it out. It wasn't that I couldn't get out; a part of me didn't want to get out. I was now on a forced vacation. My captain made me take as much time as I needed and told me not to come back until I resolved whatever issue I was dealing with. I laughed out loud, and if he wasn't my friend, I don't think he would have been as understanding. He knew what I went through in the past and what I lost just recently. He knew and he understood. He too lost a child a few years back in a skiing accident. He turned to the bottle and did reckless things like running into a house on fire without a plan. He and I are so alike, and I think that's where the friendship and extreme respect for one another came in.

I remembered that moment vividly. The heat and thick smoke engulfing me, and me not paying any attention to that. I remembered pressing forward. I had to get the bodies out. I had to save the bodies. I would not let the flames take them. I was ready for them to take me instead. I was living in hell already every day, so I felt it was a fitting way to go. At least I thought so. I thought that the flames could somehow cleanse me of my past sins and what I had done. I felt like, perhaps, if I went out this way, that my obituary would say, "He died trying to get bodies out of a fire," and not, "He died of a broken heart, a broken man, scared of his reflection."

The flames had no reflection. I would not die seeing what a coward I was. I would die trying to help. I could not stand back and relive what happened so many years ago. I could not stand back and watch death come while I stayed back and clutched my cat. I was a little boy again in that moment, only this time I made a choice to go out not by standing and watching, but by going in, even against orders.

After the fire, Trent and Jim came to visit me at home. I wasn't speaking, but they sat with me in silence for a while. After they left, I found the journal that Jim had left me.

"Write to her; write to yourself. Write to whoever helps. Get what you are feeling out. Remember that true love never dissipates. Let her know how you feel. Write and believe in what you feel, son."

The last thing I wanted to do was write to her, but I figured I would give it a try.

Dad,

Her scent was everywhere. On my pillow. On my clothes. It haunted me in my waking hours, and don't even get me started about what it did at night. She always came to me at night. With that look on her face, that look of sadness, that look of a person that just found out they weren't loved by the one they had given their heart and soul and entire being to. I wish she knew . . . I wish she knew how much I loved her.

Drew

Dear journal,

I found her scarf under my bed. I fall asleep holding it daily. Every morning I lay it out to dry. I stare at the path my tears take every night on the gray material.

I'm scared to wash it.

Scared to lose her scent and terrified of the day when it is no longer there.

I fear it might be soon.

It's been forty-three days.

I told you all once before, and I will say it again. I was a coward and do not want to be one anymore.

D.

My love,

Is everything okay? I haven't heard from you in a while. I hope you are not mad. I haven't been able to write, as loss hit close to home. Matthew died. It should have been me, but he always was a better man.

I was unable to do anything after his death, but I had to. I became a robot, unfeeling and closed off. He was my best friend. My brother. And now he is gone. I can't imagine how Shelby feels right now. How you feel.

I can't even talk about him without breaking down, so I will change the subject and we will talk about him when I return. I will return. I have to. He made sure I survived, and I'm not going to let him or you down.

I love you my lovely and fiery gal.

Forever and always,

J.

Chapter Thirty-Eight

Kendrew

It was pouring today. I couldn't help remembering my favorite rain memory with her. I remembered it as if it was just yesterday. I remembered the cold and the passion, the intense freedom a thunderstorm affords a soul. For just like a cloud, I was dark and carried all this darkness in me that I needed to let pour out. Intensity followed by a peaceful calmness.

Dark clouds loomed ahead. It was quite beautiful. Half the town was light, the other dark as night, thanks to the storm clouds overhead.

"Let's hurry. It's going to pour," I said.

She grabbed my hand and teased. "So what! You're not scared of a little rain, are you?"

"It'll be more than a little. It looks like it will be an absolute downpour." I hugged her and whispered in her ear, "Maybe I should check on the ark just in case?"

We both burst out laughing.

"Hmm . . . do you have a pair of animals ready?"

"Well, no." I seriously pondered her question. "Now that I think about it, I have a shelter, but nothing to put in it."

"Not quite Noah's ark then, huh?" she teased.

"Nooooo, but then again. I am not really a Noah. You know, his style isn't really my style."

She could not stop laughing.

"So far I only have me, but I have an idea of who I want in it besides me." I leaned in and pulled her close and kissed her passionately, leaving her wide-eyed and gasping for breath. I could not stop the kisses, even as the rain started pounding hard against the pavement. We were soaked to

the bone and she grabbed my hand and we ran in the rain, stopping every now and then and jumping in puddles. We were so happy, like teenagers that were giddy and in love.

"Shall we go to my ark, madam?" I asked her after jumping into a puddle and splashing her. I approached her, smiling, and lovingly embraced her.

"No rush," she said. "This right here is all the shelter I need."

Rain plastered our hair to our faces, and our clothes were like our second skin.

Looking back, I now knew that the moment we played in the rain was the moment that I fell in love with her. Hair wet. Clothes drenched. Eyes sparkling and her lips red from my kisses. It was almost as if Kaitlyn, combined with the rain, had saved me.

As I held onto her, with the rain falling around me, I felt myself move. She responded, and before we knew it we were dancing. In that moment, I remembered the painting I had seen in Jim's store, the one I had purchased for my home, of the couple dancing in the rain.

That day, the painting had reminded me of something, and I couldn't quite place my finger on what that was. Now I knew. It reminded me of this moment. The painting, circa 1934, captured a moment of my future. The foreshadowing gave me goose bumps, and the woman against me drove them away with the heat of her body pressed into me.

She and I were one. We were at peace just like that couple in the painting.

We had gone back inside and I had cherished her body, but I could not stop the worrying from keeping me awake.

Just like that day holding the painting, I had known that something else was hidden from me. I could not pinpoint it, yet I knew it was coming, and somehow I knew that it would try to bulldoze everything I'd built. This ill-boding feeling had terrified me, so I had hugged Kaitlyn harder, replaying the dance she and I shared in the rain, trying not to let this feeling destroy the loving and beautiful moment we had shared.

I had watched her smile in her sleep, and I leaned down to kiss her lips. She mumbled something, and I reached out my hand to touch hers, entwining our fingers. I vowed to not let anyone or anything get in the way of us.

Yet I knew I couldn't stop this vision I was having of a couple dancing in the rain, oblivious to the floodwater heading their way at a rapid speed, ready to take them underwater with its vigor. I held Kaitlyn's hand and promised her I would never let her go, yet that vision foretold what I was feeling inside. That vision haunted me, and it was worse than my nightmares. In my nightmare, I knew what to expect. The same script replayed on a nightly basis. This, however, was unknown. I didn't know what to expect, but I did know that this feeling, this sense of coming, was ridiculing me.

***

"Stay just like that, don't move." My breathy command caressed her ear and I saw goose bumps appear on her neck and arms. Instinctively she moved and pressed her butt up against me. I let out a very horny groan. I thought about nibbling her neck, but instead I surprised her and planted a kiss on her neck.

"Yes, that's perfect," I joyfully exclaimed.

"What is?" she asked, her brow furrowing. She turned around to face me and saw that I was looking down at my phone.

"So candid. So beautiful," I said softly. A smile formed on my face as I traced her in the picture I had just taken, on my phone with my index finger.

I looked up from the phone and straight into her eyes. "I didn't want a pose. I wanted to capture you how I see you. Full of passion and . . ." I tapped my chin for a moment ". . . what's the word I am looking for . . . ?" tap, tap, tap ". . . at peace and content," I said without breaking contact with her gaze.

"I'm not a big fan of pictures," she said, blushing and feeling shy all of a sudden.

"Probably because you've never had a photographer like me, that's why." I winked at her and she grinned. I pulled her in closer, giving her a sideways hug. "Take a look at these hotties." I showed her the phone.

She looked at the screen and gasped. The picture had captured a man cherishing a woman's neck and a woman who did not want him to stop.

The picture was incredible.

"You know, I gotta give it to you. This is pretty good," she said.

"Pretty good?" I said, my jaw dropping in shock. "This is museum worthy. At the very least, billboard ready."

We both laughed.

Have you ever tried to blink away tears? Thinking that the faster you blink, the better chance you have of them not spilling?

That's what I was doing right now. I had no reason to hold back these tears. I wasn't in a public place, nor was I around anyone.

I was alone, sitting in my living room, accompanied by darkness. It was a little after 2:00 a.m., and I sat there, watching her.

Raw, intense emotion coursed through my veins, keeping company with my blood. With a close of the eyes, I was brought back to that day. A day that I was so happy. A day when I wanted to do nothing but hold her and I wanted to capture that in a picture.

Memories were all I had. I opened my eyes, and memories were staring back at me from a broken screen in my hands.

I blinked rapidly, trying to keep the tears from falling. I shut my eyes tightly, the phone falling from my hands onto the floor.

Another crack in the screen.

I cringed.

What was another crack in a screen when my heart was broken beyond repair?

At least a screen I could replace. I wished I could say the same for my heart.

I could almost feel her pressing against me, and when I closed my eyes, I could smell her . . . a little floral, very fresh, with a hint of sunshine, dewy meadows, rain, and a field of cotton.

How vividly I remembered this.

How vividly I remembered pain.

I opened my eyes and could feel the wetness, obscuring my vision of her. I kept blinking, yet I knew that it would end up being futile. I picked up the phone and stared at the cracked faces of a man I didn't recognize, a man so happy that I felt my heart ripping from my chest, the pain strong as memories overcame me. Then there was her. The woman I loved staring back at me. Her eyes were closed and she looked so content and happy with my lips on her neck.

I blinked frantically to no avail. However, it did not help in this case. These tears were too big and too powerful to blink away.

I watched as my tears fell onto the screen, and I followed their path as they disappeared between the cracks.

Here one moment, ingested by the cracked apparatus the next.

My tears could not mend the phone screen, just like these memories could not replace her. Thinking about holding her did not compare to actually holding her.

I felt my heart breaking yet again, or perhaps it never stopped breaking. Perhaps I never stopped hurting and I just didn't acknowledge it. Until this very moment.

It was 2:12 a.m. when I saw clearly, through the haziness of tears. I finally let myself grieve. Something I had denied myself for too long.

Deep down I wished that these tears would mend my broken heart, all the while knowing that they would roll off of me, just like they had rolled off my screen.

The only one that could fill those cracks was no longer here.

It did not stop me from wishing she was.

It did not stop me from searching for her in the cracks of my heart.

Hi Dad,

I fucked up big time. I know I shouldn't curse, and I am sorry for that. I just wanted to be open about how I was feeling, and that curse word sums it perfectly.

I am sitting on my porch and looking at the stars. I made one more wish.

The same exact wish.

I've done that every night since she left, even on the starless nights. If you had told me I would have done that a few months ago, I would have told you that you were nuts.

How people can change when love enters the equation.

Just to be sure that my wish was heard, I said it out loud. "Please bring back the love of my life. Please."

Dad, if you can help me up from up there, I would really appreciate it so much.

I miss you.

—K.

My Mary,

What's wrong? You are starting to scare me. I haven't heard from you. Please write. Please let me know you are okay at least. Please tell me what is going on.

I feel different and I know something is happening. Please know that you can tell me everything.

Is it your mom? Has she been stealing your letters?

I couldn't send them to Shelby anymore out of respect for her mourning. I was the reason Matt didn't come back home alive, and I didn't want to remind her of that.

Please write at least one sentence so that I know you are okay.

Yours forever,

Jim

Chapter Thirty-Nine

Kaitlyn

It was going to be a long, difficult day. I felt it the moment I woke up. I was so glad that I took the day off because I was barely able to get through my morning run. My thoughts kept returning to him and to Landing Falls.

I missed him, and that angered me, and the more I tried to focus on other things, the more he popped into my mind.

I had done a fine job this past few months moving on, yet how did one truly move on when a piece of their heart and soul was still in Landing Falls?

I came home, showered, and pulled on my favorite pair of jeans, a sweater, and some ballet flats. I pulled up my hair in a bun on the top of my head. I skipped makeup, just applied a little color to my lips, and I was out the door. I was going to grab a cup of coffee at my workplace, The Bean. I knew that would do the trick. Jack, the owner of the café, always made the best and strongest coffee.

I entered the café, and the smell of coffee invaded my senses. I got in line, closed my eyes, and inhaled the beautiful scent. I smiled. I liked this town. It wasn't Landing Falls, but then I didn't want it to be. I was all about making new memories now.

"Mornin, Kait, the regular?" Jack asked while reaching for a croissant for the customer in front of me.

"Morning, Jack." I smiled at him. "Yes, extra strong for me today too."

"Can I get you anything else?" he asked over his shoulder while pouring my cup of coffee.

"No, just the coffee, thanks," I replied. I looked around. The café was full of people this morning, more so than usual. Jack approached with the coffee and looked around as well.

"Great crowd, right?" he said enthusiastically. "They are here for the jazz festival that starts tomorrow. Are you going?" he asked.

"Hmm, I don't know," I said, looking around. "I don't really like overcrowded places."

"I'm sure Mason wouldn't mind taking you." He winked at me.

"Mason is my friend. That's it." I looked him straight in the eye. "That's it, Jack."

Mason was a regular that came into the coffee shop, and he had asked me out once. I had politely declined, telling him I wasn't ready to date just yet.

Jack started to laugh. "I know, I know. I love teasing you." He looked at me softly. "You are beautiful though and deserve someone extra special."

"I had that already." I looked down at my hands, feeling a little vulnerable, discussing *him.* "I don't think something like that comes around twice." I smiled at him. "Unless you are super lucky, like you and Liam are."

Jack smiled, and his love for Liam was written visibly on his face. "It wasn't easy for us, but we made it work."

Liam and Jack had been together for five years before Liam was sent overseas, to Iraq. Liam being an active service member really tested their relationship, but they had made it through two deployments. Jack had opened the coffee shop with all of his savings to keep his mind off of the war and off of Liam's absence and danger while serving overseas. It was tough on them until Liam was back home for good. They married a year ago and were in the process of adopting a child.

Jack was the first person besides Father John that I met when I came into town. The moment I left Father John's rectory, I broke down. My mom's letter wasn't in the box; it was at home in Landing Falls all this time, and that newfound knowledge shattered me. It was like that saying goes, "The straw that broke the camel's back." Boy, had it broken mine.

I had felt so alone without Kendrew, Jess, Shelby, and Jim. I felt abandoned and did not know where to go. I walked around the town purposelessly and came into Jack's café while he was closing up. He made me a cup of coffee, warmed me up a plate of food, and sat next to me, a perfect stranger, and listened to me cry my heart out to him. That night he let me stay in his garage one-bedroom apartment, and he gave me a job at his café, training me himself.

Jack touched my hand gently, laying his hand on top of mine. "Never underestimate luck." He paused for a moment. "Or fate." He winked at me.

I went around the counter, and with arms outstretched, ran into his arms. His embrace comforted me.

"Thank you for being you," I said.

He whispered in my ear, "Never give up on love. It's worth fighting for."

I smiled and grabbed my coffee and went to sit by the window. My favorite place to people-watch.

Once a stalker always a stalker, I thought to myself and laughed. My thoughts drifted to another window, in another place, and to him. No matter where I went or what I did, he would always stay in the back of my mind.

I was finishing my coffee, and was about to leave, when a song playing in the café caught my attention.

I walked out, a spring to my step, singing along to "Our Love Is Worth Fighting For."

***

I decided to plant some flowers and help landscape Jack and Liam's lawn. It was the least I could do for Jack, as he did not accept my rent money. Every month I tried to give it to him, and every month I was turned down. So instead, I did little things, hoping that they helped the guys out a bit.

I was hunched over the flower bed, planting marigolds and wallflowers, along with some coneflowers and black velvet petunias. I also planted red geraniums and some electric-blue lobelia so that the flower bed would be as colorful as could be. The unusually warm late spring sun caressed my skin, and the gentle breeze blew through my hair. I found myself leaning back and raising my face to the sun. The sky was a perfect cloudless shade of blue. I closed my eyes and felt warmth and peace settle in me. This was wonderful and so freeing. I remembered someone once telling me that sunflowers faced the sun. That they tracked the sun's path through the sky. That was how I felt.

I smiled thinking about sunflowers in fields, and *he* promptly made his appearance in my thoughts. He looked so handsome and looked at me with so much raw love that it hit me and almost knocked me over with its force. I could imagine the feel of his hand in mine as we ran freely through the field of encapsulated happiness, with the sun warming our skin.

Then my thoughts turned, and he and I fell to our knees, not stopping our wandering hands that caressed each other's bodies, before he laid me down in the warm soil, covering me with his body. We were surrounded by yellow, and I would always look for that color wherever I went. Sunflowers and fields would remind me of him.

Who am I kidding?

Everything good would remind me of him.

When it came to him, I realized that I did not need sun to feel at peace. I felt that way around him whether it was sunny or raining or cloudy or subzero. He made me feel like a sunflower that always searched for a moment of sunlight. Although to me, he was more than that. He was my beacon at night, his arms my shelter during a storm, his smile my grounding center, and his heart, my home. Some may call me crazy, but I could swear that I heard him calling me every single day. I felt his presence as I lay in bed at night, and his face was the first one I saw when I woke up from my dreams. Sometimes the dreams were so real, his appearance so clear, his voice so raw, that I didn't want to wake up, and when I did, I found my pillowcases wet with my tears. It was like I lost him every single day all over again.

I opened my eyes and let the daydream slip away slowly, savoring the moment I had just experienced.

I looked back at my flowers, and my gaze was riveted on a tiny plant sticking out near the porch. How I had missed it I was not sure, but I instinctively knew what it was.

Every year since I left foster care, I bought lilies of the valley to plant in a pot. The cashier at the store told me that lily of the valley brought her true love, and she said that she believed that when it bloomed for me, I would have the same. She said it brought luck in love and a return of happiness and sweetness. I took hold of her words and memorized them word for word, nestling them deep inside of me. I clung to that precious short conversation with a lady whose name I didn't even know for many years to come. I secretly hoped that it was true, that her words would spring to life along with those blooms. That day, I desperately craved love and human touch, and I bought two boxes of it. Not one bloomed. I did this year after year and none ever bloomed.

Yet now, out of the blue, in an unexpected spot, one lily of the valley plant had blooms, and they brought tears to my eyes.

I guess I never stopped believing or hoping, as I planted them year after year. Except for this year, because I had run. Yet here one was, growing. Barely, but it survived in a crack in the foundation. Its flowers and scent were there, and I felt like perhaps they were there for me.

I walked over and broke the stalk and brought the delicate flowers to my nose. The fragrance was beautiful, so floral, so strong, so feminine, and so lovely.

"I met my true love too," I told the flower, feeling so giddy and happy. Just like a child that had gotten her favorite ice cream cone. Except in this case I had gotten what my heart always yearned for, always longed for: love. I held the little flower with its eight bells dangling down, to my heart, the bells and my heartbeat in sync. I raised my tear-filled eyes to the sky, the daydream and his kisses fresh in my mind, and whispered, "Thank you," over and over again.

I *had* to go to him. He was calling me. My heart beat wildly just thinking about him. I was going back. I was finally heading home. I had to tell Jack and Liam, and I would tonight.

I walked inside, heading for my bedroom and my suitcase, the flower tucked in my hand. It was coming for the ride as well.

For a girl whose wishes never came true, this felt beyond surreal. The wait, the struggle, the hurt, the pain, the delays almost seemed worth it because in the end, it was *him*. It always had been him. I just hoped he felt the same.

No matter what, he and I needed to talk. We owed each other that, but holding the flower in my hand, my gift from the soil I so loved to work, I made one more wish.

I wished that he loved me as much as I loved him. And that he was ready to welcome me and my love for him home.

I looked back at the flower and felt infused with hope. I had a feeling it would all work out. The eight dangling bells seemed to nod their head in agreement.

***

We may have a vision, an illumination, but in a blink of an eye, that vision can fade and darkness and uncertainty can take its place.

Someone once told me that life was not guaranteed to go according to our plans. It's how we adapted to the changing circumstances that really mattered.

That's how it was for me. I was so happy to go back to Landing Falls. To visit him and see everyone again. But life wasn't going to allow me to return to Landing Falls on my terms. I got a call from Irma. Jim had just been rushed to the hospital.

My Mary,

We just received word that we would be heading home. I am excited to come back to you, but worried because I have not heard from you in a very long time. I feel like something happened, something bad, and I can't shake this feeling. I hope I am wrong. I hope your letters got lost somewhere or delayed, but I have a feeling that's not the case.

My heart hurts. It feels your pain and I don't know how to help ease it. I feel like my coming home might be too late. I hope and pray and wish on all the stars in the sky that I am wrong.

Mary, I love you. Only you.

I'll be home soon. PLEASE wait for me.

Love always,
Jim

Chapter Forty

Kaitlyn

It was a sunny day. The cemetery was filled with a large number of people who came to pay their respects. There were a lot of tears but also a few murmurs about two loves finally being reunited after so many years.

I looked at the casket being lowered into the ground, and my eyes filled with unshed tears. I'd been in shock the past two days and could not accept her death. Shelby's passing deeply touched and affected me. She was such a sweet, kind-hearted lady. A link to my grandmother and most importantly, my mother, and a dear friend and confidant to me. Her love for Matt was so inspiring, and I knew she was happy alongside him now, but I would miss her vastly.

Before the cemetery, I had found out that Shelby had left her home to Kendrew and me in her will.

We were co-owners.

Even after she was gone, she was *still* playing matchmaker.

Jim was doing much better. He had suffered a heart attack, and doctors had not given him the okay to come to the funeral and burial today. They said it would be too strenuous on him, not to mention emotional. I promised to represent both of us at the funeral. He wasn't happy about not going, but surprisingly he didn't fight the doctors too much and in the end listened to them, which told me he wasn't feeling too well yet.

I felt someone's eyes on me and I looked up. I hadn't seen him since that day almost one year ago. His gaze had the ability to stir feelings deep inside me effortlessly. I looked down at the ground again.

I needed to talk to him. He was the reason I had planned on returning, before I received news of Shelby's passing. We also needed to figure out what to do with Shelby's home

My thoughts of him and what I would say to him were interrupted by a female calling his name. My head snapped up and I felt my knees shake, and I felt as if I was hit in the middle of my chest. Breathing became difficult, but I focused on it. I felt tears welling up in my eyes, and I blinked them away. As soon as I did that, I regretted it. The picture before my eyes was so clear now. Kendrew was standing next to the same woman I saw in his home that day I decided to go away.

So, he did know how to be in a relationship with one woman!

Looking at him, one would not say he looked happy. In fact, he looked miserable, and his eyes looked sad. His eyes penetrated mine, telling me so much without words, and I couldn't stand being there any longer.

I leaned down and grabbed some dirt and threw it on Shelby's casket. I took a white rose, kissed it before dropping it on the dirt, the contrast visible, the gesture making my heart ache. It was my way of saying, "See you one day, dear friend, my dear beautiful rose." It was my way of sending her my love all the way to heaven, where I imagined she and Matt were embracing now.

I walked away and was not sure where I was headed, but I walked until I found myself in front of Jim's store.

When I had visited Jim at the hospital, he mentioned that Kendrew was running it in his absence. He and a few of the guys at the firehouse took turns. I walked in, scanned the store and didn't see anyone there. Perhaps they were grabbing some inventory in the storage room? Thankfully it wouldn't be Kendrew, as he was with his girlfriend, probably heading home or already there now, undressing her and . . .

Stop it. Stop it. Stop it.

He could do as he pleased and he didn't owe me a thing.

One lily of the valley bloom and a wish made did not guarantee true love. I saw that now and wanted to cry. I had truly thought that he and I could try again . . .

I thought back to the first time I came into the store, how at home I felt there, and I smiled. So much had changed since then, but at least I still had Jim. My eyes scanned the items on display, and I was fascinated most with the new books that had arrived. Along with books, there was a nineteenth-century armoire and a beautiful portrait of a man and a woman from the late eighteenth century, judging by their clothing. The painting was called *Strolling in Hyde Park*. I was looking at it and fascinated that a portrait could capture the love they had for one another without kissing or even hugging.

It was the gentle way he was touching her hand. And the look in their eyes. I gently touched his hand and smiled. I believed I had had what they had one day not so long ago.

I didn't know how long I looked at the picture, but it must have been a while and I must have really lost myself in that painting. I was in some kind of trance, and I did not want to leave Hyde Park.

"Beautiful, isn't it?" he whispered close to my ear, and I jumped, my hand coming to my chest, my body instinctively turning toward his voice, craving it, drinking it into my parched body.

He looked so handsome in his dark suit. His hair was a little longer than when I last saw him. His face looked the same except for the deep circles under his eyes. His eyes were gazing deeply into me, before traveling over my face and settling on my lips.

I broke away from the binding spell cast by his eyes, and pointed toward the picture I was just admiring.

"Yes, it is. Is this a new painting?"

"Yes, it came in two days ago." His gaze moved from me to the painting. "I found it in Shipstown last week at an estate sale and had it shipped here. I knew Jim would love it when he got back."

"Yes." I nodded in agreement. For some reason I couldn't formulate a sentence around him right now. Something about him always managed to catch me off guard, and after not seeing him for a little over a year, I found myself nervous around him. The thoughts assailing my brain were anything but PG. I wanted to kiss him wildly and passionately. To remind myself how he tasted, even though I never forgot. I had always remembered every detail about him, from his scent to every scar and freckle on his body, to the way his eyes glimmered when he was smiling or the way his eyes darkened when he was in the throes of passion. I wanted nothing more than to take him home with me and love him properly and often. I wanted him to feel the same. To see safety and comfort in me. To see and feel the love.

I wanted to forget about the day that changed everything and just remember how right he felt beside me and in me. How right he felt in my grandmother's house, working alongside me, making that house feel like more than a building.

How right he felt in my hopes and dreams.

How being with him felt like home.

Home, sweet home.

With him by my side, I finally knew what that saying meant.

Home wasn't a location or a specific house. Home, to me, was with my rock and foundation, with the man who loved me deeply and affectionately, with the man who cherished me and protected me, with the man whose embrace alone kept away the nightmares of my past.

No, my home was more than a location or an address. It was a person.

It was one person. It was him, and it always had been.

The scary part was that I was terrified that it would always be him.

That I would live in the past yet again.

An awkward silence ensued. I knew I had to get away, but I found it hard to leave just yet.

"It's kind of you to watch the store while he is in the hospital," I murmured. Jim and the store were safe topics, so I congratulated myself on moving the conversation along. One thing I didn't need from him was talk of us, talk of the day that "us" ended, and especially not talk of his new life, with his new girl. I didn't think I would be able to withstand that without breaking.

I still loved him.

It was evident by the strong erratic beat of my heart when he looked at me. When his voice traveled to my ears, when his frame, standing mere inches from mine, seemed to scald my body, without even touching it.

"Jim is like a dad to me." His voice broke and he cleared his throat. My thoughts returned to him and what he just said. I could tell he was sad and worried. "I would do anything for him," he said softly.

I nodded my head. "I know," I said gently, my whole heart put into the next two words. "Thank you." I thanked him not only for watching out for Jim, but also for changing me. For making me who I was today and making me want to be an even better version of myself for tomorrow. I thanked him for showing me how great it felt to love. I thanked him for opening me up to the best feeling in the world. I thanked him for being him and for making me feel magic for at least a few months in time. I turned away from him and slowly started walking toward the door. A few more steps and I was within reach of the air outside. Away from him. Away from his eyes that seemed to be looking into my soul, reading me like a good book. I stopped, and over the back of my shoulder, said, "I know it means a lot to him." I grabbed the door handle and was about to turn it, when I felt his hand on mine.

I looked down, and it was just like the portrait. My heart screamed for me not to pull away. It craved his touch, but I had to pull away. I would make myself move my hand.

Just one more second.

There was one major difference between me and that painting. Kendrew wasn't my man. He was with someone else. He chose her over me.

"Drew—"

"Lynnie—"

We both spoke at the same time. I found the courage deep within and moved my hand quickly from the warmth and safety of his hand, and he watched me closely. I felt the loss of him and hated myself for putting myself through that feeling of having him and losing him all in a few seconds' time.

"What are you doing?" I ground out. I was frustrated that he still had this power over me. That one touch made me turn into a puddle at his feet.

"I had to feel you, to see if you were real." He ran his hand through his hair, exhaling the breath he was holding in a loud whoosh. "God, I missed you so much. I imagined you coming back so many times in my dreams that I had to see if this—" he pointed to me and to the hand that touched me "—if you being here was real."

I looked at him, and he looked like he was deliberating whether he should say more or not. He started to speak, and stopped when he noticed me crossing my arms and taking a step back from him.

"I'm real and I am here," I said with strength and courage that was newly rediscovered. "But not yours to touch, Drew." I glared at him and saw him flinch. Sadness crossed his face, and I watched his jaw tick. I felt tears pooling in my eyes, and I held back a curse. I would not cry in front of him. I refused to let him see that he had hurt me. That my heart still had a gaping hole that oozed sadness. "You made that decision, not me." My voice cracked and I looked to the side. Anywhere but at him. I could feel his gaze on me intently.

"I was an ass and scared of what I felt for you, but in the end I lost you anyway." He whispered the last sentence, his voice breaking, his eyes pleading with mine to hear him. To listen to the words he was speaking and those that were buried deep inside. His eyes were filled with sadness. I saw tears pooling in his eyes, and that angered me. What had happened was his decision. He told me to leave, he told me what we had didn't matter, he was the one with the naked woman in his home.

I forced myself to sound unaffected, uninterested even though my heart was yearning to embrace him and feel his arms around me. Instead, I turned the knob and said icily, "Well, by the looks of things, you didn't lose your girlfriend, so it worked out for you in the end. I'm happy for you." I plastered an unnatural smile to mask the pain I really felt inside. "Bye," I muttered and walked away.

I could feel Kendrew watching me through the glass doors. The door closed shut with a bang, and I grabbed my chest, feeling the bang inside as well.

"Wait, what girlfriend?" he whispered, looking at the door and then back at the painting of the couple. Utter silence was his answer.

Chapter Forty-One

Kendrew

The rain brought back so many memories. Growing up, I always loved it. I looked at it like a clean slate. The rain came and wiped away dirt and dust and left a clean ground in its wake. It gave nutrition to the plants and the trees and grasses and filled the rivers and ponds up that the sun had dried out a bit.

I loved the feeling of it on my skin. It had always made me feel alive.

I couldn't explain how I found myself in front of her house, but I did. I stood there exactly like that morning when I went for a run, the morning that changed everything. The morning that opened my heart up. The morning that showed me it was safe to plant my roots alongside her.

After she left yesterday, I stared at the painting for a long time. I gazed at it as if it held the answers to all of my questions. It didn't. Seeing that couple walking hand in hand and in love propelled me out of the store that I should've been running, it propelled me to turn over the Open sign so that it read Closed, so that I could get answers to what she had said.

I had no girlfriend. I didn't know what she meant by that.

Surely she didn't mean Hayley?

I needed to tell her how I felt without her and how she made me want to dream and wish and be happy once again.

Standing on the sidewalk, watching her home, working to find my courage, I found myself moving toward her porch, toward her door, ready to knock.

However, I heard a loud crashing sound that seemed to come from the back of her house. I ran down the stairs and toward the sound. My heart was beating wildly inside my chest, my worry escalating. I felt panic set in.

God, please let her be okay.

I spotted her standing in front of a big mirror that had broken. I took her appearance in and she looked to be okay. Thank heavens. In fact, she was more than okay.

She was drenched in rainwater and looked beyond beautiful. She was standing in the middle of her lawn, her gaze on me. I watched the raindrops fall from her head and fall on her face, rolling down her body. Some lucky raindrops cascaded down her shirt, clinging to her chest. How I wished I was them this moment. I knew every spot I would travel to.

I drank in her natural beauty and smiled. Only she could make ripped jeans, ballet flats, and a sweater look runway ready.

She was surrounded by furniture and looking at me, back at the furniture and back at me again.

"Hi," I said. "Need help with those?" I pointed to three chairs, an armoire, and an old distressed door.

"Hi." She nodded her head. "I painted these this morning outside and didn't think to look at the weather." I watched her bite her lip, and I took a step toward her, needing to be closer to her. "If you can grab that door, it would be perfect." She looked at me, and I watched her eyes linger on my face before falling to my lips. I watched a raindrop fall on their perfect pink plushness, and I watched as she licked it away. I groaned inwardly.

"You and I seem to always get caught in the rain, no?" I laughed, feeling so young and free around her. More like myself than ever before.

"I think that is a sign. Of the heavens crying when we get together." She rolled her eyes dramatically and laughed. I joined in, loving our back-and-forth banter.

I lifted the door and she pointed to her back covered porch. We both made two trips to the porch and back, and we were almost done.

I didn't want this moment to end. I grabbed the last chair and put it back down. I turned toward her and found her looking my way. "You know, I think it's the opposite. I think they know what comes after the rain with us and make sure we get caught in it for a reason." I winked.

She was drenched, and her once-thick sweater was now thin and outlining her breasts. Her hair was completely wet, beads of rain were holding every hair strand, and curls were framing her face. She was caught off guard by my statement and by the wink. I could tell she wanted to turn away by the blush making its way to her cheeks, but she didn't. She looked back at me with an intensity that I loved, with an honesty that I loved even more.

"Your hair always curls when it's wet." I spoke softly. I felt my body closing in on hers. The heat was intensifying with every step I took toward her. I was trying to control my breathing, to show her the effect she still had on me, the effect that she would always have on me.

My hands reached out and framed her face gently. The feel of her skin against mine was powerful. I felt it healing me. Infusing me with something that I couldn't explain, but something that I knew I could not live without. The passion in me grew, and I licked my lips. We were both breathing hard from just a mere touch of fingertips on cheeks. This was how intense it had always been between us. How different and special.

I lifted the curl from her cheek and touched it, looking at it longingly before placing it behind her ear.

Raindrops were clinging to her eyelashes, and her eyes were large and filled with hunger, looking at me.

She touched my face and we were both caught in the moment, caught in our past love story. I heard her soft voice, and it stirred something deep inside of me. "You always look so boyish when you are caught in a rainstorm."

I loved her and conveyed that message to her with my touch as my fingers traveled from her neck to her waist, reaching under her sweater. She was so wet and cold, yet she burned where I touched her. I moved my fingers under her sweater and watched as she moaned out loud. I wanted to drink in that moan and pull her closer, my mouth needing to feel her mouth. My body needing her just like it needed air and water.

This was a dream come true. No other thoughts came to mind. When she and I were like this, no one else seemed to matter.

I felt her breath on my lips, and it was almost like she was breathing for me and I was breathing for her. My gaze traveled to her eyes and I saw something that caught me off guard. Her gaze was filled with an emotion so close to love that I couldn't believe it. I looked again and saw that it was love unfiltered, love so raw, love on display for me, and I felt tears pooling in my eyes.

My eyes shone, washing away the darkness that my life had become without her. I let myself feel raw and vulnerable, even if for this moment. In the midst of this rainstorm, I wanted to be her light keeper, like she was mine. I wanted to keep her soul and heart alive and filled with love and light.

Her hand reached for me and touched my cheek. I closed my eyes and released a breath. I felt her fingers make their way to my lips. They touched my lips, and I kissed her fingers before taking one in my mouth.

She pulled away. "I'm sorry. We, umm, we can't," she stuttered. I looked at her, trying to decipher what was going through her mind. Her eyes were wide in panic.

"Why not?" My voice sounded strained, but it pleaded with her to hear me and believe me. "I love you, Kait."

"Stop it, Drew. I am not the same person I was so many months ago. I won't be another hookup again." Her voice cracked, but her eyes flashed anger.

She moved away from me and took a few steps backward, without breaking eye contact with me. Her gaze was unwavering. "I want something real and strong. I want a Mary and Jim love story, a Shelby and Matt love story." The rain fell harder, and she raised her voice. She was now practically yelling.

"Why can't we be a Kait and Drew story?" I bellowed out, my arms outstretched.

I could tell that the question surprised her. She was silent for a moment. I watched as her hands formed into fists at her side.

"Because you forgot one ingredient for that story: love," she called out, tears filling her eyes. "They all had an undying love for one another. A deep love. Not just sex, and definitely not another woman in the mix."

"I love you and I always will. There is no other woman for me. I haven't been with another woman since that day I was an asshole to you. I couldn't even think about being with another woman. You, all I could think about was you. How you felt in my bed, how it felt waking up next to you, how it felt to laugh with you and work alongside you. How it felt to sit in silence and watch reruns of *I Love Lucy* with you." I was breathing heavily. I felt the need to tell her everything, while she was still listening. I found myself speaking fast and loudly to make sure she heard me over the pouring rain.

I took a few steps toward her until I was mere inches from her. I looked into her eyes, and she was looking deep inside of my eyes. "You are the only woman I want to make love to, because—" I paused to deliver the next words slowly, emphasizing every single word "—I . . . love . . . you . . ." I lowered my face and whispered in her ear, "I love you more than I ever loved myself. I love you more than I ever thought was possible. And most importantly, I love you with a love so strong that it should scare me, but it doesn't, because I know that without you, I will never be myself again. The time spent apart only verified that." I framed her face with my hands. "You make me the man I am supposed to be. You fill the parts of me that were broken and empty and fill them with such a love and happiness that I cannot imagine. I know for a fact that if you don't want me, I don't want anyone else because I know that there is no one else there for me that will fit me like you fit me, that will compliment me like you will. So if you walk away now, know that I will be like Shelby and Jim. I would rather be alone with my memories than with anyone who is half of what you are." I got everything I wanted to tell her out, and I felt breathless. I breathed in and out heavily, awaiting her actions.

I hoped she felt the same way I did.

I wished . . . for her and her love.

I saw confusion warring with uncertainty on her face.

She turned away from me, resentment evident on her face. She took a few steps before stopping, turning around, and looking at me again. "That's not how I saw it. I did not see you suffering alone." She air quoted "suffering" and rolled her eyes at the same time. I watched her eyes narrow at me. "What about that pretty brunette?" she blurted out.

"What brunette?" My brows knit together.

"That day, I came over to apologize for snooping," she said, glancing away in embarrassment. "I wanted to let you know that I wasn't going anywhere until we talked it out." She looked up at me briefly before looking down at the puddles forming around our feet. The rain was really coming down even harder now, with lightning illuminating the dark sky every so often. "I came by to fight for you—" she walked up to me and nudged me on the chest with her index finger "—to tell you how I felt about you, but that day someone beat me to your house." Hurt seeped into her words.

"Who?" My expression was confused. I bit my lip and replayed that day in my head. I squeezed my eyes shut for a moment. "You saw her that day, didn't you? You saw Hayley?" My voice broke and I drew in a sharp breath. My hand reached for her, wanting to comfort her.

She must think that Hayley and I . . .

I expelled a breath harshly.

She pulled away from my touch, an array of emotions on display.

"Don't touch me," she said, anger filling her eyes. "She looked very comfortable being naked in your arms." A tear slipped down her cheek, and I watched as she rushed to wipe it away.

I cursed loudly. "It's not what you think." My voice cracked, and she looked at me, straight into my eyes and into my soul. I bared everything for her, wanting her to see how honest I was being with her, how open I was being. Holding nothing back anymore.

I was all in.

"Nothing happened. I swear." I tried to touch her arm again, and she took a giant step back from me.

She snorted. "It didn't look that way, Drew. I stood and watched like an idiot." Tears were now streaming down her face, and she shouted, her fists clenching and unclenching. "It was like freakin déjà vu, the day in the parking lot all over again." She wiped at the tears angrily and glared at me. "Only this time it was so much worse." Her voice broke, but she still managed to whisper, "I was so fuckin gullible." I watched as she shook her head, looking at the puddle once again. It was growing bigger and wider.

I crossed over to her and placed my arms on her shoulders. "Look at me, please," I said.

She ignored my request. I touched her cheek. She jerked away from me.

I let out a deep breath. "That must have looked . . . I can't imagine what you, how you . . . damn . . . I am so sorry, Lynn." I felt her eyes on me. My face was full of regret and sadness. "It's really not how it looked. I swear, nothing happened. It couldn't. Not after you." I looked at her lovingly.

"It didn't look that way to me. In fact, it looked like you were enjoying her dropping her coat and being naked," she stammered out.

"She surprised me. Completely caught me off guard. It took a minute to realize what was happening, but I knew for a fact that I didn't want what she offered me. I couldn't stop thinking about you."

"Yeah, I'm sure it was one hell of a surprise." Her voice was laced with icy disdain. "You might want to invest in some window blinds. Unless people watching you is your thing; then by all means . . ." Her voice sounded so cold.

"I'm sorry you saw that—"

She interrupted me. "I'm not. It saved me more hurt down the line." She looked at me with such disgust that I felt pain in my chest. "You got what you wanted, and I don't blame you for moving on—"

I opened my mouth to refute that statement, but she gestured for me to hold on. She wasn't quite done. I obliged, hoping that getting everything off her chest would help her hear me out and believe me.

"But please don't feed me bullshit now. You yourself told me to leave. That all this ever meant to you was sex, so . . ." she gestured to herself and me ". . . we are good." She plastered the fakest smile ever on her face.

I was not buying anything she was saying. She was still hurting. I needed to make her understand how much I loved her.

"Listen, no, we are not good. That's not what happened," I said, my voice rising a bit. "I thought it was you. Instead, it was her. She caught me by surprise."

"I'm sure she did," Kait said while turning around and walking away from me. She stopped for a moment before looking at me over her shoulder. "I'm sure you loved that surprise. She is beautiful, and I am happy for both of you." She turned away from me and started walking away. Her body shutting down and accepting that this was fact.

I ran after her. I touched her arm and turned her toward me. She refused to look at me. Instead she was staring at my chest. "Kait, you have to believe me. Had you waited a minute, you would have seen me put her coat back on her and send her away." I stopped for a moment, finding the courage to say the next words. The words that had lived in my heart for months now. "I told her I was in love with a woman who made me want to be a better man, a woman who made me want to reconcile with my past, a woman that I love more than anyone ever in my life." I touched her cheek, wiping away a tear that had created a trail down her beautiful face. "I'm sorry for causing you so much hurt and pain. I was going to talk to you that night, apologize and tell you everything in my past."

"It's hard for me to believe that, especially seeing her with you at the funeral."

"She always has bad timing. She is a stewardess that I used to see occasionally before I met you. She would always drop in on me in the past, and she saw Shelby's obituary and knew that I would help Shelby in the past with groceries or chopping wood, so she came to support me during the funeral," I responded.

"I want to believe you, but I don't know if I can. I want someone who I can trust, and I can't trust you right now." She bit her lip, looking at me with uncertainty in her eyes.

"Ask Jim. He knows everything," I told her.

"Jim knows about her?" she asked, shocked.

"Yes, he knows everything. I was a mess when you left. In fact, I haven't been myself since you left. It's like a big piece of my soul and heart were missing." I smiled softly. "In fact, just being around you has made me feel like myself again."

"I don't know what to say. I want to believe you, but I am terrified of being hurt again," she said hesitantly.

"I am telling you the truth. I hope, deep down, you feel it and believe me."

She looked at me and mouthed, "Give me some time."

I nodded my head and walked away from her, from my heart, feeling half hope and half gloom. Not knowing what was true, but hoping that time worked in my favor.

I couldn't lose her.

Chapter Forty-Two

Kaitlyn

As much as I loved turning pages and new chapters in a book, I was terrified to open a new chapter in my life. I was so confused. I didn't know what or who to believe right now. I spoke to Jim and he told me the same thing that Drew had. He also told me to quiet my thoughts and listen to what my heart was saying. Problem was, I didn't know how to quiet my thoughts. They were spinning in my head.

I needed her help.

I needed my mother.

I walked toward the painting I had always loved to look at. I cringed when I saw that I still hadn't replaced the faux orchid. I really had to change that out.

I turned toward the painting, the real reason I had found myself in my hallway. I ran my fingers across the painted magnolia and smiled. I took the painting off the wall with great care and placed it on the floor so that I could locate the letter.

I found it easily. It was nestled in the corner. The envelope was sealed and in immaculate condition, although time had aged it slightly.

My hands shook slightly in anticipation of seeing my mother's handwriting for the first time in my life.

I drew in a deep breath and ripped open the envelope. I was ready. I wanted to know. I needed to know. I took out the letter and started my next chapter.

Dearest Daughter,

The name you carry is a name I have chosen for you myself. It is one that is full of meaning, and much thought was put into it. I spent nine months thinking in silence of what I would name you. And then it came to me, it was all too obvious. I named you Adira. My precious, beautiful daughter. My Adira.

I am about to leave this world, and I will have to atone for what I have done. I hope you can forgive me, my beautiful girl. Know this, baby girl, even after I am gone, I will always be there for you. If ever you feel a cool breeze, that is me keeping you cool on a warm day. If you ever feel heat on your hand, that is me keeping you warm in the winter. If you ever feel alone, just call my name—Mary—and the wind will carry it to my ears.

I cried looking at you a few moments ago in the crib. You felt me nearby and you reached out your hand. I touched you and you grabbed my finger. You held on as if to remember my touch. As if you knew that this was the last time you would see me, feel me, hold on to me. Your beauty and innocence almost made me want to stay. But how would I ever tell you that you were born as a result of someone stronger imposing himself on someone weaker? I could have given you up for adoption, but I could never live with myself if I lived and you lived and we never saw each other. I loved you too much, and sometimes, I wondered how I could love you so very much when I hated him so ardently. This way you can always say your mother died. Not everyone will know how . . . I hope. This way I can always be near you and watch over you.

I love you, my angel. Please tell my darling sweetheart that I love him and that I am always near him as well. Please tell him that I had to do what I did. I wanted to spare him and you, the only two people that I truly loved, the pain. When you see him, please give him this flower for me. Even now, I have goose bumps just thinking about him.

My darling, if you ever feel such an emotion just give yourself over to it. Let it consume you until you lose all rational thought and that person lives in you. Then and only then will you will know that you are in love. Never accept anything less and never let anyone pressure you to do what you do not want to.

My love and I made it through a war unscathed, but I wasn't strong enough to survive after the rape. I am ashamed and feel dirty. Jim says he doesn't care and holds me and surrounds me with love, but Tom would destroy him. And you. He promised me he would.

I love you and Jim more than myself and put you both first. I always will.

In case you are wondering why I named you Adira, I will let you know. I hope you smile when you find out its meaning. Adira means strong, noble . . . powerful. I didn't name you alone. My love and I both named you under our favorite tree, our magnolia love tree, as we called it. It's where he and I first met.

Jim was so proud to call you Adira Morris. He considers you his daughter. My mother was livid. I hope she is a better grandmother to you than she was a mom to me. I forgive her though. I know in her own way, she thought she was doing the right thing.

She wasn't lucky to love like I was, so she didn't understand us. I hope she learns to understand that not everything is about money or power or connections. Sometimes it's as simple as who your heart beats for. Mine, even after it stops living, will beat for you and Jim.

You are strong, noble, and powerful, not to mention sweet and beautiful. My darling baby girl. I love you with all of my heart and soul. Never forget this. If you ever need me, just whisper and I will be there. Always.

Your mommy,
Mary

As I looked at the letter, the word *always* resounded in my head. It was this constant tapping, this beat that I could not silence. It was a litany to my ears. What shocked me was the emotions that I felt. No sadness, no questions, but an inner calm. The kind that washes over you when you sit on the beach, alone except for your thoughts, and the water calmingly crashes against your feet in a constant, soothing rhythm. Back and forth. That was how I felt. Calm, satisfied, content. Yes, content. That was the word.

This world was too bad for my Mom. She was an angel brought into this world and she could not survive here. Her wings were clipped... or better yet, they were ripped from her body, and she was unable to fly freely. The letter showed me that she loved me, and I believed her. I was not Kaitlyn, but Adira.

Now more than ever I believed that my mom had checked in on me through the years in spirit. I also believed that she had sent Jackson and Jess into my life. I hoped Kendrew was part of her plan as well. I had a feeling he was. I loved her and she loved me. *My mother.* My Mother and I shared a bond deeper than others. She and I went through the same trauma and although I was on the road to healing from my attack, I believed she was supporting me. Fully. Completely. Always.

After re-reading my mother's letter, I felt her spirit infused in me. I knew that Jim was the sweetheart she had been talking about. It all made sense now . . . the writing on his picture matched this writing in the letter.

I folded the letter and put it back in the envelope. I felt something on the bottom of the envelope. I took it out. It was a dried magnolia flower that was still fragrant. I inhaled the scent and was reminded of the scent at Jim's house.

Could it be my mom was there, letting her presence be known?

I felt a shiver spread throughout my body. I was reminded of the key my grandmother had returned. I ran up the stairs to my bedroom and opened the box that Father John had given me. I grabbed the key and placed it in the envelope and ran.

I ran to his home and knocked loudly. When no one opened the door, I ran to the next place that made sense. His second home. I had a feeling that he had gone back to his happy place, surrounded by memories and old things.

I ran until my legs started to burn, but I couldn't stop. I knew that Jim needed to see the flower quickly. I felt my mother cheering me on, urging me to run quicker and fanning my face with a gentle breeze when I got a little tired. When the light rain fell, I welcomed it as it cooled my tired body, revitalizing it.

I charged into the store, and Jim looked my way with a startled look on his face.

Kendrew was there as well, and his eyes were wide in surprise. He took a step toward me, his face filled with worry. I passed him, winking at him and smiling. "Later," I whispered.

I stood in front of Jim with my mom's letter in my hand. I opened the envelope and took out the magnolia blossom. I watched his eyes widen. I extended the blossom toward him, and he took it and cupped it in his palm gently. I watched as he leaned forward and smelled the flower. Peace settled over his face although his fingers were still trembling. I touched his hand, and he looked at me with questions in his eyes.

"I know." I nodded my head. I pulled out the letter and showed him. "My grandma and my mom filled me in on some things." I smiled and felt my eyes filling with tears. Happy tears.

"I have one more thing for you." I pulled out the key from the envelope, and he sobbed loudly. He reached for it quickly, touched it, kissed it, and held it to his chest.

"Dear girl, you had the key to my heart a long time ago," he whispered softly, touching the key he wore on his silver chain on his neck with my mother's key.

Two puzzle pieces that were reunited.

Jim took a step toward me and embraced me. "I knew you looked familiar that day you came into the store. I thought I was going crazy," he said. He paused briefly and continued. "You have your mother's eyes and her smile," he whispered. I was shaking and crying, and he patted my back.

How things would have been different if he had raised me. I had a feeling he would have been an amazing father. An amazing friend.

And he was.

Returning to my roots had taught me that living in the moment was what truly mattered.

"I felt such a connection to you too." I sniffled. "I hope you can tell me more about you and her. I would love that so much."

"It would be my pleasure, my beautiful Adira. I love your mom so much," he managed to say, his voice cracking with emotion. "I looked for you . . ." His voice broke.

I pulled away from his embrace only to look deep into his eyes. "I know. Grandma told me. She told me to tell you that she was so wrong about you. That you taught her what true love looked like." I sobbed, wiping the tears from my cheeks. Kendrew approached with tissues, and Jim and I both took one.

"I love you too, baby girl." Jim kissed my cheek, and I closed my eyes, cherishing this moment.

"I love you too . . . Dad," I whispered so quietly, only for Jim's ears. I kissed Jim on the cheek as well and moved away and stood next to Kendrew. I needed him now. I grabbed his hand, and he looked down and smiled.

Kendrew stood beside me. My rock and my strength. My support system. My heartbeat. Mine.

He raised our entwined hands and kissed the top of my hand. I felt butterflies. I felt loved.

Jim looked up at us and smiled. His eyes were tear filled, but happy. He looked like a young man in love again. The flower had transported him to a time where love was what kept him alive and breathing and his heart beating.

He spoke gently to us, "Never forget that love can survive parting, but also do not take it for granted. Do not waste precious moments. Love each other and be loved in return." He approached both of us. He looked at me before glancing at the flower and the key. "Thank you, my darling, for getting this to me. I will treasure it forever."

"I had a feeling you would," I responded, knowing that Jim would worship these items, my mom's gifts to him.

He turned to Kendrew and said, "Treat my daughter right or else you have me to answer to. If she is ever upset at you, try to make her forget she's upset and remind her of her love for you. Please be happy as much as you can and support one another. Be her rock and allow her to be your rock when need be. And remember that sometimes a flower can be more priceless than a diamond." He winked at them both. He walked toward a chair, sat down, and stared at his treasures. The reunion warmed my heart, and I wished for happiness for him, for me, for everyone seeking it.

Love washed over his face, and I felt like for once, everything would be okay. My wish had come true. I had found my past while building a stable present and the future . . . well, that was to be explored in its own time.

"Wait, daughter?" Kendrew asked, his jaw dropping.

I had a lot to tell him and fill him in about, but right now, I needed his kiss. I needed his body. I needed his love.

I jumped into his arms, my legs circling around his waist. He caught me and held me. I kissed him passionately. Like a sunflower, I turned toward him, my sun, knowing I would follow him everywhere he went.

He lit the candle and took it to his bedroom. He placed it on his nightstand while he sat down in the middle of the bed.

"My darling. Our daughter found us," he whispered to her, his voice breaking.

"She is beautiful, just like you, and has a heart filled with love, compassion, and goodness. She found me, she found us." He broke down.

His chest felt heavy and he started to weep openly into his hands. Suddenly he felt as if arms were embracing him.

Magnolias penetrated the air and he smiled.

He relaxed and turned to her with a smile on his lips and love in his eyes. "I love you always and forever," he whispered.

The words "our daughter, our beautiful daughter" replayed in the quiet, magnolia-scented room.

Epilogue

Three years later

Sunlight filtered through the massive magnolia tree and shone a beautiful, peaceful, warm, penetrating light on my girl. Truth be told, she was a radiant light without the sun's spotlight on her. She was the sun in my life every single day and brought me such happiness and love that I truly was the luckiest person on the planet this very moment. I smiled as I watched my Adira, or as I called her, Addie, give chase after our twenty-two-month-old little rascal named Riley Hope Batten, who was giggling and grabbing flowers and grass as she ran in zags-zags from her momma. She was a firecracker and she stole my heart from the day Adira told me she was expecting. I knew I would love her, but I didn't know how much until I held her in the delivery room. That moment for me was omnipotent. My love combined with Adira's love created this little miracle, and we could not be more ecstatic. Addie had complications throughout her pregnancy, but we never lost hope, and our faith in our love for one another pulled us through those difficult uncertain times. There were days when Addie needed me to hold her, and I did, and there were days when I needed to be hugged and held, and she did, and I am not ashamed to admit it. We seemed to sense what the other needed, and we carried that out. All these years later and she and I were still each other's rock. We were pieces of a puzzle that would not fit anywhere else. Our pieces were unique and only meant for one another.

It hurt me to see the fear on her face when I had to rush her to the hospital twenty-six weeks into her pregnancy. She begged me not to leave her side, and I didn't. I slept in the bed with her, to the disapproving looks of many nurses and doctors, but when I gave my word, I meant it. I never left her side. I even showered in her room and held her tightly every night. The only person I trusted to stay with her when I wasn't around was Jim. Her father. He loved her so much.

When I placed the ring on my beautiful wife's finger, I promised her that I would never leave her, that I would always love her and that I would always support her, in every decision and on every path that our life took us on. Little did I know that Riley was growing in her mommy's belly already and those promises meant for Addie, extended to her.

Thankfully, after a week, Addie was released from the hospital and put on bedrest at home. Man, was that difficult. I chuckled now as memories assaulted me: I'd never forget the time I bought Addie yarn to make a blanket and a DVD showing her how to do it. Her face was priceless as she threw the yarn, aiming at my head. She was not impressed. She wanted to climb trees and plant flowers and paint the nursery and help Jim at the shop and not be in bed all day long. All reasons I had fallen in love with her. She looked just as beautiful, if not more, in our bed with our baby growing inside of her. She glowed more than ever, and I fell even more in love with her daily. I remember spooning her and kissing her neck to calm her down. I told her she would be running around in no time, and look at her now. She was always chasing our little mischief maker.

The next day, Adira watched the DVD, and we still showcase and use her creations throughout the house. Some are even sold in Jim's shop. Proceeds go to the after-school program that we started at the sanctuary, which is what we turned Shelby's house and land into. The sanctuary allows kids to help with rescued animals and also get tutoring and homework help free of cost.

After we found out that we could not have any more children, we wanted to help other children as much as possible, and this was a way that made us feel like we were truly helping our community and the youth. And saving animals in the process. Win-win for both of us.

I often looked around at my heart's joy and smiled. This picture was better than any I could have painted for myself years ago. I didn't believe this was possible for me, but in fact, it was possible. The love gods were truly shining down on me, and I was eternally grateful. I would be for the rest of my life.

Today we had our two cats out with us, Sadie and Latte, our new rescue pit bull, Jakie, who was a gentle giant, and a bunny named Big Bun keeping us company. Our family had expanded in many ways, animal-wise and human-wise. Our sanctuary now housed twenty-five animals, and we hoped to rescue more. We had two blind goats, numerous chickens, a cow, a horse that was abandoned on an old farm and was starving, ducks and geese, and two pigs that had run away from an overturned trailer they were being transported in and we took them in and gave them a furever home. Addie and I joked in the past about having a Noah's ark. Well, we were kind of heading in that direction. The way Addie and I looked at it, we were rescued by love and we wanted to extend that love to other beings.

Speaking of expanding families, we were also adopting a six-year-old boy who lost his parents in a three-alarm fire. The boy, whose name was Michael, was burned throughout 30 percent of his body. I carried him out of the inferno and visited him at the hospital, and our bond formed. I knew how it felt to lose a parent, and he had lost both, and I wanted to show him that loss hurts but living and honoring the memory of those we love and lost is so important and necessary. And Michael does that every day. He will be released from the hospital next week, and we can't wait to have him in our life. For a six-year-old child, he has taught me a lot about unbreakable strength and the will to go on. He, along with my beautiful girls, with Shelby, Jim, Mary, Trent, and Jess, have shown me that the love of family is the most important gift a person can possess.

Every day that I wake up, I consider myself so lucky. We have one another, and we are bound together with love and respect and spend many hours of the day among laughter and giggles.

I just looked back and saw Adira on the swing with Riley in her arms. She must have finally caught our little Energizer Bunny. I watched Addie braid her hair, and once she was done, Riley turned around and put her arms around her mommy, holding on to her tightly. That was something that I could relate to. I had clung to Addie that same way many times. She had this thing about her that made you always feel safe in her arms. After the hug, you felt recharged and ready to face the world. My Addie had superhero strengths, and I was lucky that she chose me to share her life with. I felt my chest expanding. I couldn't begin to explain the love I had and the love I felt inside of me. It grew every single day, making me want to be a better version of myself for them and for myself as well.

"Hey, Jakie." I reached down and ran my hands over our pit bull. He wagged his tail excitedly and licked my hand. "Come with me." I motioned to him. He looked back at my girls, who were now Skyping with Auntie Jess, unsure whether he should leave them, and I smiled. He was so protective of them. I leaned down and gave him a big kiss on the top of his furry head. I whispered, "Latte and Sadie are watching them and so is Bun. Come on." I waved my hand once again.

I rose and watched him look back once more before looking at me. He let out a gentle woof, and I looked at his happy eyes.

"Come on, I need you for this." I gestured toward the house and started walking in that direction, the sound of giggles and piercing laughter warming my soul, the note Addie wrote so many years ago in my pocket, strengthening me. Giving me the support I needed right now. Giving me the courage.

I needed to do this.

I had to do this.

I wanted to do this.

I COULD do this.

I entered the kitchen, grabbed a bottle of water, and looked at the phone lying in the middle of the island, right next to the bouquet of sunflowers. Addie was in the room with me via those flowers, and I felt strong. I felt like I could truly do this. I took a sip of water, pulled out the note that was crinkled and ripped and had been taped together, and held onto it. I looked down at Addie's words and smiled. She had been, and I truly believe always would be, my strength. With her, I knew I could, in time, face my fear of driving again. With her, I realized that anything and everything is possible.

I placed the note on the counter. *Téng* ài stared back at me, and I reached for the phone and dialed numbers that I never forgot.

All those years of trying to forget and I couldn't.

They were embedded deep inside of me, and as I dialed them now, I surprisingly no longer felt pain or sadness.

I felt peace and anticipation.

I felt renewal and rebirth.

Ring, ring, ring.

I knew she would pick up on the third ring.

She always had.

She still did.

"Hello."

I heard her voice and tears entered my eyes. It hadn't changed. It still had the power to move me. I felt my chest swelling with unspoken love, with emotions I had buried for so long and finally was able to revisit.

"Mom," I said breathlessly. That one word took so much out of me. I felt myself shaking, and when I heard my mom say my name over and over again, the tears ran down my cheeks. I never thought I would hear her voice again. Yet here I was, calling my mom with the silent, in this case, yet ever-present support of my wife.

I started to laugh. Happiness overcame and won the battle with darkness and sadness.

The person who did not believe he deserved love was surrounded by love.

Love truly was stronger than fear and brighter than the darkness I cowered in before I met her.

She had shown me that.

The truth about Adira was simple, yet profound. She had a way of becoming one's life raft on choppy waters.

The truth about Adira . . .

She saved me.

***

I held the card in my hands, emotions overcoming me. He had been on my mind more so than usual. I didn't know how he knew about my marriage or baby, but he did. He sent me a congratulatory card with no return address. The only way I knew it was from him is because he signed it Jetliner Jax. Wherever he was, I hoped that he, my dear brother, knew that I loved him and missed him.

I glanced at my husband sleeping in our bed, and I smiled. I hugged the card tightly to my chest and made a wish for Jetliner Jax's happiness and thanked him for caring about my life. I placed the card back on my armoire. I would frame it tomorrow.

Now, I had slightly different plans. I tiptoed back to bed and leaned over my husband, kissing his chin gently. I smiled when he mumbled my name and reached for me, still fully asleep.

If someone had told me years ago that I would feel so loved and love so deeply in return, I might have not believed them fully. This was better than any dream I could have dreamt, better than every wish I made and hoped came true. This was so much better.

It was real.

It was mine.

The love of my life looked so at peace in our bed, with our children down the hallway, and our fur children nestled safely around the house and our land. They were always loved. Always cherished. Always cared for. Always listened to. Always provided for. Always treated with respect. Always ours. And we theirs.

Love so deep spread through me, and I got goose bumps.

I watched as Kendrew nestled deeper under the sheets. His arms tightened around me. I released a breath. He did the same. My eyes closed watching him sleeping.

A Note From Anna

I am not quite done with this fabulous trio. I look forward to accompanying you, my dear readers, on a journey together as we delve into Jessica's story as well as Jackson's.

Please feel free to follow me on the sites listed below for more information as well as updates and sneak peaks:

www.annapaulsen.com

www.facebook.com/annapaulsenwriter

www.instagram.com/annapaulsenauthor/

Acknowledgments

A very big thank you to my best friend, my Mom, for believing in me and my dream. She has always been in my corner, cheering me on whilst offering her support and unending love.

Special thanks to Marianne who managed to get inside my head and grasp what I was seeing when it came to my book cover. It's *exactly* as I envisioned it.

Massive thanks to Stacey, my editor. Thank you for your patience and your dedication to making my book the best it could be. None of this would have been possible without your help.

A *very* special shout out to Cate for understanding me and my vision for this book. Your enthusiasm for my characters warmed my heart and brought tears to my eyes. You truly understood their essence. Thank you so very much!

Huge thanks to Noemi for formatting my book. I am so grateful for your work and for being so amazing at what you do.

To my future husband, take notes from Kendrew!

Thank you to everyone who came on this voyage with me and my characters. I hope you fell in love with them as much as I did. Thank you from the bottom of my heart for the support, the blogs, and the recommendations. Thank you!

I would like to end in the words of Adira Morris Batten. I saved this quote just for this moment.

"Let the past be your canvas that you paint your present on for the future generations to see and admire. Make it memorable. Be. Cherish. Love."

About the Author

Anna Paulsen is a Native New Yorker. After winning a poetry contest in her school in the fourth grade, Anna quickly realized that writing felt like home to her. Since the fourth grade, life has taken her on many different paths, but she always finds her way back home via written words. Anna likes writing romance novels that focus on redemption, passion, hope, second chances and true, never-ending love. Anna is a proud fur mom to two cats. She adores antiques and collects old books. When she isn't writing, she loves to travel, read, run, garden and belt out her favorite songs.

Anna can be found online at:

www.annapaulsen.com

www.facebook.com/annapaulsenwriter

www.instagram.com/annapaulsenauthor/

Made in the USA
Monee, IL
22 January 2023